Sacred Sons

Sacred Sons

LINDA HUDSON-SMITH

BET Publications, LLC
http://www.bet.com

NEW SPIRIT BOOKS are published by

BET Publications, LLC
c/o BET BOOKS
One BET Plaza
1900 W Place NE
Washington, DC 20018-1211

All Kensington Titles, Imprints, and Distributed Lines are available at special quantity discounts for bulk purchases for sales promotions, premiums, fund-raising, and educational or institutional use. Special book excerpts or customized printings can also be created to fit specific needs. For details, write or phone the office of the Kensington special sales manager: Kensington Publishing Corp., 850 Third Avenue, New York, NY 10022, attn: Special Sales Department, Phone: 1-800-221-2647.

ISBN: 1-58314-460-9

First Printing: September 2005
10 9 8 7 6 5 4 3 2 1

Printed in the United States of America

Sacred Sons

Chapter One

An instrumental rendition of "Bridge over Troubled Water" floated softly from the speakers, filling the dark room inside the Baldwin Hills home with the peace of the Holy Spirit. Tears running down her cocoa brown face, lying in a fetal position, feeling anything but serene, forty-four-year-old Simone Branch could barely hear the song for the shouting and cursing in the next room. A loud thump made her flinch. It sounded to her as if a body had been thrown pretty hard against the wall. The next banging sound had her jumping out of bed and kneeling down beside it. She was so unnerved that she felt compelled to give a loud voice to her silent prayers.

Simone looked upward and then closed her eyes. "Lord, I'm trying my best to stay put and not get myself involved, but please don't let them hurt or kill each other. I can't do a thing with Tyrell, but I know for a fact that I have the wrong person trying to minister to him. Jerome Hadley is worse than my twenty-year-old son. Both of them are on-and-off addicts, more on, and neither of them have any respect for me or anyone else. All I asked my man to do was talk to Tyrell about staying out for days at a time without calling

1

home. Big mistake. It sounds like he has gone into my boy's bedroom and started World War III. Lord, I need your guidance."

Seated at the desk inside her Westchester in-home office, Sinclair Albright bucked her big almond brown eyes, staring at her Visa card bill as if it were a deadly enemy about to attack. Adrenaline pumped wildly through her as she read the list of endless charges. Her minimum payment was $500; unheard of, especially on what she made as a registered nurse. It was due next week; she didn't get paid for another two. Reality hit her right in the face. Not one of the items charged was purchased for the use of her or her husband, Charles. Marcus Albright, her nineteen-year-old college sophomore son had possession of every single item charged.

"This has got to stop," she told herself for the umpteenth time. "It has to."

The phone rang and Sinclair snatched it off the hook, responding to the caller in a less-than-enthusiastic greeting. She sighed hard when she heard Marcus's voice, her expression softening by a warm smile. "How are you, baby? It's nice to hear your voice. What's up?"

"Hi, beautiful," he charmed knowingly. "Hey, Mom, I'm in a bit of a bind. Can you send me a few dollars until I get paid next week? I didn't keep very good records and I'm sort of overdrawn on my checking account. Can you break off your baby boy a little something, something? I promise to pay you back as soon as I can."

Sinclair sucked her teeth, wishing she could resist that sweet voice of his. Denying him had always come hard for her. "What do you consider a little something, something Marcus?"

"Two hundred fifty dollars."

The response to his request was stuck in her throat. She'd just sent him $200 a couple of weeks ago. *What was he doing with his money? Eating it? Probably spending it on one of them fast behind college girls.* "The check is as good as in the mail."

2

* * *

The Four Tops, Smokey Robinson, and The Temptations had already set the mellow mood for Hannah and Robert Brentwood's romantic evening. Seated at the dinner table inside their View Park home, dining on T-bone steak, baked potatoes, and steamed vegetables, their gaze was steadfastly locked onto each other. Hannah had flirtatious hazel eyes and Robert's were a slight shade darker, a golden brown. The capricious smiles passing between them and the silly giggles were the kind teenagers shared in. Love was evident in every one of their gestures.

Though married nearly twenty-seven years, the Brentwoods still loved to share romantic dinners and a weekly dinner out and a movie date. They also tremendously enjoyed spending the rest of their evening cuddled up together on the sofa while listening to the oldies-but-goodies by candlelight. A little chardonnay never failed to put Robert in a frisky mood; Hannah made sure it was always served with their special dinners. The couple would give anything to take a spin back into the seventies. Since that wasn't possible, they often relived them via the music from that era.

Robert covered his wife's hand with his own. "Ready to go into the family room and curl up on the sofa, baby? I'm ready for a little quiet storm." He lifted her hand and kissed her palm.

Hannah's warm-beige cheeks blushed with color. "A raging storm is what I'm looking for. Let's get it on! Oh, dear brother, Marvin, how I wish you were still with us. Everybody wanted to cuddle when they heard that fantastic tune." Hannah began to sing the words to the favorite golden oldie, a timeless song loved by people all over the world.

"Mom, where are you?" twenty-four-year-old Derrick Brentwood yelled. Suitcases in hand, Derrick entered the dining room, much to the dismay of his parents, especially his father.

"I need to crash here for a minute. I'll stay out of the way. Macy kicked me out again."

* * *

Pacing back and forth in front of the picture window that looked out onto the darkened streets of her middle-class Culver City neighborhood, both scared and agitated, Glenda Richards, a licensed vocational nurse, looked down at her watch; nearly eleven o'clock. "Where are you, Anthony Richards? What have you gotten yourself into now?"

Glenda thought of calling her boyfriend, Taylor Phillips, but she wasn't in the mood to hear him tell her what she should do with her renegade son, Anthony. Only a few months shy of eighteen, he had failed to make his ten o'clock curfew, which had been imposed on him by the juvenile court. He was in violation of his probation for the third time this week alone.

The phone bell caused Glenda to jump with a start. She looked at the phone for several seconds before picking it up. Fearing that it might be the police telling her that Anthony was in jail, she threw up a silent prayer. "Tony," she said hopefully, her voice trembling hard.

Taylor Phillips sighed with obvious displeasure. "So, Tony hasn't made it in yet. What do you plan to do about it this time, Glen?"

Glenda sighed. "I don't know, Taylor. Nothing I've done so far has ever worked."

"I realize you don't want to hear me say this, but you've never let him suffer any consequences. He's going to be eighteen in a couple of months—and that means the cops aren't going to call you anymore to come and get him out of juvenile hall. As an adult, he'll be a guest of the county jail. He's the only one who can save himself from the destructive path he's on."

Upon hearing the key inserted into the lock, Glenda turned to face the front door. "He's here now. I'll call you back before I go to bed. I love you, Taylor."

"I love you, too, baby. Tough love or an even rougher life for Tony; the choice is yours."

* * *

Up to her neck in bubbles, twenty-seven-year-old Tara Wheatley, an ultrasound technician, had her head resting on the back of the tub inside her Hawthorne condominium. To keep it from getting wet, her long sable brown hair was twisted in a topknot. Candles softly lit the room and easy listening music played on the radio, as the steaming hot water, laced with a generous amount of lavender aromatherapy drops, helped Tara to relieve the stresses of the day. A half-empty glass of sparkling cider sat atop the pink wicker clothes hamper.

Missing Raymond Wilkerson something fierce, her successful paramedic boyfriend of nine months, Tara looked over at the portable phone and then at the lighted clock dial. Although they were used to talking on the phone all hours of the night, the spontaneous moments they'd once enjoyed in their relationship had changed drastically—and all too soon.

Much to Tara's dismay, Raymond had already called to say he'd be late again. They hadn't been spending nearly as much time together as they had before Raymond's fourteen-year-old daughter, Maya, had come to live with him about two months ago. Maya's mother had passed away unexpectedly from a stomach aneurysm, which had given Raymond sole custody of his daughter; a responsibility he had been more than willing to take on.

Thirty-four-year-old Raymond was downright handsome, very athletic, and had the dreamiest caramel brown eyes. He was a romantic at heart, and Tara absolutely adored the way he expressed himself to her by constantly sending her flowers and the sweetest cards. Everything about Raymond turned her on. However, just like now, Tara, as of late, often found herself waiting for the phone or doorbell to ring. She couldn't count the number of times Raymond had cancelled on her since Maya had moved in. *Was this just a preview of things to come?*

Simone leaped from the sofa, her heart in her mouth. The shouting and cursing had intensified in the other room. While rushing down the hall in her lavishly furnished home, Simone prayed hard—fast, furiously, and loudly. Upon reaching the bedroom entry, she stood stock still, listening to what was going on behind the closed door.

"You're not my father," Tyrell sobbed, "so you need to stop trying to act like it. My mom may be in love with your sorry butt, but I'm not. You need to back off me, Mr. Jerome. I *will* pull this trigger. Busting a cap off in your black behind will be my pleasure. Back off, old man!"

"Oh, my God, my baby's got a gun in there!" That Tyrell even had possession of a gun shocked Simone senseless. It also surprised her to hear her son sobbing, especially so hard. Tyrell was a hard-hearted one, a young man who rarely cried at all. Ever since his father, Booker Branch, had walked out on them eight years ago Tyrell had joined the ranks of the troubled youth.

Not knowing exactly what she was walking into, but fearing that if she didn't go in there something terrible would happen, Simone opened the door and rushed into the room. A flying object suddenly whizzed by her head, causing her to back out of the room much quicker than she'd entered. Once outside the room, her heart racing, Simone put two and two together. The flying projectile had been a bullet. Seeing the hole in the now-splintered door and the bullet lodged in the opposite wall was confirmation enough.

Feeling as if she were losing control of her sanity, Simone trembled hard from the trepidation in her heart. Thoughts of Tyrell murdering Jerome in cold blood sobered her immediately, making her realize she had to intervene. Calling the police would only make matters worse. Both men could end up dead if she called 911 and reported the incident.

"Tyrell," she screamed, "please put the gun away. You nearly shot your own mama. Please, baby, you don't want to spend the rest of your life in jail for shooting somebody."

"Not just somebody, Mama, Mr. Jerome. Your so-called man's been physically and verbally abusing me long enough. You brought him into this dang house, but the coroner's going to carry his no account behind out of here if he doesn't back up off me."

Feeling solely responsible for the grave unfolding of this entire situation, Simone burst into tears, letting them roll unchecked down her cocoa brown face. "Please let me come in, Tyrell, or just let Jerome come out. You don't want to do something stupid. Please, son. You have to end this now."

Simone already knew that Jerome was loaded on some sort of substance, illegal or otherwise. *Drugs or alcohol?* Probably both. He'd come home that way earlier in the day, much to her disappointment. *So why had she asked him to talk to Tyrell about staying away from home?* If he hadn't been high on something, he would've already backed away from the gun-toting Tyrell. Both of the men in her life were terribly troubled. Their clashing egos and the bitter rivalry for her attention were the root causes of most of the fights between them.

Jerome hated that Simone doted on Tyrell, giving in to all his whims and desires, often putting her son before her man. Jerome refused to see that his mother was the same way with him. So while he was complaining about Tyrell being a mama's boy, he was constantly taking advantage of his own mother's greatest weakness, which was him, Selma Hadley's only son.

Simone ran for cover when the door swung back forcefully. As Simone watched from around the corner, instead of Jerome walking out, Tyrell backed out of the room, still pointing the gun at Jerome. She wanted to sigh with relief, but it was too soon for that. Until Tyrell put the dangerous weapon away, all Simone could do was hold her shallow breath and pray.

Upon spotting his mother poking out her head from around the corner, Tyrell turned to face her, lowering the gun to his side. "Get him out of this house tonight, Mama. Him or me? One of us has to go. The choice is yours to make."

Simone couldn't control her shaking. "I hear you, baby, but please put the gun away."

"I will, once I'm out of this hellhole. Don't come looking for me with him still here. I'm not coming back to live here long as Mr. Jerome is. Since you're always hollering at me about what the Bible says, you might want to read what it says about the sinful situation you're living in." Without another word, Tyrell took off running. Never once did he look back.

Simone flinched when the front door slammed shut, praying hard that her son's troubled state of mind wouldn't cause him to go out into the streets and do something else crazy. Drawing in a deep breath, she gave a brief thought to Tyrell's parting shot, ashamed of what he'd really meant by it. Realizing that Jerome hadn't come out of Tyrell's bedroom, that she hadn't heard a sound coming from him, Simone inched her way to the entry and peeked inside. Her heart nearly stopped at seeing Jerome sprawled out all over the bed, his face down. *Had Tyrell shot him?*

No, only one shot had been fired, Simone told herself, sighing with relief. The thought that the bullet could've hit Jerome before whizzing through the door had her scrambling into the room and rushing over to the bed, her experience as a registered nurse clicking into high gear.

Lifting Jerome's hand, Simone pressed her fingers onto his wrist to take his pulse. He was definitely alive. Looking down upon Jerome, glad that he was probably just out cold from the substance abuse, Simone noticed the large wet spot on the back of his pants. If this had been a laughing matter, she would've cracked up. Jerome was obviously not loaded enough to have been unafraid. A gun pointed in their face would've been frightening to most folks, but alcohol and drugs often brought on false bravado. In this instance, Simone was grateful that fear had won out over drug-induced bravery. Otherwise, this situation could've easily produced fatal results.

Deciding that letting Jerome sleep it off was the best course of action, Simone walked away from the man she'd moved into her home without consulting a single soul, including her only child, wondering why she'd wasted so much precious time on a useless someone like Jerome Hadley. It wasn't like she hadn't learned right away who Jerome really was.

As Simone left the room, her head hung lower than low, and with deep shame clearly etched on her pretty face, thoughts of her only son were ablaze in her mind. Tyrell should've been laying in his own bed, she mused, in the comfort and safety of his mother's home, not a worthless man like Jerome. How her self-esteem had come to be so low was no mystery to Simone. The man behind her fall from grace was none other than Tyrell's father, Booker Branch, the man Simone Branch would eventually go to her grave still loving with an unending passion.

Simone couldn't help smiling as the handsome vision of Booker floated into her mind. Booker had been her high school sweetheart from the tenth grade on. Not only had he been a star athlete, but Simone had also thought of him as her hero. Booker had been her fierce protector back then. Because of him no one had dared to look at Simone in any way but a respectful one. Booker had adored Simone and never once had he minded letting everyone know it.

Once Booker had graduated high school and had gone off to a prestigious black college, with a full athletic scholarship under his belt, he still kept his loving relationship with Simone intact. The two were inseparable when he was home during breaks. The happy couple had married right after the NFL draft. The serious problems came a number of years after he'd become a member of the NFL, when Booker's superstar status began to loom larger than life.

Charles Albright walked into Sinclair's office and threw down on her desk a stack of envelopes containing bills and bank statements. Standing over his wife's black leather chair, he looked down on her with dismay, his warm-brown complexion flushed with the color of anger.

Eyeing her husband intently, Sinclair looked perplexed. "What's going on, Charles?"

Picking up one of the envelopes, Charles dragged his thumb across the name of the bank. "Don't play coy with me, woman. You know this stack of envelopes contains our monthly bank statements and charge card bills."

Charles dropped down onto the black futon and crossed his leg over his knee. "Now tell me this. How do I retire on what's left?"

Sinclair's mouth fell open. That Charles had discovered their troubled financial status so soon put her on edge. She had planned to discuss everything with him before he found out, but it looked as if she was a day late and more than just a dollar short. Since Charles had trusted her with their finances from day one, he hadn't been aware of the massive damage she'd done in nearly emptying the bank accounts and running up the charge cards with large cash advances.

Robbing Peter to pay Paul had long since become Sinclair's way of life, or so she'd thought it could work out that way. The financial hole she'd dug them into was deep enough to bury her entire family in. The interest charges alone were large enough to choke a horse. How Charles had come upon the statements she had kept locked away was a burning question in her mind.

Charles cleared his throat to bring his wife back to the here and now. "I guess you're wondering how I came across your secret stash, huh? The expression on your face is easy enough to read. You left them in the leather bag in the corner of the laundry room, beside the clothes dryer. I'm sure you didn't leave them there on purpose."

The leather bag. Sinclair's heart skipped a couple of beats. She'd forgotten about the bag altogether. Her intention had been to take it to the rented storage unit until she was ready to tell Charles everything. Sinclair recalled removing it from her office, but after that moment had occurred she could only draw blanks. Then she suddenly remembered the phone ringing that day, when she'd been on her way out through the garage. Apparently she'd stuck it in the corner of the laundry room to answer the phone, planning to retrieve it before leaving the house.

The phone call on that day had been from Marcus, asking for yet another financial disbursement. His voice always had a way of making Sinclair lose her objectivity. From the moment she'd heard the stress in her son's tone, Sinclair had blocked out everything else.

"Are you in outer space, Sinclair, or what? I'm waiting for some answers."

Sinclair jerked her head up and made direct eye contact with Charles. "Can we do this later?" She looked down at her slender gold wristwatch. "I have a phone consultation in thirty minutes, Charles. It'll take me at least twenty to get all my paperwork together."

"Cancel it." The tone of Charles's voice was calm but insistent.

Sinclair was taken aback by the formidable tone of voice used by her extremely mild-mannered husband. "You're serious, aren't you?"

Charles snorted. "I think you've already answered your own question, Sinclair."

Wishing this particular moment in time wasn't happening, Sinclair sighed hard. Since there was no plausible explanation for what she'd done, no room existed for squirming out of this one. Squandering away their hard-earned money with nothing tangible to show for it could never be explained away. Still, Simone felt she had to at least try to stall for more time.

Out of her frustration, Sinclair threw up both her hands. "I don't know where to start."

Charles's body language showed his impatience with his wife. "Try the beginning. How'd you ever convince yourself that exhausting our life savings was the right thing to do?"

Sinclair shook her head from side to side, wondering if dropping a few tears might make Charles back off, since it normally worked for her. The one thing her husband couldn't stomach was seeing her cry. He was a sucker for tears, though Sinclair only used the iniquitous scheme when she'd gotten herself into serious trouble, like now.

It didn't take Sinclair but a couple of seconds to rethink her unfair strategy. The expression of intolerance on Charles's face had her racking her brain for another way out.

Sinclair cleared her throat, hoping what she had to say would fly. "Charles, most of the money has been spent on Marcus's education. I've only been trying to help him out when he gets in a bind. He's in school, trying hard to make something of himself. Half of America's African-American sons are dead or in jail. If he didn't have any financial obligations, I think he'd do very well. Though his grades aren't always the greatest, I think he's giving his studies his best."

"His best!" Charles shook his head in the negative. "Barely passing most of his courses is not our son's best. For Pete's sake, he was an honor student in high school. The boy is brilliant."

"Doesn't that confirm what I'm saying? He's going to make it big one day, Charles. But if we withdraw our monetary support now, he could face hard times."

"Easy come, easy go is our son's way of thinking, which is not the solution to real problems. If you don't earn it, you don't value it is how I see this situation. It's time for Marcus to become a part-time student so he can work a full-time schedule. Your way just isn't working, Sinclair. Two years of hearing these same lame excuses from you has gotten utterly ridiculous. Marcus will never be a man if you don't let go. A boy calling himself a man, especially when his freedom as one only comes at his mother's expense, is not the definition of a real man, Sinclair."

Sinclair sucked her teeth, her heart rate quickening. "Would you rather Marcus be in a gang or perhaps out there on the streets selling drugs and robbing folks? He's in college, Charles, working on the opportunity to one day make his mark on the world. Do you want to deny him the chance to continue on with his studies so he can graduate in two more years? Or do you want him to join the workforce and completely fail at his studies? He could end up destitute."

"If Marcus were living up to his potential by getting good grades, I could agree with you and continue to support his educational needs. But let's face it. The large sums of money you're sending to our son are not going toward his educational expenses. Paying for his tuition is one thing. Financially supporting his every whim, no matter how foolish, is a horse of a different color. You need to find a clue. You're helping Marcus suck us dry under the pretext of getting a good education. It's time for you to open your eyes and see the truth."

"That's not how it is. Nothing could be further from the truth," Sinclair huffed.

That Sinclair still didn't get it bothered Charles to no end. She was lying to herself to justify not only Marcus's irresponsibility but also her own untoward actions. That astounded him. Charles didn't want to dole out ultimatums, but he felt Sinclair wasn't giving him a choice. He couldn't continue to let her lead them right into the poor house. Enough was enough.

Charles looked Sinclair dead in the eye. "Immediately cut off the financing to all of Marcus's unreasonable demands and selfish desires or I'm out of here, Sinclair. I can't do this any longer. It's insane."

Sinclair couldn't believe her ears. "Is that a threat, Charles Albright?"

Charles got to his feet. "However you want to take it, Sinclair. We're darn near bankrupt. If that's not a wake-up call for you, I don't know what more can happen here before you see the light. Bankruptcy is staring us right in the face. If that's what you want, continue financially supporting our rebel of a son who has yet to find a cause. But you'll have to do it solely on your salary, not mine. I've rerouted the direct deposits of my paychecks to a new bank account."

As Charles turned to walk away, an incensed Sinclair got to her feet, hands on both hips. "I'll continue to support Marcus, Charles. You can count on that. But how can you dare to do something as underhanded as rerouting your checks without even bothering to consult me? I think you're exaggerating this whole thing. You've blown it way out of proportion."

Charles turned back to face his wife, a deep sadness resting in his eyes. "I think not. But have it your way. And I'm only doing what you've obviously been doing underhandedly for quite a while. Just don't expect anything else from me in the way of finances for Marcus. There's nothing left for me to give in this instance. However, I'll gladly pay for filing of the paperwork."

Sinclair swallowed hard, her breasts heaving heavily, unconquerable fear tearing at her insides. "What are you talking about, Charles? Paperwork for what?"

"Divorce. I can't stay in this marriage under the present circumstances. I've always given in to you on one matter or another, but I won't give in to you over this financial debacle. Since we still haven't gotten a tenant to lease the brand-new town house, which has put us into even more debt, I'll be moving in there until this is all settled."

Sinclair could've been blown over with a feather. That her mild-mannered husband had just declared war on her came as a huge surprise. Shocked beyond disbelief, calling on God to help her deal with this grave situation, a tearful Sinclair stared after her retreating husband.

Hannah looked at her handsome husband and then glanced over at their gorgeous son, who possessed a winning combination of both his parents' good looks. Derrick had his mother's full-dimpled smile and warm-beige complexion, inheriting his father's sexy golden-brown bedroom eyes, curly black hair, towering height, and athletic build.

Hannah knew all too well that this wasn't a good situation for her to be in. There were far too many times that she'd been caught in the middle of choosing between her husband's needs and their son's wants. How many fights had there been in past years over their vast differences in opinions regarding how Derrick should be raised and disciplined? Although she had tried her best to remain quiet during father-and-son confrontations, Hannah always failed at it.

Derrick, a grown man, who'd never held down a job for more than three consecutive months, was also quite the womanizer, a choosy one to boot. He never dated any woman who wasn't financially successful. His good looks and instant charm were what had paid his way through life thus far. That women took care of his every need didn't seem to bother him one iota. Derrick's manhood was never in question by him, though his father questioned it frequently.

Hannah thought Derrick needed more time to find himself; Robert thought his son was just plain lost and that he'd never find himself. *Not as long as women were willing to foot the bills for his lavish lifestyle.* Although his son's choices in life often disappointed him, Robert loved his son dearly. As a godly man, Robert constantly preached to his son about his ungodly ways. Although he had brought Derrick up in admonition of the Lord, Robert also realized that he couldn't force his son to live by God's personal blueprint for eternal life. Derrick's life was his own to do with as only he saw fit. Robert could only continue to pray constantly for his son.

Robert pushed his chair back from the table. "Sit down, son. We need to talk."

Derrick frowned, feeling a long, drawn-out sermon coming on. His dad would talk and he'd have to be quiet and listen. "Dad, it's late. I'm bushed. Can we do this in the morning?"

Robert shrugged. "We do this now, or you can find a Motel 6. The choice is yours."

Hannah gently rested her hand on Robert's shoulder. "It *is* late,

15

honey. Can't this wait until tomorrow? We'll all be well rested by then."

Robert hated it when Hannah intervened on Derrick's behalf. It happened all too often. Rarely did he get a chance to speak as a matter of fact to his son without her input, but he never let it stop him from eventually getting his point across. There were times when he gave in to her pleadings to put it off, but not tonight. If Derrick wanted a place to sleep, he'd just have to listen to one of the sermons he'd come to hate, which Robert felt was his duty as a parent to deliver.

"There'll be no rest for the weary or anyone else in this house until I've had my say. Our evening has already been rudely interrupted and I'm still not too happy about that." Robert looked to Derrick. "I just gave you a choice, son. You can park your butt on one of these chairs or close the front door quietly behind you. By the way, give me your house key. This is the last time you're popping up in here on us unannounced."

Robert looked at his wife with gentleness. "Hannah, I need to talk to Derrick alone."

Hannah started to protest, but there was something about her husband's tone that caused her to remain silent. Besides, he'd never before asked her to leave the room. Fearing the ugly confrontation surely to come, Hannah got up and left the room, opting for the kitchen, which was close enough for her to at least hear what was said. Upon hearing her husband tell Derrick it was best to talk to him upstairs in his old room, she made a fast U-turn and went up to their bedroom.

Hannah waited until she thought the two men in her life were settled down in Derrick's bedroom and then she crept out into the hallway, tiptoeing close to the partially cracked door. Praying she wouldn't be discovered eavesdropping, Hannah promptly positioned herself.

"I'm sorry you don't want to listen to me, son, but there's a lot to be said about your lifestyle. I know you think I've already said it all, but I haven't come close. Where would you have gone tonight if you hadn't been able to come here?"

Derrick bounced an intolerant glance at his father. "I'm sure I could've found somewhere else to crash."

"If that's so, why didn't you?"

Staring hard at his father, Derrick wondered what this was all leading up to. "This is my home. That's why I came here first."

"Correction, son. Through the grace of God, this home belongs to your mother and me, a gift from God, just as it is with the bed you're stretched out on. Know why it belongs to us?"

"I guess 'cause you purchased it."

"Right you are, and we purchased it with money we worked hard for. Unlike you, both your mother and I have very good-paying jobs. Since you might need a gentle reminder, I'm a senior account executive for Global Bank and your mother is a registered nurse. We worked hard to get where we are today. We didn't get this house, our third one to date, on a whim. If you hadn't been able to find a place to stay tonight, what steps would you have taken next?"

Derrick frowned. "You mean if I couldn't stay here?"

Robert smiled with cynicism. "Exactly."

Derrick hunched his shoulders, staring down at the floor. "I would've found a place, Dad. You can be sure of that."

"Then why didn't you go somewhere else, Derrick? Why come here?"

"Dad, I've already tried to tell you why, so I guess I just don't know."

"Yes you do. You came here because it's comfortable, because it has always been a soft place for you to land. You needed a place to regroup, a decent place for you to operate out of until you locate your next unsuspecting victim."

Scowling hard, Derrick clenched and unclenched his fists, trying to ease the tension he felt. "What are you talking about now, Dad? This isn't making any sense."

Robert eyed his son with open skepticism. "I think you already know, but let me go ahead and spell it out for you. First off, when you show up here, you know your mother's going to tend to your every need, just like she's always done when you're under our roof and also out from under it. Don't you see that as kind of unfair to a woman who works as hard as she does? But you don't seem to care about that, so we'll move on. . . ."

"Dad," Derrick interrupted, looking as if he was about to explode, "is all this necessary?"

"As necessary as breathing. Everything I say to you is for your benefit, not mine. But if you refuse to listen, you're never going to get it. You get to eat here, sleep in a clean bed, shower, use the telephone, and have your mother cook and do your laundry, all for free. The sad part is that you never offer to lift a finger to do a thing to help us out around here."

"That's not true. I do help Mom out."

"Yeah, but she practically has to beg you to get you to do anything for her, big or small."

"I don't see it that way."

"Of course you don't. But let's see if you can get this. Late in the evenings you leave out of here dressed to the nines, but we never know if you're coming back that night or not. Your style of dress would put the richest of men to shame, yet you don't have a single red cent in the bank. You often drive a fancy new car, for as long as your relationship is working for you, only to arrive back here once your current girlfriend has had enough of your fast-talking bull and alley cat ways. You come here so you can chill out for free, so you can at least be comfortable until you can latch onto the next woman with a fat bank account, one who's willing to move you into her place with no questions asked. How is that for necessary? How do you justify any of that nonsense, Derrick Brentwood?"

Derrick shrugged, seemingly unaffected by anything his father had just said. "It's easy. If they're willing to give up the cheddar, why shouldn't I take it? If someone offered you an expensive car to drive and a ritzy place to stay, are you saying you wouldn't take it?"

Robert looked downright disgusted. "Wouldn't even entertain the idea of it."

"Why not?"

"I'm a man, Derrick, not a male gigolo, not a boy toy for someone to dangle expensive trinkets in front of so that I'm forever indebted to them, so that I'll do anything they command and demand of me just to stay in the lavish lifestyle. If you think these women aren't operating on their own agenda, you'd better think again. You have nothing to offer them, so what do these highly successful women really need you for? That's something else you might want to give some deep thought to. What you can't seem to understand is that you *are* paying a price for these expensive privileges afforded you by these rich women, a very high one, Derrick. You have yet to learn to live in the world and not be a by-product of it."

"How do you figure I'm paying the price for it?"

"That's something I want you to answer, Derrick. Let's talk later on in the week, after you've had a chance to really think about this conversation. Give it enough thought to really let what I've said sink in. When you come down for breakfast, you'll find on the refrigerator door a list of things I need your help with. See you in the morning."

Robert started for the door but turned around before he reached it. "By the way, you have a month to get a job. No job, no room available at this inn. I won't even mention attending church, since you already know that's a prerequisite for living under my roof."

Upon hearing Robert's last words, Hannah scrambled down the hallway and entered the master bedroom, her heart breaking for her son. A month was barely enough time for Derrick to get acclimated to being back at home again, let alone find any meaningful work. Forcing anyone to go to church, especially an adult, was archaic. Derrick was still young, and he had a lot to learn, but he wasn't going to get it through constant browbeatings. She'd have to talk to Robert and get him to understand he couldn't force anyone to do anything, especially an adult.

"Adult," she repeated aloud. It was hard for Hannah to think of Derrick, her baby boy, as one. Regardless of how old he lived to be he'd still be her baby. Hannah could only wish that Robert knew what it was like to carry a child, give birth to one, and then take care of the baby until he or she was old enough to begin functioning under his or her own power. That was something men would never have the privilege of experiencing. If they only knew the joys and pains of motherhood, they might not be so quick to judge everything a mother does for her child.

Hannah looked over at the door. Seeing her husband looking so defeated caused her heart to go out to him. Why was it that she was always torn between the two people she loved most in the world? Robert and Derrick were her life; there was no one choice to make between them.

Frowning heavily, Glenda reached up and grabbed her tall, lean son by the shoulders and shook him firmly. "Where have you been, Tony? Don't you know how to tell time, son?"

Anthony pushed past his mother. "Don't start with me tonight. I'm not trying to hear that noise. You don't know what it's like out dere in them streets. I'm nobody's punk. What you think is gonna happen to me if I tell my boys I gotta go home and check in with my mama?"

Glenda gave a frustrated sigh. "It's not your mama you have to worry about checking in with. If your PO calls and finds you not here, that spells big trouble for you."

Anthony shook his head, laughing derisively. "I ain't hardly worried about him, Mom. Mr. Steve Castor's nothing but a thug himself. He ain't gonna do nothing if he calls and I ain't here. Don't even bother to sweat that old man."

Cringing at Anthony's improper language, Glenda took a seat on the sofa, encouraging her son to sit next to her. Much to her surprise and relief, Anthony took a seat, even if it was in the leather re-clining chair, a good distance from the sofa. "Tony, please help me understand your fascination with the streets. You're not from the streets yet you seem to love it out there."

Anthony Richards was a highly intelligent young man, whose grades were always way above average, and he came from a good home. Since his father's untimely death several years back he'd given himself over to the call of the streets, indulging in criminal activities. His grades had begun to suffer terribly as a result of his newly acquired lifestyle.

Anthony looked totally disinterested. "How many more times you gonna ask me that, Mom? You've already asked it a thousand times."

"Until you give me an answer. I don't understand how all this began, but I want to."

"The streets are my teachers. I learn a lot from them."

"Learn what, Tony?"

"How to survive. The streets ain't gonna run out on me either, not like Dad did."

Glenda's autumn brown eyes misted up. "Why do you keep re-ferring to your father's death as him 'running out on you'? You know that's not what happened, Anthony Richards."

"It's not? He got killed doing something illegal, didn't he?"

"That has never been proven. I knew your father. He wasn't a criminal, never even had so much as a speeding ticket. Your dad may've worked as a long distance trucker, but when he was in town, he was at home with us. I believe he was merely a victim of circum-stance, Tony, that Antoine Richards simply got caught up in the wrong place at the wrong time."

"In a crack house? He wasn't at home with us that night over four years ago. And what about the prostitute found shot dead right next to where he was cut down?"

Hearing that soul-crushing comment caused Glenda's heart to

throb painfully. While there'd never been a reasonable explanation for anything that had occurred that insane night, the issue of the prostitute bothered her the most.

Prostitution had once been a serious issue in the marriage. With Antoine on the road so much, he had had an occasion to indulge with questionable women. The sexually transmitted disease he'd brought home to his wife had brought that horrific situation to light. But that had long since changed before his death. The fact that he was in town that night hadn't quite convinced Glenda that Antoine hadn't been physically involved with the prostitute, even though she'd always been there to meet her husband's every need.

There was evidence as to whether Antoine had been with the female victim, but Glenda hadn't ever been able to bring herself to hear the truth one way or the other. That was one question she just didn't want to know the answer to. Her marriage to Antoine had been all that she'd needed it to be before his death. The possibility of marring those wonderful memories wasn't something she was willing to do, especially when nothing could ever be done about it.

The truth didn't always set you free. Forgiveness did. . . .

Glenda leveled her gaze on Anthony, wishing he could let go of the strange circumstances surrounding his father's death. It was destroying him and it was also killing her spirit. Antoine had been a wonderful father to his son, but all that had happened had caused Anthony to lose respect for his dad despite the fact the actual truth was still unknown.

"He wasn't shot inside the crack house, Tony, and you know it. He was found dead on the street. As for the prostitute, I'm not even going to get into that with you."

"That's not how the word on the block has it, Mom."

Sick and tired of hearing about what was still being said on the streets, Glenda cringed inwardly. "Why is it easier for you to believe the people on the streets over your own mother? I lived with your father every day. Not a single one of those people even knew him personally."

"Not every day. Dad was gone out on the road a good bit of the time. If Dad was into selling or buying illegal drugs and sleeping with prostitutes, and you didn't know anything about it, that proves you didn't really know him like you're saying you did."

"None of those are facts either. It's all speculation by the cops and everyone else in this city. No one really knows what happened that fateful night. Are you forgetting that there were no eyewitnesses? No one saw a thing."

"I'm not trying to forget any of it. That's why I'm not gonna end up like Dad, not as long as I have protection out on the streets. My boys got my back."

"Your boys! Are you telling me you've now gone from being a follower to a leader?"

"That only happens in a gang, Mom."

"Gangs, isn't that what you're really in to, Anthony Richards?"

"No!"

"If you *are* in a gang, you may very well end up exactly like your dad—dead—though I'll never believe he was in to any organized or unorganized crime. Not without rock-solid proof; no one will ever make me believe my husband was a drug dealer or out seeking prostitutes." Not during that time frame, Glenda added in her thoughts. "No one. Your anger over your father's death is terribly misplaced, Tony. So far it has gotten you into nothing but trouble. In case you've forgotten, you're on probation for grand theft auto and receiving stolen property. Since they have your back, why didn't your boys talk you out of committing those crimes?"

Anthony smirked. "I wondered when you were gonna go there. I didn't do any of that stuff, Mom. If you can believe Antoine Richards was in the wrong place at the wrong time, then why can't you believe that about me, huh?"

Glenda couldn't answer that question, didn't even want to respond to it. What good would it do, anyway? She didn't want to believe Anthony had committed those crimes, but the evidence had already proved otherwise. It was late and she had to work the next day. To continue this conversation with Tony was fruitless. He was going to believe what he wanted to believe regardless. That had been proven over and over again. Her son was simply in denial.

"Can't answer me, can you? Keep on believing them lawless folks." Anthony got up from the recliner and stormed out of the room.

Wasting no time at all, Glenda dropped to her knees. It was time to consult her Maker.

Tara looked at the clock again and yawned, hoping she could stay awake until Raymond got there. It was already well after ten o'clock and she had to work the next day. She was all for her man taking care of his daughter, glad that he was a great father, but she missed him. Since Maya was only fourteen, Raymond's responsibility to her would hardly end anytime soon.

Tara had spent some quality time with Maya in the beginning, but their outings had been far and few between, since Maya had once lived fifty-five miles from L.A., in the city of Fontana. Raymond used to drive up there on his visitation days. Maya's parents had never married, but Raymond and Maria had maintained a very good relationship after the breakup. Maria wanted marriage but Raymond wasn't ready at twenty. After breaking things off with the father of her child, Maria moved on. According to Raymond, it hadn't taken her long after that to find a man who had no problem committing to her.

Raymond was deeply hurt at first, but after seeing how happy Maria was with Lionel Waterman, a civil engineer, Raymond had given her his blessings. Lionel would've been thrilled to have Maya stay in Fontana with him, but Maya had desired to live with her natural father and still maintain the healthy relationship she had with her stepfather.

The phone rang and Tara instantly reached for it, hoping Raymond was turning onto her street. He always called her as he rounded the corner. Her heart dropped when she saw his home number on the caller ID box, which meant he hadn't even left yet. She drew in a shaky breath. "Baby, is everything okay? I see you're still at home."

"Yeah, things are cool. Sweetie, I'm sorry, but I can't make it. Maya needs my help with some complicated homework. Why she waited this late to tell me about it I'll never know."

"What's she been doing with her time since she got out of school, Ray?"

"Watching television, I guess, instead of getting her homework done. The girl should be in bed asleep by now. Tomorrow is a definite for us, Tara. I won't let you down."

Tara sighed inwardly. "Okay, Ray. I'll talk to you in the morning, before I go to work."

Tara didn't like that she'd been disappointed once again, but she hoped that she, Raymond, and Maya would eventually find more quality time to spend together. Time spent with Maya also meant more time with Raymond. That they'd hopefully become one big happy family often crossed her mind, but Tara didn't see it happening any time in the near future.

However, if God were for them, who could be against them? If it were in His plan for them to become a family, they would be. Since it was already set in stone, one's destiny couldn't be rushed. Tara believed that divine plans were always in order and always right on time.

Chapter Two

Seated at a corner table in the staff break room, located on the fifth floor of Los Angeles Memorial Hospital, where she was employed as a registered nurse, tall, curvaceous, and extremely attractive Sinclair Albright had been keeping a vigilant watch on the entry door, impatiently waiting for her best friend–coworkers to show up for their daily break time. The five women all met at the same place and at the same time every workday for both breaks and lunch, unless someone was off duty or too busy to take the regularly scheduled time-out.

Sinclair's nerves were stretched to the absolute limit regarding the financial trouble she'd gotten into with her husband, Charles, who was actually going through with his threatened plan to move out of their home and into their rental property. Having gotten very little sleep over the past few days, Sinclair looked as haggard on the outside as she felt inside.

Watching Charles snatch up and toss things haphazardly into the suitcases before she'd come into work had nearly caused Sinclair to have a nervous breakdown. Her heart had told her to drop on her knees and beg him to stay, but her stubborn mind and arrogant attitude simply couldn't be so bothered as to hear any pleading moans coming from her own mouth.

During the few days since Charles had first made the discovery over their dire finances, Sinclair had tried numerous times to get him to listen to reason, although she'd refused to ask him to reconsider leaving her. The only thing he'd wanted to hear from her was her promise to sandbag Marcus Albright's free ride. Since Sinclair had no intention of pulling the financial rug right out from under their son's feet, she hadn't been able to make that kind of oath to Charles.

The door to the break room flew open and in walked slender but curvy Simone Branch, carrying a small brown bag, looking like she'd just traveled through a war zone. For someone who always kept her hair neat as a pin, Simone's head looked as if she'd lost her comb and brush. Though normally clean and impeccably pressed, her white uniform was spotless but noticeably wrinkled. The bags under her dark brown eyes seemed to suggest she'd had as many sleepless nights as Sinclair. Both women had had several days off and hadn't seen each other.

Simone dropped down onto a chair on the opposite side of the table from where Sinclair was seated. She then took an orange from the bag. "Morning, Sinclair. How you doing, girl?"

Sinclair frowned, not daring to spill out her troubles after seeing Simone looking so distraught. "I think I should find out how you're doing first. What's up? You look like hell!"

"I feel like hell, too." Simone sighed hard. "I guess I should be used to all the drama by now, but every time Jerome and Tyrell get into a fight I realize I might not ever get used to it."

Knowing it was nothing but the same old stuff Simone always brought to the break table, Sinclair sighed with relief. Sharing her personal problems was always easier when one of the others wasn't going through something even more serious than her issues. "What are those two hardheads fighting about this time?"

"It was much bigger than a fight this time." Tears welled in

Simone's eyes. "Tyrell threatened to kill Jerome with a gun he'd somehow managed to get his hands on."

Sinclair's almond brown eyes widened with disbelief. "Say what, girl? A real gun!"

Simone nodded. "The real thing. I'll wait until everyone else gets here to tell you what happened. This gun scenario isn't something I want to keep repeating or continue to relive."

No sooner than the words had left Simone's mouth in through the open door came the rest of the lively break-time crew—Tara Wheatley, Glenda Richards, and Hannah Brentwood—all employees of Los Angeles Memorial Hospital. Simone, Sinclair, and Hannah were all registered nurses; Glenda was a licensed vocational nurse. Tara, the youngest of the group, by at least thirteen years, was an ultrasound tech. The entire group also attended the same church.

"What's that I heard about a gun?" Hannah asked, plopping down in the chair next to the one Sinclair occupied.

Since it was Tara's turn to retrieve coffee or juice for everyone, she quickly executed her duties and then took a seat next to Simone, which was also right across from Glenda.

Simone waited until everyone had settled in and fixed their coffee to their liking before she began telling her latest tale of woe. This close-knit fivesome was used to sharing all the dramatic episodes that occurred in each of their lives, but some of the stories they told had a tendency to be downright soul rocking. With all eyes trained on Simone, the silence was near deafening, as everyone waited with bated breath for her to give them a full accounting of the story about the gun.

Several minutes later, once Simone had finished her unenviable story, Tara's hand flew up to her mouth. "Thank God Tyrell didn't shoot Jerome. Where is Tyrell now?"

Simone shook her head. "I don't know. I'm used to him not showing up for days at a time, but in this instance his disappearance has me more than a little crazy. I don't even know whom to call on anymore."

"God is the only one you can call on. He's the only one who can resolve our problems," Glenda chimed in. "All the rugs in my house are so knee worn they're threadbare. If I didn't know better, I'd believe my Tony and your Tyrell were brothers. They sure act a lot alike."

Simone laughed, but her heart didn't feel the least bit joyous. "Tell me about it, Glenda. The cops have been at your house almost as many times as they've been to mine over the past year or so. How *is* Tony coming along? You haven't mentioned him over the past week or two."

Glenda wrung her hands together, her anguish obvious. "Just remember you asked the question, Simone. So, ladies, here goes my megadrama of the week." Glenda went on to tell her friends the last volatile thing that had happened with her son inside her home.

With her story over, Glenda sighed with discontent. "Taylor is constantly on my case about practicing tough love with Tony. He has no children, so that's easy for him to say. I sense that he's getting impatient with these ever-rising confrontations between Tony and me. He fears for both of us. I just don't know what to do anymore. Taylor is such a good man—one of the best—but I'm afraid he's growing weary. I expect him to just get up and walk out of my life one day. Men have no concept of the powerful dynamics between mothers and sons."

Everyone was well aware of the mystery surrounding Glenda's husband's death. No one was surprised when she told her friends that Anthony was still questioning his father's morals and his alleged criminal activities, or even that his anger at his dad was still way out of control. Anthony violating the conditions of his probation was at least a twice weekly occurrence.

Although the other four women wouldn't think of voicing it to Glenda or even dare to discuss it among themselves in Glenda's absence, Antoine's death was still a big question mark in each of their minds. None of what had occurred that September night made sense to anyone. That Glenda might be in total denial over who

Antoine really was as a husband and a father was a sentiment shared separately in thought, yet still a theory shared by all.

Sinclair had flinched at Glenda's last two statements. She hadn't ever expected Charles to up and leave her, but he was doing just that—and for the very same reason Glenda's man might walk: out-of-control sons. Charles just *didn't* understand her relationship with Marcus. Not ready to reveal her story just yet, Sinclair was content to sit back and listen to the others. None of the situations had topped hers so far in severity, so she thought it best to save her drama for last.

With Glenda's story completely unfolded, just another familiar episode, Hannah took up the baton, going into great detail about the latest battle of wills between her husband and son.

"Robert and Derrick had another of their usual clashing of opinions and gnashing of teeth. Suitcases in hand, Derrick showed up right in the middle of one of our romantic evenings, just when we were ready to end up on the sofa."

Hannah giggled, blushing all over the place. Everyone was used to her silly giggling and passionate blushing every time she talked about her and Robert's wonderful romantic escapades. All the women thought it was actually a refreshing thing to witness. A happy marriage was rare.

"Macy has thrown Derrick out for the third time in less than a month. I know for a fact Derrick's still trying to find himself, but Robert isn't buying into that for a second. My husband is fed up with our son's lifestyle. He's given Derrick a month to find a place to stay. Even took his house key away. That's a real change in Robert's attitude. It seems to me he's had enough."

"These are grown men you're all talking about," Tara weighed in. "Tony's not yet eighteen, Glenda, but he will be shortly. Things are going to change drastically once he reaches that so-called magical age. No one will ever again have to consult you about anything that goes on in his life then." Tara turned to face Hannah. "Derrick has lived with at least six women in the four and a half years since we've all been hanging out. That says a lot about his character, but, Hannah, you simply dismiss it as him trying to find himself. How's that?"

"Because I believe that's all it is, Tara. Men simply don't mature as quickly as women."

"Okay, but if you had one, what would you think of your daughter dating a man who was just like Derrick Brentwood, Hannah?" Tara inquired, a questioning eyebrow raised.

Hannah had to take a minute to think about the question. Although she resented it coming from someone so much younger than she, Hannah had to admit that the question posed was something she hadn't given any thought to. "I don't know, Tara. But I promise to think about it," Hannah voiced, holding a tight rein on her anger at Tara's judgmental observations.

Simone rolled her eyes at Tara. "Tara, you have no kids, so you don't have a clue," she charged. "Maybe you can speak to our situations once you have your own children."

Ignoring the obvious dismissal, Tara felt compelled to continue on in saying her piece.

"Simone, speaking of situations, this tumultuous relationship between Tyrell and Jerome has been going on since the day Jerome moved into your place. If you have to make a choice between the two men, knowing exactly the kind of man Jerome is, your choice should be an easy one. You all are mothers of *men*, not baby boys. Don't you think it's time for you to let them grow up? So what if they have to struggle a little. Strife builds character. Can't you see that you and your husbands and lovers are locked in deep conflict over your sons? Don't you think you should really listen to what your men are saying? This is really serious stuff, girlfriends!"

"Tara, what's going on in your relationship with Raymond? You seem really upset today. Do you have something to share with us?" Glenda asked, hoping to take the heat off. The others appeared grateful for the timely intervention. It had gotten a little too hot for all their comfort.

Tara's story of the week didn't hold much interest for any of the other women, as she laid out what she considered her insignificant problems with Raymond. Especially when compared with the others'. The older women just couldn't seem to ever relate to her issues. First of all, they didn't understand why she'd gotten herself involved with a man who already had a child, which had never set well with Tara. Everyone's problems were always more important than hers.

It hurt Tara that the others always seemed to dismiss her troubles as minor ones. She was either too young to understand or she hadn't had enough experience in the world to give a worthwhile opinion. No one ever really took her seriously, which was the main reason she hadn't ever gone into the heart-rendering pain of her past. Tara's painful past had made her wise far beyond her twenty-seven years.

If her older friends, whom she had once looked up to as parental figures, only knew what she'd been through, she didn't think they'd discount her feelings so easily. The bad choices each of them constantly made in regard to their adult sons caused Tara to see them as anything but role models for parenting. Tara had already experienced firsthand what each of these women was going through with their sons and mates. Those awful days of her bittersweet youth were forever emblazoned upon her soul. Bad parental decisions had cost her what she'd loved most.

Tara Wheatley still blamed her older brother, Timothy, for the bitter divorce of their parents, Joanna and Jamaica Wheatley, and the untimely death of their mother, a loving woman who'd gone to her grave from trying too hard to please the boy she'd never let grow into a man. Tara hadn't spoken to Timothy since their mother's funeral, well over five years ago. Her older girlfriends didn't even know a Timothy Wheatley existed in Tara's secret world.

Sinclair bit down on her lower lip. "Now that you all have had your say, I have something to contribute to yet another of our get-it-off-your-chest sessions. "Charles was busy moving out of our house when I left for work this morning. He's leaving me."

Simone looked shell-shocked "Oh, no! Another woman?"

Sinclair snorted. "That might be easier to bear. At least that's something I could compete with, and probably win out over. Finances have come between us. To be more specific, my financing Marcus's every desire is the major issue. Charles doesn't feel he can retire because of the dire straits of our financial future. He gave me an ultimatum. Cut Marcus off or else."

Sinclair's heartbreaking story only rivaled Simone's dramatic one as the shocker of the week. The others found it hard to believe that softhearted Charles was leaving his beloved wife over finances, of all things. It would've been easier for the group to believe the "other woman" saga, especially as good-looking and successful as Charles Albright was.

Sinclair and Hannah were often touted as the spoiled ones of the group because their husbands were so good to them. The two women often sang their husbands praises, except for when it came down to matters concerning their adult sons. The differences in opinion on that sensitive subject had Hannah and Sinclair jawing nagging complaints about their significant other. There were times when the other women were given the impression that the two men were downright evil, that they may even be jealous of their own flesh-and-blood sons.

On the other hand, Simone and Glenda would jump through a series of hoops in order to land wonderful husbands and terrific fathers like Charles Albright and Robert Brentwood. Taylor Phillips was a darn good man, but he wasn't Glenda's husband, and she wasn't sure he'd ever be.

The minutes seemed to have ticked off the clock much faster than usual on this dreary Monday morning. Hannah was the first to notice that time had run out on their soul-bearing session. "Our break is over, ladies. We can pick things back up during the lunch hour. In the meantime, let's bow our heads for our parting moment of silent prayer."

* * *

Simone rushed headlong through the front door, hoping to catch the phone before it stopped ringing. Breathing heavily, she snatched up the receiver, gushing her breathless greeting into the mouthpiece. Sweat trickled from her forehead, as she tried to calm herself down.

"Hello, Simone."

Simone's heart stopped right in the middle of a strong beat, her eyes wide with incredulity. Then her heart restarted with an unusual pounding, accompanied by echoing sounds thumping loudly in her ears. While holding the phone in a death grip, her breath came in short, raspy gasps.

"Are you there, Simone?"

Stretching the phone cord to its maximum length, Simone dropped down in one of the living room chairs. Had she stood a second longer her legs would've folded up on her like an accordion. Taking a clean tissue from her uniform pocket, Simone wiped the sweat from her face. "I'm here. But why are you calling me?"

"It's about Tyrell."

The lightning speed at which Simone's heart had suddenly started beating had her covering her chest with a flattened palm. Her eyes glazed over with the mist from her unshed tears. "My baby! Where is he? Is he okay?"

"He's here with me, Simone. Tyrell is safe."

"Where's here?"

"Marina del Ray."

"As in Marina del Ray, California? If so, for how long?"

"I've been back in southern California for several months now. Simone, I called to talk to you about Tyrell. He was really upset and depressed when he showed up here. Did you know that this kid carries a gun?"

"This kid! Tyrell is your son, Booker Branch. How dare you refer to him as 'this kid.' He's your flesh and blood. You're his biological father. But you seemed to have forgotten that fact on the very day you walked out on us."

"Not now, Simone. This isn't about what happened way back then. This is about here and now—this moment. Tyrell wants to stay here and live with me. How do you feel about that?"

Feeling as though her heart was about to give out, Simone sucked in several deep breaths. The pain in her chest was immeasurable, but she was aware that the aching strain came from all the stress she was under. She wasn't having a heart attack, though it felt like the "big one" Fred Sanford always referred to in his once very popular television sitcom.

Tyrell going to live with his father may've been welcomed by Simone when he'd first entered puberty. To have Booker suggest it now seemed like a nasty insult, and it hurt as much as any hard slap across the face. After she'd put in all the hard time, had happily invested her very being into Tyrell, not to mention every dime she could get her hands on, Booker now wanted to take away the son she'd nurtured and loved like crazy, all during his father's eight-year absence.

Booker's comments about Tyrell coming to him suddenly struck an out-of-tune chord within Simone. "How did Tyrell know where to find you, Booker?"

"I called him when I first moved back here. I told him where he could find me and then I gave him my phone number. He never tried to make contact with me before he showed up here."

"I know you're not wondering why the contact didn't occur." Simone quickly decided to cast the sarcasm aside, realizing her bad attitude wouldn't help matters. "How is Tyrell?"

"Other than being totally upset over whatever went down with him and your man, he's fine. Who is this guy, anyway, that you got living up under your roof?"

Resenting the question, detesting the tone in which Booker had asked it, Simone fought hard to keep the cap on the rising steam of her temper. "What matters is that I know who he is."

"Okay, Simone, I see that you're hell-bent on making this as difficult for me as you possibly can, so let's get on to the other reason I called. Tyrell needs his things. Can I bring him to your place to get them? I can sit out in the car and wait for him if you prefer it that way."

"Damn straight you'll stay outside. You're not welcome here. If Tyrell has needs, why don't you just go out and buy him all new things? That would be such a touching gesture, since money is the only thing you've ever contributed toward his life and upbringing. However, if you do decide to come here and wait for him, you just might have a long one. You need to know I intend to do everything I can to talk Tyrell out of this foolish move."

"Why's it foolish, Simone?"

Simone wished Booker would stop calling out her name. The way he said it caused too many wonderful memories to try to come to the surface. He'd always said her name as if it were the sweetest word that ever rolled off his tongue. It sounded no different to her ears today.

"Because he doesn't know who you are, Booker Branch, not at all."

"He wants to get to know me and I desperately want to know him. Tyrell's a grown man and he can make his own decisions. Your permission on this isn't required, but your blessings are. He's already told me he's not coming back home as long as your man is living there. Would you rather have him out on the streets than here with me? I'm a changed man, Simone. I've got God in my life now. I can hardly believe all the remarkable changes He's made in me."

Did he say God? He couldn't have. "Who are you kidding? Booker, you don't know the first thing about God or His Son, Jesus. You shouldn't even be using His name. It sounds like blasphemy coming out of your lying mouth."

Booker cleared his throat, unable to ignore the deep hurt caused by Simone's cold remarks. "Don't be so quick to judge me, Simone Branch. Aren't Christians supposed to be above that kind of behavior? You *are* still a Christian, aren't you?"

Booker calling her by his surname caused her indignation to rise further. Though angry enough to spit fire, Simone controlled her desire to slam down the phone in his ear, banging it hard enough to damage his hearing. *Who was he to question her spiritual nature?*

Booker had struck his blow right at the heart of whom she'd always claimed to be. Though her awful attitude toward her estranged husband gave credence to the devil, Simone did believe she was a Christian, a weak one at times, but nonetheless a Christian. Simone believed in and loved God with her whole heart, mind, body, and soul. But that didn't make her perfect.

Feeling her emotions slipping out of her control, Simone had to lower her head for a moment of prayer, silently asking God to please refill her empty cups of mercy and compassion.

"Have Tyrell call me when he wants to come by and get his things. I want to make sure I'm home when he gets here. Thanks for calling, Booker. Please give Tyrell my love."

After disconnecting the line, Simone sat in stone silence, staring at the phone, wondering if Booker was going to call right back. She hoped not. Her heart and emotional stability couldn't stay strong enough through another conversation with him. The main issues for Simone had already been resolved. Tyrell was safe and she now knew where he was staying. Booker living so close to the city that she herself resided in was unbelievable. That he had actually contacted Tyrell to tell him his whereabouts was even more astounding to Simone. It was a miracle.

Booker Branch had walked out on them for the high-rolling, fast-paced living of an NFL superstar. Without Booker ever sending Simone his personal address or phone number, he had his lawyer send out all the monies he paid to Simone. Booker hadn't contacted his immediate family either, according to his parents and three siblings, two brothers and a sister. Other than everyone knowing which football team he played on, not one of them had known exactly where he resided. After a couple of years of watching him play football on television, Simone had finally given up on them ever getting back together. Yet neither of them had ever filed for divorce.

When Booker had taken off and deserted his family, he'd taken Simone's precious heart with him. She had yet to get it back. Now that he was back in town perhaps she could make an attempt to retrieve it. On second thought, she didn't want it back. Not if it was still hurting today like it had been back then. The pain of her heart being ripped right out of her chest had been the most unbearable thing she'd ever gone through, the most unforgettable, a pain that had never fully healed. Keeping most of her feelings trapped protectively inside her was just fine by her.

The thing puzzling Simone the most was why Tyrell hadn't confided in her regarding his father making phone contact with him. Booker had said he'd been back in California for several months. Had she and her son grown that far apart? Did Tyrell feel that he couldn't come to her any longer? Had she alienated her only child? Did Tyrell feel that she'd put Jerome Hadley before him? Did her boy feel as though she'd deserted him, just like his father had done?

The deep aching in Simone's heart could not be massaged away or disregarded.

Sinclair stood at the kitchen counter, pouring herself a cup of freshly brewed coffee. A glance at the clock revealed the time as ten minutes after seven. She'd been home from work for over three hours, with no word whatsoever from Charles. No messages had been left on the answering machine. If this was what loneliness felt like, it was an awful feeling for her.

Sinclair had been left home alone on numerous occasions, even for days at a time, when Charles, a top-notch building contractor for the U.S. government, had had to travel for business. Loneliness hadn't come into play for her then, because she'd known Charles would eventually return home. She normally had a million and one tasks to perform, which was what had kept her from ever feeling lonely. At evening's end she'd have no problem falling asleep.

Feeling way too sorry for herself, Sinclair picked up the phone and then punched in Simone's home phone number. After several rings, only the voice on the recorded message greeted her. Hannah's was the next number that came to mind; same results as the first call. Glenda's number just rang and rang. No message device picked up the line. Calling Tara was only a fleeting thought, one Sinclair quickly dismissed. All the women loved Tara, but confiding in one so young seemed somewhat preposterous to Sinclair. What advice could she give anyway? Tara was still soak and wet behind the ears.

The phone rang at the exact same moment Sinclair cradled it. Praying that it was Charles, Sinclair grabbed up the receiver in haste.

"Hey, Mom, it's your baby boy. What are you up to?"

Sinclair smiled, relaxing back in her seat. "Hi, Marcus. Just having myself a cup of coffee. What's on your agenda for the evening?"

"Just chilling. I called to thank you for the money. It really helped me out of a jam."

"What sort of a jam, Marcus?"

"I'd gotten a little behind on my bills. That's all."

"What bills? I didn't know you had any bills."

"Sears sent me a charge card a long time ago. I also have a department store clothing account and a Discover Card."

Sinclair groaned. "How much are you into them for?"

Marcus laughed nervously. "You don't want to know, Mom. But I got it covered."

"Yeah, I *do* want to know. How can you have it covered if you're getting money from me to pay your bills?"

"Hold on a minute, Mom. Someone is at my door. I'll be right back."

Listening for voices, Sinclair strained her ears. Dead silence was all that she heard on the other end. While waiting for Marcus to come back on the line, she took a few sips of coffee.

"Mom, I have to call you back. I have company."

"Marcus, wait. You were about to tell me how much money you owe on your credit cards. I need to know now."

"I can't discuss that in front of company. If it's not too late when my friends leave, I'll call you back tonight. Love you, Mom. Bye."

Sinclair believed Marcus was lying to her, doubting that anyone had even been at his door. He was so creative in getting himself out of sticky situations. Marcus was hiding something. She was sure of it. *Lord, just don't let it have anything to do with more money. I'm in enough financial hot water as it is.*

It was imperative for Sinclair to learn the balances on Marcus's credit cards. If he didn't call her back, she'd call him and insist on the truth. Sinclair could only pray that Marcus hadn't run up his credit cards like she'd run up all of hers.

Sinclair's thoughts turned to Charles. *Where was he? What was he doing? Did he miss her?* She sorely missed him. *Had Charles turned on a phone at their town house? Was he sitting in the house, all alone, wondering about the same things she was?*

A sudden noise behind Sinclair caused her to turn around. The subject of her very thoughts stood there in the doorway. The absence of Charles's beautiful smile was upsetting to her. But he was here in the house, right across the room from her. Her longing for him increased.

Charles held up his laptop. "Forgot this. Sorry for the intrusion. Hope you have a good evening, Sinclair."

"Charles," Sinclair called out to him, "what about joining me for a cup of coffee? I just made it a few minutes ago. I'd love the company."

Charles shook his head in the negative. "I have a couple of budget reports to prepare for an early morning meeting. Thanks for the offer, Sinclair, but I have to run. Goodnight."

Sinclair rushed across the room and stood right in front of Charles. "Why are you doing this, Charles? Why? Isn't this something we can try to work out?"

"We've already discussed this matter over and over again, Sinclair. You've made your intentions known and I have to stick to mine. We'll eventually have to sit down and talk everything through again, but not anytime soon. We need the space until we can figure everything out." He leaned over and kissed her cheek. Before she could respond, he was gone.

Sinclair felt incredibly lousy. She couldn't ever remember Charles being so adamant with her about anything. Her husband had always given in to her, but he'd suddenly changed on her, but why so drastically? "For better or worse," she whispered, wishing she could turn back the hands of time. "Till death us do part."

Freshly showered and dressed in blue denim jeans and a crisp navy blue polo shirt, Tara had been keeping her eyes on the clock. Raymond had called to say he'd be late once again. Over an hour had passed since she'd last spoken with him. Maya needed sneakers for gym class, but she hadn't told her father until the last minute. Tara could imagine Raymond running all over the mall to fulfill his daughter's needs. He was doing his best to be the greatest father who ever lived.

Knowing time wouldn't slow down, no matter what she hoped for, Tara began checking on the food she'd begun preparing for a quiet dinner with Raymond. For the evening meal Tara had chosen grilled chicken breasts, green beans stir-fried in olive oil, baked sweet potatoes, and a tossed salad. Crazy for the taste of sweet potatoes, Raymond ate them at least three times a week.

As the doorbell pealed, Tara smiled, hoping Raymond had finally made it. She had rather expected him to call from the mall to say he couldn't make it. Tara had every intention of flinging herself into Raymond's arms, but that was before she saw Maya standing beside her father. Tara's heart fell a little. Although she'd expected to spend the evening alone with Raymond, she welcomed Maya with much enthusiasm.

"Come on in, you two." Tara hugged Raymond and then momentarily grasped Maya's small hand. "So nice to see you, Maya. This is certainly a pleasant surprise."

"Same here," Maya said, her voice soft and timid-like.

Raymond kissed Tara lightly on the mouth. "I hope you don't mind Maya tagging along with me. Had I taken her home first, there's no telling what time I would've made it here."

"Of course not. You are always welcome to bring Maya here with you."

Raymond and Maya followed Tara into her comfortable, upscale-furnished living room, where a crackling fire burned brightly in the black and gray marble fireplace.

"Have a seat you two. Would you like something to drink?"

"Do you have a Pepsi?" Maya asked.

Tara shook her head. "Coke or 7-Up. That's all I have. Will one of those do?"

Maya smiled softly. "Coke is okay."

"What about you, Ray?"

"Coke is fine for me, too. I'll come in the kitchen and help you with the drinks." Raymond turned to face Maya. "Be right back, sweetie. Tara has a lot of good magazines on the table there, including *Essence*."

"It's okay to make yourself right at home, Maya," Tara suggested, smiling sweetly. Winning Maya over would be a big plus. Besides, Tara loved kids of all ages.

The second Tara and Raymond reached the kitchen he took her into his arms, hugging and kissing her passionately. "I missed you, baby. You look so good." He nuzzled her neck. "And you smell so sweet. Did you miss me?"

Blushing heavily, Tara kissed Raymond gently on the mouth. "Yeah, very much so. I was hoping you'd get here, but I was beginning to think you might not be able to make it again."

Raymond looked slightly abashed, pressing his forehead against Tara's. "I know that I've been late a time or two recently and that I've had to call and cancel a few times. But normally when I make a promise I do my best to keep it. I promised you I'd see you today. I've kept it."

Tara softly brushed her knuckles down his cheek. "You certainly have, Raymond Wilkerson. You're here now. That's what matters most. Have you guys eaten?"

"I was hoping the three of us could go out to dinner. Is that cool with you, Tara?"

"Fine by me, but I did make one of your favorites, baked sweet potatoes. I also have grilled chicken and stir-fried green beans."

"So that's what smelled so good before I got a whiff of your sweet-smelling perfume."

Tara laughed at his complimentary remark. "Still want to go out and eat, Ray?"

"And let what you cooked go to waste? Not a chance! We can go to dinner over the weekend. Bring on the sweet potatoes, girl."

Tara laughed heartily. "Great. Go get Maya and bring her in here. I'll start warming up everything. Would you mind putting on some music while you're in the living room? Maybe you can let Maya choose what she'd like to hear. I have Usher's latest."

Smiling, Raymond winked at Tara. "Sure thing, baby. I think she'll like you allowing her to make the choice. As always, you're so thoughtful. See you in a minute or two."

Tara looked up at Raymond and smiled broadly. He smiled back, as he left the room. This is nice, Tara mused, hoping Maya would love her cooking as much as Raymond did.

Tara loved to cook and entertain in her home. Though she'd only been to their homes on a few special occasions, her four best girlfriends loved to convene at her house when they all had a chance to get together outside of work. They absolutely loved the way Tara pampered them. The two married ones of the group, Hannah and Sinclair, rarely had a social event in their homes. Simone and Glenda occasionally liked to entertain their friends and families in their home, but not nearly as much as Tara did. Tara also went all out for her girlfriend get-togethers.

Tara's childhood home at one time had been filled with dinner guests, especially on Sundays and holidays. Joanna Wheatley had an open-door policy in her home, always offering love and good down-home cooking. Joanna had kept the same policy after the divorce, but she never seemed to enjoy herself as much as she'd done when Jamaica was there to help her host.

Tara prided herself on being so much like her mama, a woman with a spirit of gold, yet she was so different in many ways. How she would've dealt with a troubled son like Timothy was one of their major differences. Tara was certain that she would've kicked Timothy out long before it got to the boiling point it had eventually reached. Long before her mother had died of a heart attack from all the stress and unbelievable drama Timothy had brought into her life.

Thinking of her loving father always filled Tara with joy. They only got together twice a year, but those were the times she lived for—good times. Jamaica had moved back to his native Birmingham, Alabama, shortly after Tara's mother had died, not long after he'd retired from the automobile industry. Although he'd never remarried, Jamaica was now considering doing so. Tara had yet to meet Anna Clay, the new woman in his life, but she was very eager to do so.

Upon going into the refrigerator to retrieve the butter, Tara saw that she had very little left and not nearly enough for everyone. Raymond loved to lavish butter on his sweet potatoes. There was only one solution. She'd have to run down to the convenience store, which was just around the corner from her place.

As she was on her way out of the room, Tara met up with her

guests at the entry. Tara laid her hand on Raymond's arm. "I'm just about out of butter. I need to run down to the corner store real quick. Can you keep an eye on things here in the kitchen while I'm gone?"

"I'll do one better by running down to the store for you. Is the butter all you need?"

"What about a couple of Pepsis for Maya, since she prefers it over Coke?"

Raymond fought the urge to bring Tara to him and kiss her for being so darn sweet. Her thoughtfulness had a way of warming him through and through. "Done deal, Tara. I'm out."

Tara felt a little awkward about being alone with Maya, but she quickly tamped down the fluttering butterflies, suggesting that Maya have a seat at the table. She reminded herself that Maya was only a teenager, not some big bad female wolf dressed in cute designer clothes.

If she wanted to have Maya as a friend, Tara knew she had to become one—a good one. Tara had no desire to fill Maria's, Maya's late mother's, shoes, but she did hope for Maya to one day consider her a confidante, someone she could talk to about anything and everything. A father could meet most of his daughter's needs, but a woman's touch was magical. Only a woman understood exactly what another woman had to contend with, the same as with a father and son.

"Do you like sweet potatoes, too, Maya?"

"They're okay. My mom used to fix them for my dad when he visited us. Daddy used to tell her that no one could make them better than she did. He always made a big fuss over hers."

Although she got an uneasy feeling about Maya's comment, Tara decided to let that remark go right on past her. Besides, a baked sweet potato was just a baked sweet potato. Throwing it into the oven to bake wasn't a major task by any stretch of the imagination. Outside of overcooking or burning it, there wasn't much you could do to ruin a sweet potato.

"No one can ever cook anything compared with the way our moms do it, but I do hope you'll enjoy the dinner I fixed. Your dad loves to eat my cooking too."

"Daddy's standards don't seem to be all that high. He seems to settle for way less than what he should. Now that I'm living with him, I hope to change at least that much about him."

Wondering if those remarks were made as insults against her, Tara glanced over at Maya to check out the expression on her face. Maya's sweet smile led Tara to believe otherwise, yet she decided to remain wary of the cute person behind the baby-soft voice and smile-curved lips.

Maya looked Tara right in the eye. "You think my dad's going to marry you, don't you?"

Tara was instantly taken aback by Maya's pointed question. How to answer it without returning the obvious attempt at sarcasm would be difficult. There was no mistaking Maya's intent in this case. Her razor-sharp tone of voice had set the record straight for Tara.

Tara silently prayed for tolerance. "Marriage has never come up, Maya."

"It won't either. Thank God for that. My dad never married my mom, so I know he's not going to marry you. You're just wasting your time with him. If he had to do it all over again, Daddy told me he'd marry my mom in a heartbeat. He still loves her, you know."

"Yeah, I do know, Maya. He's told me enough times," Tara said, hoping to deflate Maya's overinflated sails. This mannerless young woman had set out to hurt her intentionally. Maya had succeeded, but Tara would never give her the satisfaction of letting it show.

Going on with her kitchen duties, Tara did her best to remain calm. Fighting fire with fire was never a way to put out one. When one person escalated, the other had to keep his or her wits. Dousing this fire wouldn't be an easy task, but Tara was determined to take the high road—and keep the flame retardant handy. Getting into a verbal sparring match with a teenager was just not her style. She loved her peace far too much to end up charging into a boxing ring to put up a fight she couldn't possibly win.

Tara had also refused to enter the ring with Timothy. A war was not winnable for her with any of Satan's staunchest warriors. Although she knew God had her back, that He'd fight her battles for her, Tara was more concerned with her own salvation. Walking away from it all had been easier at the time, even though there were times when she'd wished she'd stayed, wished she'd fought against Satan to unequivocally win back her brother for Christ.

Tossing up yet another silent prayer, one for reinforcements in patience, love, and kindness, Tara sucked in a deep breath. "Would you mind putting the rolls in the oven for me, Maya? If we pop them in now, they'll be ready by the time your dad returns."

Unable to believe Tara actually wanted her help, Maya eyed Tara with open curiosity.

By the skeptical look on Maya's face it was obvious to Tara that Maya hadn't gotten the kind of reaction from her she'd been shooting for. But Maya had gotten a reaction all right, but good, because Tara's stomach was burning something fierce.

Maya raised an eyebrow. "You really want me to do that for you?"

Tara smiled gently. "I really do. You have to hurry if you're going to take care of the rolls for me. Your dad will be back any minute."

Maya's every step was a reluctant one, as she slowly came over to the kitchen's island counter. Without looking at Tara, she began arranging the rolls on a cookie sheet. Tara could feel Maya's eyes on her as Maya moved about the room, seemingly unsure of herself or of Tara.

Tara's thoughts were turbulent, but her outward demeanor belied the turmoil from within.

At the same time Raymond returned from the store, Tara and Maya had everything prepared and already on the table. Delicious cooking smells filled the air, increasing everyone's appetite but

Tara's. Maya's unsavory food for thought was the only thing Tara could chew on.

Raymond looked from Tara to Maya. "Everything is okay with my two girls, isn't it?" Raymond asked, letting go of a nervous chuckle.

Tara sensed that Raymond could feel the tension between her and his daughter. Hating the situation she had suddenly found herself in, her hopes for them to be a happy threesome all but dashed, Tara grasped Raymond's large hand. "Everything is cool. We're just hungry and ready to dig in. Please pass the blessing for us, Ray."

Raymond leaned over and kissed Tara on the forehead. "My pleasure. Let us join hands."

Chapter Three

"Hello, Simone."

Looking into the handsome, golden brown face of the man Simone once adored was nothing short of surreal. His star-studded, dark brown eyes were still heart rendering. Booker Branch hadn't shrunk an inch in height and not an ounce of body fat was visible anywhere on his anatomy. His six-foot-five athletic physique appeared as strong and as solid as it had in the days of his youth. So many years had passed them by, years of unbearable longing for him and the endurance of incredible loneliness. Memory after memory of their years together, desperately in love, tumbled recklessly through her throbbing head. Simone bravely fought the urge to cry.

Simone felt as if her armpits were sweating seahorses. Being in the company of her estranged husband was more than unsettling. That she was still in love with the hunk of unsweetened, dark chocolate came as no surprise. Booker had been her only boyfriend, her only lover. Numerous years had passed, but none had changed her feelings about the man standing before her.

There were times when Simone was angry with Booker, felt deep resentment toward him, cursing him innumerable times, but her love for him remained steadfast. She would always believe that he'd been a victim of circumstance. Too young, with too much money, too soon, and with too little experience in the world, he'd made the same mistakes a lot of rich athletes made. Booker began to believe that money owned his salvation and not God.

Simone struggled to speak, praying that her voice wouldn't desert her now. A silent Simone could only mean one thing. In no way did she want Booker to know that his presence had rendered her speechless. Everything about him had her at a loss for words.

Simone cleared her throat. "Hey, Booker." She had more to say, but her voice had disappeared once again. Fear played a large role in her inability to communicate. The fear of saying the wrong things, inflammable remarks fueled by anger, was the biggest issue for Simone.

Tyrell stepped into the front hallway and pulled Simone into his arms, hugging her tightly. "Hi, Mama. Sorry for getting you so upset. I don't like to worry you like that, but I seem to do it anyway." Tyrell looked to his dad. "It'll only take me a few minutes to get my things together. I won't leave you waiting too long."

Simone flinched inwardly. It amazed her that Tyrell was concerned about making Booker wait too long when his dad had left him behind to wait all these years for him to come back. Her son was definitely stronger for the experience, though he didn't know it yet, but she wished it hadn't happened to him at all. No loving mother wanted to see her child in pain.

"Take your time, son. The car stereo equipment works. I'll be entertained." Booker turned to walk away, only to turn back around before taking another step. "Nice to see you again, Simone. I'm glad to see you looking so well." His eyes appreciatively ran the length of her body.

Simone wrung her sweating hands together, wishing she could be as cruel to him as he'd been to her and Tyrell. "Please, Booker, you can wait inside. I really don't mind if you come in."

Stunned by her offer, Booker lifted an eyebrow. "Are you sure, Simone?"

"Positive. Please come in and have a seat. I'm sure you remember where the living room is. It's still in the same spot." Her nerves a jumbled mess, Simone started down the hallway.

The heavenly smell of homemade bread baking in the oven wafted across Booker's nose, grabbing his immediate attention. "From the smell of things, Simone, maybe I should wait out in the kitchen for Tyrell. It seems that some divine things are going on out there."

Simone couldn't hold back her smile. "The delicious aromas have gotten to you, huh?"

Booker grinned. "What kind of bread are you baking, Simone?"

The answer to Booker's question brought a sudden look of dismay to Simone's face. *Pumpernickel.* Had she unconsciously baked her estranged husband's favorite bread? If it wasn't so, he would more than likely think that it was, Simone mused. The truth was that she'd never baked pumpernickel bread in his absence—and she couldn't explain why she'd done so today.

"Rib-eye steaks, collard greens, and red potatoes." She'd purposely left out the bread.

Booker sniffed the air. "I don't smell any of that. But I do smell the bread. It's pumpernickel, isn't it?"

Simone hoped he wouldn't make anything of it. "You guessed it. Would you like some?"

Booker licked his lips. "Sure, Simone, if you don't mind."

"Help yourself to anything else you want. Everything you need should be easy to locate. If you have a problem finding something, holler. I'll be upstairs with Tyrell."

"Thanks. I promise to leave you and Tyrell a little something," Booker joked.

Simone felt good that she'd been able to act civilized with Booker. For all practical purposes her home was still his. He'd sure enough paid for it, lock, stock, and barrel, though the deed was in both their names. Booker making himself at home in his home-on-paper wasn't a problem for her, because she was sure he wouldn't return there again once he and Tyrell left.

Talking her son out of living with his father was no longer on Simone's agenda. Tyrell had needed his father for such a long time. Now he had him back in his life. Who was she to take that away from him? If Tyrell had issues with Booker, she wanted them to be his own, not hers.

Simone had made it a point never to talk down Booker to her son, never to give her son the impression that his father was no good. Ripping apart the other parent was never right. He had at least taken care of them financially, very well at that. It was her desire that Tyrell find out who his father was for himself. Had Booker not run away from everything she would've been only too glad to share Tyrell with him, even while living in separate households.

A child needed both parents, always and forever.

Simone would've done everything in her power to see that Tyrell never felt as if he had to choose one parent over the other, or feel any guilt over loving both. Putting children in the middle of personal battles was a gross mistake made all too often by feuding parents. If parents, including her, could only remember that it was all about the child's happiness and security.

One parent could not have a child independent of the other, unless an adoption was involved. It was up to the adults to work things out and make sure their children were brought up in a stressfree, loving environment. Unfortunately, that wasn't the way it normally worked out.

Simone silently thanked God for not allowing her to give in to her raging anger and go on the attack against Booker. Allowing this complicated situation to play itself out was the best thing for her to do. Badmouthing Booker would only serve to make it all more complex. She knew she needed to have a talk with Tyrell but thought it was best to wait for another opportunity. *Was the timing wrong?* With Booker in the house, Simone thought so. She and Tyrell needed to have a private one-on-one. But he also needed to know he had her support.

Feeling a sudden weariness, Simone dropped down on the very top step, unable to go any farther. Her entire body ached yet she also felt numb. Leaning her head against the wall, Simone closed her eyes, wishing she could go back in time just to see what she could've done differently.

Simone was fascinated with the powerful-looking muscles of the moving men, which were gleaming from a heavy sheen of sweat. She'd never seen so many buff men in one place. Carrying the massive loads of boxes and heavy furnishings appeared effortless for them.

Bounding down the steps like an Energizer Bunny on speed was a young man about her age. Fourteen or fifteen, she figured. Simone thought he looked pretty cool in his worn jeans and Chicago Bears sweatshirt. She didn't know the first thing about swooning, but she felt faint.

Simone smiled at him when the young man looked at her with interest. "What you doing wearing that Chicago Bears sweatshirt in L.A.? This is Raider and Ram territory."

He looked surprised, but he was also impressed. "What do you know about football? You're nothing but a girl."

"A smart one too. I probably know as much as you do about the game. My daddy is a football fanatic. So there."

Seriously doubting her, he waved her comments off. "What's that got to do with you? Just 'cause your daddy watches football doesn't mean you know anything about it."

Simone jutted her chin out in defiance. "Ask me some questions and find out."

Laughing inwardly, Simone remembered the ninety-nine football questions Booker had fired at her on the very first day they'd met. She'd never forget the stunned expression on his face, after she'd correctly answered each one.

"Who taught you all that?"

"My daddy, Ellison Madison. Don't you remember what I said about him?"

Booker looked dazed. "Oh, yeah. He's a fanatic. I don't know any girl who knows as much about football as you do. I guess you're pretty okay. What else you know about sports?"

"I know a lot, boy. I also know you didn't answer my question."

"Which one?"

"About you wearing that Chicago Bears sweatshirt in L.A."

"I lived in Chicago. Just moved here. Cut my teeth while watching the Bears."

Simone's eyes widened in wonder at Booker's response. She'd never met anyone from Chicago, but she'd heard plenty of exciting stories about the Windy City.

"Do you have any vinegar, Simone?" Booker asked from the bottom of the stairs.

Upon hearing Booker's deep bass voice, Simone snapped her head back. "Vinegar? Oh, vinegar," she remarked, fighting hard to pull herself out of the grasp of yesteryear. "I keep it in the fridge, Booker."

"Are you okay, Simone?"

Simone looked perplexed. "What are you talking about?"

"You look lost, Simone."

"Lost how?"

Booker shrugged. "I don't know. Maybe you should tell me. You look dazed."

"I don't feel that way, Booker."

Dazed was a grossly understated word for what Simone felt. Stuck under the massive wheels of a semi was closer to it. Although Simone had known it wouldn't be easy seeing Booker again, she had horribly miscalculated the deep impact it would have on her emotional stability. This was the only man whom she'd ever entrusted her heart. And look what he'd done with it. Torn between her undying love for Booker Branch and the fathomless hatred for what he'd put her through was a tough ditch to climb out of. And she didn't own a sturdy ladder.

Al Green's "How Do You Mend a Broken Heart" suddenly came to her mind. Sighing deeply, Simone wished she had the answer to that one.

Tyrell saved the day by appearing at the top of the steps, where Simone was still seated. Being in Booker's presence had gotten terribly awkward for her. Making any sort of polite conversation with the man who'd trampled all over her heart wasn't something she considered a pleasantry. Thinking outside the box was impossible for Simone, especially when she felt so utterly trapped inside it.

Tyrell stooped down, resting on his haunches. "Mama, do you know where my black Nikes are? I can't find them."

Simone shook her head in the negative. "No clue." She reached up and grasped Tyrell's hand. "I'd like for us to go downstairs so we can all talk for a minute or two. Is that okay with you?"

"Talk about what?" Tyrell asked, frowning.

Simone smoothed Tyrell's hair back. "This move you're about to make."

"There's nothing to say. I just checked your bedroom closet. Mr. Jerome's clothes are still in there. That settles it for me, Mama."

"Maybe for you, but it doesn't settle it for me, Tyrell. We still need to talk." Simone was not going to get into anything heavy, but she'd decided she might be making a big mistake if she said nothing. Despite her earlier considerations, she simply didn't want Tyrell to leave home. If she didn't voice her dismay over him leaving home, he might think she didn't care about him.

Booker pointed toward the kitchen. "Come on down, son, and have a seat at the table. You need to hear your mother out. I'm just going to finish my food and listen."

Sighing hard, Tyrell stood up straight and practically ran down the stairs. "I hope we can make this quick. It won't be long before that sorry Mr. Jerome comes home from work. I don't want to be here when he does."

Once everyone was seated in the kitchen, Simone looked over at Tyrell. "I understand your feelings about Jerome, son. Now tell me this. Do you feel that moving out is really going to solve anything, Tyrell? You've only lived in this house all your life."

Tyrell eyed his mother strangely. "You should already know the answer to that, Mama, unless you've forgotten what happened between Mr. Jerome and me. I can't forget it. I'm not a violent person, but I could've pulled that trigger in the blink of an eye. It also made me realize I need to change me. That I could do something like that scared me even if it didn't scare you."

"It did, and it still does," Simone confessed, recalling the devastating images of that fearful night. "I'm not trying to discourage you, Tyrell, but you don't know your father that well yet. You were so young when we split up. Wouldn't it be better if you took a little time to get to know him before you moved into his place?"

"I didn't know Mr. Jerome either, but you moved him in here with us, anyway." Tyrell looked at his father. "This is my real dad. Mr. Jerome was and still is a stranger to me. Someone could get hurt real bad if I stay. We both have problems. Don't you know that by now, Mama?"

Simone's hand went up to her chest, covering her heart. Talking Tyrell into getting to know his father first had failed. Hearing what her son had to say made her think that perhaps Tyrell would be better off living with Booker. Jerome had to go, eventually, but she needed to give him enough time to find a place to stay. No doubt his mother would take him in, but that had to be his choice. She couldn't see herself kicking him out in the streets with nowhere to go.

Simone pulled Tyrell to her and hugged him tightly. "I accept your decision to go live with your dad, Tyrell. I don't want to see you involved in anything worse than what has already happened. The gun incident was bad, but not as horrible as things can get. You have my blessings, son, but you are always welcome to come home. This is your house, too."

Booker's sigh of relief was loud and clear. "Thanks, Simone. Tyrell coming to live with me is what's best for now. Everything will eventually work itself out."

Simone appreciated Booker's comments, but they didn't ease the pain in her heart one bit. It suddenly dawned on her that she didn't know if Booker had anyone else living with him. He wasn't remarried, unless he was a polygamist, which she doubted seriously. Oh, well, all of these things would come to light soon enough, she mused, though she wasn't the least bit eager to learn if he had a live-in girlfriend. Somehow that would cause her more hurt if it were true.

Tyrell looked over at his father. "Ready to go, Booker?"

With an incredulous look on her face, Simone raised her eyebrows. "Excuse me! What did you just say, Tyrell?"

Tyrell looked confused. "I asked if he was ready to go."

Simone scowled hard. "No, no, I'm referring to the name you called him by."

"I called him Booker," Tyrell responded, puzzled by his mother's sudden outburst.

"Not in my house or in my presence, mister. You're an adult, but you'll never be that grown. If you can't bring yourself to call him 'dad,' you'd better find another respectful handle to use instead. Don't you ever again let me hear you call your father by his first name."

"Simone, I gave him permission to call me by my first name," Booker said. "It's okay."

"No it's not. I didn't raise him to be disrespectful to anyone. You just can't come in here and undo what I've tried to do to bring up Tyrell right, Booker. That's not fair."

Booker threw up his hands. "I only agreed to it until he gets to know me better. I have to earn the right to the title 'dad.' I know that I also have to gain Tyrell's respect. Think you could let me handle things now? I promise not to undo any of what you've managed to accomplish."

A look of defiance settled in Simone's eyes. "As I said before, Tyrell will be respectful in my house and in my presence. What you two do when you're alone is your business."

That was as close to an approval from Simone for Booker to handle things his way, but only in his space. It was becoming clearer to her by the minute that Tyrell desperately needed his father. Perhaps Booker could set the record straight and redirect her son's path. If he could accomplish that, she would take her hat off to him. Lord only knew what she'd had to contend with once Tyrell had hit puberty. Booker's sudden reappearance in their lives just might be God's answer to her constant prayers. It certainly wasn't a minute too late.

Upon hearing the key in the lock, Simone's body grew rigid. Jerome was home early. She could only hope that he wasn't strung out. If he was, drama like nobody's business might very well occur. The last thing she needed was to witness another confrontation. Booker would stand up for his son against Jerome, forcefully so. There was no doubt in her mind about that. Booker had always been a warrior at heart, had never been known to run from a fight.

Hearing her name echoing into the room caused Simone to flinch. Instead of waiting for Jerome to find her, she got up from the chair and went out to meet him. Keeping Jerome and Tyrell apart was the only thing on her mind.

Simone rounded the corner and came face-to-face with Jerome. His bloodshot eyes told her all she needed to know. He was definitely strung out. Jerome tried to hug her, but she rejected his awkward affection. The smell of stale alcohol nearly made her gag.

Jerome eyed her curiously. "Whose fancy car is in my spot in the driveway?"

"That's what I want to talk to you about, Jerome. Can we step into the study?"

The voices coming from the kitchen caused Jerome to push past Simone, nearly knocking her over in the process. "Who you got in here?"

Tyrell leaped to his feet the same moment Jerome entered the cavernous room. Simone's hopes were immediately dashed. That Jerome was higher than a kite was evident to everyone present. The anger in his bloodshot eyes made him look like a crazed lunatic.

Jerome pointed a shaky finger at Booker. "Who's this joker up in my house?" Jerome slurred, teetering and tottering on unsteady legs.

Booker instantly got to his feet, rearing up his six-foot-five frame, causing Jerome to take several steps back. By the expression on Jerome's face, he clearly hadn't determined the size of the person he'd just confronted.

Booker raised both eyebrows. "Your house? That's interesting, since I paid cash for this house quite some time ago. It seems to me that you're in my home. Care for proof?"

Simone saw the need for her to intervene before things got out of hand. She moved farther into the room. "Jerome, this is Tyrell's father, Booker Branch. We were having a family meeting. If you could excuse us, we'll be through in just a minute."

Fire blazed in Jerome's eyes. "Family, my butt! How can you call the likes of him a part of your family after what he's put you through?"

Seeing Tyrell's fists clenching and unclenching wasn't a good sign. Simone grew alarmed. *Lord,* she prayed in silence, *please diffuse this situation before it goes any further.*

Booker put his arm around Tyrell's shoulders. "I think we should go now. No good can come from this situation." Booker looked to Simone. "We'll finish our talk later."

"The hell you will," Jerome challenged, his tone loud and boisterous.

Before Booker could tighten his grip on his son's shoulders to calm him, Tyrell was throwing wild punches at Jerome. Already unsteady on his feet, Jerome rocked and reeled from side to side. A powerful shove from Tyrell sent Jerome flying across the room.

Simone's desperate screams brought everything to a screeching halt. Without a moment's thought, Booker rushed to his wife's side, drawing her into his arms. He then held her at arms length. "Try to calm down, Simone. I'm sorry. This is my fault. I shouldn't have come inside."

"You have more of a right to be here than he does," Tyrell shouted, pointing at Jerome, who was trying to get to his feet. "I see who means more to you, Mama. If you really cared about me, he would've been gone by now. Let's get out of here before I kill him," Tyrell shouted.

Booker walked over and put his arm around Tyrell. "You have to calm down, too. This will all work itself out. Go on outside. I want to say something to your mother in private."

A look akin to hatred filled Tyrell's eyes. "She's not my mother. As far as I'm concerned, she's dead and buried. I never want to see her face again. Her choice is clear to me."

Booker squeezed Tyrell's shoulders hard enough to make him wince from the pain. "Don't ever let anger do your talking for you. Go wait for me in the car. Right now."

Visibly shaken by Tyrell's parting shot, Simone's entire body trembled with the deep anguish she felt. Hearing her only child referring to her as *dead* had shattered her very existence. Why did children get so angry with the parent who'd done the most for them, who'd been there to see to their every need, the parent who'd lay down their life for them? How had everything gotten so complicated? Booker's sudden reappearance had made things even more complex.

Booker took a moment to check on Jerome to see if he was okay, but he didn't get too close. If Jerome were to swing on him, Booker didn't want to have to take him out. Satisfied that Jerome's inability to get to his feet came more from intoxication than anything else, Booker gave a huge sigh of relief, glad that the paramedics didn't need to be called.

Booker walked back to Simone and stood in front of her, placing both his hands on her shoulders. "I don't think you should stay here with him in the condition he's in, Simone. Is there somewhere you can go until he sobers up?"

Simone shook her head in the negative. "No need. I can handle things. I've done it many times before. I'm more concerned about Tyrell right now. Go to him. He really needs you."

"I need him, too. You can't even imagine how much. I've made a lot of gross mistakes in the past, but I'm back here to try to rectify as many of them as I can. Please be patient with me. Everything will be okay, Simone. You'll see."

Simone sighed wearily. "I hope so, Booker. I can't take too much more of this."

Booker removed his wallet from his back pant's pocket and then pulled out a business card, which he handed to Simone. "Call me if you need anything. Although I feel responsible for a lot of this, I'm not taking on any responsibility out of guilt. I'm a man now. I've put childish things away. I've also made my peace with God. And I hope to one day make my peace with you and our son, Simone. I know that forgiveness may come hard for you. Just know that I understand. I'm not here to pressure you in any way. I'm here to do what I have to do."

Corinthians I, Chapter 13 came to Simone's mind. "We'll see. Time, Booker. Time will tell all. It always does. I'll give Tyrell a couple of days before I try to contact him."

"That's a good idea. I'll see you." Booker looked over at the man who was still struggling to get to his feet, glad to see that he hadn't been seriously hurt. Booker could only shake his head in dismay. "Are you sure you'll be okay?"

"I'm fine. Now get going, Booker. Tyrell is probably ready to come back in here and tear into Jerome again. We don't want that to happen."

A worried look on his face, Booker waved at Simone as he headed for the front door.

Rubbing her temples in a circular motion, Simone looked down on the shadow of a man who'd only managed to get to his knees thus far. Although only ten minutes or so had passed since Tyrell had flattened Jerome, it seemed like an eternity to Simone. Jerome looked as though he had no idea what had hit him so hard.

Unable to keep from feeling so sorry for him, Simone bent over and attempted to help him up. Jerome's fist flying into her right eye wasn't something she would've ever expected. He'd never even attempted to strike her before now, though verbal abuse from him wasn't that uncommon. Simone struggled hard to keep from falling backward and losing her footing. The hard tile floor could do serious damage to her skull if her head were to meet up with it. After a few seconds of swaying from side to side, she managed to regain her balance.

Simone's head felt as if it were splitting in two. It couldn't hurt any more if she'd actually landed on it. The throbbing pain in her eye was also unbearable. Calling the police was only a fleeting thought. That would only make things worse. Leaving her comfortable home wasn't an attractive option but it was the most feasible one, the safest. Simone thought of her four closest friends, but she wasn't sure she wanted them to know that Jerome had dared to strike her.

Simone's heart raced as she gave more thought to facing her friends and coworkers all bruised up. *How in the world was she going to hide a black eye from their probing eyes?* She couldn't, not if she planned on going in to work. The thought of calling in sick for a few days just might be the solution, but knowing how understaffed the hospital was made her also rethink that idea. Simone decided just to tell her girlfriends what had happened and leave the chips to fall where they may.

In the course of Jerome swinging on Simone, he had lost his balance and fallen down to the floor once again. Helping him up wasn't even a remote consideration for Simone. Getting out of the house was uppermost in her mind. Checking into a hotel nearby her job was the most convenient for now. Then she thought of Tara, the only one of her friends who lived alone. Tara would welcome her into her home with open arms. The idea of being alone in a hotel wasn't the least bit appealing. Tara's presence would help bring her some level of comfort.

Simone stood over Jerome, looking down upon him. "As soon as you sober up, gather your things and get out of my house, Jerome. You have gone way too far this time. Don't let me come back home and find you still here. You will need Jesus and a host of His angels if you decide not to move out. The road has come to an abrupt end for you and me."

Although Tara tried to hide her feelings, the troubled look in her eyes was hard to conceal. Deciding if she should mention to Raymond the scene between her and Maya wasn't an easy decision to make. Would he understand? More so, would he believe her? Maya appeared so innocent, smiling sweetly, as if she hadn't just verbally raked Tara over the hot coals.

Why Maya felt the way she did was puzzling to Tara. Maya hadn't shown any resentment toward her before now. The death of Maya's mother had been a recent occurrence. Tara could relate to how she must feel, since she still missed her mother more than she could adequately express. Upon deciding to shelve all her thoughts until later, Tara tuned into the conversation between father and daughter. The ballet lessons Maya was taking was the topic.

"Daddy, do you remember when you and Mommy came to my first dance recital? We had such a good time that evening, huh?"

Nodding his head, Raymond smiled. "Yeah, baby, I do. You were super."

"I'll never forget the look in Mommy's eyes when you drove into the parking lot at the same time we did. She didn't think you were coming. We were both so happy to see you." Maya dropped her head. "I miss Mommy so much."

Raymond leaned over and massaged Maya's back. "I know, baby. We all miss her. But maybe we should change the subject for now.

It's only making you feel worse. We also need to show some respect for Tara. This *is* her home, you know."

Maya lifted her head and stared at Tara, her eyes wide with innocence. "I'm sorry. I didn't think it would upset you to hear me talk about my mother. I didn't mean to disrespect you. It's just that I really miss my mom."

Although Tara recognized that it was all an act on Maya's part, she wouldn't think of calling her out. "I'm not upset, Maya, nor do I mind you talking about your mom. No apology for that is ever necessary. Talking about Maria will help keep her memory alive."

The annoyed expression on Maya's face told Tara that Maya had once again been stunned by her refusal to engage. Tara really didn't mind Maya talking about her mother. What she resented was that Maya was trying to use Maria as a weapon against her. As sad as it was, it was true. Tara had been a daddy's girl so she knew how that could be. But she couldn't imagine herself being viciously rude to someone her father was involved with under the same circumstances. It wasn't as if she'd come between Maya's parents. They'd parted long before Tara had ever met Raymond.

"Thanks, Tara. I knew you'd understand," Maya remarked.

Tara bristled inwardly at Maya calling her by her first name. It was totally unacceptable, disrespectful. She hadn't done that before, and Tara wasn't going to allow her to get away with it a single time. No fourteen-year-old girl should ever call an adult by his or her first name.

Tara smiled softly. "Maya, please revert back to calling me Miss Tara. I'd like that."

Maya looked Tara dead in the eye. "Why's that?"

"It's a sign of respect, that's why," Raymond responded before Tara could. "You've always called her Miss Tara, so it shouldn't be a problem for you to continue doing so."

"Okay, Daddy. Again, I'm sorry if I upset you, Tar, uh, Miss Tara."

"Again, I'm not upset." Hoping the urge to strangle Maya would hurry up and go away, Tara clasped her hands together. "I hope you're both enjoying your dinner."

Raymond smiled at Tara. "The food is great, honey. Tastes like my mama's cooking."

The look of disapproval in Maya's eyes was not lost on Tara. It seemed that Raymond's compliments had Maya's nose a little disjointed. Tara couldn't help wondering if this was the beginning of a nightmare. If it were, it wasn't going to take Tara too long to wake up. Tara had no intentions of charging into battle with a teenager. It just wasn't going to happen.

"Now that we've eaten, what about me taking my two favorite girls to the movies?"

Waiting for Maya's response before she committed to Raymond's query, Tara discreetly sucked in a deep breath.

Maya frowned. "I'm really not feeling well, Daddy. My stomach is upset. The food might've been too overseasoned for me. Do you think you could just take me home?"

"Sure, baby. I don't want you home by yourself, so I'll drop you off at Aunt Susan's."

Maya's eyes grew wide with surprise. "I didn't want to go to your sister's last night and I don't want to go to her house now. I want to sleep at home in my own bed."

Raymond looked helplessly at Tara, as if he needed rescuing.

Tara hid her disappointment very well, pasting on a smile of empathy. "Take Maya on home. We can do a movie another evening. Hope you're feeling better soon, Maya."

The arch of triumph was visible in Maya's eyes. Tara was not surprised by it.

Raymond leaned over and kissed Tara on the cheek. "Thanks for being so understanding, sweetheart. I'll help you clean up the kitchen before I leave."

Tara reached over and patted Raymond's hand. "I've got it, Ray." *We wouldn't want Maya to die from my cooking, so please get her out of here before my eager hands end up strangling her after all.*

Tara instantly scolded herself on her corruptive thought. Maya had worked her nerves this evening—and she was in dire need of a soft place to land. Raymond's arms were the preferable spot, but it was apparent that that wasn't going to happen tonight. Sure, she'd wanted to spend time with Raymond, lots of it, but things just hadn't turned out in her favor. Tara felt like crying, but tears served no purpose in this instance. Tara wondered if Maya treated Raymond's sister, Susan, the same way. It would be sure enough interesting to find out.

The doorbell rang just as Tara opened it for her guests to leave. Seeing Simone standing there was rather shocking. The most surprising part of it was Simone wearing sunglasses at night. After hellos and good nights were exchanged between Tara and all her guests, Tara ushered Simone into the living room, where they both took a seat.

Tara crossed her legs. "What's going on with you, girl? And why the sunglasses?"

Simone slowly took off her sunshades and then pointed to her swollen, discolored eye. "Does this answer your question, Tara?"

Tara's hand flew up to her face. "My word!"

Taylor Phillips placed a cup of hot tea in front of Glenda, who looked terribly weary. Taylor glanced at the clock on the kitchen stove. It was well after Anthony's curfew, but he hadn't come in yet. Glenda had called everyone she'd thought of, those whom Anthony might be with, or those who possibly knew of his whereabouts. No one had seen him or talked to him in the last couple of hours. Glenda had already exhausted the familiar calling list.

After pouring himself a glass of Coke, Taylor joined Glenda at the table. He hated seeing her looking so distraught, but there wasn't much he could do about it. He'd tried countless times to talk Glenda into letting him counsel Anthony, but she'd always told him it wasn't his place.

Since her son rebelled against most authority figures, Glenda didn't believe he would make Taylor an exception. While he had never disrespected Taylor, the two males had had very little interaction. Glenda made it a point to keep them at a distance from each other.

Taylor's fingers gently massaged the back of Glenda's hand. "Would you like me to run you a hot bath, Glen?"

Glenda shook her head in the negative. "I think I'll just shower tonight. But thanks."

"A hot bath will help you relax more, but I accept your decision. You look really tense and worn out, girl. How much longer do you plan to keep up these late-night vigils?"

Glenda shrugged. "I don't know. I just can't fall off to sleep until I hear Tony come in. Talking to him does no good, so I don't know why I keep trying to get him to listen to reason. I'm so scared for him, Taylor."

Taylor rubbed Glenda's shoulders in a soothing manner. "Tony is the one who should be scared, Glen, but he's not. As long as you continue to cover up for him, he has nothing to fear. I'm afraid that good fortune is going to run out on both you and Tony. Very soon."

"I don't cover up anything for him, Taylor. Why do you always say that?"

"Have you reported his missed curfews to his PO, Glen?"

Glenda glared at Taylor. "Why would I? That would get him into even more trouble."

"Then what you're doing is called covering up. You may not see it that way, but covering for him is exactly what you're guilty of. I know you'll only reject the idea again, but I still think you should consider letting me get involved with Tony. It just might do him some good."

Just to get Taylor to back off, Glenda nodded. "Okay. I'll think about it."

Taylor chuckled. "Liar," he said jokingly. "You just want me to butt out."

Glenda had to laugh too. "Too obvious, huh?" She smiled sweetly at Taylor. "I know you mean well, but I'm afraid to get you involved. I don't want Tony to turn on you. So far he hasn't had anything negative to say about our relationship and I really don't want that to change."

"I understand that, Glen, but he may think I'm being indifferent to him. You do your best to keep us apart, so I wouldn't be surprised if he thinks I don't want to be bothered with him. We both know that's not the case. Do you see what I'm saying?"

Pondering Taylor's question, Glenda picked up her cup, took a sip of the lukewarm liquid, and then put it back down. Keeping her son and male friends apart was definitely by design. Anthony never liked the men she'd dated in the past and he'd made sure they all knew it. One serious argument between him and one of her long-ago suitors was the main reason why she'd made the decision to keep the men in her life separated. Less risk was involved that way.

Taylor was such a great guy and Glenda would hate to see him and Anthony end up on a bad note. Things were at least amicable between them, even though they were like two ships passing in the night. One was always coming while the other was leaving. Familiarity did have a way of breeding contempt and she didn't want that to occur between Anthony and Taylor. Anthony had already built up enough resentment during his short tenure on earth. Glenda plainly feared the outcome if she were to risk such a venture.

Glenda took Taylor's hand. "I do appreciate your wanting to counsel Tony, but I still don't think it's a good idea. I don't want him to come to resent you. Please try to understand."

Taylor nodded. "I already do. More than you know. But if you ever change your mind, I'll be here to help out. I'd be glad to try to help Tony see his way clear."

Glenda smiled softly before kissing the back of Taylor's hand. "You're a very special person, Taylor Phillips. I'm blessed to have you in my life."

A gentle kiss was shared between Glenda and Taylor, followed by a few warm hugs.

"Same here, Glenda."

Upon hearing the alarm system chime, Taylor instantly got to his feet, glancing down at his watch. "Tony's home now. I'm out of here. I'll call you in the morning." Before heading for the front door, Taylor gave Glenda another soft kiss. "I hope you get a good night's sleep, Glen. Your body won't be able to take much more of this physical abuse. I worry about you."

"I know you do. I appreciate your concern, Taylor. I really mean that."

Glenda followed behind Taylor as he vacated the room. Anthony was busy taking his shoes off when they reached the front foyer. Glenda grew tense, hoping her son wasn't in one of his foul moods tonight.

Taylor nodded. "Hey, Tony. Nice to see you, man."

"You, too, Mr. T."

Anthony had been taught to respect all of his elders by Glenda, but he only respected those who returned the favor. Glenda didn't know exactly when her son had begun referring to Taylor as Mr. T., since they saw so little of each other, but it pleased her that he had always treated Taylor with respect. It didn't appear to her that Taylor minded being referred to that way.

Anthony had a look of uncertainty, shuffling his feet back and forth. "I hope you're not leaving 'cause of me, Mr. T. You seem to do that every time I come home."

Thinking of the point he'd tried to make earlier about how Anthony might feel about him, Taylor shot Glenda a knowing glance. "It has nothing to do with you, pal. It's late and I have an early morning wakeup call. I was sticking around until you got home so your mom wouldn't be alone. My leaving is nothing more than that, Tony."

Anthony nodded. "That's cool. Thanks. See you next time, man."

Taylor pumped his fist in the air. "Good night, Tony."

Glenda looked completely astounded. Anthony making light conversation with Taylor had surprised her, but pleasantly so. They'd spoken to each other before, but never anything more than a toneless hello or good-bye. The question Anthony had asked of Taylor had also stunned her. Maybe there might be something to what Taylor had mentioned to her. It wouldn't hurt to explore the possibility, Glenda mused, though she was still unsure that anything would ever come of Taylor and Anthony building a relationship. Glenda couldn't help seeing it as a very risky proposition. Fear had a way of paralyzing the mind, body, and soul, all at once.

After once again promising to phone Glenda the next morning, without further ado, Taylor took his leave. Already forming in her mind what she'd say to her son for being late again, Glenda closed the door behind the man she'd come to care so much about.

Upon entering the kitchen, Robert's mouth flew open. "Look at this kitchen," Robert voiced loudly. "Derrick has left this place a holy mess, Hannah."

Hannah looked around at the untidiness, wishing Derrick had thought enough of them to clean up after himself. "I'll take care of it, Robert. It'll only take me a second."

"Oh, no, it's not going to take you any time at all. Derrick is cleaning up this mess all by himself. You're not lifting a finger."

"But, Robert, it's one-thirty in the morning."

"It could be four o'clock, Hannah, and it wouldn't matter to me!" Robert shouted at the top of his lungs, heading for Derrick's bedroom.

"Don't, Robert!" Hannah yelled after him. "I don't feel like hearing the drama at this hour of the morning. I'm ready to go to bed."

Robert turned around and popped his head back in the doorway.

"Good night, Hannah. Close the door and go to sleep. I promise to keep my voice down. You won't hear a thing, unless . . ."

"Unless what?" Hannah interjected, looking fearful.

"Derrick decides to challenge me. Then all hell *will* break loose."

Feeling one gigantic headache coming on, Hannah slapped her palm against her forehead. Too tired to get into a shouting match with her husband, Hannah wearily dragged herself up the stairs. At the door of Derrick's room, she stopped and watched Robert pulling the covers off their near-comatose son. Derrick had always slept like a log, even through some of the earthquakes.

Derrick suddenly sat up straight in the bed, looking wide eyed and crazy. "What's wrong? What you doing, man?"

Robert snatched the covers up and tossed them on the floor. "I got your man! Get your butt out this bed right now, Derrick. You got some work to do."

Derrick rubbed his eyes with his fists. "Do you know what time it is? Dad, what's up?"

"You, as soon as you get on your feet. The kitchen is calling out your name."

Derrick scowled. "What?"

"Don't what me, boy! Get your butt downstairs and clean up that kitchen. I want it put back exactly as you found it. This is not a hotel. There are no maids living here. Now move it."

Grumbling under his breath, Derrick clambered out of bed.

Robert cupped his ear with his hand. "What's that? You got something to say to me?"

Derrick shook his head. "No, but I'm moving as fast as I can."

"Not fast enough for me. If that phone rang, you'd already be on it."

Derrick looked out into the hallway at his mother. "Can you help me out in the kitchen?"

"Not so much as the lifting of her little pinkie," Robert responded for Hannah. "Your mother's not the one who messed things up down there. You're wasting time, son. The sooner you get things done, the sooner we can all go to bed and get some sleep."

"What? You planning on standing over me, Dad?"

Robert smirked. "Every second."

Hannah thought Robert was being very unreasonable with Derrick, as usual. Getting someone up out of bed in the wee hours of the morning was downright cruel. The kitchen could've waited. It certainly wasn't going to get up and walk away. It seemed to Hannah that Robert wasn't going to be happy and content until he completely alienated Derrick from the family. She was so fearful that Derrick might one day leave home and never come back.

Hannah had already experienced the devastating pain of someone leaving home and never coming back. Her older brother by five years, her only sibling, Harold Burrell, whom she had adored, had left home because of their strict father, never to return.

Harold had run away from home at the tender age of seventeen. At twenty years of age he had been killed in a logging accident in an Oregon national forest. Her brother had chosen hard labor over the unrealistic expectations of their father, Edgar. Harold had once told Hannah that he'd rather join the military and fight in a war than live under the same roof with Edgar Burrell.

As for their mother, Ruth, she had pampered Harold in pretty much the same way as Hannah coddled Derrick. However, Ruth had never let her son get out of his responsibilities, always holding him accountable for his every action. Unlike Hannah, who could never hold Derrick's feet to the fire for more than a few minutes, Ruth was a tough-love mother. Harold was a darn good son, which had made it very easy for Ruth to raise him up. She gave her love abundantly and freely to both of her offspring, but Hannah always knew that Harold was Ruth's favorite, just as she'd been Edgar's special baby girl.

In her early seventies now, Ruth still pined away for her son. Edgar was rather frail but sound in mind and just as stubborn as he'd always been. Hannah took care of their personal needs when she was off duty and had hired someone to look after them when she worked.

The Burrells resided in a senior citizen's apartment a couple of miles from Hannah's residence; their financial picture was very secure. Though they'd had everything needed for survival, and then some, Edgar had worked hard and had believed in saving his money for life after retirement. The only reason her parents hadn't come to live with her was that Edgar had outright refused. His independence was important to him, so his daughter hadn't fought him on his decision. Tampering with Edgar's dignity was the last thing Hannah had wanted to do.

Robert slid into bed next to Hannah. When he tried to pull her into his arms, she pushed him away, moving to the far side of the mattress. Robert quickly sat up in bed and looked down on his wife, whose back was now turned to him. "I see we're back to being at odds again, huh? Why is it that every time Derrick moves back into the house an icy wedge suddenly gets lodged between us, Hannah? In his absence we're closer than close. Why does this always happen?"

Hannah sucked her teeth. "I don't want to get into that with you, Robert. There are only a few hours left before we have to get up and go to church."

Robert shoved his hand through his hair. "Same situation, same responses. I guess nothing ever changes when it comes down to our opinions of our son. I think if you had to make a choice between him and me, I'd find my weary behind out in the cold. It's amazing that we've been married all these years yet I've never held the top position in your life. Amazing indeed."

"I gave birth to Derrick, Robert, not you. There's just something different about mothers and their children, especially their sons.

We carry these babies inside of us for nine months, which forms an everlasting bond. I'm sorry if me loving our son so much bothers you."

Unable to believe his ears, though he'd heard the same remarks from Hannah time and time again, Robert slid down in the bed and pulled the covers up over his head. There was no reasoning with Hannah and he wasn't going to try. He loved Derrick every bit as much as she did, but it was high time for their son to become a man; he wasn't going to apologize for that.

Robert's earlier words suddenly thundered through Hannah's ears, forcing her to think hard about what he'd said. Choosing between her husband and son wasn't something she'd ever want to be faced with. Robert's comments brought Sinclair's marital problems to mind.

Charles had given Sinclair a choice and she had chosen Marcus. Hannah couldn't help wondering what her choice would be if she were ever faced with the same situation. It didn't take her but a second to determine that she couldn't possibly exist without both Robert and Derrick. Hannah would fight to her death to keep her two men in her life forever.

Deeply regretting the cold shoulder she'd given her husband, Hannah huddled her body up against Robert's back. "I'm sorry, Robert. I need you to hold me."

Robert's nonresponse brought tears to Hannah's eyes, yet she knew she deserved exactly what she'd gotten from him. Hannah turned over on her side and buried her face in the pillow, praying for God to please make everything be all right in the morning.

Chapter Four

Simone was the last to arrive in the cafeteria. Her friends were all seated and each of them had already gotten their meals. Having brought her lunch in a brown bag, Simone walked over to the long table and sat down. Only a second had passed when the loud gasps began.

Tara was the only one who showed no signs of shock. She already knew Simone's story.

"What in the world happened to your eye, Simone?" Sinclair asked, looking concerned.

"Compliments of Jerome Hadley's fist," Simone responded calmly. "I never knew he had such a mean right hook. And I've never had a shiner before either. It's not fashionable and I don't want to be the one to start the trend." Simone was the only one who laughed at her tasteless joke.

Hannah looked totally upset. "How can you joke about a man hitting you like that, Simone? From the looks of your eye, he could've blinded you. I know he's in jail. Right?"

Simone shook her head. "Wrong. But he's out of my house, though, not completely. He left a few things behind, probably as an excuse to come back over there. I'm going to give him an opportunity to get the rest of his stuff. I've already packed it up in boxes. If he doesn't come for them in a reasonable amount of time, everything goes out on the curb for the trash truck."

Sinclair shook her head from side to side. "Am I hearing you saying you're going to let Jerome come back inside your house? Tell me it isn't so, Simone Branch."

Simone chuckled. "It isn't so, Sinclair. When I know he's coming to get his things, I'll just set them outside the door for him. He can never come back inside my home. You all don't have to worry about that. I ended up staying with Tara for a couple of days. I went over to her house not long after all the drama occurred. She's been so gracious. Thanks again, Tara."

Tara smiled. "You know you're more than welcome, Simone. I'm always happy to help out my best friends." Tara was awfully worried about Simone. Joking about her serious injury was a sign of Simone's deeply hidden pain, the kind of torment people stuffed way down inside.

"What about the locks, Simone?" Glenda queried, hating to see Simone looking the way she did, so worn out and disheveled. "Have you changed the locks?"

Simone looked as if a bolt of lightning had suddenly hit her. While muddling over Glenda's question, fear momentarily flashed in her eyes. "No, I haven't. Furthermore, I hadn't even thought about it until you mentioned it." Tyrell had keys, too, Simone mused.

Changing the locks would mean Tyrell couldn't get in if he tried to gain entry when she wasn't there. Taking a new set of keys to her son meant that she'd possibly have to see Booker again. She wasn't in any way ready for that. The locks would have to wait, but she wasn't about to announce her decision and have all her friends go ballistic on her.

"Thanks, Glenda. I'll deal with the locks," Simone said, leaving it at that, hoping no challenge was forthcoming. "But, girlfriends, you haven't heard the half of it. Getting beat down wasn't the only dramatic happening that evening. The rest of my story is incredible. Ladies, I'm about to knock your shoes right off your feet, so you'd better crunch up your toes if you don't want to lose them. Tyrell is now living with his father out in Marina del Ray. How's that for unbelievable drama?"

Mouths fell wide open and more loud gasps echoed about the room. Glenda reached over and grasped Simone's hand, squeezing tightly, as if Simone needed something to anchor her.

Hannah dropped her fork. "Say what? Could you repeat that?"

For the next several tension-wrapped minutes, Simone filled in her friends on all the juicy details of Booker's unexpected return to the area. Everyone was so tuned in, so intent on what she was saying it would've been easy to hear a cotton ball drop to the floor. Faltering off and on from the emotional stress, Simone went over the entire evening in painstaking detail.

The mention of Jerome coming home while Booker was there had everyone on the edge of their seats. Simone then explained that she'd gotten the black eye when she'd tried to help up the alcohol-besotted Jerome. The assault was the most difficult part for Simone to explain.

In a loving gesture, Hannah pushed back a few stray hairs from Simone's face. "How did you feel about seeing Booker again after all these years?"

Simone wrung her hands together. "Weird. Downright confused and totally disoriented. He'd phoned first to let me know Tyrell was at his home with him, but that hardly prepared me for seeing him face-to-face. Booker Branch can still make my heart beat like a fast-moving race car. That big old man is finer and sexier than ever. I guess true love never dies."

Glenda sighed with impatience, her eyelashes fluttering. "How can you possibly still love him after what he's put you through, Simone?"

Simone sharply raised an eyebrow. "Don't you still love, Antoine? And we all know how much drama you went through with him before he finally started to settle down into the role of husband and family man. When it comes down to love, possibilities are endless. Unfortunately, we don't always get to choose the one we're going to love. Our hearts seem to make the choice for us. How does someone my age stop loving the man they've loved since high school?"

Glenda smiled weakly. "I see what you mean. I guess I was being a little judgmental. Sorry, Simone. No harm intended."

"It's okay, Glenda. We often judge others for the very same thing we're guilty as sin of. We can't see the mirror image of ourselves in others 'cause we're too busy looking and pointing fingers at everyone but the person staring back at us from in the looking glass. It's human nature, girl, that's all. At any rate, love is a hard thing to get over," Simone concluded. "Real hard."

"Tell me about it," Sinclair remarked on a sad note. "I just hope I don't have to get over Charles. I don't think I can bear it if this separation turns into divorce."

Simone patted Sinclair's hand. "You can handle anything that comes your way if you just continue to lean on God. Sometimes I have a hard time practicing what I preach. I seem to always call on Him after I've gotten myself into a jam rather than before it occurs. But I really hope and pray to God that you don't have to go through a divorce, Sinclair. Constant prayer."

"Thanks for that, Simone," Sinclair said, wiping an errant tear from the corner of her eye.

A thoughtful expression crossed Simone's face. "I often wonder if I could've moved on with my life had I gone on and divorced Booker. Year after year I waited to be served papers from him, but none ever came. I didn't divorce him because I believed wholeheartedly in the vows we took: 'until death us do part.' The sad thing is I still believe in them."

Tara felt sorry for both Simone and Sinclair. Each woman appeared emotionally shattered. A silent prayer had her asking God to protect her heart from the same kind of devastating destruction.

Tara remembered all too well the pain her mother had gone through when her father had left. Like all the women seated before her, her mother had chosen her son over her mate. All Jamaica had wanted to do was to teach Timothy how to become a man. The apron strings proved to be too strong and too long for Jamaica to cut Timothy loose from.

As though she'd felt Tara's inner turmoil, Hannah leveled her eyes on her young friend, smiling sympathetically. "How are things going with you and Raymond, Tara?"

Tara raised her hand in the air, turning it from side to side. "So-so. Maya is such a trip, not a typical fourteen-year-old. She's a clever little something." Tara quickly explained what had happened at her home the evening Raymond had brought Maya along with him for a visit.

"Clever is a mild observation compared with what we just heard," Simone commented. "The child sounds downright menacing. So what are you going to do about it?"

Tara shrugged. "I don't know yet. But I can promise you all this. I'm not taking too much more of this from Miss Maya. I understand she's grieving and all over her mother, but that doesn't give her a license to slice and dice me up. If Ray can't handle his daughter, I'm gone."

"Really. You'd walk out on him just like that?" Glenda inquired.

Tara snapped her fingers. "Just like that!"

Hannah looked skeptical. "Then you must not be in love with Raymond, Tara, not if you can just up and split on him that easy."

Tara gave a hearty harrumph. "I'm in love with him all right. I'm just nobody's fool. I guess you all didn't believe me when I said I'd never take anything off no kid."

"Yeah, but Maya's not yours. You didn't give birth to her. That's why it's so easy for you to say that, Tara," Hannah responded, as a matter of fact.

"Wrong! I said it 'cause I meant it. If a kid doesn't respect his or her parents, chances are he or she won't respect anyone else. Maya doesn't have to love me, but I will demand her respect. Whether or not to tell Raymond about the things she's said to me behind his back is my biggest issue. I'm fearful that he won't believe me, since she comes off as such an innocent. I'm still having a hard time believing it myself. Her sudden change in behavior really caught me off guard. I was of the opinion that Maya liked me until she showed me otherwise," Tara lamented.

"I wouldn't tell him just yet, Tara," Glenda offered. "Maybe Maya was just having an off day. I'd wait and see what happens the next time you're in her company. Teenagers are so unpredictable these days. I know none of us have forgotten the raging hormone syndrome. Well, maybe some of us have. That was a very long time ago for most of us."

"Yeah, but not so long ago that I don't remember," Hannah said, with a chuckle. "That's an unforgettable period in the lives of most folks. But I'm sure we'd all love to forget the fiery trials and tribulations of that particular time in our lives. Being a teenager was frightening. If I had the opportunity to go back and live over parts of my life, I'd definitely choose to skip my teens."

"Not me," Simone said. "If I could go back, that's where I'd start; right back to the very first day I met Booker. That was a sweet time for me. Booker was everything a girl could possibly want in a boyfriend. I was the girlfriend of the most popular jock around town. Wearing his team letter jackets and his class ring around my neck made me the envy of every girl in school. It still hurts so much to know that his popularity is exactly what tore us apart so many years later. He was so unaffected by his superstar status in our youth. He remained the same throughout college. I never dreamed Booker would one day outgrow me. But he did. Money and fame put him so far out of my reach that he may as well have been on the moon."

Tara was nearly brought to tears by Simone's reminiscing, but she fought them back. Otherwise, everyone else would start crying. In her desire to end the pity party sessions, Tara loudly clapped her hands together in order to command attention. "Okay, girls, it's time to lighten things up. No more 'woe is me' for today. It seems to me that it's time we go out and have some fun. We've gotten too down in the mouth in here today," Tara said. "Since it's the beginning of the weekend, what about having dinner out tonight somewhere? We can also rent a video movie for later. I'd like to see *The Passion of the Christ* since I didn't see it when it was in the theaters, eons ago. Anyone else interested?"

"The dinner sounds great, but if we're going out to have fun, the movie choice for later needs to change," Hannah suggested. "It won't be any fun watching our Savior being beaten and crucified. Violence is never uplifting. We can rent *The Passion* another time, because I definitely want to see it, too. I'm up for an evening out. But I'll have to check with Robert first to see if he has already made plans for us. Who else is in on this outing?"

All the other women's hands went up in agreement.

"I have another suggestion for us," Glenda remarked. "In speaking of being uplifted, I just remembered there's a gospel concert at our church this evening. Since it starts at six o'clock, we could go to First Tabernacle for the beginning of our outing and on to dinner afterward. Sister and Reverend Covington's son, Malcolm, and their godson, Todd, are both on the program. Those two boys are doing great with their inspirational rap. Reverend Jesse will give only a minisermon, but you know he's still going to work it for us, as he always does."

"Don't leave out First Tabernacle's choir. They always rock the house, too," Simone commented. "I like the idea of attending the gospel. Let's do it. I need to be uplifted."

Tara palmed her forehead, looking a bit dismayed. "I forgot that I'm on call this weekend." Tara gave a minute thought to her situation. "Oh, well, that's okay. I can put my pager and cell on vibrate. It's not like I haven't done it that way before. If you all are riding together, I won't be able to go with you. I'll take my own car in case I have to make an early exit."

"I'll just meet you all at the church, too," Simone responded. "I've got a few places to stop after we have dinner, that is, if it's not too terribly late, so I'll need my car. Going to the twenty-four-hour Wal-Mart is on my list of things to do before the weekend is over."

Hannah looked at Glenda and Sinclair. "I guess that leaves just us three to figure out how to do the transportation. Shall I pick you all up in the Suburban?"

"That works for me, Hannah. Once you find out what Robert's up to, let us know right away," Glenda said, glad she didn't have to drive. Night driving wasn't her favorite thing to do.

"Works for me, too. What are the chances of Charles calling me to make plans for us to talk this evening? Nil and none," Sinclair said, answering her own question sarcastically. "He seems to have forgotten that I exist."

Hannah felt bad for Sinclair but thought it best not to comment. "I'll call Robert as soon as I get back to my station. He hasn't mentioned going anywhere so I can't imagine him having plans for us. But I'll call your extensions and let you know one way or the other."

Coming home to find Tyrell sitting on the front porch immediately upset Simone. As she rushed up the front steps, she just knew something was wrong. "What's going on, baby? You look so sad. Did you and your dad fall out already?"

Tyrell shook his head. "Nothing like that. I forgot most of my videos and some of my older CDs. I just came back to get them. Is that okay?"

Looking rather shamefaced, Tyrell recalled his hurtful parting words to his mother. The last thing he wanted was for his mother to die and leave him behind. Simone had been his only lifeline, all his life. He wanted to apologize to her, but he just didn't know how. The right words wouldn't come to him. Nothing he might say would ever be adequate. He had been so unfair.

"That's fine. But why are you sitting out here? You could've just gone in and gotten them. How'd you get here?" Simone's heart started beating fast, wondering where Booker was.

"He brought me. He was going to let me use one of his cars, but I was scared to drive either of them. Both his cars are really expensive. A white Mercedes and a black Corvette. I didn't go inside 'cause your car wasn't in the drive. I didn't want to chance running into Mr. Jerome. His car isn't here, but I thought he might come home before I got a chance to leave."

"Jerome isn't living here any longer, baby. He's history. You said your dad brought you over to the house. Where is he?"

"He's waiting around the corner. Said he didn't want to cause anymore trouble for you."

Simone's heart skipped a beat as she opened the door and entered the house. "That was very thoughtful of Booker, but he wasn't the problem. Come on in and get your things so you won't have to leave your dad waiting." Simone smiled at her son. "I miss you, Tyrell. A lot."

Having been worried that she'd hate him since he'd been so hateful to her, Tyrell smiled with relief and looked up at his mother. Upon noticing her black eye for the first time, he nearly freaked out. "What happened to you?"

The shameful look on Simone's face was a dead giveaway.

"No, don't tell me that fool hit you. That crazy man must've lost the rest of his freaking mind." Tears filled Tyrell's eyes. "Where's he staying, Mama? I'm gonna get him if it's the last thing I do. I can't believe he did this to you. Your eye is all messed up."

Simone cursed under her breath. She had left the sunglasses in the car. It then dawned on her that even with the glasses on Tyrell would've asked why she was wearing the dark shades in the house. When Tyrell pulled out a cell phone equipped with a walkie-talkie, she groaned loudly, thinking that Booker was already trying to buy his son's affections with expensive toys.

Tyrell pushed in a button. "Are you there?"

"Yeah, son. Are you ready to be picked up?"

"I need you to come to the house. Mama has been badly hurt. Hurry up."

Simone tried to snatch the phone from Tyrell, but he quickly pressed in the button to turn off the two-way speaker. "Why did you tell your dad that, Tyrell? He's going to think I'm in serious trouble. What if he calls 911 on his way here?"

Tyrell scratched his head. "I hadn't thought of that. But he's probably already outside. He was only parked on the next block. He let me use this phone to call him when I was ready."

Simone looked exasperated, though relieved the cell phone was only a loaner. "I wish you hadn't done that, boy. By the way, all you've been referring to Booker is as 'he.' Is that what you call him when you're alone?"

"I call him by his last team's city, Tampa Bay. Sometimes I shorten it to T.B."

Simone laughed. "Good morning, Tampa Bay or good morning, T.B. Is that it, Tyrell?"

"Yeah, for now. You told me not to call him by his first name."

Booker rushed up the steps and into the open door. Expecting Simone to be sprawled out on the floor, laid out on the sofa, or possibly stretched out upstairs in her bed, he was shocked to see her standing on her own two feet. He looked from Tyrell to Simone. Then he noticed the black eye. "Oh, I see." Booker formed a steeple with his hands. "The Simone I know wouldn't take a whipping from no man, so I don't even have to go there. How'd it happen, Simone?"

Another telltale look from Simone not only gave away the answer to how it had happened, but also revealed the identity of her attacker. Deep regret and shame was awash in her eyes. The two people she loved most in the world were seeing her in one of the most vulnerable states she'd ever been in. Tyrell had occasionally heard Simone being yelled at and called stupid and other unattractive names, but there hadn't been any physical abuse whatsoever for her son to witness. She was sure that she wouldn't have ever let it go that far. Now Simone wasn't too sure about much of anything. Because of her bad choices in men, Simone's life was in shambles.

Was one kind of bad treatment really worse than any other type of mistreatment? Abuse was abuse, no matter the form it came in. The entire situation embarrassed Simone and saddened her to no end. The cracks in her strong resolve were never more apparent than they were right now. All Simone could do was hide her face in her hands and break down and cry.

Booker looked as if he was hopelessly out of his depth. Simone's loud sobbing tore viciously at his heartstrings. "Get your mother some water, Tyrell. Bring it into the living room."

Cupping his hand under her elbow, Booker helped Simone into the living room and then assisted her down onto the sofa. "You want to stretch out?"

"No," Simone said, her voice cracking. "I'm fine just sitting up. Thanks."

Booker plumped a pillow and put it behind Simone's back. He then took a seat beside her. "I'm not the one to lecture you, since I'm also guilty of hurting you pretty badly, but I hope you gave this guy the boot. If he's capable of hitting you, causing that much damage to your eye, what will he do next? Did this happen as a result of me being here when he came home?"

"Not really, Booker. I don't want you taking the blame for any of this. When a man's mind is chemically altered, he's totally unpredictable. And he did get the boot. A royal one."

Booker fought the urge to chuckle at her comment. Simone getting punched out wasn't a laughing matter. "Good for you, Simone. How many times has this happened before?"

"Never, at least nothing physical. He can be pretty mouthy when intoxicated, but I swear to you he's never even attempted to hit me. I'd never stand for that, and you know it. However, I have put up with too much other crap from him. Anyway, it's all under control now. I'm fine. I have to get moving so I can get showered and dressed for my date this evening."

"Into another relationship already?" Booker asked, raising an inquisitive eyebrow.

"I'm not going to answer that, Booker. But I need to say something to you before Tyrell gets back. He told me he was going after Jerome. Please don't let him out of your sight for a while. I don't want to see Tyrell get himself into serious trouble. His anger may get the best of him if he dwells too much on Jerome hitting me. Keep him in check, Booker. Please. You also need to know that Tyrell can get quite out of hand, especially when he's angry. Maybe you can get him to understand the things I couldn't. Tyrell just may be ready for change. I don't know."

"I got it under control. Thanks for letting me know all that. Are you feeling better now?"

At that moment Tyrell came into the room and carefully handed Simone a cold glass of water. "You want something else, Mama?" Tyrell asked, looking terribly worried.

"Nothing else, Tyrell. Thank you, baby. I'm much better now."

Booker quickly got to his feet. "We'd better get moving, son. Your mother has to get dressed for her date this evening."

Tyrell looked surprised. "Date! With whom, Mama?"

"Just a nice evening out for a change, Tyrell. Don't worry about it. It's no big deal."

Simone knew Booker thought he'd been very clever with the announcement he'd just made to Tyrell, but she'd seen right through his ploy. Why he was so interested in whom she was going out with completely eluded her. She'd never give her estranged husband the satisfaction of telling him her date was with her girlfriends. Simone was sure Booker had thought she'd tell Tyrell whom her date was with, but he'd just have to think again. It wasn't any of his business.

Simone didn't think her heart could break into any more pieces, but watching Tyrell go off arm in arm into the sunset with Booker shattered her heart even more. There was something terribly wrong with that picture. A very important element was missing:

her, the wife of Booker, and the mother of Tyrell. The Branch family portrait was not complete without Simone in it.

After closing the door behind her family, Simone went back into the living room, where she picked up the Living Bible and then took a seat. Once she'd opened it up, she turned the pages until she found the passage she was looking for.

"A worthy wife is her husband's joy and crown; the other kind corrodes his strength and tears down everything he does" (Proverbs 12:4).

Simone went on to find the next passages she was interested in.

"A wise woman builds her house, while a foolish one tears hers down by her own efforts" (Proverbs 14:1). "Wives, submit yourselves unto your own husband, as it is fit in the Lord. Husbands love your wives, and be not bitter against them. Children, obey your parents in all things: for this is pleasing unto the Lord" (Colossians 3:18–20).

Moments of silent prayer were what Simone needed to shore up her strength and courage.

The shadowy, empty house immediately darkened Sinclair's upbeat mood. As a well-established contractor, Charles could pretty much set his own hours and was normally home when she made it in. Sinclair missed his engaging presence more than she'd ever imagined.

The entire place was often lit up like a warm Christmas Eve in the evening hours. Lightly scented candles were usually aglow all over the house and a blazing fire burned in the fireplace in the fall and winter months, making for a relaxing and romantic atmosphere. Charles asking her if she'd like him to draw for her a hot bath came right after his warm welcoming kisses and hugs. A delicious hot meal would've been prepared, and the sparkling cider chilled, all things having been taken care of by her loving husband.

Freshly brewed coffee, a bakery dessert, and a great two-way conversation always came at the end of the meal.

As Sinclair thought about life before Charles had left her, it began to dawn on her that those special things had been absent for a while. She'd obviously been too busy working loads of overtime in order to meet her mountain of bills, to notice the not-so-subtle changes. Had Charles been unhappy over a period of time or had he just started feeling this way? Was it possible that his decision to move out was one that he'd been pondering for a long time? Arguments between them over Marcus happened frequently, but they'd always made up rather quickly.

The thought that Charles just might have another woman waiting in the wings momentarily caused Sinclair an unbearable amount of grief. The more she thought about it, the more it didn't make sense to her for him to just up and move out without any warning. Maybe he was actually using the financial situation as an excuse to leave her just so he'd be free to be with someone else. Imagining Charles with another woman was heartbreaking. It just couldn't be.

Sinclair moaned loudly, pressing her palm against her heart, praying that nothing she'd thought of could be even close to the truth. Losing Charles over finances was one thing, but losing him to another woman wasn't something she'd relish. Although Sinclair believed she could compete with a mistress, and more than likely win, she didn't want to have to find out.

Sinclair looked over at the telephone, wondering if it would hurt to call Charles just to see how he was doing. That wouldn't be so unusual since he was still her husband. But would he think she was running after him? After glancing at her watch, Sinclair saw that she didn't have a lot of time to get ready for the church concert. Hannah would be there before too long. Thinking she had just enough time to shower and change clothes, Sinclair dismissed the idea of calling Charles, which was just as well. Her call may not be a welcome one, she concluded.

A loud banging noise caused Sinclair to turn her attention toward the entry of the living room. Believing it was Charles, she patted her hair down and smoothed her uniform, wanting to look her very best for him.

As Marcus bounced into the room, shock and then signs of disappointment registered on Sinclair's face. Her son was the last person she'd expected to see in the middle of the fall season. Thanksgiving break was still weeks away. "What are you doing home, Marcus?"

Marcus grinned, shrugging his shoulders. "I just came in for the three-day weekend. I don't have classes on Monday." Marcus strolled across the room and took his mother into his warm embrace. "Now that's more like it, Mom," he said, squeezing her tightly. "I was beginning to worry. You didn't look too happy to see me. Where's Dad?"

Sinclair panicked, wondering how she was going to explain Charles's absence. She had hoped they would've resolved their issues so that Marcus would never have to know about the separation. What was she supposed to tell her son? What reason could she possibly give for the estrangement? The truth would hurt Marcus too much. She definitely couldn't tell him his father had left her because of him. Sinclair took a deep breath, hoping to quiet the nervous butterflies swarming in her stomach. "He's out of town on business, Marcus."

For all Sinclair knew, she just might be telling the truth. Charles traveled on business quite a bit. But the fact that she really didn't know where Charles was didn't make her feel any better about lying to her son.

"When will he be back?"

"Early next week." Sinclair wished Marcus would stop grilling her so she could stop lying to him about his father's whereabouts. She didn't want the lies to continue mounting. They could only come back to haunt her later, especially if the truth ever came into the light of day.

"Darn! I'm going to miss seeing him. There were a couple of things I wanted to discuss with him. I guess I could call him on his cell phone."

The idea of Marcus calling Charles had Sinclair shaking in her shoes. No doubt that Charles would tell him what was going on between them. Now what should she say to that? "That might not be such a good idea. You know how busy he is when he's out of town. Maybe you could just share things with me. You think?"

Marcus eyed his mother with deep curiosity, thinking she appeared to be awfully jittery. She didn't seem like herself at all to him. He couldn't help wondering if she wasn't feeling well. "Not really, Mom. Just guy stuff. Did anyone cook? I'm starving. All they serve on these airlines are peanuts and pretzels. The airfare continues to rise and the service keeps going down."

"There's a pot roast and vegetables simmering in the Crock-Pot. I put the food on before I left for work this morning. I'm afraid I won't be able to hang out with you this evening, Marcus. My girl-friends and I are going to a gospel concert down at the church. We're having dinner out afterward and then we're later renting a video. In fact, I need to hustle and get dressed. Ms. Hannah is picking me up in just a few minutes."

"That's cool. I have plans, too, but I should be here when you get home. Have a good time and tell everyone I said what's up. Before I eat, I need to put my things up in my room."

Sinclair looked after Marcus as he made his way up the winding staircase. It was so unlike him to come home unannounced. That had Sinclair worried. What was really up with him, she wondered. His airline ticket had probably cost a small fortune, unless he'd made reservations with a fourteen-day advance notice. That didn't seem likely, though. To her it seemed like Marcus had come home on the spur of the moment. Why he was really there was a big concern for her. Marcus clearly had a hidden agenda.

Thinking about the cost of the airline ticket made Sinclair recall their last phone call on the subject of finances. She had yet to find out about his credit card debt. Now that she could sit down across from Marcus and look him dead in the eye, she planned on revisiting the subject with him before he returned to school. She hoped that more unpleasantness wasn't in store for her, fearing that she couldn't take much else. Sinclair was already at breaking point.

Simone and friends were still reeling from Reverend Jesse's soul-stirring sermon on forgiveness. Although it had only lasted thirty minutes, he had certainly gotten his point across, accomplishing his mission from God with relative ease.

As the first gospel singer began to further fill the hearts and souls of the audience, the thrilling sounds coming from the young woman's mouth were nothing short of incredible. In a matter of minutes the crowd was on its feet, cheering and clapping to the deeply moving lyrics of the song and the dynamically arranged music.

The next song, "His Eye Is on the Sparrow," was a favorite hymn to many. Leslie Acres was making this wonderful song her own, singing it as if it were written and arranged exclusively for her. She had the kind of voice that produced chilling goose bumps, the kind that caused tears to flow unchecked. Her sultry rendition of the old gospel tune was breathtaking.

Hannah loved gospel music, especially the older hymns, the truly unforgettable ones. While she was somewhat into the younger gospel singers like Kirk Franklin, Yolanda Adams, and Mary Mary, just to name a few, she positively loved Shirley Caesar, Andre and Sandra Crouch, Wintley Phipps, all the Winans, Bobby Jones, the Hawkins clan, and a host of other gospel greats. Hannah wished that Robert were there to experience the concert with her.

In Hannah's opinion, First Tabernacle Choir could give the best gospel groups of today and yesterday a good run for their money. This spirited group of brothers and sisters knew how to grip tightly and then hold the undivided attention of the audience with joyful, blended voices.

Sinclair was having a great time even though she was having a hard time concentrating fully on the performances. Charles was heavy on her mind, so much so that she was thinking of dropping by the town house to pay him a visit. Since they hadn't discussed the idea of sharing their marital problems with Marcus, she wanted them to get that out in the open before their son found out on his own. The weight of their separation should be shared with Marcus in the presence of both his parents. Sinclair refused to take on such an unenviable task alone.

Glenda couldn't have been happier with the stellar performances, yet she was worried if Anthony would make it home on time. He had promised her that he'd make his curfew so that she could have a good time out for a change. Taylor had offered to stay at the house with Anthony, but, as usual, Glenda had turned down his generous suggestion.

Tara had thoroughly enjoyed the gospel rap tunes performed by Malcolm and Todd. She had been surprised to learn the two young men had written all of the songs for their act. Eight-year-old Marjani Davis had also compelled the audience from its seats. She possessed such an amazingly strong voice for such a little girl, belting out sounds in an adult manner. Tara believed that Marjani, with her angelic voice, could certainly hang with the very best in gospel singers.

Song after inspirational song brought a sense of peace to each of the five friends. For a solid two hours the women were entertained and ministered to in premier fashion. Once the concert was over, they congratulated the performers and then hung around to mingle for a bit with the other concert attendees. It was later decided that they'd all meet up at the popular Coffee House rather than patronize a full-service restaurant. No one was hungry enough for a full-course meal. Coffee and appetizers were quite adequate for a late-evening repast.

While sipping on hot coffee and snacking on appetizers of hot wings with ranch dressing for dipping, quesadillas, potato skins layered with cheese and sour cream, along with fried mozzarella cheese sticks, the five girlfriends couldn't praise the concert enough. Their desire to have their spirits uplifted had been totally fulfilled.

"What'd you guys think about Reverend Jesse's sermon?" Hannah asked.

"It was off the hook, as always," Glenda responded. "Forgiveness and the different ways to praise God are themes he never seems to tire of. His messages are so thought provoking, every single time. Reverend Jesse is a gifted man. His love for God and his faith in Him are apparent in everything he says and does. I often wonder if I'll ever have that kind of faith. I sure want to."

"The scriptures he gives to back up his sermons are always enlightening. I know by heart the ones on praising the Lord, but I don't use them as often as I should. This concert was a perfect example of how we're to praise him," Simone said.

"Make a joyful noise unto God, all ye lands. Sing forth the honor of his name: make his praise glorious" (Psalms 66:1–2).

"Praise ye the Lord. Praise God in his sanctuary: praise him in the firmament of his power. Praise him for his mighty acts: praise him according to his excellent greatness. Praise him with the sound of the trumpet: praise him with the psaltery and harp. Praise him with the timbrel and dance: praise him with stringed instruments and organs. Praise him upon the loud cymbals: praise him upon the high sounding cymbals. Let everything that hath breath praise the Lord. Praise ye the Lord" (Psalms 150:1–6).

Tara knew how to effectively praise God in many ways, but she struggled badly with forgiveness. It always caused an attack on her conscience when she thought about it, like now. She rather believed that her life would probably be a bowl of cherries if only she could forgive her brother. Easier said than done, she mused. The unrelenting anger she felt for Timothy had kept her from reaching out to him all these years. But he hadn't reached out to her either, which made her think that he felt the same about her as she did him. The olive branch extended both ways. Stubbornness was another major problem for Tara.

"As for the topic of forgiveness, people struggle with forgiveness on a daily basis," Simone added, "including us Christians. Forgiving Booker isn't as much as a challenge as I thought it would be. The funny thing is that I don't feel any malice toward him, which is hard for me to believe. I used to sit around and think up all the nasty, low-down things I'd say to him if I ever saw him again. Though I've spouted off a few heated words to him, none of them have been close to what I had imagined me saying. Deep-seated anger spearheaded a lot of my caustic thoughts about him. It was easy for me to slay him in my thoughts and out of his presence."

"Do you think you two will ever get back together since you have confessed to still loving him?" Tara inquired, hoping Simone wouldn't be offended by the question.

With uncertainty blazing hotly in her eyes, Simone furiously shook her head. "That'll never happen. Loving Booker is one thing. Living under the same roof with him again isn't something I'd even consider. Do me once, shame on you. Do me twice, the shame is on me. Although I haven't actually thought of divorcing him, I really should look into it now that I know where I can have the papers served. Though it's still very hard for me to conceive, not to mention extremely painful, we'll never be able to live as husband and wife."

"Never say never," Tara sang out. "If you two haven't divorced each other in all this time, there's a good reason for it. You just might want to explore it. I think you owe it to yourself to at least find out why neither of you ever filed."

Simone sucked her teeth. "Don't even go there, Tara Wheatley. Let's change the subject. This one for sure is a dead issue."

"Have I got a subject for you," Sinclair jumped in. "Marcus is home unexpectedly. Popped in not too long before Hannah picked me up. He doesn't know about the separation, so I'm planning on stopping by the town house to see Charles to discuss it. Since I don't have a phone number for him other than his cell, do you all think it's wrong of me just to drop by unannounced?"

"Why can't you just call his cell?" Hannah asked.

Sinclair chewed on her lower lip for a couple of seconds. "What if he refuses to let me come by if I give him prior warning? That'll just devastate me."

Glenda looked perplexed. "Why would he refuse, Sinclair? That doesn't sound like the Charles we all know. Unless there's more to this separation than what you've been telling us, I don't see the problem."

Sinclair wouldn't dare to tell her friends that she'd been entertaining the idea of Charles having another woman. No one would believe it, anyway, because she didn't either.

"The Charles you all know wouldn't have up and just left his wife either," Sinclair sounded off rather loudly. "Believe me, Mr. Albright has changed. I thought for sure he would've had a change of heart by now. I can't tell you how much I miss all the attention he once paid to me. I'm afraid I'm guilty of having taken Charles for granted. He has made himself very scarce since he moved out. I don't mind telling you all I'm terrified of this mess I've made."

"I find that hard to believe," Tara remarked impatiently. "Charles had already told you what it would take to work things out, but you don't seem to want to deal with that, Sinclair. Marriage is all about compromising. If financing Marcus is costing you your marriage, then you have to decide what's more important to you. We can't make that decision for you."

Sinclair shot Tara a sarcastic look. "If it's all about compromise, why aren't you willing to negotiate with Raymond on his situation with his daughter?"

Tara scowled hard, rolling her eyes at Sinclair. "I didn't know this was about Raymond and me, Sinclair. I'm not the one sitting here asking my friends for advice on my troubled relationship. I already know how I plan to deal with my situation if things keep going the way they are. Besides, I'm not married to Raymond, nor do we have any children together."

Trying to bring about calm, Hannah held up her hand and

waved it in the air. "Okay, ladies, this isn't the way we want to do this. Support, support, support has always been our motto. But, Sinclair, I have to agree with Tara on this one. It's really hard for us to advise you when you're the only one who knows what you want. The ultimatum has already been given. Now it's up to you to adhere to it or dismiss it. I know it's an unfair position for Charles to have put you in, but he has. I don't think anyone can decide the outcome for you. In plain English, your marriage is on the rocks. It seems to me that you don't have many choices available to you. Put up or shut up?" Hannah shrugged. "It's all up to you, girlfriend."

Feeling as though she was being ganged upon, Sinclair was thoroughly exasperated. "That still doesn't answer my question. Should I go to see Charles without trying to contact him on his cell?" The anger in Sinclair's tone had everyone exchanging bewildered glances.

The house was darker than Sinclair's stormy mood. It irked her that Marcus hadn't thought to leave on any lights, knowing she'd be coming in late. She didn't know if her son was in the house and it surprised her that she didn't even care one way or the other.

Sinclair quickly realized that she didn't have the heart to go up to her bedroom, where all she'd find was sweet memories and utter loneliness. After taking off her suit jacket, she flung it over the sofa back. Feeling miserable was an all-too-often occurrence these days, she mused, stretching out fully on the divan. Still unhappy that her friends seemed to have turned on her, Sinclair closed her weary eyes.

Although no one had offered her any advice on whether she should visit Charles, she had called his cell. Only after she hadn't received an answer had she asked Hannah to drop her by the town house. If Charles was in, Sinclair had convinced herself that he'd give her a ride home.

Charles hadn't answered the door either, but Sinclair was relieved that she'd asked Hannah to wait to see if she got a response before leaving. Her spare keys to the place were inside her parked car at home. Sinclair was grateful for that, thankful that she hadn't decided to drive to the concert. Letting herself into the town house would've been the next step taken.

Marcus turned on a light as he rushed into the living room, looking thoroughly upset. "What's going on around here, Mom?"

While her eyes adjusted to the sudden burst of light, Sinclair managed to pull herself upright on the sofa. "Explain, son. I don't know what you're talking about."

"None of Dad's clothes are in his closet. I went in there to borrow one of his bathrobes to put on. All of his clothes are missing out of the drawers, too. Where's Dad?"

Sighing wearily, Sinclair picked up one of the sofa pillows and buried her face in it momentarily. Tell me this isn't happening, she mused, fighting back her emotions. Deep down inside Sinclair knew that Marcus would more than likely found out about her and Charles while he was at home. But that hadn't stopped her from praying it wouldn't happen.

Sinclair reached for Marcus's hand, prompting him to come and sit down beside her, hugging him once he was seated. "I was hoping against hope we wouldn't ever have to have this conversation, Marcus. We're separated, son. Your dad is currently living over at the town house."

Marcus looked as if he was in total shock. "Why, Mom? When did all this happen?"

"We aren't seeing eye to eye these days, Marcus. We have a few serious issues to work out between us. He's only been gone a short while. It'll be okay. We'll eventually work it out."

"Do you have another man, Mom? Is that what this is all about?"

Sinclair was horrified, completely taken aback by Marcus's objectionable question. "What in the world would make you think that, son? And if there were a third party involved in our marital problems, what makes you believe I'd be the one guilty of infidelity?"

"'Cause Dad wouldn't think of cheating on you. Never. You're the one that's always off somewhere doing whatever you find so much to do. I may not live here full-time anymore, but I haven't forgotten how busy you always are. I remember all those nights Dad was here alone."

Sinclair's heart felt as though it were about to leap out of her chest. Her son's low opinion of her had her totally distressed, not to mention disappointed. "Are you suggesting that I'd cheat on your father? If so, thanks for the undeserved assassination of my character."

Looking both disturbed and chagrined, Marcus shook his head in the negative. "I didn't mean it that way, Mom. I guess it came out all wrong."

"Yeah, I'd say so. Neither your dad nor I am a cheater. You can rest assured of that." Sinclair saw that she had to change the subject before they got any deeper into her marital issues. Protecting Marcus from the truth was still important to her. "Want some tea, hot or cold? Your choice."

"What about a Coke, Mom? Do you have any out in the garage? There's none in the kitchen refrigerator."

"I don't know, but I'll go out and check. The only time I stock it is when I know you're going to be here. By the way, why *are* you home, Marcus? I'm not buying your story of you just popping in for the weekend. What's the real reason for your unexpected visit?"

Not wanting to have this particular conversation, at least not at this moment, Marcus put his head down. He had come home to ask for more money. The telephone wasn't the proper vehicle for this big of a deal. The large amount of cash he needed to ask his mother for had to be dealt with in person. His mother was going to have a fit either way, but he thought he stood a better chance of buttering her up if he was seated right in front of her. It was hard for Sinclair to deprive Marcus of anything that he told her was very important to him. He often banked on that.

Lying to his mother didn't make Marcus proud of himself, but she'd never give him such a large sum of money if she really knew what he needed it for.

"Mom, under the circumstances I think we should wait until morning to talk about why I'm here. There's a lot I need to say. But I'd like to sleep on it another night."

Sinclair couldn't imagine what all Marcus needed to say, but it sure had her worried. "You might be right. We'll let everything rest until tomorrow morning, son. Then I expect total honesty. I have a lot to say, too."

Chapter Five

Frustrated to the max, Taylor once again watched Glenda pace back and forth across the room in a maniacal fashion, which was par for the course. He was surprised the carpet in her home wasn't completely worn out. The girl had put in some serious mileage on her flooring while constantly worrying herself to death about Anthony.

Anthony's probation officer had sent him back to juvenile hall for a seventy-two-hour period. After he'd called the house and got no answer, Steve Castor had tracked Anthony down through the electronic leg device Anthony had recently been ordered to wear by the judge. According to Castor, he had been by the house several times, unbeknownst to both Glenda and Anthony, and Anthony hadn't been there. Glenda had gotten off work late and hadn't been there to answer the phone the last time Castor had tried to reach Anthony. Those were the incidents that had led up to Anthony being hauled back into court, thus the tracking device.

Glenda was starting to realize that she couldn't keep covering for Anthony. Once the probation department had decided to follow Anthony electronically, it would know exactly when he wasn't where he was supposed to be. The inconsistency of his probation officer checking up on him was one of the things that had made Anthony think he could get away with being out after his curfew in the first place. Anthony never believed that anyone was going to check up on him after ten o'clock at night, because older folks were already in bed by that time, his probation officer included.

"Why don't you come and sit down, Glen? There's nothing you can do for Tony now. He's not coming through that door tonight, late or otherwise. You should take this opportunity to get some rest. Tonight you know exactly where he is."

Glenda looked over at Taylor, her expression soft. "I know you mean well, Taylor, but this is my boy you're talking about. It's hard for me to rest knowing he's locked up."

"Soon to be a man, Glen. Only a few months left until Tony's eighteenth birthday. The choice for him to be sent to juvenile hall will suddenly up and disappear."

Agitated by Taylor constantly repeating the same old comments, Glenda roughly massaged the kinks in the back of her neck. "Do you have to keep reminding me of that?"

"Until it sinks in. You need to look at Tony's eighteenth birthday as the day of reckoning for both of you. I'm a parole officer for hard-core adult prisoners, Glen. I know exactly how these things play out. The system is a hard road for anyone to trek, but more so for men of color."

"I know. I know. The police aren't going to call me and tell me to pick up Tony. He'll remain a guest of the county jail if he's arrested after he turns eighteen. I've heard it all before."

"Unless you're willing to pay bail money by putting up some serious collateral, Tony will stay behind bars until he either pleads out or opts to go to trial."

Glenda walked across the room and plopped down on the sofa, next to Taylor. With her eyes filled with tears, she looked up at the man she admired and greatly respected. "What's a mother supposed to do when she's given all that she can to her children?"

"The only thing a mother can do is to turn them over to God.

Put your trust in Him. Trust that He knows what's best for His children. Trust in God, Glen."

"But I do, Taylor, wholeheartedly. I pray for Tony all the time. My knees are practically worn out from hitting the carpet. If this keeps up, I'll need knee replacements before I'm fifty."

Taylor wiped away Glenda's tears with the pads of his fingers. "Yeah, but you pick the heavy load right back up in the same instant you get off your knees, Glen. If you continue to carry the burdens, believing you can fix them, you really haven't turned it over to God. Once you ask Him to take on your troubles, you have to leave them in His hands. He's capable. Trust me. I know. You also know what He's done in my life. There are a couple of passages from the Bible that come to mind—Matthew, chapter eleven, verses twenty-eight to thirty: 'Come unto me all ye that labor and are heavy laden, and I will give you rest. Take my yoke upon you, and learn of me; for I am meek and lowly in heart: and ye shall find rest unto your souls.' Jesus said these things for those who are weary from their heavy burdens, much like yourself."

Glenda rested her head against Taylor's shoulder. "Thanks for that. And, yes, I do know what He's done in your life. You are a walking, talking miracle, Taylor Phillips. You're also a walking testimony. Those guys who mugged and beat you so badly thought sure they'd left you for dead. But God had other plans for your life."

The memories of that night, a night he'd never forget, brought tears to Taylor's eyes. "Tell me about it, lady. With two broken legs and a host of other fractures and internal injuries, God gave me the strength to crawl out that back alley to where I'd be spotted. Then he sent me an angel to tend to the rest."

Knowing he was referring to her as the angel, Glenda smiled softly. "When I saw you on the pavement, as I drove by that fateful night, I thought you were just another drunk who'd passed out from too much liquor. Seeing your style of dress made me rethink my initial assessment. Not too many people living on the streets wear designer suits."

Both Glenda and Taylor chuckled at that.

"As a Christian and a nurse, I had to stop and check things out. There's no way I could've drove on without knowing your physical condition despite the lateness of the hour. If I hadn't worked overtime that evening, I never would've been out so late."

"That may be true, Glen, but God didn't allow me to crawl from that cold, dark place for nothing. Had it not been you, another angel would've come along." He gently kissed Glenda's forehead. "I don't know if I would've fallen for another angel the way I've fallen so hard for you. I'm glad that I don't ever have to wonder about it since I'm real content with the perfect angel He sent my way."

Glenda reached up and ran her fingers through Taylor's wavy hair. "That's so sweet of you to say. I don't know what would've happened to you had I not been trained as a nurse." Her fingers then roved his smooth, clean-shaven face.

Becoming a nurse had been a lifelong ambition of Glenda's. In fact, she came from a long line of nurses. Her mother, Geraldine, had proudly worn the starched whites, as did Geraldine's mother and her two sisters. Glenda and her sisters had followed in their mother's footsteps. The four siblings came out of nursing school, one right after the other. The sisters were like stair steps, as there was only a year between each of them. Glenda was the youngest.

Unlike Glenda, who was an LVN, the others were all RNs. This was a family of women who loved to serve and care for others. Glenda's father, Dudley, a loving Christian man, had passed away when she was a teenager. He had been employed as a mechanic with GMAC.

All of Glenda's family still resided in Memphis, Tennessee, where she'd grown up. Glenda had moved to California after she'd married Antoine. For many years, prior to Antoine's death, Glenda believed that she had failed him as a spouse, only to later realize that her husband had failed her, miserably.

Glenda knew that she was still in partial denial over Antoine's true character. Not to face the hard facts had become second nature for her when it came down to dealing with all their issues, which she'd truly believed had been resolved. Then the mystery surrounding his death had unexpectedly come into play.

Wishing she could be everything Taylor needed her to be, Glenda sighed. As long as she had Anthony and his mountain of issues to deal with, she couldn't be anything significant to anyone. That saddened her deeply. Besides being a nurse, all Glenda had ever wanted to be in life was a great mother and a good wife to a wonderful man.

Touching Taylor's face this way made Glenda's desire stir, which caused her to withdraw her hand quickly. This wasn't the time for her to be playing with fire, yet she ached for the day when she'd be free enough to let herself go completely. Taylor desperately needed that from her.

"I never dreamed you'd look this beautiful once you healed, Taylor. You had so many cuts and bruises on your face, not to mention the awful swelling. Your warm brown eyes were practically closed shut. I'll never forget the first moment I actually saw them open. The beauty of those magnificent orbs nearly took my breath away. And it still does."

Taylor put his arm around Glenda's shoulder and brought her in closer to him. "I'll never forget that moment either. I really did think I'd died and gone to heaven when I saw this dark beauty, all dressed in white, standing over me. I remember how I kept wishing you'd turn around so I could see your wings."

Glenda laughed heartily. "I'm sorry, but I have to crack up every time I hear you say that. Boy, that was just the Demerol working you over. You were in so much pain for the first couple of weeks. I was in constant prayer for you, praying hard that you would recover fully."

Glenda moaned at the sudden visions flashing inside her head, images of Taylor's broken and bleeding body tearing at her resolve. While wiping the horrific memories from her mind, she smiled up at Taylor and then nestled her head against his chest.

Taylor blew out a gust of relief, glad that Glenda had begun to relax. He loved to see her beautiful smile, a rarity as of late. If only he had the power to take away all her troubles, he'd gladly do so. Taylor knew that Glenda's peace couldn't be achieved until she placed her burdens at the hands of the Almighty. The last couple of minutes had been extremely stressful for her. He'd seen the anguish in her eyes. Bad memories had a way of dismantling peace without any warning. It used to happen to him often, but that was before he'd learned to trust in God.

"I'm not too sure about your thoughts on my drug-induced state, Glen. You were a stunning sight to behold, Demerol or not. I can only believe that God intended for you and I to come together. No one can ever make me believe otherwise. We're destiny realized, Glen, though not yet completely fulfilled."

Glenda was aware that Taylor was talking about marriage. He'd only asked her to marry him five times already. But his proposals hadn't come without conditions, which was the main reason why she hadn't accepted. Although she loved him to life, allowing Taylor to take control over her son wasn't something Glenda could ever come to terms with. He wanted to teach Anthony how to become a man, desired to equip him with the tools he'd need for success in life.

On the other hand, Glenda didn't think Anthony would accept guidance from any male figure, because of his bitter feelings about his dad. Fulfilling Taylor's conditions for marriage wasn't an open option for her. Besides, Anthony was practically a man himself, though he hadn't quite turned sixteen when she and Taylor had first met.

Taylor knew he'd traveled into forbidden territory by the way Glenda had begun to fidget. The subject of "destiny" had always come with the same unpleasant results. She'd shut down on him and he'd have to wait out her moodiness. He'd also have to deal with the inevitable distance she'd put between them, which could last up to a week or more. Taylor wondered if it would make any difference if Glenda knew his patience was starting to grow thin.

Taylor nudged Glenda's shoulder. "Sorry, Glen, I know I've treaded into forbidden waters again, but, honey, you have to know how much I love you. *Do* you really know that?"

With her eyes blinking nervously, Glenda nodded. "I do. But until I get Tony settled down I can't commit to anything more than what we have now, which hasn't been going very good in my opinion. At least, not lately."

"Too bad my opinion doesn't count."

Stung by the rejection she'd heard in Taylor's voice, Glenda jerked her head up and looked him in the eye. "Your opinion has always mattered to me, Taylor. It always will."

"What if you don't ever get Tony settled down? Are you willing to live out the rest of your life alone, Glen? Tony is about to enter into manhood, agewise, and there's nothing you can do to stop that. Though he's not mature enough to handle the responsibilities of a man, he'll be required to do so, especially when it comes down to the laws governing this land."

"Taylor, I know he's not prepared for the world, but I don't know what else I can do to get him ready for the avalanche that's sure to bury him alive. I've tried to tell him, have done my very best to teach him the right things, and I've always been there for him. But Tony has a mind of his own. He dances to the tune of his own drummer."

"My point exactly. If only you could hear yourself, you'd recognize the solutions. No matter what you do, Glen, he's going to do as he sees fit. If he hasn't gotten what you've tried to teach him by now, he's not going to. He may eventually get it, but, unfortunately, it'll more than likely come to him the hard way. Life's experiences are the best teacher, but they can be tough."

Glenda sighed hard, flailing her arms in the air. The anger in her eyes was crystal clear. "I get your point, Taylor. There's nothing more I can do. Is that it? Is that what you're saying?"

Nearly frustrated out of his mind, Taylor closed his eyes for a brief moment to gather his wits. "What you can do is accept my help, Glen! I'm not going to abuse your boy, and I think you know that. He needs a man's guidance. As sure as I'm breathing, that boy is crying out for help. In my line of work I've seen this same scenario time and time again. A lot of the men that report to me were once troubled boys just like your Tony. Won't you at least let me try?"

Feeling weak and helpless, Glenda eyed Taylor, uncertainty written all over her face.

"Please hear me out. If you let me help out, and we don't see any changes in him within a couple of month's time, I'll agree to bow out. You owe it to yourself and to Tony to let me make an honest attempt at trying to help him turn his life around. I desperately need you to see that."

Glenda still didn't appear convinced. "I don't know, Taylor. I'd hate for him to lash out at you the way he does me. Tony can be very cruel verbally. He's so angry. I'm afraid, Taylor. So scared to let you get caught up in all this madness. I'm also fearful of losing you over this. I don't want that to happen."

Unable to bear the anguish in her eyes, Taylor pulled Glenda into his arms. "That's not going to happen, Glenda, not if you don't want it to. But we have to be a team, have to play on the same side. You also have to lose the fear. Fear is nothing more than the absence of faith."

Taylor grew thoughtful for a moment, his mind turning like the massive blades of a windmill. His vast experience with guys who'd once been like Anthony was his strongest ally. He'd already won over some pretty hard-core adults and he wasn't going to allow himself to believe that he couldn't win over another misguided boy. Anthony had a long, hard journey ahead of him if he was ever to become a man. Taylor believed he could help make it happen.

"Let me run this by you. Why don't you arrange for me to pick up Tony from juvenile hall when he's released? His reaction to that will give us some idea of what page he's on. We have to start somewhere, Glen. Are you willing to let me give it my best shot?"

Although she gave a resigned sigh, Glenda still looked reluctant. "Okay, but if he rebels against the idea of having you in his life in a new capacity, you have to back off immediately. Can you agree to that, Taylor?"

"Not only can I agree to it, but you have my word. I promise to take things slow and easy. I believe I can get Tony to trust me in due time. I refuse to believe otherwise."

Glenda laughed nervously, still unsure if this could work out or not. "I just hope you're not setting yourself up. Tony's distrust of males runs very deep. What I trust is that you'll keep your word to me. Thanks, Taylor, you've been a godsend since day one. Let's eat now."

Upon hearing the front door open and then close, Hannah looked up from the inspirational novel she held in her hands. Her eyes began to light up. Seeing Robert and Derrick hanging out together made her smile. Hearing them laughing had her heart rejoicing.

A lot of yelling and threatening had gone on in their house over the past week or so, the majority of it being done by Robert, but things had started to calm down. Derrick didn't seem to be trying Robert's patience as much, and it appeared to Hannah that Robert was trying to be less impatient with their son. Robert's waking Derrick up in the middle of the night to clean the kitchen had apparently given Derrick a wake-up call in more ways than one.

The two men in Hannah's life had taken to watching sports programs together again and they'd even had lots of fun playing a few hands of dominoes and talking trash about who was the best. The guys had even tampered under the hoods of the cars out in the garage, one of their favorite pastimes. Derrick hadn't been staying out all hours of the night over the last few days, which was definitely a change for the better.

Hannah was grateful for the miracle of peace in her home, hoping it would last forever. However, she knew that that was more than likely wishful thinking on her part. As long as Derrick played by his father's rules, they could coexist in a peaceful atmosphere. But the minute Derrick stepped out of line or over it, Robert would be right back in his face. She'd seen it happen too many times before, but Hannah was keeping her hopes up for better results this time around.

Robert leaned over and kissed Hannah on the mouth. "What about take-out for dinner? I'm in the mood for Chinese. What about you?"

"Sounds fine to me, Robert. Do you want me to go pick it up?" She looked down at her loose pants and oversized sweatshirt, her favorite lounging attire. "I'd have to change first."

Robert held up his hand in a halting motion. "No, no, Hannah. You're fine just as you are, nice and comfy. This is my bright idea, so I'll call and order the food and then go get it."

Hannah looked over at Derrick. "Are you going to join us for dinner tonight?"

"I got plans for later on in the evening, Mom. If it's okay with you and Dad, I'll take a pass on the Chinese."

Hannah wanted to run over and check Derrick's temperature. He had never cared a jackrabbit about what was or wasn't okay with them during the past several years. Although she was happy that he was being considerate of them, she was wary of his motivation. Perhaps all the private conversations he'd had with his dad were responsible for the change. Robert and Derrick had also been talking to each other in the open a lot lately, causing her at times to feel totally excluded.

"You still have to eat, Derrick, unless you're planning on eating out," Hannah said, talking down to him, as if he didn't know his own mind. "I don't see why you can't eat with us."

"Hannah, the boy knows whether he wants to eat dinner with us or not. He's already stated his choice. Can you just leave it at that for a change?" Robert asked.

Robert's impatient tone of voice grated on Hannah's nerves even though she knew he was right. If only she could stop treating Derrick like he was a small child, she mused, things might be better for everyone. "You're right, Robert. I apologize, Derrick, for dismissing your decision on dinner. I have to keep reminding myself on a daily basis that you're a grown man."

Derrick was so overly dependent on Hannah, which was why she treated him the way she did. It was a habit she needed to break, a really bad one. Even when Derrick was living with a woman, he depended on his mother to handle so many things for him. Hannah was beginning to realize she may've crippled him by doing everything for him, including washing his clothes and keeping his room clean. Robert would have a fit if he found out she was the one making Derrick's bed and cleaning up his bathroom practically every day since he'd moved back in. He hadn't bothered to do it simply because he knew his mother had always taken care of it for him.

Hannah had to wonder if Derrick might've turned out differently had she let Robert be the more dominant guiding force in their son's upbringing. Shielding Derrick from every little negative thing he'd come up against had become a way of life for Hannah. Standing up for him when Robert scolded him had happened more often than not. For her husband to lay hands on Derrick would've been out of the question had Robert not ignored her pleas when he believed there was no other way to handle Derrick's unruly behavior. But there had been a high price for Robert to pay after any physical punishment, a costly one. Hannah had made sure of that. Ignoring her husband's physical needs for days at a time had been her weapon of choice.

Old habits were surely hard to break and they died even harder. It was hard for Hannah to admit that Derrick was so dependent on her because that's the way she'd trained him. That was a hard pill for her to swallow. A Bible truth that her father had spouted over and over again in their home, day in and day out, came to Hannah's mind: "Train up a child in the way he should go: and when he is old, he will not depart from it" (Proverbs 22:6).

The minute Robert left the room Derrick came over to the sofa and sat down next to his mother. He looked at her and smiled broadly. "I need a favor."

Hannah turned her body a little, nestling her back into the corner of the couch. She then looked at Derrick and chuckled. "Your charming smile let me know that much. What's up?"

Derrick had to laugh at how easily his mother could see through him. "Do you think you could iron the shirt that I want to wear when I go out later?"

"Of course I can," Hannah said, without blinking an eye. Her mental reference of the Bible passage had already flown from her mind. "I'll need to do it while your father is out getting the food. Otherwise, I'll have him yelling at me about how I need to let you do things for yourself. Everyone can't iron. Your Dad's one of them, but he uses the excuse that he just prefers to take his shirts to the cleaners. The truth is your Dad's too stubborn to admit that he can't iron them himself and he refuses to let me do them."

Robert popped his head in the doorway. "Did I just hear my name mentioned? I hope you're not bad-mouthing me in here," Robert joked, not knowing he'd hit the nail on the head.

A bit ashamed of what she'd just said about her husband, Hannah's cheeks colored slightly. "Are you on your way out now?" she asked, purposely avoiding his question.

"Yeah, but I won't be long. I have to drop off some letters in the outdoor boxes at the post office, but I plan to do that before I pick up our dinner."

"Okay. See you when you get back," Hannah said.

"Son, do you want to ride along with me?"

"Thanks for asking, Dad, but I need to start getting myself together to go out later."

Robert nodded his understanding. "No problem, Derrick."

Upon hearing the front door close, Hannah leaped from the sofa. "We have to move fast, Derrick. Go get your shirt and bring it down to the laundry room while I set up the ironing board and iron. I want to have it done before your dad gets back."

Derrick got up and started out the room. He then turned back to face his mother, wearing a thoughtful expression. "Maybe Dad doesn't want you to do his shirts because he thinks you already have enough to do." Without further comment Derrick rushed from the room.

Hannah was so stunned by Derrick's comment, which sounded a lot like something Robert would say, that she had to take a minute to think about it. Derrick's remarks certainly had been in defense of his father. The not-so-nice things she'd said about Robert prior to him interrupting her conversation with their son instantly echoed inside her head.

It disturbed Hannah to know what she'd done, had obviously been doing all along; hating that she may be guilty of constantly playing father against son—and vice versa. That Derrrick seemed highly aware of it bothered her the most. Then another revelation hit her hard. Derrick had probably learned right from her how to play one side against the other. A perfect example of that was what had just transpired in the living room. She'd armed Derrick with ammunition.

Hannah remained thoughtful as she set up the ironing equipment. There were definitely some things she needed to change, but she didn't have a clue how to undo the damage she'd done thus far. It then dawned on her that undoing anything from the past was impossible. However, she could start working today toward making a brighter tomorrow for her and her family.

"Here's my shirt, Mom," Derrick said, interrupting Hannah's musings.

After taking the shirt from her son, Hannah looked up at him and smiled. "You know something. The remark you made before you left the room hit home with me. You're more than likely right about what you said about your dad. So, with that in mind, I'm going to teach you how to iron your own shirts. I *do* have enough to do already." She stepped away from the ironing board and then thrust the iron into Derrick's hand.

Derrick frowned heavily. "I can't do this, Mom! Why you going back on your word?"

"I'm not. You should know by now that it's a woman's prerogative to change her mind. Besides that, I've decided that it's high time you started fending for yourself."

Derrick grimaced. "Now you sound just like Dad."

"Good, since he's right most of the time. Do you want to get this shirt ironed or do you want to continue sparring with me?"

Wishing he'd kept his big mouth shut, Derrick sucked his teeth. "I guess I don't have a choice in the matter if I want to wear this shirt tonight."

Hannah beamed brightly. "You're absolutely right about that, son."

Proud of herself and how she'd handled the ironing chore with Derrick, Hannah smiled as she checked her appearance in the mirror. While taking the quickest shower ever, thinking over that little scenario with her son had helped her to see a few things a lot clearer. It had also prompted her to lose the baggy clothes and dress up a little for dinner, even though this wasn't Wednesday, her and Robert's normal date night. Slim black pants and the Oriental-designed red, black, and gold silk blouse were perfect for the evening. Eating Chinese take-out by candlelight would be just as romantic. Robert would think so, too.

Knowing Robert would be back any minute, Hannah sprayed on a light perfume and then made a mad dash for the stairs, hoping she'd have the table set and candles lit before he arrived. Soft music always put them in the right mood. Thinking of spending a spontaneous, romantic evening with Robert had Hannah smiling all over. Her sensuous thoughts were purely delicious.

Out in the upstairs hallway Hannah ran right into Derrick.

Derrick looked puzzled. "What you in such a hurry for? And why you all dressed up?"

Hannah chuckled. "Boy, if you don't get out my way, in the next second you'll wish you had." She started down the steps and then stopped abruptly, turning around to look back up at Derrick. "What time are you leaving?"

Derrick shrugged. "I don't know."

Hannah smiled solicitously, batting her eyelashes playfully. "Do me a big favor by making it as soon as possible. Your father and I need some time alone."

Derrick shook his head in dismay. "Whatever!"

"Whatever indeed," Hannah said, bubbling inside with eager anticipation of whatever was to come later. Robert would no doubt make their evening rendezvous intriguing, as always.

All finished with her last case, Tara began to shut down her ultrasound equipment, since she'd already performed the necessary cleaning. Her sterile white workroom, which she had brightened cheerfully by hanging on the walls a few pastel watercolor paintings, had been a busy place from the start of her shift. She'd done so many ultrasounds she'd lost count hours ago. The tension in her body was a killer and she couldn't wait to get home and soak in a relaxing aromatherapy bath. Raymond was also coming to see her later. Without Maya, she hoped.

"You have a STAT case on the way down from the ER, Tara," a deep male voice remarked. George Whitehall, an ER nurse, was one of Tara's coworkers.

Tara faced George, whose head was poked halfway in the door. "Is it serious, George?"

"Possible kidney failure," George responded. "He was flown in via Life Flight. That should give you some idea of what we're deal-ing with," he said, before rushing off.

Tara took in a few deep breaths of air. Needing no further expla-nation, she leaped into action, quickly turning back on all the equip-ment. Though she was sure she'd have to do the ultrasound with the patient on a gurney, she still put a sterile paper liner on the leather table.

Knowing that her plans for the evening might very well disinte-grate before her very eyes, she prepared herself for what might lie ahead. It wasn't that she didn't need the overtime pay, but if she had her way, she'd prefer to spend her time relaxing in the company of the man she hadn't seen for several days. Talking over the phone just wasn't cutting it.

Despite the fact she'd been eager to get home, Tara, a real trooper, was committed to her job. She loved what she did. Being a vital part of a team of professionals working in a life-saving envi-ronment made her proud to be a public servant. Her job as an ultra-sound technician was an important one. Her profession always came before her pleasures. When duty called, she heeded.

Tara's back was to the door when her patient was wheeled in by one of the ER attendants. She quickly turned around to face the visitors. A cursory glance at the man on the gurney let her see that he was African American. A closer look at him caused her complex-ion to turn grayish.

The still form on the gurney was Timothy, her estranged brother. Believing that her eyes were deceiving her, Tara closed them and opened them repeatedly. Loud gasps of air tore from her lips when reality checked in. Tara stepped right up to the gurney and looked down into the man's face. He wasn't dead, but he looked the part, his honey brown complexion dry and ashy.

"Mr. Wheatley was heavily medicated to keep him calm," the at-tendant informed Tara. "The guy's kidneys are in bad shape. Are you going to be okay? You suddenly look a little odd."

"Yes, yes. I'm fine, Rodney. If you don't mind, I need to get started on the ultrasound. I was already told by George that this was a STAT order."

"No problem, Tara. Call the ER when you're finished and I'll come back for him."

While sending her fervent prayers up to God, Tara's lips moved as rapidly as her hands in preparing things for the medical procedure she was about to perform.

How could this be? Not knowing exactly what was wrong with Timothy had Tara gravely concerned. He looked as if he was in critical condition. She could barely believe that she was face-to-face with her brother after all this time. Tara suddenly felt so sorry for the part she'd played in their absence in each other's lives. Squeezing back the tears, Tara quickly sobered, shutting her emotions down. Time was of the essence. The attending physician was awaiting the results. STAT procedures weren't ordered without just cause.

All during the procedure Tara's thoughts took her back to a time when she and Timothy had been inseparable. Only three years apart in age, Tara was the youngest sibling. Their mammoth backyard flashed into her mind, causing her memories of that time to come alive.

Hide-and-seek had been one of their favorite games to play outdoors. They hadn't been allowed to go out into the front yard, so behind the numerous backyard trees and in the dark shadows of the shed house and garage were the only places they'd had to hide. As they'd grown older, they had loved to roller skate and play all sorts of board games. Checkers had been one of Timothy's favorite games because Tara hadn't ever been able to best him at it. The thought of their summer lemonade stands brought joyous tears to Tara's eyes. The two siblings had made quite a sales team back then.

Since they'd once been so very close, for her and Timothy not to have spoken to each other in five years was indeed a travesty, Tara mused, wiping away her tears with one hand. Her mother would be so displeased with their estrangement, not to mention terribly hurt. She had prided herself on teaching them to love and take care of each other in good times and bad.

Tara could plainly see that Timothy had recently run into some not-so-good times. For a guy who had once been a great high school athlete, who had looked so healthy, and who had been chockful of energy, he appeared so gaunt, as if he hadn't been eating properly. Tara could only imagine that alcohol and drugs had played the leading role in his kidney problems.

Timothy had started drinking beer in his late teens and hard liquor came shortly after, which had later become unmanageable for him. The couple of different rehabilitation programs their mother had convinced Timothy to attend hadn't worked simply because he hadn't worked them. Joanna's only son did not share her enthusiastic desire for him to be clean sober.

After finishing up with the ultrasound of Timothy's kidneys, Tara called the ER to let Rodney know that his patient was ready for pickup. While waiting for the attendant to appear, Tara began cleaning her equipment in a mechanical fashion.

Tara hadn't felt this numb since the day her mother had died from an overworked heart. Was Timothy going to die, too? She had to wonder, shuddering hard at the dark thought. He hadn't moved a muscle or batted an eyelash during the entire procedure. Although she knew the heavy doses of medication had him in a near-comatose state, her fears were not the least bit lessened. Kidney problems weren't something to recover from easily. She wasn't a doctor, but she had done enough procedures to know when a patient's physical condition was very serious.

Tara didn't even look up when Rodney first swept into the room. She didn't want her coworker to see her tears. He had already mentioned earlier how odd she'd looked. Using discretion, Tara wiped away the rolling moisture before she made eye contact with Rodney. "Mr. Wheatley is all ready for you."

"Thanks. The doctor is anxious to get this patient admitted. The on-call urologist is on his way in to view the findings. But we already know this guy's kidneys are a wreck. If the Life Flight team hadn't gotten him here when they did, he probably would've died."

Tara's insides trembled at the thought of her brother dying. While battling her emotions, she squared her shoulders and took in a few calming breaths of air. "Rodney, you need to be careful about what you say in the presence of a patient. He may be able to hear you, you know. He's only medicated, not in a coma. Many people believe that some comatose patient's can hear what's going on, including me, so we have to be careful with our words."

Rodney looked abashed. Then a flicker of light came on in his eyes. "Hey, it just dawned on me that this guy has the same last name as yours. He's not related to you, is he?"

Rodney's question had caught Tara off guard momentarily. Although she wasn't ready to reveal the truth of the matter, she just couldn't outright deny Timothy's relationship to her. That would be like continuing to deny his existence, which she'd been guilty of long enough. "Yeah, he is, actually. We're all sisters and brothers in Christ."

Rodney laughed. "I guess that answers my question. I'm out of here."

All Tara had enough strength to do, once Rodney had left, was to drop down onto a chair and close her eyes. "God, help me," she pleaded. "Please show me how to soften my heart toward my own brother. I know you know that I love him. Guide me toward making all my wrongs right. I can't do it alone, God. I need you to show me the pathway to forgiveness."

Since Jesus had cried out to the Father from the cross He was dying upon to forgive those who had hated Him and had wanted Him dead, why couldn't she forgive the brother whom she still loved dearly, the brother whom she truly wanted to live forever?

It then came to Tara's mind that hers wasn't a multiple-choice question. There was only one answer. Therefore, she couldn't possibly get it wrong. Not if she believed in the promises. Tara knew that she had no choice but to forgive Timothy in order for her multitude of sins to be forgiven by God. Knowing what she had to do and getting it done were two different things.

Only with God's help and following His instructions would Tara become triumphant.

Mark, chapter eleven, verses twenty-four to twenty-five: "Listen to me! You can pray for anything, and if you *believe*, you have it; it's yours! But when you are praying, first forgive anyone you are holding a grudge against, so that your Father in heaven will forgive you your sins too" she voiced aloud.

Tara picked up her cell phone and dialed Raymond's home number, hoping that he was still there. When Maya answered the phone, Tara frowned slightly, since she didn't know what to expect from this unpredictable teenager. "Hi, Maya, how are you? Is your dad in?"

"No, he's gone back to work. He was called in to cover the night shift for a coworker." Maya slammed down the phone without further comment.

Tara held the phone away from her, looking at it in total disbelief. "No, Miss Girlfriend didn't just hang up on me!" Tara laughed nervously, checking the line for any signs of life. "Yeah, I guess she did."

Upon calling Raymond's cell number, Tara listened to the phone ring until his voice message came on. Deciding not to leave a voice mail, she promptly hung up, knowing her number would come up on his phone anyway. He'd eventually see the missed call.

Tara was somewhat glad that Raymond was working. For all her earlier desire to see him, she now wanted to be alone. She had so many things to think through. Tara knew her work was cut out for her if she was to make amends with Timothy. She groaned loudly. *If* wasn't an option. *When* was the operative word in this instance. Making peace with her brother was imperative. Too much time had elapsed already.

Tara tried to think of what she'd tell her friends about all this.

Keeping a sibling a secret wasn't something best friends normally indulged in. Was there a good enough reason, or any reason at all, for that matter, for her not ever mentioning Timothy to her girlfriends? Especially since they'd shared so much of their personal affairs with her. Tara suddenly felt like a hypocrite, her mind flipping and flopping between telling all or nothing.

Frightened to go home and afraid to stay at the hospital alone, Tara turned off the lights and then locked up her work space. Slowly, she went down the long corridor, coming to a complete stop at the large double doors leading into the ER. Tara looked up at the windows above the doors, wondering which treatment room Timothy was in. She doubted that he'd already been admitted and sent up to a room. ER procedures took a long time. Finding an empty bed could take even longer.

"Hi, Tara," a cheerful voice said, from behind Tara.

Tara turned toward the direction of the voice, immediately smiling at the older woman. "Hey, Ms. Millie, nice to see you. How have you been?"

Millie gave Tara a warm hug. "I'm fine, thank you. Good to see you, too. Since your shift is already over, what are you doing down here in the ER? Did they call you for another emergency case?"

Tara shook her head. "No, I'm on my way out. I was wondering about the last patient I had. He seemed in really bad shape."

"Oh, I'm sorry, but he just died a few minutes ago, Tara."

Tara nearly doubled over, feeling as though she needed to throw up. Beads of sweat popped out all over her forehead, making her feel faint. No, Timothy, Tara cried inwardly. *I needed to tell you that I loved you. Oh, God, I'm too late. I missed my chance at redemption.*

Concerned over how upset Tara appeared, Millie put her arm around the young woman's shoulders. "Don't stress yourself, sweetheart. Mr. Harper was ninety-seven, Tara. According to his son, his father lived a good life. He's at peace now."

"Mr. Harper!" Tara felt instant relief, though she felt horrible for the older man and his family. Tara gave a silent thanks to God for sparing Timothy's life. "I got so upset because I thought you were talking about my very last case, the younger black guy."

"Oh, no, not him. I'm sorry if I misled you. I see why that would upset you. He's only thirty. He's in bad shape, but alive, though in guarded condition. He's already been moved to intensive care. A hospital bed opened up really quick. Unusual, huh?"

"You can say that again. Tara felt herself growing even weaker from the relief, wishing she could just break down and cry her heart out. Timothy was alive. Rejoicing was more in order for such a liberating occasion. God had given her another chance to make it right. This was an opportunity that she wouldn't let go to waste. Awake or asleep, she would tell Timothy how much she loved him, how much she wanted him to live and to be a part of her life again. God had answered her earlier prayers. Now she had to do her part by obeying God's instructions.

Tara quickly made her way up to the intensive care unit where Timothy had been taken. Without inquiring of his exact whereabouts, Tara took a seat in the visitor's waiting area. In dire need of a brief respite, Tara closed her eyes, her emotions chaotic. The first memory that instantly came to her mind was not a peaceful one by any stretch of the imagination.

That fateful Saturday morning had been a cold and rainy one. Tara was twenty-two at the time. She'd gone over to her mother's to spend the night because Joanna hadn't been feeling that well. Tara remembered sweating when her old bedroom had gotten too hot, so much so that she'd had to kick the covers off. The unbearable heat had kept Tara from getting a good night's sleep. Because her mother was always cold, Tara had suffered through the discomfort.

Loud voices had awakened her just before dawn. The loudest voice was male, but it hadn't been her father's, because he had moved out a long time ago. Rarely had Jamaica come by the house after the legal separation. Tara had always visited her father in his

cozy one-bedroom apartment, where she'd spent some of the hap-
piest moments of her life.

Tara recalled creeping to the door and opening it slightly, looking up and down the hallway, without stepping out of her room.
The arguing had come from her mother's bedroom, where the
door had been left slightly ajar. It was then that she'd seen Timothy
running out of her mother's room, carrying Joanna's purse. While
he'd rustled through the black leather shoulder bag, the look in his
red eyes had been a wild and crazy one. Once he'd removed all the
cash and change he could find, he'd dropped the purse and run toward the front of the house.

Seconds later the front door had slammed shut. Worried sick
about her mother, especially after seeing the doped-up state her
brother was in, Tara had dashed into her bedroom, where she
found Joanna sprawled out on the floor, her eyes rolled to the back
of her head. She had thought her mother was dead until she'd taken
her pulse, which was barely there. Tara had then called her father to
meet her at the hospital immediately after she'd dialed 911.

If Tara lived to be a hundred, she was sure she'd never forget
seeing Timothy with her mother's purse that night, nor would she
ever forget that death-defying ride in the ambulance. Shortly after
arriving at the hospital, not long after the unclear encounter she'd
had with her own flesh-and-blood son, Joanna had died from the
massive heart attack she'd suffered.

The police had never learned of the strange incident with
Timothy and Joanna's purse. Jamaica Wheatley was the only other
person whom Tara had ever shared the story with.

Chapter Six

Seated comfortably in her living room, where she'd been working on a crossword puzzle, Hannah's jaw nearly dropped to the carpet, practically floored at the sore sight before her eyes. Derrick had brought a lot of women over to meet his parents, but this one took the cake.

Hannah and Robert's son loved older woman, who were usually from five to eight years his senior, but the woman on Derrick's arm had to be close to Hannah's own age. Or the sister was living one hard life. Spotting the diamonds seeming to drip from every part of the woman's anatomy, Hannah decided that perhaps life hadn't been so hard for Derrick's female companion, at least not financially. However, if she was correct in her assessment of the lady's age, this liaison was downright ridiculous.

It wasn't that the woman wasn't attractive—she was absolutely stunning. Not a single gray hair resided in her dark brown, shoulder-length hair. The appearance of her widely spaced, cinnamon brown eyes definitely pointed more toward the age of wisdom. Despite her knock-dead girlish figure, Hannah was willing to bet that she hadn't seen her twenties in a few decades. She actually looked old enough to be a mother to someone Derrick's age.

Hannah quickly decided that she should check herself. She really didn't know what their relationship to each other was, since Derrick hadn't even made the introductions yet. Hannah glanced over at Robert, who sat quietly in his favorite leather recliner, with the daily newspaper spread out on his lap. He also looked as if he'd been hit right between the eyes with a stun gun. His pupils had grown rather large with incredulity.

Derrick gently placed his hand over his companion's hand, the one that now held onto his arm tightly. "Mom, Dad, this is Raquel. We've been dating for a while now, so I thought it was time for her to meet you two." Derrick looked up at Raquel, who was a couple of inches taller than him, and smiled endearingly. "Raquel, these are my parents, Mr. and Mrs. Brentwood."

The worst-case scenario was now laid out for Hannah. She was speechless. Though never one to be outright rude to anyone, Hannah just didn't know what to say. Trying to get her mouth to move just wasn't happening. Derrick's introduction of his friend had shocked her senseless.

Upon seeing his wife's stunned reaction to Derrick's announcement, Robert laid the paper aside and then got to his feet. "Nice to meet you, Raquel. Come on in and have a seat."

As if she were trying to snap out of a trance, Hannah blinked hard. "Yes, please do," she finally managed to say, her mouth feeling as dry as sawdust. Hannah still couldn't help wondering what in heaven's name was going on in her son's mind. No, she thought, Derrick no longer had a mind. He'd totally lost it. Derrick Brentwood was certifiably insane.

Raquel smiled broadly, promptly seating herself at the other end of the sofa. "Thanks so much. It's really nice to meet both of you. Derrick has told me a lot about you."

Hannah sighed a breath of relief when Derrick seated himself between her and Raquel. She then shot her husband a bewildered glance. The expression on Robert's face let her know he was enjoying this little scene to the max. She'd seen that twinkle of devilment enough in his eyes to recognize it right off. That Robert found her discomfort amusing had her fuming inside. Hannah couldn't wait for them to be alone so she could tell him what she thought about him having such pleasure at her expense. In fact, she could hardly wait to get this entire matter off her chest. Hannah's gut felt like it was about to burst wide open.

"We're only going to be here a minute," Derrick announced. "We're on our way to a concert at Arrowhead Pond."

Thank God for small favors, Hannah mused. It seemed to her like they'd already been there over an hour. Holding her tongue in check was darn near impossible. She had so many questions in her mind. None were so important to Hannah as learning Raquel's exact age.

"Who're you going to see?" Robert asked.

"Will Downing. Raquel's crazy for his music. She has every CD he's ever put out."

Raquel's choice in music was just another indication of her age, as far as Hannah was concerned. Since Derrick only listened to loud hip hop music, at least when he was at home, she couldn't imagine how he was going to sit through the entire concert without getting bored. Will Downing was an exciting performer and a magnificent balladeer, but his style of music just wasn't what Derrick was used to grooving on.

"I love Will, too," Robert remarked. "The brother can croon."

"Mom, you like him, too, don't you?" Derrick inquired.

"Very much. We don't have all his CDs, but we own quite a few. I've never seen him in person, but I hear he's a premier performer," Hannah responded.

Raquel smiled, showing off her beautiful white teeth. "Had I known you two were so into Will as well, I would've purchased two extra tickets. The concert would've made a nice first-time outing for all of us. We'll make sure to check with you the next time we plan to go to one."

Hannah groaned inwardly. Double dating with her son and his

older woman was the perfect gift, the kind of present she'd always wanted for Christmas. Not! The very thought made her feel like tossing her dinner. Knowing their few minutes of visiting time should be up, Hannah glanced at the clock, anxious for this little meeting between girlfriend and parents to be over.

As if Derrick had read his mother's disingenuous thoughts, he got to his feet. "It's time for us to roll. We don't want to be late." Derrick reached for Raquel's hand, helping her up from the sofa. "We're out. Don't you two stay up too late now," Derrick joked with his parents.

Hannah wanted to ask Derrick if he'd be coming back home tonight. But under the circumstances, she knew he'd be livid with her if she did. Robert wouldn't be too happy with her either. Minding her own business in the case was the only way to go, Hannah concluded. However, Derrick was her business—and she had every intention of sticking her nose all up into his the first chance she got. This was one situation Hannah wasn't about to keep quiet about.

Robert offered to walk Derrick and Raquel to the door, but Hannah remained seated, bidding the departing couple her polite farewells from the sofa as they left the living room.

While waiting for Robert to return to the room, Hannah was beside herself with anger. The nerve of that woman coming into her house thinking that it would be acceptable for her to be dating their son, who was probably half her age. If Raquel thought she'd gone over well with them, that they were okay with this unhealthy relationship, she'd better think again.

Robert walked back into the room and sat down next to his wife. "Okay, Hannah, let it all out before you burst. I can clearly see that you're not going to let this one get by you."

Sinclair and Marcus had already eaten the delicious egg, pancake, and turkey sausage breakfast she had prepared for the two of them.

To satisfy Marcus's craving for pastries, baked cinnamon rolls, warmed in the oven, had also been served. The table had been cleaned off and the only items left on it were two mugs of fresh coffee. The only thing missing from the family gathering was Charles, the husband who had seemingly disappeared without a trace.

Sinclair had phoned Charles all through the night, to no avail. He was either out town, which still didn't explain to her why he wasn't answering his cell, or he was purposely ignoring her calls. She hoped the latter wasn't true since it made her feel even worse. Nightmares of her husband with another woman had plagued her up until the wee hours of the morning.

Now that it was time to get down to business with Marcus, Sinclair briefly went over in her mind what she needed to say to him. *Money* would be the early morning topic of conversation. What Marcus had done with all the money she'd sent him was more precise.

Sinclair picked up her coffee mug and took a small sip of the strong, black liquid. Eyeing Marcus curiously, she set the cup back down. "Marcus, exactly how much money do you owe on your credit cards? Whatever you do, don't lie to me, son."

Marcus fidgeted in his seat, looking terribly uncomfortable. "Between the two of them I owe over fifteen hundred dollars. I'm sorry, Mom. I know that's a lot of money, but I just made the mistake of letting things get out of hand."

Sinclair pounded her fist down hard on the table. "Just! There's nothing *just* about it. And your mistake is a huge one, Marcus Albright. So how do you plan to pay off these high bills on your nonexistent salary?"

Marcus frowned, not daring to look his mother right in the eye. He lowered his head, staring down at his white designer tennis shoes. "I don't know, but that's one of the reasons I'm here. I came home to ask you to loan me the money to pay them off. I'm really behind in my monthly payments. If I don't clear my debts real soon, my credit will be affected. I'm hoping I can avoid that by taking care of them before it's too late."

Unable to stomach what she'd just heard from her son, Sinclair nearly gagged from shock. Fifteen hundred dollars was a lot of money. But after she'd compared it with what she already owed on her bank cards, Sinclair saw it as a mere drop in the bucket. She could either give Marcus the money or see his credit ruined for the next seven years. If that were to happen, he'd have a hard time reestablishing a good credit report, which might even negatively affect his ability to purchase a house later on in life.

Marcus reached over and took Sinclair's hand, squeezing it gently. He looked as desperate as he felt. "I know I messed up big time. But, Mom, if you trust me with the money this one last time, I promise to eventually make it right. I think I've learned my lesson with this one. I didn't realize how important it is to have good credit up until now. It's so easy to get used to pulling out the plastic instead of using cash."

"But of course it is, Marcus! Especially when someone else is footing the bill. I don't know why you opened up these credit cards in the first place, knowing you had no means to pay for them. But then again, I guess I know exactly why you did it. Mom will bail me out if I overextend my credit line. She'll fix it for me like she always does. Isn't that what you told yourself? Mom's my own personal banker. Isn't that how you really see me, Marcus?"

Sinclair bit down on her lower lip to keep from screaming her head off. Slugging something or someone hard was the only thing that might make her feel better. She'd taught Marcus to use her this way and she'd also taught him to be irresponsible and inconsiderate. This was the monster child she'd created single-handedly. Now she had to deal with him on her own.

Admitting that Charles had been right on target about everything to do with her financing Marcus's every whim still came hard for her despite all the evidence to support his charges. A mother wanting the very best for her children wasn't a crime. Wanting everything good for them wasn't the bad part. The crime was in either doing nothing at all for your kids or overdoing it.

Marcus had taken gross advantage of Sinclair's good heart in this instance. Just as she'd been taking advantage of Charles all these years, Marcus had watched and had learned how to play the very same game with his mother. Batting her eyelashes and coming on to her husband in a flirtatious way had worked every time in getting Sinclair exactly what she wanted. Dropping a few tears in Charles's lap had worked even better. That was, until recently.

Marcus's sad looks and stressful voice played on Sinclair's emotions the same way hers had played on her husband's. It was sinful of both mother and son to use unfair tactics to get their own way. Sinclair felt ashamed of herself, but not enough to ignore Marcus's pitiful pleas.

"Children listen to what you say but watch what you do" was a perfect analogy for what had obviously happened in her home. Marcus had simply followed by example. "Do as I say do 'cause I said it" just didn't apply to this generation of youth. They simply did as they pleased.

Sinclair brought her tearful eyes level with Marcus's. "Your situation tells me that you need to get a full-time job and become a part-time student." Sinclair had heard what she'd just told Marcus, but she couldn't believe it had come out of her own mouth. Mimicking Charles's words of wisdom had her a tad worried about her already hanging-by-a-thread sanity.

Marcus looked horrified, his eyes stretching wide. "That's insane! I can't work and go to school. I need to concentrate on my grades," Marcus protested rather loudly.

Sinclair raised an eyebrow. "Since when? You haven't been getting good grades for quite some time now. I think you've forgotten what an A looks like, boy." Although Marcus had been a good high school student, his grades were suffering terribly at the college level. Sinclair couldn't remember the last time she'd seen an A on his grade sheet.

"Are you saying you're not going to help me pay off those credit cards?" Marcus asked.

Sinclair heard the stress in her son's voice, which immediately weakened her defenses. Seeing him looking so distraught broke her heart. What would it hurt to bail him out yet again if she made him understand that this was the last time she'd come to the rescue?

In bailing Marcus out of his debts, Sinclair knew that she was only digging a deeper financial hole for herself. If Charles didn't come back to her, bankruptcy would be her only way out. Adding $1,500 more to what she already owed wasn't going to make her situation any worse than it was if she had to file in bankruptcy court. Although she was concerned with her jaded thought process, Sinclair decided it was better to help Marcus out than it was not to. And she'd come to that conclusion without ever figuring Charles into the equation.

"Did you bring your bills home with you, Marcus? If so, I need you to go get them."

"I didn't even think to pack them. Does this mean you're considering helping me out?"

Sinclair hated herself for the answer she was about to give to his question, but she didn't know what else to do. She certainly couldn't ignore his serious dilemma. "Then you'll have to send them to me when you get back home. Once I get your statements, I'll write the checks out and send them in for payment."

Marcus frowned. "That's not going to work. Not enough time to do all that. Why can't you just write me the check and let me deposit it in my account? That way, I can pay the bills right away. These accounts are way overdue," Marcus lied willfully.

"Since you're going to have to pay a late fee anyway, what does it matter that they're a few more days late?" Sinclair inquired.

Marcus was growing impatient. Now that he had his mother on the hook, he didn't want her to suddenly get loose. "Okay, whatever you want, Mom. I just don't see why you can't give me the money and let me take care of it. I guess you're always going to treat me like a child."

Sinclair was totally shocked by Marcus's statement. She'd given him plenty of opportunities to act like an adult, but all he'd ever shown her was how irresponsible he could be.

"I'm not going there with you, mister. If I write you the check, you have to promise me that you'll send me the statements to the bills showing they've been paid. That's the only way I'll agree to give you the money."

Sinclair cringed inwardly. She'd first have to do a cash advance on her one last credit card that had a hefty line of credit on it. The more she thought about it, she wasn't sure she hadn't already used the one card she kept only for emergencies.

"Marcus, you're going to have to give me some time to work on this. I need to check out a few things before I write this check. I'll get back to you later today."

Knowing Sinclair would come through for him no matter what, Marcus gave his mother a bear hug. "I appreciate it. I have to go up to my room for a minute, but I'll come back and clean the kitchen for you. I can do at least that much to show my appreciation. Thanks, Mom."

The doorbell rang, much to Sinclair's dismay. Since Marcus had already gone upstairs, she'd have to answer it. Wondering whom it could be, she left the kitchen and headed down the hallway. Would Charles dare to start ringing the doorbell? Although she couldn't warm to the idea of him doing such, she still hoped it was her husband at the door. Her worry over him not calling or coming by had increased. This kind of objectionable behavior was so unlike Charles.

The U.S. Marshall standing before her caused Sinclair to suck in a shaky breath. Something had happened to Charles. That's why she hadn't heard from him. Fear shook her very foundation as she stared at the tall black man wearing an impeccable uniform, the man who'd come to bring her bad tidings. Then reality hit. This government officer wasn't here about any accident. He was here to confirm her worst fears.

"Sinclair Albright?"

Sinclair grimaced, knowing what was coming next. "Yes, officer, I'm Sinclair Albright."

The officer handed Sinclair a large envelope. "Consider yourself served." He then turned around and walked off the porch.

All Sinclair could do was stare after him. She then looked at the return address in the top left-hand corner of the envelope. Her heart rate quickened at the sight of the name. She was very familiar with this firm, had used it on many occasions. Definitely a conflict of interest, she mused, totally disgusted with the entire situation. So much for these people being her friends.

Then a sickening feeling took hold of Sinclair's stomach. With shaking hands, easily guessing at what was inside, Sinclair tore the envelope open. The first few lines she read came as no surprise, yet she felt as if a bullet had been fired into her gut. Charles had filed for divorce.

Irreconcilable differences . . .

Simone was surprised to find Booker at her front door. He hadn't called first. Fear filled her up as she thought of what his visit might mean. Was Tyrell okay? Had he gotten himself into some kind of trouble? So many questions whizzed through Simone's brain, causing her worry to increase. "Tyrell," she uttered, her lips quivering. "Is he okay, Booker?"

Booker momentarily lowered his eyes to the ground. "No, he's not, Simone. That's what I'm here to talk to you about. Can I come in?"

To allow Booker entry, Simone pushed the door farther back. "Please do."

With every step she took toward the living room, Simone's fears grew and grew. What was wrong with Tyrell and why hadn't her son called on her if he was in need? Why did Booker have to be the one to tell her anything about the child she'd raised alone? Why was Tyrell confiding in the man who'd abandoned him, and not his mother, the one person who'd attended to his every want and need? Why was she suddenly the outsider in Tyrell's life?

Simone knew she should offer Booker something to drink or eat, but it was getting harder and harder for her to be polite. He was the enemy who'd invaded her camp without any warning. Forcing herself to be charitable is what she had to do, now that her son was living in the enemy's camp. Simone resented that. "Can I get you something to drink or eat before I sit down?"

Booker looked at his watch. "No thanks, Simone. I have a lunch date when I leave here."

Jealousy arose in Simone before she had a chance to blink her eyes. Although Booker hadn't mentioned that his date was with a woman, she felt sure that it was. The smug look on his face caused her instantly to revisit her initial thought. Was this Booker's way of paying her back for keeping her evening's plans from him the night of the gospel concert? She was suspicious.

Simone cleared her throat and then her wayward thoughts. She couldn't put the inevitable off any longer. Putting off this conversation wasn't going to make it go away. "You said you came to talk to me about Tyrell. What's happening with him?"

"Anger, lots of it. It seethes from every pore on his body. Ever since he learned that Jerome moved out, all he talks about is coming back home."

"Then why doesn't he? This has always been his home."

"I challenged him not to, dared him to be a man about it. He needs you to cut the apron strings. Only then will he be free enough to become a man."

The venom-filled look on Simone's face was a clear indication as to how she felt about Booker's comments. The brush of a gifted artist couldn't have defined any better a portrait of hate etched on a woman's face.

Simone leaned forward in her seat, her eyes never leaving Booker's face. "What gives you the right to say the things you just did? You may be Tyrell's father, but you haven't acted very much like a man in my opinion. You don't fit the description or the MO of a father or a man. How can you dare to talk about our son becoming a man, when you've given him no examples to follow? You not only cut the strings to your own mother's apron, but you also cut the ties that bind a family. Where were you when I was struggling to raise this boy on my own, Booker? Where were you when I was watching him play sports, helping him with his homework, taking him to Boy Scout meetings, and running him here and there? Where the heck were you?"

"In the streets, Simone, running all kinds of women. Out there in the world living life like there was no tomorrow, thinking of no one but myself. That's the honest to God truth."

Simone was thoroughly stunned by Booker's candid response. His honesty had surprised her, since she'd expected him to make sorry excuses for his whereabouts. What could she say to the honest to goodness truth? How did she argue with the cold, hard facts he'd just presented?

"I know I haven't been here for Tyrell, Simone. You can't make me feel any worse than I do or call me by any vulgar name that I haven't already called myself. You have no idea how hard it was for me to pick up the phone a few months back and call Tyrell. You can't begin to imagine what that felt like."

"If it was as easy for you as walking out on us, I can imagine. Vividly. You're the one who has no idea, 'cause you weren't here to see what we had to go through. While other boys' fathers were attending their sporting events, Tyrell didn't have a male figure out in the crowd to cheer him on. He didn't have his dad to be proud of a job well done. All he had there was me." Simone wiped the tears from her face, her anger escalating by the second.

"If anyone needs to imagine something, it's you. Imagine your father being a superstar athlete, playing in the NFL. You see him on television all the time, grinning up in the cameras, but he won't have anything to do with you. Imagine that all he ever did was send money to cover your expenses, just like he's donating to some charity case. Not that the money wasn't important. Don't get me wrong on that. I don't even want to imagine what we would've done without the money. But Tyrell would've forgone all his needs just to have you in his life; just to sit up in the football stands and watch you play. It hurt my heart to hear Tyrell say how much he wished he could visit with you in the locker room and to be able to meet your teammates and their kids. What little you did for your son will never pass as enough, Booker. As a father, you have been derelict in your duties and in your responsibilities to our son. There's no nice way to put it."

Booker lowered his head a tad, ashamed of what he'd allowed to happen to his family. "I deserved that, Simone. Again, there's nothing you can say to me that I haven't already said to myself, on a daily basis. There's nothing more anyone can say."

"Oh, yes there is, Booker! And I have plenty more to say. You just need to get out of our lives and leave us alone. Go back to wherever you came from. You're not needed around here. Tyrell and I have done just fine in your absence, Booker Branch. Just fine!"

Booker shook his head. "No you haven't, Simone. Stop lying to yourself. My absence is exactly what has caused all these disasters in your life. Tyrell didn't have to tell me what your life's been like. Seeing a drunken man living here with you was only one of the clues I've picked up on. That black eye of yours was another. Your life has been a living Hades since I walked away from this house, Simone. You'll never be able to convince me otherwise."

More blatant truths than she'd ever wanted to face had dealt Simone's emotions another hard blow. There was no comeback for this round. Booker was dead right. She could tell him that he was all wrong, that she was happier than she'd ever been in her life with him in it, and that she was content with things just the way they were. Saying nothing at all was better than opening up her mouth and spewing out a bunch of more lies. Lies. All of what she might say in retaliation would be nothing but a pack of barefaced untruths. His absence *had* nearly destroyed her life.

While reverting to her stoic mannerisms, Simone squared her shoulders. "Let's get back to Tyrell. Other than the topic of our son, I don't want to discuss anything else with you, ever."

Clasping his hands in front of him, Booker leaned forward and rested his elbows on his thighs. "Tyrell needs to enter a rehab program, as soon as possible. As well as getting his addictions under control, he can learn to manage his anger better. I fear that he's going to kill someone or be killed if he doesn't get help. I, for one, don't want you or me to become a victim of his apparent anger, since most of it is directed at us."

Simone raised an eyebrow. "Us! Why are you including me in that?"

"Because he's almost as angry with you as he is with me. Moving someone like Jerome into your house is what he's most angry with you about. He says you didn't take his feelings into consideration when you did it, believes you're way too intelligent to be with a man like that. Tyrell feels that he's been a distant second in your life and that he knows without a doubt that he hasn't even placed in mine. Tyrell is not an out-of-control addict or alcoholic by any stretch of the imagination, but he told me that he does abuse drugs and alcohol from time to time. When his stress levels get too high, he uses certain substances to combat it. He fears it may get worse."

Rehab for Tyrell had come to Simone's mind on several occasions. Just bringing the subject up had caused him to withdraw into himself and to shut her out. That had always resulted in him locking himself into his room for hours at a time. He hadn't been able to land a decent job because most potential employers require a drug-screening test before hiring. Although she agreed with Booker on the idea of a rehab program for their son, she wasn't so sure that Tyrell would.

"What about your hospital, Simone? Do they offer a drug rehab program?"

The thought of Tyrell being admitted to a drug program at her place of employment was a downright unpleasant one. The idea of such was frightening. Gossip would run rampant, as if there wasn't enough of that going on already. The hospital grapevine would be all abuzz over her private affairs. Simone could already imagine the low whisperings and the strange looks that would come her way from those who lived for the grapevine gossip, those who didn't have a life.

Simone's sensibilities began to kick in. Then her common sense took over; her motherly instincts entered the arena. What was a bunch of gossip compared with her son's life? Would she prefer to keep the gossip at bay or help save her young son from a deadly fate? Tyrell still had a chance to get it right, still had a full life ahead of him. How could she deny her child anything that would enhance his well-being? The answer was a simple one. She couldn't. Simone, now wishing she had shielded him from the likes of Jerome, realized that protecting her offspring at all costs was how she had to look at it. That was one mistake she'd never be able to rectify, not in a million years.

Simone gave a resigned sigh. "We have an excellent drug and alcohol program, Booker, one of the best in the country. I'll check into it as soon as I get back to work."

Booker looked relieved. He wanted to grab Simone and hug her, but he knew better than to do something that could get him and his feelings hurt. "Simone, it's Tyrell's only chance. If he gets help now, he'll make it. We don't want him to die out there on those streets. I know how it may seem to you, but I'm not here to take Tyrell away from you. Quite the contrary. I'm here to get him back for you. Tyrell has been lost to you for some time now. He has also lost himself to things he really doesn't have a clue about. Those are his words, Simone, not mine."

The lump arising in Simone's throat was painful, making it difficult for her even to swallow. "Thank you, Booker," Simone finally managed to say. Her tear-filled eyes then connected with Booker's in an intense way. "Why did you leave us in the first place? Was it something that I did to cause you to run out on your son and me?"

Booker didn't so much as flinch a muscle, nor did he turn away his gaze from Simone. He'd known these questions would come one day. And she had every right to expect the answers, honest ones. "I was insane, Simone. That's the only explanation for what I did. Money changed me. For the worse, I might add."

Booker took a moment to reflect on all the money he'd run through his first couple of years in the NFL. He'd bankrolled more foolishness than anyone could ever imagine. He'd had lots of friends, or so he'd thought, until he began to recognize them as nothing more than hangers-on. He'd later come to understand that if the money ran out, they'd be gone, too. His bank accounts, often bursting at the seams, hadn't diminished in the least, but his patience had worn thin with all the users, losers, and takers masquerading as friends.

"Money was all powerful, Simone, and my bank accounts were full of it. I really believed that if I sent you enough money for you to buy anything you and Tyrell could ever want, you'd be content without me. I thought money made everything all right. I eventually learned the hard, cold facts, but not nearly soon enough. No, Simone, it wasn't anything you did or even said that made me act like a darn fool. I was a boy with a big man's bankroll. As I said, I was insane. It's not the money that's the root of all evil. It's the love of money. That's the crux of the problem."

Years into Booker's heralded sports career, tragedy struck the team, which was one of the things that had caused him to take a serious look at himself and his out-of-control lifestyle. The young incoming rookie for his team, a superstar running back, had been diagnosed with cancer several months after the completion of training camp that year. Booker had been touched deeply.

Just like Booker had done, Trent Micheaux had married his high school sweetheart, Jasmine. Seeing their love and dedication to each other had reminded Booker of how it had been with him and

Simone. Booker had loved Simone with every fiber of his being; that hadn't changed. But he'd somehow convinced himself over and over again that Simone would be okay without him, as long as she had his money, more cash than she'd ever know what to do with.

After so many years had passed by without him making any contact with his family, Booker was sure that Simone wouldn't give him a mere glance, let alone a second chance. Calling Tyrell that day had taken more courage than he'd ever had to muster up. He was so glad now that he'd made the call. Booker knew that he and his son desperately needed each other.

That Booker believed she was in it for the money made Simone's heart throb painfully. The money had certainly helped her run her household, but she hadn't spent it frivolously. Most of it was sitting in a bank account just waiting on Tyrell to decide to use it for college. Not knowing if Booker had set up a college trust fund for Tyrell had prompted Simone to start up one. Not once had she ever taken a dime out of that account. The money belonged to Tyrell, but she'd only release it to him when he'd matured enough to handle it wisely. Simone still had high hopes of him continuing his education. He was far too intelligent not to become a success in life.

"I know I can't ever make up for the lost years, but I can make today count for something. I've learned not to look too far ahead. When I pray to the Lord, I ask Him for this day, my daily bread. I have a lot to atone for, Simone. God is the only being that I have to give an account to. I want your forgiveness—want it badly—but it is only God's forgiveness that will grant me eternal life. Do you think you can ever forgive me, Simone?"

Pondering Booker's tough question, Simone licked her lips, wishing he hadn't asked it. There had been many times she'd asked this very question of herself. Although she knew the right answer, she wasn't quite sure that she could fully concede, or that she was even ready to do so.

"I don't really have a choice in the matter, Booker, not if I want to be forgiven by God. The forgiveness can't come until I calm the raging storms of anger. I don't want to be angry, don't like how it makes me feel inside, but there are those times when I can't seem to control my inner rage. I'm more hurt about you abandoning Tyrell than anything you've ever done to me. Your absence in his life has been very hard on him. If I were you, I'd be more concerned about Tyrell forgiving you. He's the one who's been hurt the most."

"I appreciate your honesty, Simone." Booker got to his feet, looking down at his watch. "I've got to run now. If you can see what it takes to get Tyrell admitted to the program at your hospital, I'll work on getting him to agree to it. Let me know what you find out."

Simone nodded in agreement. "Instead of waiting until I get back to work, I'll make a few inquiries by phone."

"Thanks for hearing me out." Booker turned to walk away, only to turn back to face Simone. "Would you like to join my date and me for lunch, Simone? I'd love to have you come along to the marina with me."

Just the thought of having lunch with Booker and one of his women had Simone bristling inwardly. She had a hard time believing he'd even asked her something like that, especially after he'd just asked her about forgiving him. He sure had a way of pouring salt into old wounds. "I think not, Booker. That's an awkward situation to put your lady friend in. Don't you think?"

Booker grinned, happy that he'd at least gotten a small rise out of Simone. Did the jealousy simmering in her eyes mean she still cared for him? Or was he mistaking the look? It could be hate he saw in her eyes, he mused, hoping that wasn't it. "Yeah, it would be awkward if that were the case. My date for lunch is our son. I'm supposed to pick him up at the Fox Hills Mall. Does that change things for you?"

Simone didn't know whether to throw something at Booker or just crack up at being led astray so easily. Having somewhat of an idea of how he'd felt when she wouldn't tell him whom she was going out with, she opted for the latter, rolling with laughter. Booker joined in. "Let me run a quick comb and brush through my hair. I'd love to see Tyrell. I miss him terribly."

Sad that she hadn't been able to get into the intensive care to see Timothy, having been told that she probably couldn't see him until the next day, Tara had decided to go on home and get a couple hours of sleep. The head nurse had promised to call her if there was any serious change in his condition, but she'd only agreed to it after Tara had confided in her that Timothy was actually her biological brother. Only close relatives were allowed to visit with patients admitted to ICU. Tara and Jamaica were the only kinfolks Timothy had. As far as Tara knew, her brother hadn't ever married. But that wasn't a certainty, since they hadn't been in touch.

All sorts of questions trekked through Tara's mind as she drove toward home. Would Timothy want to see her or would he bar her from visiting him was the one question that had her truly worried. The last time she'd seen Timothy was when the lawyer had read Joanna's will. Jamaica had also been present for the reading. Timothy had showed up drunk, had come only for the money. That he'd had the nerve to show up at all had had Tara incensed that day. After all, Tara had held Timothy solely responsible for their mother's death.

Upon pulling her vehicle into her driveway, Tara was surprised to see Raymond's car parked there. She then saw that he was sitting inside of it. Maya had said he'd been called into work. *Had she been lying?* No, Tara thought, anything could've occurred. She didn't want to go jumping to any wrong conclusions about his daughter, since she had yet to hear the facts.

After turning off the engine, and setting the alarm, Tara got out of the vehicle and walked over to Raymond's. He was asleep, so she tapped on the driver's side window to get his attention, hoping not to frighten him.

The tapping instantly jarred Raymond awake. Upon seeing Tara outside his window, he wasted no time in opening the door and stepping out. "Where have you been, Tara? How could you stand me up like this?" He pointed at the cell phone stationed on her belt. "Doesn't your cell work? Or is it not on? You could've called me, you know. I've only called you a dozen times."

"Whoa, whoa! You need to get your facts straight, Ray, before you go popping off at me. You're accusing me of something I'm not guilty of." Upset by the cutting way in which he'd spoken to her, Tara took a couple of steps back to put more distance between them.

"What facts, Tara? Did we not agree to see each other this evening?"

Tara turned away and walked to the front door, where she inserted her key, and then went inside. She wasn't about to stand outside and argue with him, not to mention disturb her neighbors. After disarming the alarm system, she headed toward the back of the house. As she had expected him to, Raymond followed behind her, after securing the door.

Once she'd dropped her personal effects on a chair, Tara sat down on the sofa, looking like she was ready to burst into tears. "Do you want to talk about this calmly or do you want to continue ranting and raving at me?"

Raymond dropped down at the other end of the sofa. "I'm sorry for the way I talked to you outside. I shouldn't have gotten so upset. I've been worried sick about you, though that's no excuse for disrespecting you. Would you mind telling me how I got my signals crossed, if that's the case, Tara?"

"Where's your cell, Ray?"

Raymond looked puzzled. "Right here." He held the cell up for her to see. "Why?"

"Please take a look at your missed calls and then the incoming ones."

Raymond did as Tara asked. Seeing her cell number come up on the screen had him cursing himself under his breath. "So you did call. But why didn't you leave a message?"

"Because I was in the middle of an emergency case. We're not supposed to use the cell phones in certain areas of the hospital, but I did it so that you'd see I had called. By the way, I phoned your house first."

"Did the answering machine come on?"

Tara took a deep breath. "Your daughter answered." Tara sat back and waited for his reaction to that.

"Didn't Maya tell you that I was on my way to your house? She knew where I was going, because she was upset that my sister was coming over to stay with her while I was gone."

Raymond's last statement explained everything for Tara. Maya had been intent on revenge. It had become obvious to Tara some time ago that Maya didn't think she should have a baby-sitter, that she thought she was too old to have someone looking after her.

Tara didn't like what Maya had done, but she wasn't sure that she should tell Raymond about the blatant lies. Tara had no desire to come between father and daughter. She understood the strong bond all too well. Where was she supposed to fit into the relationship when Maya clearly didn't want her around?

Raymond narrowed his eyes, suspicious that something was out of sorts. "What exactly did Maya tell you, Tara?"

Is this my out? Tara wondered. Raymond had asked a specific question. Either she could join Maya in lying about it, or she could simply tell the truth. "Maya told me you were called into work to cover for a coworker."

Raymond laughed. "Why that little minx! She'd do anything to keep from having a baby-sitter. She just can't understand that she's not old enough to be left alone."

Tara couldn't believe Raymond was actually laughing over his daughter's deception. That he didn't see the real existing problem had her concerned. It looked as if she had more than just Maya to contend with as an adversary. If Raymond thought Maya's behavior was acceptable, then they were miles apart in their way of thinking. Their relationship couldn't possibly survive if this was how Raymond looked at parenting. Tara wasn't one to wink at lies and deceit.

Tara got to her feet. "You can let yourself out. I'm going to bed."

Raymond jumped up. "What's wrong with you all of a sudden?"

"If you don't know, I'm sure not going to stand here and explain it to you. I'm really tired and I have a lot on my mind. Good night, Ray."

Raymond grabbed Tara by the arm. By the vehement look on her face, he realized he'd made another big mistake. "I know what Maya did was wrong, Tara, and I plan to talk to her about it. But you have to understand what she's been going through since her mother's death."

Hands on her hips, Tara stood toe to toe with Raymond. "No, I don't have to understand anything to do with Maya. That's your job. If you're going to laugh at the seriousness of this situation, then you and I aren't on the same page. The one thing I won't put up with is a disrespectful child, not one of mine, not any of yours. In fact, I don't care whose child it is. Not only did Maya lie, but she hung up in my face. Deal with it any way you see fit, Ray, but you need to know I'm not dealing with it, period. I take parenting seriously even if you don't."

"So what are you saying, Tara? If I don't go home and beat Maya down about her lies, are you saying that it's over between us?"

"Those are your words, Ray, not mine. For the last time, good night!"

With each breath coming faster than the last, Tara watched as Raymond turned on his heels and stormed toward the front door. If he thought she was going to run after him, he'd better think again. Running after a man was a sure sign of weakness. All she planned to do was take a hot shower and fall into bed. Her day had been long and horrific.

Tara also had Timothy to think about and how terribly ill he was, which was a monumental problem in itself. Her brother could be dying and she wouldn't dare to spare a moment worrying about losing Raymond over his teenage daughter's deceptions. Maya was Raymond's problem, not hers, just as she'd told him. It was totally up to him to provide Maya with a good upbringing. Tara hoped that Raymond would come to understand that he could be a parent and a good friend to Maya, but that he had to keep the two boundaries well defined.

Tara was the kind of woman who went after whatever she wanted in life. Everything she'd pursued thus far she'd achieved. However, there was one exception, the one thing she'd failed miserably at.

Davis Parker had been her one true love, her only love, until he'd broken her heart into a zillion pieces. Although she'd been crazy in love with Davis, Tara hadn't put up a fight to keep him in her life. It had taken her a long time to figure out why she hadn't gone after him with a vengeance to try to win him back. He simply hadn't been good for her. The truth was he'd brought out the worst in her. Loving someone didn't always add up to compatibility. Davis just hadn't been the one, not the one who could enhance her happiness. Tara had easily come to the conclusion that her life was better off without him in it despite her deep feelings for him.

Love should never hurt and Tara wasn't going to allow herself to be harmed by it yet again. She'd seen too many people's hearts destroyed by that four-letter word. Her father had loved her mother dearly and her mother had loved Timothy to the point of obsession, but they'd all been irreparably hurt by letting their emotions dictate their actions.

Love had held each of Tara's loved ones hostage, had eventually torn them apart. Was it really love they'd felt for each other? She had to wonder.

Chapter Seven

Simone couldn't help reflecting over the wonderful lunch date she'd had with Booker and Tyrell. There were moments when it had seemed like old times between them. Other diners had smiled endearingly at the trio, as if they were a loving family, having no earthly idea what serious troubles lay so deep beneath the surface. Off and on, during the course of the meal, Simone had been happy and smiling. But reality, only a blink of an eye away, had constantly stepped in, causing her to remember the very worst of times.

At one time the love between Simone and Booker had been so honest, pure, and warm. She could never forget how he'd once cherished her. There was nothing in the world that had been too good for his Simone. The glory days had been like a fantasy for her back then, fun and fulfilling. Riding around in his convertible with the top down had been one of their favorite things to do on lovely summer evenings. Their love for each other had always outshone the stars.

Fond memories came to mind of the day he'd sent countless bouquets of flowers to the beauty salon she'd patronized. He'd also had lunch catered for Simone and everyone inside the shop that day. Booker had been out of town then for an away game, but he'd always made sure his presence was felt during his absences. His phone calls to Simone had been constant.

The look in Booker's eyes the day he'd learned that Simone was pregnant with his child was another unforgettable memory. He had cried like a baby at the good news. There wasn't a person that Booker had come into contact with whom he hadn't told about their blessing. It hadn't mattered if he'd known them or not. Loving Booker had been so easy then. He had proved himself to be a great man and a wonderful husband in every way imaginable. Simone had expected fatherhood to be one of Booker's greatest accomplishments ever.

Then the totally unimaginable had occurred, turning their marriage topsy-turvy, and tearing the family completely apart. Booker had unequivocally failed his family.

For someone who, at one time, hadn't been able to wait to get home to his wife and son, Booker's occasional nights out had become more frequent and had eventually grown later and later. Fearing for his safety had often kept Simone up all night. She hadn't called the police on the advice of his coach, who'd obviously known what Booker had been up to during his sudden frequent absences from home. The code of silence that existed among men still amazed Simone.

Like most wives, Simone had been the last to know that her husband had gone astray. She used to feel so sorry for the other women who'd talk about their men's infidelities, never dreaming it could happen to her. The endless cash flow had kept a lot of the wives from divorcing their husbands, and some hadn't been the least bit ashamed to say so. *I'd rather be rich and unhappy than broke and miserable.* That had been the general consensus for many of the women.

Simone really didn't know how much more she would've been able to put up with from Booker, because he'd deserted his family before any decision by her had been reached. She'd always remember how shocked she'd been upon finally realizing he wasn't coming home to her.

Paradise year-round had suddenly been taken off Simone and Booker's personal calendar.

As though Booker hadn't shocked Simone enough, she was dumbfounded when he told her how deep he'd gotten into service for the Lord. Retired NFL star Booker Branch was using his celebrity status to reach kids all over America. Inner-city youth commandeered the majority of his time, because he felt he owed them the most, owed what he hadn't given to his own son.

The same man who couldn't stay around his family and be a husband and father was now going around to churches, schools, and youth organizations to talk about his successes as an NFL star. The most important topic on Booker's agenda was his unsuccessful bid at becoming a faithful mate to his wife and a devoted dad to his only son.

Booker was also targeting his male counterparts, especially the high profilers in the world of sports, to share his incredible life story with, both the best and the worst of it. That Booker was out there in the world trying to keep others from making the same colossal mistakes he'd made had Simone admiring him all over again. His agenda told her that he really had changed, that he truly regretted all the horrific life-altering decisions he'd made. Winning souls for Christ was also a part of his spiritual journey. Winning his son's love and respect was his top priority.

Glad for the interruption into her deep thoughts, since the trip down memory lane was exhausting for her, Simone reached for the ringing phone. Why she continued to go down the unpaved road of her past with Booker was a mystery to her. All that traveling upon that uneven, rocky path had ever brought her was dark despair, but yet the road was so very familiar. It was the same address on memory lane in which she'd discovered unrequited love and immeasurable joy. Then, much to her heartbreaking dismay, unspeakable sorrow had dropped by her special address for an unexpected visit.

With Booker back in California, back in her life, no matter the limited capacity he played in it, Simone was sure that she'd be forced to revisit the painful past time and time again.

Hearing Sinclair sobbing her heart out instantly caused Simone to take the focus off of herself. "Calm down, Sinclair. I can't understand a word you're saying."

Sinclair, thankful that Marcus wasn't there to witness her unmanageable distress, did her best to compose herself, but she couldn't stop the tears from falling. "Charles is divorcing me," she sobbed brokenly. "I've already been served the papers."

Simone had to take a minute to regroup. Charles divorcing Sinclair was yet another unimaginable event. Although Simone hadn't gone through the painful process of such, what she had been put through emotionally had been tantamount to losing someone to death. She still mourned the unexpected loss of her runaway husband, far too often to her liking.

A phone conversation about something so serious just wasn't going to work for Simone. It was too impersonal and it was obvious by her emotional state that Sinclair needed a friend's shoulder to cry on. "Are you at home, Sinclair?"

"I called in sick today. Can you come over, Simone?"

"I'm as good as there. Just hold on to God's unchanging hand. See you in a few minutes."

Simone hung up the phone and rushed upstairs to change out of her bathrobe and into street attire, glad that she'd already taken her morning shower. So much was happening in all their lives. It seemed as if their worlds had suddenly gone plum crazy. There had always been a certain amount of drama surrounding them, but what was now happening to each of them bordered on insanity. Simone hoped that the very worst of it had already presented itself.

Tara awakened when she heard footsteps on the uncarpeted floor, surprised that she'd even managed to fall off to sleep. While stretching her arms high above her head, she smiled, nodding her greeting at the young woman who'd entered the room. As it was time for shift changes, Renee Biggs, the RN in charge of Timothy, had only come in to take his vitals.

Having been called just before midnight by the head nurse from ICU, Tara had spent the wee hours of the morning cramped up in a chair at Timothy's bedside. The last several hours had been touch and go for him, harrowing for her. Fearful that she might lose her brother had kept her wide awake, but it appeared that her body had rebelled against her at some point.

Looking over at Timothy gave Tara an eerie feeling. The ravages of drugs and alcohol were deeply etched on his face. Even in sleep he looked troubled; no peace had he found. It suddenly dawned on Tara that she *had* missed her brother. But she hadn't missed his horrific behavior, which had occurred when he'd been under the influence of one substance or another.

Joanna's desperate cries for the Lord to save her only son from himself resounded in Tara's mind. There'd been so many nights she'd heard her mother crying and praying, and then praying to God some more. Sleep had rarely visited her mother during the covering of darkness, who succumbed to forty winks only after Timothy had.

Timothy had been a night owl, had slept by day and had run the streets at the onset of dusk. Tara used to wonder if her brother might be a vampire of some sort, since he'd hibernate in his room until the setting of the sun. Tara had come to despise Timothy's late-night goings and early morning returns. It had been terribly disruptive, affecting everyone in the family

"Are you okay, Tara?" the nurse asked, looking a bit concerned. "You look so upset."

Tara smiled, but it didn't quite reach her bleary eyes. "Worried more than upset, Renee. How do you think my brother's doing now?"

"As well as can be expected under the circumstances, Tara. Dr. Patterson Wright is a good urologist, as I'm sure you already know.

He'll figure it out once all the lab tests are in. Timothy's in good hands."

"He's also in God's hands. Thanks, Renee. If you hear anything, please let me know."

"Sure thing. See you later, Tara."

Tara knew many of the African-American nurses and other workers employed by the hospital, since a lot of them made it a point to get to know at least each other's names. Like her friends, none of the other employees had known she had a brother. The only nurses who had learned of his existence, thus far, were the ones assigned to ICU.

Tara watched Nurse Biggs step out of the room as quietly as she'd come in.

All too soon, the deafening silence was back again, surrounding Tara like a blanket of darkness. Though she loved her peace and quiet, Tara would welcome any amount of noise in this instance. The peculiar stillness wouldn't allow her to focus on anything but the frail man lying so still in the bed, looking so ill, so hopeless.

How had she and Timothy allowed their relationship to come down to this? In reality, they had become nothing less than strangers. They had in essence lost that sister–brother bond.

Tara couldn't help thinking about her mother and what it would do to her to see her son so sick and in a near-comatose state. Rather than an actual coma, the heavy medications were what kept Timothy fast asleep. Since he had been a recreational drug user for so long, he probably wouldn't enjoy the high from these narcotics, if he were awake to experience the effects, Tara concluded.

Neither Joanna nor Jamaica had drunk alcohol, smoked tobacco, or taken drugs. Their mother hadn't believed in putting so much as an aspirin or a Tylenol into her mouth. Jamaica had taken blood pressure medicine at one time, but after he'd lost more than forty pounds, his pressure had stabilized. His doctor had then taken him off the meds altogether.

As though it were summoning her, Tara's eyes were drawn to the

Bible on the nightstand next to the bed, which was normally kept inside the drawer. With the Holy Spirit nudging her up from her chair, Tara went over to where the Bible lay and picked it up.

Tara sat back down and placed the Good Book on her lap and then laid her hand atop it. "*Open it,*" instructed the small voice inside her head. Psalms, chapter 23 was the text that immediately popped into her head. As it appeared that Timothy had entered into the valley of the shadow of death, Tara began to pray that he'd fear no evil. She was in no doubt that the Lord was with him.

Minutes later a soft moan from Timothy caught Tara's attention. After standing up, she carefully placed the Bible in the chair. Tara then came and stood over her brother's bed. Although her hands itched to smooth his hair back from his forehead, she kept them at her side.

Thoughts of the tents they'd often pitched in the backyard, made of old blankets, caused her to smile, warming the ice-cold spot surrounding her heart. Tara and Timothy had only pitched the tents, had never slept in them, though it had always been their intent.

The eerie sounds of night had eventually driven them back inside the safe confines of their home. Timothy had always relied on Tara to run scared first so that he wouldn't look too bad in the eyes of his baby sister; he had been just as fearful of the night as Tara. Neither of their parents had ever teased them about being afraid. Joanna had always left the back door unlocked for them, knowing her easy-to-scare babies would come back inside sooner rather than later.

Looking down on her brother, remembering the good times, brought tears to Tara's eyes.

As Timothy's own eyes slowly fluttered open, Tara held her breath. When their gazes eventually connected, she blew out a gust of air. The recognition of her in her brother's eyes brought her much relief, since his mental condition wasn't yet known. Drugs and alcohol did strange things to the brain. Serious brain damage often occurred from long-term drug abuse.

Leaning over the railing, Tara gently pressed her lips onto Timothy's forehead. For a brief moment her hand caressed his cheek, hoping he could feel her love. "Welcome back, big brother. You've been out for a while. How are you feeling, Tim?"

Timothy nodded, pointing at the water pitcher, wondering how his sister had found him. None of his friends knew she even existed, so how did she come to be here? Tara quickly poured a glass of the now warm liquid and inserted a straw. She then held the striped plastic tube up to his mouth. The medical staff, prior to it being placed in the room, had already determined that he could have the water. Tara was glad for that since his lips were dry and cracked.

Proceeding with caution, Tara periodically pulled back the straw so that Timothy wouldn't take in too much liquid at one time. His thirst seemed insatiable. "Just sip slowly on it, Tim. I don't want you to choke."

Nodding his understanding of Tara's request, Timothy began taking in tiny sips of liquid through the straw. Once he'd signaled Tara that he'd had enough water, Tara placed the glass back on the nightstand. For the next several minutes Tim seem to drift. Then he looked alert.

Tara quickly pulled her chair up closer to the bed and sat down. Finding the right words to say to the brother she hadn't spoken to in years was a difficult task. "I missed you" was certainly an inappropriate phrase. "I love you" was even more unsuitable, yet she did love him dearly. It had just been safer for Tara to love Timothy from a distance. Up close and personal with him had already proved to be too dangerous and emotionally taxing. Only a short time had elapsed—less than an hour—since Tara first realized that she *had* missed Timothy.

Upon feeling his hand on hers, Tara nearly leapt out of her seat. Timothy's touch had startled her. She had been so lost in her thoughts. Tara's heart broke as she watched him struggle to speak. Joining her two fingers together, she touched them to his lips. "Don't try to talk, Tim. It's too much of a struggle for you right now. Give it more time. You've had a traumatic experience. The medication is also playing a role in your inability to communicate with ease."

Timothy blinked his eyes, battling the heaviness of the sleep weighing him down. "I'm glad you're here," he rasped. "Thank you for coming, but how'd you know I was here?"

"I work here in the hospital, Timothy. I was the ultrasound technician on duty when you were brought in through the emergency room. I was the one who actually performed your test."

Timothy was speechless, though glad that she'd been there. *Was God's hand in this?*

Tara winced at how hard of a time Timothy had had in speaking. She squeezed his hand, wishing by some miracle that she could remove all of his pain and suffering. He looked as if he'd already been to the grave and back a few dozen times. It appeared to her that he'd been through a heck of a lot of emotional stuff. He didn't look much like his former self, though Timothy was still handsome despite looking far older than his thirty years.

The sudden image of her mother lying on the bedroom floor, all the color drained from her beautiful brown face, shook Tara up. Remembering that Timothy had put Joanna in that horrible shape had Tara working hard to tamp down the resurfacing bitter resentment of him.

Joanna had given to Timothy until she'd had no strength to give any more. Their mother had scraped up every dime she could manage to find whenever Timothy had called on her for financial support. It seemed that every day of the year Timothy had needed something from Joanna. Unfortunately, the thought of giving something back had never crossed his mind.

Timothy's guilt over Joanna's death had been quite obvious at the funeral. He had cried like a baby and had moaned the loudest of everyone in the church. He had to practically be carried away from the casket when it came time to close it. At the cemetery, he'd acted up even worse. His grief had been so out of control that Tara had thought he might jump on top of the casket as it was lowered into the ground if several of their male cousins hadn't held him back.

Timothy reached for his sister's hand. "What are you thinking about, Tara? You seem so far away." His voice was weak and scratchy and he looked so vulnerable.

Tara's first thought was to scold Timothy again about forcing himself to talk, but she saw in his eyes the need to do so. Besides, he was a grown man, one who hadn't ever listened to anyone before, so why should she expect him to hear what she had to say now?

Tara forced a crooked smile to her lips. "I was just thinking of how we're going to get you all better. Sorry for being so distracted, Tim. Your health is heavy on my mind."

Though the majority of his strength was gone, Timothy managed to lightly squeeze Tara's fingers. "Do you hate me, Tara?"

The very direct question sank into Tara's heart and soul. *Did she hate Timothy?* It took her less than a second to consider her answer.

Obeying the earlier desire of her hands, Tara smoothed back Timothy's hair. "I never hated you, Tim, just the things you did, hated the wrongdoings of the person you'd become. I love you, Tim. That will never change."

An undeniable look of relief washed over Timothy's face. Tears slid from his eyes, bursting into wet splotches upon his cheeks. The pain in his eyes revealed the many crosses he'd had to bear over the years, his guilt being the heaviest one of all to carry. "How in the world can you love me when I can't seem to love myself, Tara? Please tell me how."

Knowing that once she got started crying she wouldn't be able to stop, Tara fought back her tears. "You're my brother, Tim. We were raised to love each other. As for loving yourself, you can still learn how. It's not too late. Loving ourselves frees us to love others and to have them love us back. Hatred and self-loathing bring about the same attitudes from those we display it to. We get back the same type of energies we put out there, both positive and negative. Love is a miracle, Tim. A miracle from God. He also commands that we love one another."

More tears rolled from Timothy's eyes. Tara raised her hand to wipe the liquid away, but then she quickly pulled it back. Crying was one of the best ways to cleanse the soul. If anyone needed a spiritual cleansing, Timothy was the one. Tears had a way of releasing heavy burdens.

"Do you think we can become close again, Tara?"

As opposed to Timothy's last one, it took Tara a little longer to think about this question.

Did she really want to be close with her brother again, only to have him hurt her like he'd devastated their mother? Timothy had been an overt user, had often become an abuser when he hadn't been able to get his way. His verbal attacks on Joanna and Tara had been brutal. Calming him down during his drug-induced tirades had been an impossible task, had always ended with him storming out of the house; the best thing for everyone concerned. It could've been much worse had he resorted to physical force. Never once had he taken any responsibility for his horrendously bad behaviors. No apologies had ever been necessary, because Timothy had believed he hadn't done any harm to anyone. His out-of-control behavior had been Joanna's undoing.

"Us getting close is possible, but only if the old Tim is back—the loving, kindhearted Tim I once knew. I can't imagine us finding our way back to each other if you haven't changed. I won't put up with what Mom took from you. Not for an instant. Have you changed, Tim?"

Deep despondency filtered through Timothy's eyes. He could feel the depths of his sorrow right down to his feet, and his brain was weighted down from the heavy burdens of his unfathomable regret and shame. "Let's just say that I know I need to change."

"Because you've fallen ill, Tim?"

Looking thoroughly chagrined, Timothy blinked hard. "Partly.

But I've been sick for a while, Tara, although I haven't abused any substances for over three months now."

"A whole three months. Wow!" Tara instantly felt awful over her sarcastic remarks, but they were out now. She couldn't take them back. Besides, if she hadn't truly felt the cynicism in her comments, they wouldn't have come out like that.

The pain in his eyes deepened. "I know, Tara, that three months isn't a very long time. But when you've been using for seventeen years, it's a start."

Tara was surprised and alarmed by the number of years Tim had confessed to using drugs. Since he was only thirty, that meant he'd first started getting high at the age of thirteen. Tara had always believed his habit had started a few years later than what he'd stated.

Regret for the pain she'd caused him showed in her expression. "You're right, Tim. I won't apologize for what I said, 'cause I meant it. But I am sorry for hurting you. If you've been using that long, three months clean and sober is a great accomplishment. You *have* come a long way. You should be proud of yourself, Tim."

"That may never happen, Tara. I've nothing to be proud of. Not a single thing."

"That can also change. You've made a good start. That you've managed to stay clean and sober for even a day is highly commendable. I only want to encourage you. Sarcasm is a form of discouragement. I don't want to be guilty of that, especially with you. Where are you living?"

Tears once again filled his eyes to the brim. Telling his sister that he lived downtown on the mean streets of L.A. just wasn't something he could do. He'd had the same opportunities as she'd had to achieve success, but he'd made other choices, no matter how unwise they'd been.

Timothy thought of the makeshift housing him and his group of homeless friends huddled into during the nights. Cardboard boxes and large rags often served as blankets. In the summer months they'd find shelter at the beaches, under the piers. He shivered at the images. Like avid shoppers, he and his buddies went from shelter to shelter to see what was good on the menu. They chose their dining facilities according to their tastes, opting to split up for meals, though more often than not they didn't even have a choice. It had become a way of life for them. Eating and sometimes sleeping in the shelters was as good as his life ever got as one of the homeless.

"I live with a couple of guys, Tara."

"Where?"

"Downtown."

"Where downtown, Tim?"

Tim knew that if he mentioned certain downtown streets, the ones with numbered names, Tara would more than likely figure out with ease the whereabouts of his living quarters. The homeless had practically taken over an entire section of downtown Los Angeles. When folks heard the street names and numbers, they automatically knew it was in the heart of skid row.

"Near Olivera Street. It's just an average place, but it's home." There was nothing average about his digs, especially since he had nothing but the sidewalks and alleyways to sleep upon. The dirt, filth, and stench of the streets were obscene, but the streets were where he called home.

Tara sucked her teeth with impatience. His evasiveness bothered her to no end. "What's your specific address, Tim, just in case I need to go there for you while you're in here?"

For whatever reason, Timothy's silence and the darkening of his eyes frightened Tara. Either he didn't want to answer her question or he didn't want her to know where he lived, which was actually synonymous. She could find out his address easy enough, simply by reviewing his medical chart, so she decided not to press him any further. Tara also knew when to leave well enough alone. Something in his large brown eyes was telling her to let this one go.

Tara looked down at her wristwatch. "I'd better go, Tim. I need to get some sleep before my next shift. I've been here a long time now. And you also need to get some rest, plenty of it."

Timothy reached for Tara's hand, squeezing her fingers gently. "Will you come back to see me, Tara?"

The fear in her brother's eyes nearly brought Tara down to her knees. Timothy was scared and lonely, a deadly combination. "Of course I'll be back, Tim. Who else is going to see to it that my only brother gets well taken care of? When everyone finds out that you're my sibling, you'll quickly become a VIP in this hospital. That's how we always do it around here."

Timothy managed a bright smile. "Thanks, Tara. I needed to hear you say that. Maybe I can rest in peace now."

Rest in peace! Was he talking about dying? Did he already know everything there was to know about his medical situation, something that he hadn't yet made her privy to?

"It'll be nice to get a few nights of peaceful sleep. Knowing you're going to be around to look after me makes things seem much brighter. I've missed you, Tara bear."

Tara bear! She couldn't remember the last time she'd heard Timothy call her that. Her host of teddy bears, which came in all sizes, dressed in all sorts of costumes, had earned her the nickname from her brother. In fact, Timothy was the only person whoever called her that.

Too emotionally full to respond verbally, Tara leaned over the bed and kissed Timothy's forehead. She then turned and walked out of the room. Realizing that she had a lot to contend with, a lot of serious issues to come to terms with, Tara threw up a silent prayer.

God's love and tender mercies were the weapons she'd have to use against such an unbelievably strong adversary as Satan, the only ones powerful enough to overcome the evil objectives of the prince of darkness. God's help was on the way, simply because she'd called upon Him to take over this battle for her. Tara now just had to sit back and let Him do His thing.

The minute Tara got situated in her car she thought about Simone. Tara felt that she needed someone to talk to, a mature, understanding ear to hear her out. An even deeper spiritual connection had occurred between her and the older woman during the few days Simone had been a guest in Tara's home. They'd shared never-before-discussed confidences. Still, Tara hadn't revealed Timothy's existence to Simone. That was all about to change. Simone would be the first to know everything there was to know about Timothy Wheatley, the good and the not so nice.

After punching into her cell the code to Simone's home number, Tara inserted into her ear the hands-free microphone device. Disappointment set in on her when the answering service retrieved the call. From a previous conversation she knew that Simone was off duty for a couple of days. Tara thought of calling Simone on her cell phone but quickly decided against it.

Sinclair then came to mind. Tara really didn't want to bring her troubles to Sinclair, since her and Charles's marriage issues had already caused her enough strife. Because she desperately needed to talk to someone, she rang Sinclair's home number anyway. After allowing several rings, disappointed again, Tara was about to hang up. Then Sinclair's voice came on the line.

"Hey, Sinclair, it's Tara. How are you?"

"Not so hot, but I'll make it, Tara."

Tara was deeply affected by the darn near tangible sadness in Sinclair's voice, making her wonder if she should put off her visit, not wanting to add her own burdens to the mix. "Do you need anything, Sinclair?"

"No, not at all. Simone is here with me."

"Oh, really. I was trying to reach her." Knowing that Simone was with Sinclair had Tara reconsidering the visit. Her need for guidance was dire. "Mind if I stop by for a few minutes, Sinclair? I'm not doing so hot either. I could use some advice from my dear friends."

Sinclair knew that she was the last person Tara needed to seek counsel from. Her own personal affairs were in shambles and she didn't have an inkling of how to fix them. She'd been buried beneath her never-ending bills, and now Charles had reached down and pulled the entire floor out from under her. Still waters ran deep; her troubles were definitely of the drowning kind.

"I could use some of that, too," Sinclair muttered. "Come on by, Tara. We'll be here waiting on you. The coffee is on and the tears are flowing hotly. If you need somewhere to drown your sorrows, you're headed in the right direction."

It didn't take Tara long to realize she'd definitely dropped in on Sinclair at the wrong time. Sinclair was so unhappy and distraught over Charles's decision to divorce her. And Simone was lamenting and agonizing over Booker's suggestion of getting Tyrell into a rehab program for treatment. This was clearly not the time for her to bring Timothy up, but Sinclair and Simone were insisting that she reveal the reason for her sudden drop-by visit.

Tara frowned, her need greater than her desire to resist. "Oh, I don't know guys. You all seem to have enough on your plate for now. You both have some heavy-duty stuff going on."

Sinclair dismissed Tara's concerns with a wave of her hand. "Haven't you ever heard that misery loves company? Even among best friends. And if it's good news you're bringing, we can definitely use a heaping helping of that."

Tara folded her hands and placed them in her lap. "It's certainly not good news." Stunned by what she'd just said, Tara stopped to think about it. "I guess it is good news. At least, in a way. It has to do with my brother."

"Your brother!" Simone and Sinclair exclaimed simultaneously.

"We didn't even know you had a brother, Tara," Simone continued. "Why haven't you ever mentioned him to us before?"

Looking regretful, Tara shook her head from side to side. "As far as I was concerned, he didn't exist. I've been angry with him ever since our mother died. Timothy is one of those sons whose so-called manhood only came at the expense of his mother. Mom died of a massive heart attack because she couldn't let go of the boy she'd never allowed to become a man."

Sinclair wrung her hands together. "My word! Did she have a bad heart already?"

"No, that's the worst part of it. Mom didn't have a thing wrong with her heart. She had an altercation with Timothy just before her death. He came home in the middle of the night, high as the sky above, looking for money to get his next fix. Tim somehow ended up with Mom's purse that night. When I realized what was going on, my brother was already rushing down the hallway, rustling through Mom's bag for what he probably came for. Drug money."

Simone gasped loudly, her heart going out to Tara. "Everything is so clear to me now. You've actually experienced the things you've been telling us about in regards to our sons. You've lived vicariously what we've been living with, through your own mother."

Tara nodded. "That's so true. If only I could've made Mom see the error of her ways. But that can never happen now. She's gone on home to be with the Lord. God knew she needed rest for her weary soul. I pray that all you mothers of men will come to understand that your sons can grow up to be strong, upstanding men only if you set them free to do so."

Neither Simone nor Sinclair had anything to say in response to Tara's factual statement.

"Your brother, what does he have to do with the advice you're seeking?" Simone asked.

The tears came and Tara let them flow unchecked. "Do you remember John Wilson, the paramedic who arrived at the scene of a fatal car crash, only to learn it was his wife and three kids who'd been killed by a drunk driver?"

The two women nodded. All of them knew John from his frequent visits to Memorial Hospital's ER. A lot of the paramedics also used the hospital cafeteria during mealtimes. That was how Tara had met Raymond. He'd asked to share her table while she was having lunch in the cafeteria. The two had hit it off right away.

"Well, I had an ultrasound case from the ER, serious kidney problems . . ."

"No," Simone uttered, "not your brother?"

"Yes, my brother. Seeing Timothy on that gurney had me an emotional mess. I talked with Ms. Millie later, after performing the test. From what she'd told me, I thought Tim had died. Learning that the person she was talking about wasn't Tim and that he was still alive resulted in an awakening of mercy. I knew it was time for me to face my demons. I never stopped loving Tim, but my uncontrollable anger at him still festers deep inside. I'm afraid that it may resurface if we become close again. I'm very scared. What's your take on it, ladies?"

Simone looked at Sinclair, as if to ask her permission to take on this one. Sinclair nodded her approval for Simone to take it away.

"Tara, first off, I'm sorry your brother is ill. Before I get into anything else, what's his prognosis?" Simone inquired, with genuine concern.

Tara shrugged. "I don't know. I haven't seen the official medical report yet. I do know that his kidneys are in really bad shape. I plan to talk with his doctor tomorrow. That is, if Tim gives me permission to do so. Since he's able to act on his own behalf, they won't consult me."

Simone smiled sympathetically. "Let us know, Tara. We'll be praying on it. Once the word gets out among the staff that Tim's your brother, everyone will be looking out for him, as well as praying him back to health. As for your anger, I know exactly what you mean. I'm experiencing the same thing with Booker. I'm glad that he's back in Tyrell's life, but at the same time, I wish I didn't have to come into contact with him. But I do. And I will continue to for our son's sake. Showing anger is not the answer to anything. Most of the time the people we're angry at could care less about how we feel. We have to work through this in a manner that doesn't harm our physical well-being. Anger is a silent killer. Make no mistake about it."

"I'm no stranger to anger," Sinclair confessed. "This whole divorce mess has me angrier than I've ever been in my entire life. I have no clue on how to channel it. I want to direct it all at Charles, but I'm the one who should receive the full brunt of it. I'm in this miserable fix because of my own doing. As much as I want to strike out at Charles, I know I'd be dead wrong."

"What's he saying about all this, Sinclair?" Tara asked, knowing that her problem was already lost in the shuffle. All of them had serious burdens to bear.

"That's the biggest part of the problem. Charles is not saying anything. I can't even get him to respond to my calls. It's like he has up and disappeared from the planet." Sinclair's perplexed expression quickly turned to one of shame. "I hate to admit this, but I dropped by the town house to see him. He wasn't here. However, I later returned with my own set of keys and let myself inside. Once again, he was out."

Simone scowled hard. "Why would you dare to go there like that, Sinclair? It doesn't make sense. Unless . . . Do you suspect that there might be another woman in his life?"

Sinclair's eyes watered up. "I've considered the possibility a couple hundred times or more. What else can it be? I just can't accept that he's through with me all of a sudden over money. There has to be more to this separation than just our financial stresses."

Tara raised an eyebrow. "*Is* it all of a sudden, Sinclair? Are you sure there haven't been signs from Charles that you've simply chosen to ignore?"

"Could be," Sinclair responded dryly. She hunched her shoulders. "Maybe so."

"Even if there were signs that you ignored, Sinclair, I still think you're completely understating the money issue. From what you've told us, you've practically exhausted your and Charles's life savings. And the fact that you have nothing to show for it makes it even worse. Another woman or another dollar, either way, Charles is also more than likely hurt by what's occurred between you two," Tara remarked. "This is not just about us and what we're feeling. Booker, Charles, and Timothy all have feelings, too. I guess I should include Raymond in that, since we've also been getting hot into it over his drama princess of a daughter."

Simone rolled her eyes in the back of her head. "What's little Miss Maya up to now?"

Tara first launched into her latest experience with Maya and then went straight into her confrontation with Raymond. "Those two need to understand that I'm just not having any of the disrespect. Love is not going to make me lower the standards I've set for myself. My boundaries are clear and will not be violated with compromises. I don't intend to make the same mistakes I saw my mother make. Choosing to cater to her son over the love of her husband put her right into divorce court. My mother died a lonely woman. Tim was never home, except to sleep, so he wasn't there for her to help fill the voids left by my father's absence."

Sinclair pursed her lips. "Is there a message somewhere in there for me, Tara? It's not like you to signify. You normally just come right out with it."

Tara raised her hands and drew them back toward her shoulder. "My message is for every woman who has a son she's overextending herself for. If the shoe fits, wear it. Some moms don't realize that they're setting their kids up for failure. When they can't live the lifestyle you've made them accustomed to, have you ever thought about what could happen?"

Sinclair shook her head in the negative. "It never crossed my mind."

"Mine either," Simone added, eager to hear more of what Tara had to say.

"Some folks will beg, borrow, and steal to maintain the designer lifestyle their parents set them up for, especially when they can't get it any other way. Some grown children want what their parents have without ever understanding all the hard work it took them to achieve success. It's really not fair to put them in that position. Most of America's young adults are at least five thousand dollars in debt and many have the worst credit imaginable. Why? Because they've never been taught to value money; they don't know how to use it wisely. Parents earn it; children spend it. Just hand over the plastic and sign on the dotted line. Paying no interest for six months to a year traps them every time. They see it as getting something for free. Credit cards are sent to college kids by these companies with them already knowing they have no means to pay for the charges when the bills come in. It's crazy out there in the real world. If children aren't taught at home about managing finances, they will end up learning the hard way."

Simone laughed heartily, admiration for Tara gleaming in her eyes. "You are at least twenty years older than your biological age, Miss Tara Wheatley. For someone who has yet to experience the joys and pangs of motherhood, you are very wise in the ways of parenting. I think you'll make a great mother one day. I normally dismiss most of what you have to say on the subject of parenting, since you don't have kids, but I think I need to start listening a lot closer to what you say. You make perfect sense. I know I overextended myself with Tyrell in trying to make up for the absence of his father. I tried so hard to make up to him for what he wasn't getting from his dad. Those were shoes I just couldn't begin to fill."

"Nor were you intended to fill them, Simone. God gave you your role in Tyrell's life, and you took it seriously, did the best you could with what you knew to do at the time. Booker didn't. That's his cross to bear, not yours. He has to answer for his neglect of Tyrell, not you."

Sinclair eyed Tara with deep curiosity, beginning to see the younger woman in a totally different light. She agreed with Simone. Tara had made a lot of valid points, which allowed Sinclair to view her own errors. "What about me, Tara? Where did I go wrong with Marcus?"

Laughing, Tara playfully poked Sinclair in the arm. "I think you already know the answer to that. But since you're relying on me to give it to you straight, I will. You and Marcus are both codependents. You feed off each other in a strange sort of way. For whatever reason, both of you are very insecure. You have taught him over the years to rely on you for every little thing, and he does exactly that. Even with the things he can do for himself, he relies on you to get it done for him. You never disappoint him or make him step up to the plate."

Sinclair frowned heavily. "What exactly do you mean by that, Tara?"

"Marcus is an emotional and financial cripple, Sinclair, and you're his crutch. By giving in to his every whim, you've taught him how to use you, especially for money. When his addiction to spending money kicks in, you're his supplier. You have the same addiction to spending money that he does, but it never quite satisfies either of your needs, a strong indication that something else is lacking in your lives. But what really puzzles me is that you really don't know what he's doing with all the money you give him. You don't hold him accountable for a single red cent of it. You believe what he tells you it's for, without ever demanding any proof. What if he's doing something illegal with all that money you constantly send him?"

Sinclair jerked her head back. "Illegal how? Like what?"

"Drugs, gambling, prostitutes. I don't know," Tara said, on a shrug. "You should be the one who has all the answers to where your money is going. But you don't have a clue, have not even thought to question it. If I were in your shoes, I'd start making Marcus accountable for every dime I sent him. If you really want to

172

help him become a man, perhaps you should consider letting him work for his supper. That should get him motivated."

The three women burst into laughter, which instantly helped to lighten things up.

Simone reached for Tara's hand, squeezing it for a brief moment. "Before we end this pity party, let's get back to you, Tara. Why do you feel that your anger may resurface?"

Grateful that Simone had turned the attention back to her issues, Tara silently thanked God for the dear sister-friends He'd put in her life. That they had begun to listen to her, and now seemed to be taking her serious, made her suddenly feel validated by the older women.

Tara wrung her hands together, hoping she could get through this moment without crying. "Because I still hold Tim responsible for what happened to Mom. He was already getting all of her, every ounce of her blood, sweat, and tears. Then she was suddenly taken away, in a single blink of an eye. I was devastated. Because it was then that I knew with certainty that I'd never have what I so desperately needed from my mother."

"What was it you so desperately needed that you weren't getting, Tara?" Sinclair asked, feeling Tara's pain in spades.

"Attention. Once my father left our home, I didn't get very much of it. All of Mom's time was spent on Tim. I felt totally neglected, like I didn't even exist in her life. Tim's problems consumed Mom morning, noon, and night. The weekends that I spent with my father were the best times of my life. But that was only on two days of the week out of the entire seven. The other five days left me begging for someone to notice me."

Simone reached over and gave Tara a quick hug. "I'm really sorry that you had to go through the pain of that, Tara. I have only one child, so Tyrell didn't have to deal with that issue. But in having several siblings, I think I know what you're saying."

"Since I'm an only child, Tara, I don't know your experiences," Sinclair said.

"It's like this. When there's more than one child in the family, parents don't always recognize that each child is different, that they each have a totally different personality from the others. Each child has a separate set off needs and desires that should be nurtured," Tara said.

"Explain in a little more detail," Sinclair requested, intently interested.

"Parents just can't raise all their children the same way; they're simply not the same people. I didn't get what I needed from my mother because she was too wrapped up in Tim and what he needed to notice that I had needs, too. My excellent grades and good behavior went unnoticed by Mom. Tim's multitude of troubles overshadowed any of the good things I ever did. That's why a lot of kids act out on their pent-up emotions."

Sinclair nodded. "I see what you mean now."

"Whether it's for good behavior or bad, children come to the point where they merely want to be noticed by their parents," Tara continued. "Thank God I chose to draw attention from others by doing everything to the best of my ability. I could've easily chosen the same path as Tim in order to get someone to notice me. I chose the positive over the negative."

The three ladies tabled a few more of Tara's troubling issues before deciding it was time to insert some positive energy into their unscheduled get-together.

"Who's ready to get totally wasted on a bottle of sparkling apple cider?" Sinclair asked, hoping to keep her friends around a bit longer. Loneliness awaited her with open arms, she knew.

In total agreement with Sinclair's suggestion, Tara and Simone cracked up.

"Bring it on," Simone said, on a burst of laughter. "Break out the crystal glasses."

Although Tara was aware that she should go home and get some rest before her next shift, she had no desire to be alone either. "If you don't have anything good cooked to go along with the cider, let's get the pizza man on the line. We may as well pig out, too."

Chapter Eight

Lights were turned down low and soft music played on the stereo inside Glenda's place. Cologne and perfume collided in midair, mixing with the aroma of lightly scented vanilla candles. This was a rare moment for Glenda and Taylor. A romantic aura surrounded them, another rarity. She was more relaxed than he had ever seen her and that thrilled him to pieces. Although sirens periodically pierced their tranquility, Glenda and Taylor remained completely focused on each other. The loving smiles passing between them were shylike yet flirtatious.

The large glass bowl filled with salad greens, tomatoes, cucumbers, and shredded cheese topped with loads of grilled chicken and a light sprinkling of croutons was situated on the dining room table, between the couple. While sharing the meal from the same serving dish, their forks clashed occasionally, causing their laughter to rent the air. Glenda's portion of the salad had Italian dressing on it and Taylor had chosen blue cheese for his. Just as their forks had come together, the tangy flavors of the salad dressings also met up, creating a very tasty blend.

Taylor eyed Glenda closely, yearning for so much more than he'd gotten from her thus far. For her to set up this enchanting evening for them was promising. Even after a couple of years of exclusive dating, there were times when Taylor felt as if he was Glenda's brother, and not the man she professed to love. This was the slowest-paced relationship he'd ever been involved in. The passion between them was kept at a bare minimum. Although Taylor desired so much more for them, he still kept coming back. Glenda was like no other woman. Despite her numerous issues she was a very special lady. Her energy had always been focused on Anthony, so this was a definite change in climate. "This is nice, Glen. Don't you think?"

Smiling beautifully, Glenda nodded in agreement. "Real nice. It's so quiet and peaceful. If only it could be this way all the time. If only this moment could last forever."

About to make yet another trek into forbidden territory, Taylor poised himself for the possibility of rejection. The peace between them would more than likely get shattered, but he was sick and tired of everything being about what Glenda needed. He had needs and desires, too. "Is there any reason why it can't, Glen?"

"You already know the answer to that, Taylor. It's impossible."

"Impossible for whom?"

Glenda shot Taylor a mildly scolding glance. "You know my situation, Taylor. All too well, I might add. We've only been hanging out with each other for two years."

"Your situation is only what you make it, Glen. I don't want to pressure you, but life is passing us right on by. We're missing out on so much. All we do when I come to see you is sit and watch the clock and commiserate over Tony's missed curfews. Don't you want us to do something exciting for a change?"

Glenda felt bad for the situation they were in, but she didn't know how to change it. The way it was now was the exact way it had been from the start. "Until I see Tony safely on the right path, I can't offer you any more than what we have now."

Taylor's brow furrowed. "Sorry to hear that. But I don't know whom to be sorrier for, you or me, Glen."

Glenda sighed hard. "Nothing's holding you down to this relationship. If you want more than this, you should try to find exactly what you're looking for in someone else."

"I hate to disagree with you, but I do. There's a lot holding me here. None of my reasons for staying come close to rivaling the main one. Love, Glen. My love for you is what keeps me holding on to us for dear life."

Swallowing hard, Glenda's heart ached to receive all that Taylor was offering her. Love held her down, too. It was her love for Anthony that kept her from accepting Taylor's love without conditions. "It's unfair of me to ask to you to be patient just a while longer, not when I can't give you a set time frame. I'm sorry, Taylor."

"Me, too, Glen. But at some point, you're going to have to start living your life for you. Sorry, but I have to say it again. Tony will be eighteen soon. I can only continue to remind you of that. If you already feel you don't have any say in his life, you're going to have even less. I don't want to see you go through the rudest of awakenings, but I can clearly see it coming."

Glenda frowned, hating to hear the truth. "Yeah, I know. You've told me enough times. Think we can get back to the peaceful part of our evening, Taylor? I set up this nice little quiet evening, which is certainly different from the norm. Can we please try to enjoy what's left of it?"

Feeling her sentiment in every way possible, Taylor cracked up. "You have so many nice ways of telling me to shut up. Sorry for crash-landing our peaceful high."

Glenda had to laugh. "As always, your apology is accepted." Glenda extended her hand across the table and took Taylor's. "Thanks for being the most understanding man on the planet."

Her charming smile did what it always did to Taylor—it took his breath away. He was putty in her hands; it sometimes bothered him to think that she knew that, without a doubt. If he made her think otherwise, would that change their situation? If she had to go without him for a few weeks, or even a month or two, would she begin to see that she needed him as much as he needed her? The answers his brain was transmitting to his questions weren't very optimistic.

Glenda was Glenda, plain and simple. *Take her or leave her?* If the choice were his alone to make, it might be easier on him just to walk away. Since his heart was heavily involved in the decision-making process of whom to love, he didn't feel as if he had much of a choice. Loving Glenda had happened instantaneously, the moment he first laid eyes upon her. God had had a purpose for putting this beautiful angel of mercy in his life. Believing wholeheartedly that God didn't do anything without good reason, Taylor was going to see this relationship through to the very end. Until God instructed him to do otherwise, Taylor planned to stay in it for the long haul.

"I love sharing romantic moments with you, Glen. We just don't do it often enough." To choose his words wisely, Taylor paused, not wanting to cause another minidisturbance for them. Still, he needed to see if he could nudge Glenda into giving their relationship just a wee bit more.

"Before we fall back into the mundane, Glen, why don't we go to a museum or do something else fun this evening, or perhaps take in a movie, preferably a light comedy? No tragedies or violence, since we see enough of that on the evening news. What do you think?"

How could she turn him down? She couldn't, not in all good conscience. Anthony would be away the rest of the weekend, so she really had no valid excuse. In all the time they'd been seeing each other, she could count their social outings on one hand—and still have fingers left over. Just as Taylor had stated, all their evenings together had been spent in her home, with nothing but their conversations, an occasional DVD movie, and music CDs for entertainment. Most of the conversing had been about Anthony, which was hardly entertaining.

How more boring could it get for them? Yet Taylor kept coming to her home to spend time with her. That said something for their relationship, Glenda mused, but not nearly enough.

Glenda gave Taylor her best smile. Laughing inwardly, she hoped he didn't have a heart attack after he heard her response to his questions. If nothing else, he'd be downright shocked. "As soon as we've eaten the rest of our food, let's take a look at the newspaper and scan the entertainment section. The museum sounds great. I've never been to one before. If we have enough time, maybe we can do a movie, too."

Taylor didn't make a liar out of Glenda. The look on his face showed his astonishment. Glad that he'd given her that one last gentle nudge, he smiled broadly. "We're on, lady!"

Taylor was eager to get through the rest of the meal for fear that Glenda might change her mind. Besides the salad, she had fixed smothered chicken, baked potatoes, and fresh spinach. There was a double-fudge chocolate cake for dessert, but Taylor was going to try to put off the consumption of that delicious-looking delight until after their outing. Saving dessert for later would also serve as a good excuse for him to come back inside when they returned to her home.

"That you haven't ever been to a museum surprises me, though I guess it shouldn't. You could say the same thing about coming to my place if I hadn't insisted on us stopping by there one of the evenings I picked you up from work. That seems like it was a century ago." Taylor grinned. "I wanted you at least to see where I resided and what type of environment I lived in, so you wouldn't have to wonder if I stayed in a pigsty of some sort."

Glenda laughed away the remainder of her tension. The thought that Anthony might call while she was away from home had her second-guessing the decision she'd made to go out for the evening. She had to will herself not to go back on her word. "You insisted more than that, Taylor, if I recall correctly. I also remember giving in to going to your place at least three times."

Taylor howled. "If you call coming inside for fifteen minutes, max, giving in, then okay. Girl, by the look on your face that first time, someone would've thought I was leading you to the gas chamber. But I was always glad when you dropped in for a few. It meant a lot to me."

Glenda looked pensive. "Why is it that you don't seem to require much of anything? You've never really made any serious demands on me, though the lectures on parenting have been plentiful." She smiled to soften the criticism. "What's your secret to serenity, Taylor?"

Taylor took a couple of seconds to ponder the questions. "Keeping God first. I guess you can also say I'm content with me. I try not to expect anything from anyone that I'm not willing to give in return. I've never been demanding with anyone but myself. But I do demand respect."

Glenda pursed her lips. "Do you think I've been disrespectful to you?"

Taylor instantly shook his head in the negative. "I'm still here, aren't I? The only person you're disrespecting is yourself, Glen. You deserve so much more than you allow yourself to have. Until you see it for yourself, nothing will ever change. I'm willing to wait on your lightbulb moment. I want to be around when it happens. I want to be caught up in the glow of it."

At that very moment Glenda felt Taylor's love for her, deep down in her soul. "That's just fine by me, Taylor. I desire change. Just don't know how to effect it."

Taylor speared a piece of chicken with his fork and then held it up to Glenda's mouth. "Let's finish eating to that! Then we can be on our way to effecting some positive changes."

Hannah looked around her kitchen for the towel to wipe off her flour-covered hands. Spotting it on the table, she sauntered across the room, picked it up, and carried it back to the sink. She then turned on the water and stuck her hands under the warm flow. Yeast rolls was one of her favorite things to bake for her family. Both Robert and Derrick loved her freshly baked goods, especially the different kinds of breads. Hannah baked all her goods from scratch. No cake mixes, canned biscuits, or frozen rolls ever came out of her oven.

As soon as the heavenly smell reached their noses, her guys always came into the kitchen and posted themselves at the table after retrieving the butter from the fridge. Today would be no exception. In about twenty minutes or so, once the aroma reached them, Robert and Derrick would be bursting through the kitchen door. Smiling happily, she popped the tins into the oven.

Hannah had just barely finished her warm thoughts about her men when Derrick came through the door. She watched her son as he headed straight for the refrigerator and pulled out a bottle of water, taking it over to the table, where he sat down.

After tossing back a few swallows of the cold liquid, Derrick looked up at Hannah. "When will the rolls be done?"

Not surprised by the question, Hannah laughed. "In about twenty minutes or so. I wasn't expecting you or your dad to show up in here until after you smelled the aroma."

"We both knew they should be just about ready. I've been hungry for a while, but I've been putting off eating until they were done." Derrick grew quiet, looking at his mother pensively. "You got a minute to talk, Mom?"

Surprised by his question, though thrilled by it, Hannah came over to the table and took the seat opposite her son's. "What you got going on, young fellow?"

Derrick made direct eye contact with his mother. "That night, when I brought Raquel over here, I think you were kind of rude to her. What was that all about?"

Highly offended by his remarks, Hannah rolled her eyes dramatically. Although she had talked herself into not broaching this subject matter with Derrick, mainly because Robert had told her she should tend to her own business, Hannah saw this as an opportunity to say just what had been on her mind ever since he brought Raquel to their home. Since Derrick had brought the matter up to her, Robert couldn't accuse her of meddling in their son's private affairs. Telling her son what she thought of his recent conquest was one of her strongest desires.

Hannah sat back in her chair and tried to relax, though she knew the tension was about to mount. "I didn't think I'd been rude to her. In fact, if I'd said what was on my mind that night, it would've been nothing less than impolite. I thought I'd been nice, considering. What did you expect from me, Derrick, bringing a woman in here that's probably my age or older? Raquel has to be at least fifty if she's a day. How old is she, Derrick?"

Looking uncomfortable, Derrick shifted around in his seat. "What's age got to do with it? Why are you hung up on that all the time?"

"Look, player, you started this conversation, not me. If you didn't want to hear what I had to say, you should've kept your trap shut. You brought this to me. Now that you have, you're going to hear what I have to say about it. Since you won't answer my question about her age, I'm going to assume I'm right. So, what do you see in someone old enough to be your mother?"

Unnoticed, Robert had come into the kitchen, just in time to hear Hannah's question to their son, but not what had prompted it. "Hannah," he said sternly, "I thought you promised not to get into this with Derrick. Don't you think you need to leave it alone?"

The glaring glance Hannah wired Robert was sharp enough to cut. "FYI: If it brings you any comfort, I have kept my promise. Your son brought this matter up to me."

Robert laughed sarcastically. "Oh, so he's just *my* son now? How convenient."

"Whatever, Robert! Can you please just let us finish our conversation?"

"Sure thing." Robert dropped down on one of the stools at the breakfast bar. "Go right ahead and put your foot all up in it, Hannah. This won't be the first time or the last."

Although Robert joining them unnerved Hannah, obviously his intent, she wasn't about to bite her tongue. Derrick had started this and she had every intention of finishing it. "Now that we're past the rude interruption, I'd like an answer to my question, Derrick."

"You never answered my question about what age has to do with anything, Mom."

"Yeah, you're right. So I will, though my question did come before yours. Age has everything to do with it, Derrick. If you can't answer the question about what you see in someone that old, maybe you should ask yourself what the heck she sees in you. You don't have a steady job, so it can't be finances. You don't have a car, so it can't be that. You live at home with Mom and Dad, so that can't be it. Do you want me to tell you exactly what it is? I can spell it out for you in bold black letters. All you could possibly have to offer her is a good roll . . ."

"Hannah," Robert shouted, "you don't need to go there! You're out of line."

"I don't think so!" Hannah's indignation was apparent. "You've said the same things to him about the rich women he dates and often ends up living with, so why can't I tell it like it is? These old women only want him for his young body. I could've said it in much plainer terms, but I think you all get my drift. If you keep this up, you're not going to have anything to offer the woman you may one day marry. You'll be so sexually burned out you won't have much of anything left to give in the physical sense. Why do you let these women use your precious body this way?

Robert came over to the table and took Hannah by the hand. "That's enough. You need to get up and check on the rolls. I'm sure they're done by now. You don't want to burn them."

Hannah pulled her hand away. "*You* check on the rolls! I'm busy checking my son, if you don't mind. He desperately needs this long-overdue reality check."

Robert chuckled, hoping to lighten the situation up. "So now he's just *your* son. Okay. I can deal with that, but you still need to take the bread out of the oven."

Hannah gave a hearty harrumph. "They can burn black for all I care, Robert Brentwood. If you haven't figured it out yet, let me enlighten you. I'm not leaving this table until I get through to this boy. To let the rolls burn or not to is all up to you. You men eat more than I do."

Derrick leaped to his feet. "I'm out of here. I don't need to hear any more of this crap."

"Derrick Brentwood," Hannah yelled, "you'd better show me some respect by sitting your tired behind back down. If you leave this room without hearing me out, you need to march right upstairs, pack your clothes, and then phone Tyrone! Or should I have said call Raquel?"

The dead silence in the room was darn near deafening. The two men in Hannah's life had been shocked out of their shoes. Neither male dared to question her conviction, or the power behind it. The strong ultimatums that had come out of her mouth hadn't been heard before, not when it came down to Derrick. This was the first time Hannah had put things right on the line.

The determination in Hannah's eyes was palpable. Robert thought it best that he retrieve the rolls. It was time for him to step. Derrick was out there on his own with this one. But Robert had to admit to himself that he was eager to see what their son was going to do with the challenge he'd just been handed. It was exactly the same as the one Robert had served up the first night Derrick had moved back into their home. Pulling no punches whatsoever, Hannah had made the options perfectly clear. *But did she really mean it?* Robert had to wonder.

"Derrick, I'm waiting. What's it going to be? My way or the highway?"

Robert's question had just been answered for him. Hannah had meant every word of it.

Derrick snatched the chair out and dropped back down onto it. "I'm listening."

"Very wise choice." Hannah was so relieved she felt like crying. She had prayed that Derrick wouldn't take her up on the challenge. Like Robert, she wasn't quite sure she'd meant it. Sending Derrick into the arms of the woman in question would've made Hannah downright ill.

The small hospital waiting area seemed to be closing in on Tara, making it difficult for her to breathe. The lump in her throat felt as if it were the size of a grapefruit. Swallowing hard did very little to help in her attempt to dislodge the painful obstruction. The comments she'd just heard had her brain in an absolute tizzy.

How was she ever to converse with Dr. Patterson Wright, Timothy's urologist, if she couldn't get rid of the lump? He looked as if he were eager for her to open up dialogue with him. Once last attempt at swallowing the grapefruit seemed to work, but she gulped again to make sure she could speak. "I . . . knew it . . . was serious, but I had no clue it was this bad. A transplant. I'm overwhelmed by the bad news, so I'm sure Tim is also. This is incredible."

Dr. Wright smiled sympathetically at Tara. "He *is* taking it pretty hard, Miss Wheatley. Your brother is going to need a lot of love and support from his family and friends."

"Of that, I'm sure. I talked with our father last evening about Tim's illness, but I never dreamed he'd need a transplant. I can't imagine my father not wanting to come here and offer his son his support. I'll call him before I go in to see Tim. I'm glad I found out before I visited him. I can better prepare myself now, if there's actually a way to do that. Tim's the only sibling I have and I love him so much. I don't want to lose him."

The doctor had a weird expression on his face. "You seem to care very deeply for your brother, which has me a little puzzled. Since you love him so much, why is Tim homeless?"

Tara could have been knocked over by a feather. Bigger than the previous one, another gigantic lump had forced itself into her throat. Homeless! Then Tara's mind went straight to the conversation she'd had with Tim about where he lived. The thought of him being homeless had fleetingly crossed her mind, but she had totally dismissed it as ludicrous. If nothing else, Tim had always been resourceful. He'd always found a way even if it wasn't the right way.

Tara finally looked over at Dr. Wright, her eyes awash with disbelief. "I didn't know. I'm sure that's hard for you to believe, but it's the truth. My brother and I have been estranged for several years now. I had no idea he was homeless. I only learned of his whereabouts when I came face-to-face with him in my work area. I did the ultrasound."

Recognition instantly flashed in Dr. Wright's eyes. "I thought I recognized you. I just didn't know from where. I guess everyone looks different out of uniform. Boy, I imagine this is a tough one for you to get through. I'm glad you and Tim are reunited. That you were on duty that night is a blessing. With everything out in the open regarding his medical needs, are you considering doing the testing to see if you might possibly match as a donor?"

Tara looked totally flabbergasted. No, she hadn't considered it, nor would she ever. Donating one of her kidneys to Tim just wasn't an option. How did the doctor even dare to suggest such a preposterous idea? It was easy for him to offer up her kidney, since it wasn't his body they'd have to slice into.

Dr. Wright cleared his throat. "Did I step out of line with that question, Miss Wheatley? If so, I do apologize. It's just that siblings are often good matches. As a medical professional, you may very well know that donors of any type are hard to come by."

Wondering if the doctor was trying to make her feel guilty, Tara only stared at him. If that was the case, it hadn't worked. What did she have to feel guilty about? The operative word was *donor*. No, she didn't want to give up one of her kidneys.

Before Dr. Wright could ask her another thing, Tara got to her feet, extending her hand to him. "Thanks for talking to me. I'm glad Tim allowed you to do so. I need to go in and see about him now. I'm sure he's wondering where I am. He relies on me to visit him, at least a few times a day, especially when I'm on duty. Goodbye, Dr. Wright. Have a good one."

Waiting for no response, Tara hightailed it out of the visitor's waiting area. The doctor had shaken her very foundation. She felt like crying, but she was too numb. The thought of calling Raymond was quickly dismissed. He'd never understand and he had enough to worry about with Maya and all her grief. Raymond hadn't called her and she hadn't called him.

Tara hated to admit that Raymond's decision to cut her off without so much as a word about it was just fine with her. For all purposes and intent, she had cut him out also. She didn't need the hassle. Aggravation was something she could live without her entire life. Tara hated conflict of any sort. It was easier for her to run away than it was to stay and deal with all of life's overly dramatic episodes.

Upon reaching Timothy's room, Tara put the brakes on. Checking her emotions at the door was what she needed to do for her brother's sake. He didn't need to see his sister acting the part of a wimpy, weepy girl, much like she'd done when they were little. Timothy needed her strength and her courage, not to mention her support and constant encouragement.

"God," she pleaded, "please give me enough strength for both Tim and me to operate under. Please recharge my brother's engine. He's almost completely out of steam. Thank you for hearing my prayer. I'll be listening for your answer."

Tara took two steps toward the door, only to back up ten. She couldn't go into Timothy's room, wasn't ready to face him just yet. The image of her brother looking so sad and pathetic had her backing up even more. As though she were being chased down by the devil, Tara turned completely around and ran in the opposite direction. Getting home where she could quietly sort out all these patience-trying events was the only way she could deal with the issues right now.

Not only was Timothy gravely ill, but he had nowhere to live. The hospital would be hard pressed to release him back to the streets, whenever he was well enough to leave. So, as his sister, she had to come up with some kind of plan. The thought of him coming to live with her was a troubling one. But it was one idea that she'd have to consider, at least as a temporary measure. Talking over Timothy's situation with their father would help her sort this all out.

Jamaica still had serious issues with his son, but he'd never deserted him in a time of need—and he wouldn't do so now. He'd done all that he could for Timothy before and after the divorce. Joanna had helped turn his son into something Jamaica wasn't very proud of. No father wanted to see his son living the kind of wildly unpredictable, out-of-control lifestyle that Timothy had resorted to. Jamaica's heart had been terribly broken by both Joanna and Timothy.

The tension in the well-appointed four-bedroom town house's family room was as thick as thieves. The décor of soft colors in the large room was in direct contrast to the presiding dark moods of the two occupants. The bright sun shining through the slightly open plantation shutters did little to uplift downtrodden spirits.

Sinclair's nerve endings were frayed, causing her to chew on her nails. Glaring at Charles had gotten her nowhere, thus far. Tears hadn't worked either, which had been her first attempt at getting him to soften up. Believing that he no longer loved her was hard for Sinclair to do, but Charles had shown no evidence to the contrary.

"Why did you come over here, Sinclair, if all you're going to do is sit there and give me hateful looks? I thought you said you had something important to say to me."

Sinclair's eyes quickly narrowed to tiny slits. "What do you expect from me, Charles? I've hardly heard from you since you moved out. You don't answer your cell and you haven't been here when . . ."

Charles waited a couple of seconds for her to continue. "When what, Sinclair?"

Sinclair had purposely left her sentence unfinished, wishing those particular words hadn't come out of her mouth in the first place. Her emotions were starting to get the best of her and she couldn't allow that to happen. Letting Charles know that she'd dropped by the town house unannounced on several occasions was something that should be left unsaid. He didn't need to know that. "Forget that. Let's get back to my original question. What do you expect from me?"

Charles shrugged with nonchalance. "Not a thing. You made your position clear to me from the start of this. Why should I have any sort of expectations about anything to do with us?"

"You expect me to sign those divorce papers, don't you, Charles?"

Charles turned his mouth down. "Only if you want to, Sinclair. Divorce is just a legal formality. It's also just a state of mind. People divorce each other all the time without ever going through the legal process. They often go their separate ways without one or the other changing domains. Two people can live in the same house and never interact with each other, eventually becoming virtual strangers. We're living proof of that, since we've been doing it for years now."

Sinclair took exception to those caustic remarks, just as she'd taken issue with all the other things Charles had put her through by walking out on their marriage. "Is that how you see it, Charles? Do you really see me as a stranger? Are you divorced from me in your mind?"

Charles nodded in the affirmative. "Yes, to all of your questions. That's exactly how I see it, Sinclair. Have seen it that way for a long time but couldn't figure out what to do about it. I hope you didn't think I'd just walk out on a whim. I'm not that kind of man."

"Then what kind of a man are you, Charles? You have deserted your family, you know."

Charles pushed his hands through his hair in frustration. "Sinclair, I'm tired. Tired of waiting in line for your attention, sick and tired of being the last to know what's happening inside your head, the last to find out what's going on in my own house. You have more secrets than a stack of one-hundred-year-old diaries. You can't imagine how I felt when I found out that you'd dwindled away our life's savings. *On what?* is the question you've never answered. But I suspect it's because you don't even know all of what you've spent it on. But I do know for a fact that Marcus has gotten a large chunk of it. I don't doubt that for a second."

"Are we back to that?"

"Stuck on it, Sinclair." Charles got to his feet. "I'm going to go out for a while. When you have something new to talk about, maybe we can try this again. Stay here as long as you need to. Just please lock the doors behind you."

Sinclair looked as if she'd been mortally wounded. It had been a long time in her getting to see Charles, and now he was leaving, without a single one of their issues resolved. There had been so much she'd wanted to discuss with him, but she had let her emotions take over before getting them out in the open. She had wasted too much time on nothing but being angry and difficult.

"Charles, before you go, what do we tell Marcus? He already knows you've moved out."

"The truth, Sinclair. Tell him the absolute truth. He has a right to know."

Sinclair's jaw dropped. "The truth is that you've left me over him. How can I tell him that? It will no doubt hurt him something terrible. I can't put that heavy burden on him."

Charles dropped back down in the chair and leaned forward. "I did not leave you over our son. And you know it as well as I do. I didn't leave you over money either. Those are the things you choose to believe, because they keep you from facing the facts. You're in denial."

Sinclair shot him a defiant look. "Then why did you leave?"

Charles groaned. "I left because I want to be more to you than just a paycheck deposited in a bank account. I'm gone because my wife left me a long time ago, taking with her the passion and love in our union, when she emotionally removed herself from everything to do with the marriage. A man and woman marry because they desire constant companionship with the one they love, but you're hardly ever home. I'm lonely, Sinclair. So I decided if I have to be a lonely man while living with someone, I'd rather be lonely all by myself. Marcus and the money issues were just the last pile of straws that overloaded this old camel's back. Nothing more or less."

Sinclair wasn't emotionally moved by his remarks. He was lying to her. Had to be. There was no other plausible explanation for all that he'd just said. Charles was definitely covering up something. "Do you love me, Charles, or have you fallen out of love with me?"

His troubled expression momentarily softened. "That's easy enough for me to answer. I love you as much as I ever did. Do I like you, the woman you've become? I haven't been able to reach a conclusion to that one yet. Sometimes love is just not enough, Sinclair. We should also like each other. We seem to have grown apart. Married people aren't supposed to be lonely. We've had somewhat of an empty nest for a while, yet we're both sleeping in beds with empty spaces in the spots that you and I used to occupy. We're just not on the same page anymore. In fact, we're not even in the same book." With nothing left to say, Charles got to his feet again.

Sinclair moved to the edge of her seat, ready to try to physically stop him from leaving if necessary. She couldn't let him walk out on her yet again. "Charles, please sit back down. We still have so much to talk about. We can't hope to resolve our issues if we don't discuss them."

Charles threw up his hands. "I don't see that there's anything left for us to talk about. Sinclair, I gave you my conditions weeks ago. You made your choice and I've made mine. The divorce settlement is all there is left for us to discuss. I really don't want much of anything we have, though not much is left. Still, we have to come to specific terms on things. Since we can't see eye to eye, maybe we should just let our lawyers mediate for us. That's probably best."

Feeling wearier than he'd ever felt in his entire life, Charles walked over to Sinclair. Leaning down over her, he reached out and ever so gently touched his wife's face. "Forever didn't last as long as I had imagined or had hoped for us." With that said, Charles turned around and strolled toward the front door, his shoulders slumped in defeat.

"Charles," Sinclair cried out in anguish, burning tears flowing, "who the heck is she?"

Feeling as though she were frozen to the spot on her bedroom floor, Tara stared fearfully at the phone number on the caller ID screen. If she were to answer it, Raymond just wouldn't understand that she was in no mood to talk with him. Their last conversation about Maya hadn't turned out very well and she had no desire to get into that topic again. She was sick of hearing "Maya this and Maya that." Although she was happy Raymond had broken down and called her first, his timing couldn't have been worse. The only person she wanted to talk to was Jamaica.

Although she thought it was against her better judgment, Tara picked up the phone. "Hey, Ray. How you doing?"

"I'm in a bind, Tara. Need your help. Can you come over here and stay with Maya tonight? I have to pull a double shift and Susan is busy. Can I count on you?"

This is not happening, Tara mused, trying to muster up enough courage to turn him down. It seemed that Raymond's problems with his daughter were eventually going to consume him. Even before their major falling out, he'd been asking her for advice. Since he always disagreed with whatever suggestions she gave, Tara felt that her input was useless, so why bother.

"I don't think so, Ray," she finally said. "I'm the last person Maya wants to be with."

"Forget what she wants, Tara. She's the child and I'm the parent. I'm the one who's in control here. I'm asking for your help, not her. She can't be here alone and I'm not going to walk out of this house and leave her by herself. Are you going to help me out or not?"

Raymond's statement about being in control didn't exactly ring true for Tara, but she decided not to take issue with it. Being true to the part of her that often put others' needs and desires before her own, Tara agreed to stay with Maya, though instantly wishing she hadn't.

"What time do you have to leave home, Ray?"

"About an hour and a half. Can you make it by then?"

"Yeah, I'll be there." She grew silent for a moment. "Ray, does Maya know you're asking me to come stay with her?"

"Not yet, she doesn't. I'll tell her as soon as we hang up."

"That's a good idea, but I think you should call me back with her reaction. I don't want to walk into a lion's den, because I have very little fight left in me this evening."

"Don't worry. Maya has no choice in the matter, so her reaction isn't going to change anything. I'll see you when you get here."

Tara didn't like the sound of Raymond's last statement. Everyone had a choice in this life, including minor children. "Wait a minute, Ray. Maybe you should drop Maya off here. I can't be in charge of what goes on in your house, but I know how to control my own turf. Besides, I have a couple of phone calls to make and I desperately need a hot shower. If you bring her over here, I can accomplish what I need to do before you arrive."

"I see what you mean, Tara. See you shortly. Thanks. I knew I could count on you."

Raymond always counting on her was part of the problem, Tara mused, hanging up the phone. If he thought she was going to allow him to turn her into a child-care attendant, he was way off on that ideology. An emergency situation was one thing, but baby-sitting Maya on a regular basis wasn't in the cards for her. This was one dealt hand she wasn't going to continue to play out. Raymond would have to understand her position on that up front.

Praying that her father was at home, Tara sat on the side of the bed and then picked up the phone again. Her smile came bright when she heard Jamaica's loving voice. "Hi, Daddy. How are you?"

"Hey, sweetie face! I'm fine. How 'bout you?"

Tara sighed. "I wish I could tell you everything is okay, but it isn't. Daddy, Tim has resurfaced. He's been admitted to my hospital. Severe kidney problems." Tara went on to explain to Jamaica all that had happened so far with Timothy's health and their relationship. Telling him that his son needed a transplant was the hardest part for Tara to relay to Jamaica.

"A transplant, huh? Does it have anything to do with his drinking, Tara?"

Jamaica had failed at his attempt to hide from his daughter his anguish over the bad news. Tara had heard the distinct stress in her father's voice. Much like his daughter, Jamaica was a very emotional man. He deeply felt everything that had to do with his family.

"More than likely, Daddy. Alcohol abuse normally affects the liver, but it can also wreak havoc on the kidneys. The doctor asked me about testing as a donor. I can't lie to you. I'm freaked out about that. That's not something I think I can do. Am I wrong not to at least test?"

"Tara, as I've always taught you, you have to do what's best for you. And only you know what's best for your life. If you don't want to do this, you'd be doing yourself and Tim a great disservice to go through with it. If you test, and find out that you're a match, your dilemma is not going to get any easier. Not knowing is one thing. Knowing for sure is going to make your decision an even harder one, especially if you turn out to be a match. Do you see what I mean?"

Tara cringed inwardly. "Yeah, I do, but it doesn't ease my burden. If I can help and I don't, then Tim dies. I'll never be able to live with my decision. You see my problem?"

"It's crystal clear. But only you can make the decision one way or the other. I don't know if it will bring you any comfort or not, but I'll test to see if I'm a match. Tim's my son, Tara. And just as I'd do for you, I'd try to move heaven and earth to make him well again. Don't fret over this any longer, little girl. I'll get on the road first thing in the morning."

Tara felt so relieved. "Why don't you fly, Daddy? I'll pay for the airline ticket."

"You know how I like to have my own wheels. If I fly, I'll have to rent a car. And I wouldn't think of you buying my ticket. I'm not broke by any stretch of the imagination."

"What's so bad about renting a car? In the interest of time, I think you should fly."

Jamaica was silent for several seconds, making Tara wonder what he was thinking. She knew he was feeling a lot of pressure over this, but had she not told him what was going on with Timothy he would've been crushed.

"I see your point, Tara. I'll fly. This may seem insensitive to you at a time like this, but would you mind terribly if I brought Anna with me? I'm sure she'd love to come along."

Understanding what his silence had been about, Tara laughed gently. "Oh, Daddy, I think that's a wonderful idea. We're all going to need as much support as we can get. I've been dying to meet Ms. Clay, so I see no problem with it. Once you have your plans firmed up, let me know. If you don't mind taking me to work and picking me back up, you can drive my SUV. Okay?"

"You got a deal! See you in the next couple of days or so. Maybe even tomorrow."

"I can't wait, Daddy. Talk to you soon."

Although she didn't have much time before Maya's arrival, Tara remained seated on the bed, thinking about why she hadn't told Jamaica that Timothy was homeless. Knowing that it would've hurt her father deeply was one very good reason. Wanting to do it face-to-face was another one. Shame had also played a part in her decision not to reveal to Jamaica Timothy's living arrangements, or lack thereof. For whatever the reason, Tara felt terribly ashamed of her brother's perilous plight. People who had families should never find themselves in such a sad state of affairs. Tara didn't have a lot to offer Timothy as far as finances were concerned, but she did have a spare bedroom. If only she had known . . .

Since she'd run away earlier from seeing Timothy, Tara knew she had to make contact with him so he wouldn't think she had deserted him. There were no telephones in the rooms in ICU, but she could have one of the nurses tell Timothy that she'd be there to see him first thing in the morning. Once Raymond picked up Maya, which would more than likely be very early, Tara could then be on her way.

If the situation with Raymond hadn't come up, Tara probably would've gone back to the hospital later on, since her fears had started to subside. Talking to her father had brought her the comfort she'd come to expect from Jamaica's counsel. Seeing him again would provide her with the dose of strong medicine she needed. Wrapped up in the comfort of her father's love was always healing for Tara. Perhaps his love and support would help heal Timothy, too. That the three of them could become a family again seemed a real possibility. God willing.

As Tara studied Raymond's daughter, she thought that Maya was every bit as pretty as her father was handsome. In many ways, despite her waspish attitude, Maya knew how to carry herself in a mature manner. But with her lips poked out in a childish pout, she wasn't showing very much maturity at the moment. Maya hadn't spoken a word to Tara since she first arrived, over thirty minutes ago, though Tara had given her quite a warm welcome.

Although she was sure that she'd only be shot down again, Tara decided it was worth it to make another attempt at engaging Maya in conversation. Before speaking, Tara shifted her body around on the sofa until she obtained a more comfortable position. She then stretched her arm along the back of the divan. "Do you like living with your dad, Maya?"

Maya shrugged with nonchalance. "It's okay, but I'm sure it'll get better with time."

Feeling encouraged by Maya's willingness to respond, Tara smiled. "I'm sure of it. Your father is such a good man and he's so happy to have you living with him."

Maya sharply raised an eyebrow. "I don't need anyone to tell me a thing about my dad. I've been in his life a lot longer than you have, so what suddenly makes you the expert on him?"

Although she had halfway expected an outburst of some sort to come sooner or later, Tara was still totally taken aback by Maya's comments and her surly tone. She quickly bit down on her tongue to stop the nasty retort from escaping her mouth. "More bees with honey," Tara recited in her head. "Maya, I didn't mean to upset you. I'm sorry that I did."

"Yeah, I've heard all that before. If you think you're something special to my dad, you're not. All of his women are just alike. By being so nice and friendly to me, they thought that that would draw him closer to them. As you can see, they're not around anymore, and you won't be either, not for very much longer."

Tara wasn't really surprised by where this conversation was going, but it hurt her to her heart to see so much anger residing inside such a wisp of a girl. Where had all the anger come from? Then Tara recalled being very angry, too, at that age, only she had handled her anger in a more constructive way. If someone didn't help Maya to redirect her anger in a more positive way, she was going to have a miserable life. If her anger stemmed from her mother's death, Tara certainly could relate to that, but it shouldn't ever be used as an excuse for hurting others.

There were times when Tara was still desperately angry with her mother for dying, for leaving this life without ever having been attentive to her only daughter's needs. Tara resented that she never really got to know her mother the way she'd wanted to, that the bond between them had never become an unbreakable one. Timothy and his multitude of issues had kept a healthy mother–daughter relationship from ever developing between Joanna and Tara. Simply put, Joanna had lived for Timothy—and had died because of him.

Tara looked Maya directly in the eyes, knowing she had to proceed with caution. "Are you saying I'm being nice to you to win points with your dad?"

"Exactly! There hasn't been one of you who hasn't tried to use me as a way to win over my dad's heart. I'm not a pawn, but what does that matter to any of you? You desperate women want what you want, when you want it, and to heck with your pride. If you ever had any."

These vilifying comments sounded as though Maya had heard them from someone with far more experience in life than her mere fourteen years. Who had she heard say these sorts of unsavory things about other women? Her mother or perhaps her aunt? Tara had to wonder.

"I'm not trying to change your opinion of me one way or the other. But as far as me using you to get to your dad, that's downright absurd. I'm sorry, but you've gotten the wrong impression of me, Maya. A very wrong one! And there's nothing desperate about me."

"What's absurd is you trying to convince me I'm wrong about you. Good looks and money are two of the things women like you are most interested in. My dad has both. The majority of you are nothing but gold diggers."

Tara got up from the sofa. "This conversation isn't going any-where, but I am. I won't sit here and listen to you insult me, not in my own home. Whenever you get ready to go to bed, the guest room is all made up for you. You know where it is. Good night, Maya."

"Maybe I should just call a cab and go on home. It was obvious you didn't want me here in the first place. Daddy had to practically beg you to stay with me so he could work the double shift. I heard the entire phone conversation."

"Unless you were on the extension, all you could've heard was what your father was saying to me. So please don't make assumptions about anything that has to do with me, Maya."

Maya smirked. "If I was on the other line, you'd never know it. I got skills."

That Maya might be listening in on her and Raymond's phone conversations had Tara alarmed and worried. The off-color things she and Raymond sometimes talked about over the phone were far too provocative for the delicate ears of a teenager. God forbid, Tara mused.

Determined not to play into Maya's devilish hands, Tara sat back down. Her decision to stay up was also fueled by the fear that Maya might leave the house while she was in bed. At this point, Tara wasn't going to put anything past little Miss Maya, who certainly seemed bent on exacting vengeance against her. "You know what, Maya. I've changed my mind. I think I'll just sit up with you until you're ready to go to bed. Want to see what's playing on BET?"

Maya said nothing, only stared hard at Tara.

"I'll take your silence as a 'yes.' I think I'll even fix us some pop-corn in case there's a good movie on." With that said, Tara reached for the remote and turned on the television, flipping channels until she reached the desired one. Tara then got up from the sofa. "Excuse me. I'm going to change into nightclothes real quick. Maybe you should get comfortable, too, since we have all night to have loads of fun," Tara said, flashing Maya a triumphant smile. She could see that the teenager was a sore loser. The rage in Maya's eyes caused Tara to shudder within.

If looks could kill . . .

Chapter Nine

Seated at Taylor's kitchen table, all ready to devour the delicious-smelling dinner he'd prepared for them, Glenda was fidgeting around in her chair like she was sitting on hot pins and needles. "How was it?" Glenda asked Taylor. "I'm eager to hear everything."

Taylor laughed at the dying-to-know tone in Glenda's voice. "Maybe we should eat first. You can wait that long, can't you?" he joked. "Okay, okay," he said at the menacing look Glenda had just bounced off him. "Actually, Glen, it went even better than I had expected. Tony was certainly surprised to see me there instead of you, but he didn't protest it one bit. After signing him out, we went to the car and got in. During the drive home, we made small talk. I explained to him why you hadn't picked him up, but I didn't get into the reasons why you hadn't visited him."

"That's okay." Glenda's eyes stretched wide. "What excuse did you use, Taylor?"

"I told him you had to work overtime, that you weren't able to get away to come pick him up. He seemed to accept that. If not, he didn't question it any further."

Even though it was a lie, Glenda felt relieved. "What else did you two talk about?"

"Not a lot. I asked how he was doing and such, and he told me he was okay. We didn't talk at all about his stay in juvenile hall, since he didn't bring it up. I knew enough to respect his privacy on that issue. We spouted off a little sports talk and, later, when I dropped him off at home, he thanked me and went inside. That was it."

Glenda sighed hard. "I can't tell you how relieved I am that everything seemed to go so well. But the real test is yet to come."

Taylor scowled. "What do you mean?"

"If Tony's resenting you picking him up, I'm the one he'll let know about it. And in no uncertain terms. That's why I wanted to come here and talk to you before I faced him at home. Thanks for letting me drop by, though I didn't expect dinner, or to be here this long."

Taylor grinned. "You never do, so what else is new?"

"Okay, so you got me there. Back to what we were talking about, I'm really nervous about seeing Tony since I don't know what to expect from him. He's so unpredictable."

"Do you want me to be there when you get home, or arrive shortly thereafter?"

Glenda looked thoughtful for a moment. "That's not necessary. Tony may pop off at the mouth a lot, but I'm in no physical danger from him. He's not crazy, just troubled. At least, I don't think he's nuts. Are you going to be around home all evening?"

"Sure. What do you need?"

"Just to have you standing by for me to call and talk if Tony explodes all over the place."

"What if he doesn't go ballistic, Glen, do you still want to talk to me?"

Glenda smiled sweetly, her breath catching. "I always want to talk to you, no matter what. Is that okay with you, Taylor Phillips?"

Taylor's heart began to pump faster than normal. "You said just what I wanted to hear. If I have to run out for a minute or two, my cell will be on. I love you, Glenda Richards."

Blushing like a young schoolgirl, Glenda did all but swoon at Taylor's feet. "I love you, too. I'm glad you love me back." She looked into Taylor's eyes. "By the way, I had a wonderful time with you over the weekend. Thanks for bringing me back to life, for helping to bring me so much joy. I didn't know I could have all that fun. The museum was fantastic and I really enjoyed the drive down to the beach. The stroll on the Santa Monica Pier and the Ferris wheel ride were just what the doctor ordered. I don't know when we'll get another chance to do something fun like that, now that Tony is back home. But I do want that special magic to happen for us again."

Taylor reached across the table and covered Glenda's hand with his. "It will happen again if you just relax and go with the flow of it. Glen, you can't allow yourself to fall back into the same old rut. I don't think Tony's going to begrudge you a night out on the town two or three times a month. He doesn't need a baby-sitter. What he needs is for you to let go and begin to trust him. He can't take responsibility for himself if you don't allow him to." Taylor lifted Glenda's hand and kissed the dead center of her palm. "Dinner out this Friday night?"

A slow, bright smile spread across Glenda's face, lighting up her complexion and her eyes at the same time. "You don't ever stop challenging me, do you? Friday night it is."

Taylor grinned broadly. "All right now! That's my girl. I'm going to plan one heck of an evening for us, one that you'll never want to forget."

"In case I haven't told you, I don't ever want to forget a second that I've spent with you. More than that, I don't think I could forget if I wanted to. You're good for me and to me, Taylor. Your patience has brought me so far. Please don't give up on me. I don't think I could bear it."

Taylor couldn't stay in his seat a second longer. Kneeling down in front of Glenda, he pulled her into his arms, kissing her passionately. Seconds later, he held her at arm's length, looking deeply into her eyes. "Giving up on you would be like giving up on myself. I'm not about to do that. And you're not going to have to bear anything, at least not alone, 'cause I'm not going anywhere. As long as you continue to show me there's hope for us, I'll be right here."

After showering his face with a few moist kisses, Glenda kissed him gently on the mouth. "I promise to keep the flames of hope burning brightly." She got to her feet. "Now I have to run on home and hope that Tony is there when I arrive. The fried fish dinner was delicious. Thank you, Taylor. I appreciate all your special pampering. It means so much to me."

Taylor put his arm around Glenda's shoulders and pulled her in closer to him. "You're welcome. And I'm not even going to ask you to help me clean up the kitchen. How's that for keeping everything special for my fair lady? Just like that fish I cooked for you, I'm a darn good catch, Glen. Although you're good at keeping tempting bait on the hook, you'd better go on and reel me in, girl. Swimming in deep waters can get pretty cold and lonely for a brother my age."

They both had a good chuckle over that, which elated Taylor to no end. Speaking in terms of bringing permanency to their relationship most always put Glenda in a sour mood. Her joyful laughter had shown him his remarks had done otherwise this time.

Deciding to leave things on a good note, and not push the proverbial envelope, Taylor kissed the tip of Glenda's nose. "Come on, Glen, I'll walk you out to your car."

Acutely tuned in to every nerve ending in her body, Glenda turned the key in the lock and slowly opened the front door. The surround-sound silence greeting her set her nerves on edge even more. The absence of loud rap music normally meant that Anthony wasn't home. It wasn't near time for his curfew, but she thought for sure he'd be home when she returned, especially since they hadn't seen each other since he was sent off to juvenile hall. It had been hard for Glenda not to visit her son at the facility, but Taylor had convinced her that she should let Anthony get a little taste of what it would possibly be like without having her to lean upon.

Well, the unplanned side trip to Taylor's house had her coming in later from work than usual, she considered. Perhaps Anthony had gotten tired of waiting for her. Hoping he would honor his curfew this time around, Glenda started down the hallway leading to the kitchen. Preparing his favorite foods as a welcome-home meal for Anthony suddenly popped into her head, making her smile at the great idea. Glenda also hoped it would keep her son's anger at bay.

Delicious food scents wafting in the air had Glenda picking up her pace. Something cooking in the kitchen meant that Anthony *was* home. Glenda's nervousness increased at the thought of him being angry with her about not being there when he'd needed her. It was now show time. She had nowhere else to run off to. A mere swing of the kitchen door would bring her face-to-face with the son she loved and adored regardless of his feelings for her.

"God," she prayed, "please allow this reunion to be a calm one. Thank you."

The broad smile on Anthony's face upon seeing her standing in the doorway immediately put Glenda at ease, causing her once again to thank God. Him rushing across the room toward her had her opening her arms wide to receive him. The embrace was warm and loving, making Glenda cry out joyously within. This special greeting was more than she could've ever hoped for. With God only being a prayer away, she knew that everything was possible through Him.

Anthony pulled a chair away from the table. "Sit down, Mom. I fixed dinner for you. Your favorites, liver and onions, mashed potatoes and gravy, and Hungry Jack biscuits. I hope you're good and hungry. I'm glad you taught me how to cook, though I always fought you on it."

All Glenda could do was smile outwardly and giggle from deep within. She was so full of Taylor's food that she thought she might burst if she ate another bite. But there wasn't a thing in the world that would stop her from eating this meal, the first one her son had ever prepared in her honor. She might get sick in the stomach later, but she'd cross that bridge if she ever came to it.

"Tony, this is so thoughtful of you. I can't wait to taste it all. It sure smells wonderful."

Anthony grinned, appearing proud of his culinary skills. "You deserve it, Mom. Oh, by the way, Mr. T called just before you came in. He invited me to go along with him to some kind of sporting event this weekend." Anthony suddenly looked doubtful. "I told him I couldn't give him an answer till I talked to you about it. Do you mind if I go?"

Glenda had no control over the tears springing to her eyes. Taylor, wonderful Taylor, always paving the rocky paths for her, she mused happily. His phone call had done just that.

But Anthony's question had Glenda stunned. *Would she mind if he went?*

That statement said to her that Anthony wasn't sure how she'd feel about him being in Taylor's company, and that he was also being considerate of her feelings. Had she been wrong to keep them apart all this time? It appeared so. While she wasn't going to conjure up a father-son image of the two, she was happy that Anthony was actually considering the invite.

"The most important question is, do you want to go out with Taylor, Anthony?"

Anthony still looked unsure of himself. "Only if you don't mind." He grew pensive for a moment. "Yeah, I'd really like to go, Mom. Mr. T's been real cool. He's been so cool that I invited him over to have dinner with us. He's on his way over here. I hope you don't mind."

"Of course I don't mind." Glenda got to her feet in record time. Pulling Anthony into her embrace, she hugged him fiercely. "I'm so happy to have you home, son. Everything's just fine."

*   *   *

After removing her personal belongings from the shelf in her treatment cubicle, Tara sat down at the desk, though her shift was already over. All during the workday her mind had stayed on her situation with Raymond and Maya. The previous evening had turned out worse than it had begun. Although Maya had sat up with Tara to watch television for a while, everything that had come out of the young girl's mouth had been negative. Not a single show on the entire television network had pleased her. Hearing her touting it all as a bunch of trash was unsettling for Tara. When Maya eventually went off to bed, her lip was still poked out, her mood sullen.

It was Maya's parting shot that made Tara fully realize what she was really up against.

"You can count on me to do everything I possibly can to break up you and my dad. And you have no idea what I'm capable of saying or doing to accomplish it. He's not going to choose you or any other woman over his own flesh and blood. I'm willing to bet on it. Are you?"

Feeling relieved that she'd been too stunned to make any sort of response to Maya's malicious comments, at the time they'd occurred, Tara shook her head, still in disbelief of what Maya had said to her. She couldn't count the number of times she'd started down the hallway to go into the guest bedroom to have a confrontational showdown with the surly Maya. Each time she started out common sense and mature thinking had won out over Tara's hot indignation.

Levelheadedness hadn't stopped Tara from conjuring up all sorts of abusive things she'd like to do to Maya. Waking up the teenager out of a deep sleep and slapping her silly had been Tara's constant musing for the rest of the night. Sleep hadn't come in to embrace Tara until the wee hours of the morning and she had welcomed the blackness with open arms.

The ringing phone pulled Tara away from her troubled thoughts. She quickly looked up at the clock, wondering if she should answer the call or not, since she was officially off duty. Performing an emergency ultrasound was the last thing she needed to have happen right now. Although she wasn't the emergency on-call technician, she was fair game just by being in the building. Getting upstairs to visit with Timothy was a daunting enough task in itself.

Tara's workload had been constant throughout her shift, so she hadn't been able to visit with Timothy during her breaks or even at lunchtime. Reassuring her brother of where her loyalties lay was important to her. Talking to him about the transplant was a totally different matter altogether. Tara could only wish that she could put off that conversation forever.

The desk phone stopped ringing. Then Tara's cell-phone chimes took up where the other ringer had left off. Recognizing her father's number on the tiny blue screen, she clicked on the talk button. "Hey, Daddy, what's happening?"

"Just wanted to let you know I'll be in L.A. tomorrow at 4:07 P.M. on Continental Flight 777. Will you be able to pick us up from the airport?"

Tara laughed. "Us! I guess that means Ms. Clay will be with you. Am I right?"

"On the money," Jamaica joked. "I hope you're really okay with this visit, Tara. I'm going to marry this lady very soon, so I thought it was high time you two meet. Having Timothy back in our scope is another good reason for it to happen now versus later."

"I'm fine with it, Daddy, or I would've already told you otherwise. The sleeping arrangements might prove a little tricky, since I only have one guest room, but we'll work it out."

"You still have that sleeper sofa in your home office, don't you? I have no problem stretching out there, or I can get a hotel room for Anna. Whatever works best for you, Tara."

"You just gave me the solution to the problem. I hadn't thought about the sofa bed. It'll be okay, Daddy. I'm getting ready to go up and see Timothy now, so I'm wondering if you want me to let him know you're coming. Or would you prefer I keep your visit a surprise?"

"Leave well enough alone, Tara. He's going to see me face-to-face whether he wants to or not. But if you tell him I'm coming, he may find a way to get out of that hospital or even try to have himself transferred to another one before I get there. Timothy and I have got to come to terms with each other. There's no time better than the present. I'll see you tomorrow. And please don't start worrying about what might or might not happen. God is in control of this situation, just as He is with every other one imaginable. Bye, sweetie face. Love you."

"Love you, too, Daddy."

Tara rushed out of the elevator and into Timothy's room, happy to see him sitting up in bed and looking very alert. The bright smile he gave her had her smiling back. She had been worried about his mood, but he didn't seem to be as down as she had imagined he might be. The doctor had said he'd taken the news hard, so she'd expected to find him somewhat depressed, understandably so. Needing a transplant was enough to throw anyone into a deep depression.

Leaning over the bed railing, Tara kissed Timothy on the cheek. "Sorry I haven't been able to get up here to see you before now. How's it going?"

Timothy turned his palms upward and shrugged. "As well as to be expected. I guess you've heard the bad news already. What do you think about it?"

Plopping down in the chair beside the bed, Tara looked thoughtfully at Timothy. "A bum deal, huh? Thanks for letting your doctor talk to me. I felt honored to have your trust."

"And to think I didn't want you to know how ill I was. I didn't know I needed a transplant, but I was aware of being really sick. I wish I could've spared you. But then I realized you'd want to know. What are my chances of even getting a donor, Tara? I don't want to die."

Tara wanted to shrink away from the subject, but she knew it wasn't possible. To do that would probably make Timothy feel that he was without hope. That just wasn't true. As long as he had breath in him, he had a fighting chance. If he became so weak that he couldn't fight any longer, God would take up Timothy's cross and make the final decision as to what to do with it. Timothy's life was in God's hands, His alone. As to the outcome, God would have the final say.

"I don't have the answer for you, Tim. I wish I did. A lot of prayer could work wonders. If you turn it over to God, He'll supply you with all the answers. Think you can do that?"

"I'm surely going to try. Prayer hasn't been a part of my life in a long time." A watery sadness suddenly filled Tim's eyes. "Tara, I need you to do a favor for me. A really big one."

Tara nodded. "If I can. What is it?"

Timothy's eyes began to blink uncontrollably. "I have a three-year-old daughter, Tara. You have a niece."

Tara gasped loudly, feeling both giddy and nervous inside. "I do? A niece!"

"Yeah, you do. I need you to go see her mother for me. Carolyn should know what's going on with my health. Although we've been apart for over a year, she still tries to be there for me when I show up at her door from time to time. Essence is my heart, but I've failed her as a father. Ironically she looks just like me. She resembles you, too. If I'm going to die, I want to spend as much time with my daughter as I can before then. Can you help me out by going to see Carolyn and telling her what's going on in my life?"

"Essence," Tara breathed, "is that her real name?" None too happy with Timothy's request of her, Tara ran her fingers nervously through her hair, wondering what she should do.

"Essence Joanna Wheatley," Tim said proudly. "I know Mom would love her to death."

Tara winced inwardly. *Just like you loved Mom*, Tara mused, *to death*. Sorry that she'd allowed her mind to go there, Tara gave herself a silent scolding. Letting bygones be bygones wasn't always easy to do, especially when the hurt was deep. *Am I ever going to get over it?*

Tara forced a smile to her lips. "I love her name. I can't wait to meet my niece. Wow! I have a niece." Tara's expression sobered rather quickly. "Tim, I've only had a minute to think about what you've asked of me, but there's only one answer to this. Telling Carolyn the news is something you should do, not me. She doesn't even know me. Sorry, Tim, but it's not my place to tell her. It would be unfair for her to hear something so serious coming from a stranger."

Tim stroked his chin. "You're right, especially since she doesn't even know you exist."

So, there it is. He didn't tell anyone about me, either. We sure had that in common, Tara mused. She knew what her reasons were for not telling anyone about Timothy, but she couldn't begin to imagine his reasons for keeping her a secret. She wasn't the one who'd ruined their relationship. Maybe she'd ask him about it one day, but today wasn't the day for it.

Timothy looked up at Tara and shook his head. "This is a tough situation I find myself in. I know you may not want to get into this with me, but, Tara, we need to talk about what happened with Mom and me that night. . . ."

"No, we don't!" she shouted, cutting him off before he could finish his remark. "I don't want to talk about that; not now or ever. It's not going to bring Mom back."

"I don't think we can afford not to talk about it. It's the very thing that has stood between us for the past five years. Even if it won't be any comfort to you, I need to make peace with what went down. Since you refused to talk to me, I couldn't tell you that Mom was already ill when I got there. She was having a hard time breathing when I first came into her bedroom. . . ."

Tara leapt out of the chair and began pacing the room. "Oh, great, so you snatched up her purse already knowing Mom was ill!

211

Is that what you're saying, Tim? If so, that makes you an even worse person than I thought. Sick is what you are."

"That's not what happened, Tara. Will you please let me tell you everything before you go off the deep end?"

"No, I don't want to know, don't want to hear any more of your rhetoric. I've got to get out of this room before I do or say something I'll one day live to regret."

"Wait, Tara!" Timothy yelled as Tara turned to flee. "I need to know if you're going to go see Carolyn for me. Please do this for my daughter if you feel that you can't do it for me."

Tara glared at Timothy. "You manipulative . . ." Tara stopped short of calling him a bad name. "It's sad to know that you're not above using your own daughter to get what you want. You haven't changed. And that's regrettable. I'll go see Carolyn for you, but after that, I'm not sure I can come back here, Tim. Go ahead and give me the information on how to contact her."

Tara was already living to regret her actions. Timothy was very ill and she'd all but picked a fistfight with him. He was in no shape to get into an emotional altercation with anyone, let alone a healthcare professional who should know better than to upset a patient.

Hearing Timothy trying to explain away what had happened to their mother had set Tara off. She didn't need him to tell her what had occurred that night. Seeing him running down the hallway while rifling through Joanna's purse had been evidence enough for her. No one would ever convince Tara that Timothy hadn't been robbing his own mother, thus causing Joanna to have a massive heart attack. That he'd even try to convince her otherwise had Tara fighting mad.

Wishing Timothy would stop staring at her like she had suddenly grown horns, though she felt as if she had, since the devil had definitely come out in her, Tara reached into her work satchel and took out a pen and paper. "I'm ready to write down Carolyn's address and phone number if you're ready to give it to me, Tim."

Stroking his chin thoughtfully, Timothy openly stared at Tara for a few more seconds. Knowing that he was at her mercy and that he desperately needed his sister caused him to swallow the rest of the things he wanted to say to her. Tara had always stood in judgment of him. It appeared as if nothing had changed with her, either. He wasn't sure she even knew how judgmental she could be, since she'd always come off as this perfect being. If it were the last thing he ever accomplished before he passed from this world, Timothy was determined to make Tara listen to the truth about the night Joanna died. The assumptions had gone on long enough.

Timothy called out Carolyn's personal information to Tara. "The home phone number might not be the same, but her work number should be. She's been with the same major insurance company for years. She's an adjuster."

After writing down the information, Tara put the pad and pen away. "I'm going now." Wishing she could take all her ugly comments back, she looked down upon her brother. "Please be patient with me, as I will try to be more patient and understanding with you, Tim. I'm trying to get there. I'm just not there yet. I feel awful for upsetting you at a time like this. I'm sorry."

Timothy reached for Tara's hand. "It's okay, Tara bear. We both have a ways to go. But I'm sure we'll get there, eventually. I love you, Tara."

"Love you, too, Tim."

Tara moved toward the door. Before exiting she turned to face Timothy. "I *will* be back."

That Tyrell wanted no part of being admitted to a rehabilitation center came as no surprise to Simone, but it looked as if Booker hadn't prepared himself for this particular outcome. Seated across from Simone in her living room, Tyrell's father looked like he could chew up a group of nails and swallow them with ease. For the past half hour Simone had been listening to Booker angrily voice his disappointment in Tyrell's decision not to have himself admitted to the drug rehabilitation program at her hospital.

Since only a couple of hours were left of the evening, Simone figured she wasn't going to get a chance just to relax and watch television before it was time to go to bed. She'd come home tired and weary from working a twelve-hour shift and had only wanted to stretch out somewhere and do next to nothing. Booker had rudely interrupted her plans. He had appeared at her front door before she'd had a chance to close it behind herself. Booker had looked so emotionally disturbed that Simone hadn't exercised sending him on his way as an option.

Simone folded her hands and placed them on her lap. "Why are you so angry about this, Booker? Didn't it ever cross your mind that Tyrell might totally object to the idea of rehab."

Booker shrugged. "It didn't. I was so sure that he wanted help since he's the one who'd mentioned needing it in the first place. If he thinks he can do this alone, he's mistaken. Cold turkey isn't the answer for everyone. Tyrell could greatly benefit from a rehab program, especially from an educational standpoint. He could use the anger management portion as well. He needs to be educated on what can happen to him if he keeps up the addictive behavior."

"Has he been high lately?"

"Not that I've noticed."

"What does that mean, Booker?"

"Just what it means. I haven't noticed him being high on anything."

Simone looked agitated. "It seems to me that you may not even know what's going on with your son. I could always tell if he was on something, just by looking at him. That is, most of the time. But all you can say is you haven't noticed. How much time *do* you really spend with Tyrell, Booker? Or is he over at your place locked in his bedroom like he used to do here?"

A flash of anger glinted in Booker's eyes. Simone questioning his parental skills was downright unsettling for him. It was obvious to him that she hadn't yet come to trust him with Tyrell. He understood her need to voice her concerns, but he didn't always have to like what she had to say. Simone didn't need to keep reminding him of how he'd failed as a father. He was well aware of all his inadequacies, including badly failing Simone as a husband. His thoughts were only entrenched in them during every waking minute. Owning up to his shortcomings just didn't seem to be enough for her. It seemed to Booker that Simone still wanted his blood.

"For your information, Tyrell and I spend a lot of time together, Simone—quality time. When we're not watching television or playing a board game together, we sit and talk for hours on end. I invite him to go practically everywhere I go. He's with me quite a bit. Everything is not hunky-dory between us, Simone, nowhere close to that, but Tyrell and I are constantly working on our issues. Believe it or not, we have made a lot of progress."

Knowing his next remark could start a domestic war, to prepare for the verbal attack, Booker sucked in a deep breath. "As for Tyrell being locked away in his room, the circumstances you had him living under were the reason for that. He kept himself secluded because of the tension between him and your man. Maybe you should stop pointing fingers at me long enough to figure out what role you may've played in the tough things Tyrell's faced with today. We've both had a hand in upsetting this young man's life. You need to come down off that holier than thou pedestal you've placed yourself upon so we can start working together to help straighten out our son. This is not just my problem, you know. This is a family quandary."

Furious was an understatement for what Simone felt about Booker and his insulting comments. Ready to verbally wrestle him to the carpet, though she'd rather take him down by sheer physical force, she moved to the very edge of the sofa. "There are some things you just shouldn't ever say to me, Booker Branch. You have stepped out on thin ice, very thin. For you to question me about anything to do with Tyrell takes a lot of gall on your part. The word *family* wasn't in your vocabulary until recently. You weren't here, so you had no say in what went on. Had you been in Tyrell's life, you'd be well within your rights to question the choices I made. As it stands, you don't have any rights whatsoever to inquire about what I did or didn't do."

Not one bit surprised by her righteous attitude, Booker threw up his hands in indignation. "It seems as if it's okay for you to say exactly what you want to me, but I can't speak my mind. If you expect me to sit here and listen to you constantly putting me down, without responding to you, you're barking at the wrong person. Grinding my failures into my face at every turn is not your job. God has that gig taken care of. He's my judge, not you. If you've been living so righteously, so much so that you can stand in judgment of me, why is your life in the toilet?"

Red hot with anger, Simone picked up a paperback and threw it aimlessly across the room. "Booker, you've said enough! In fact you've said way too much."

"Oh no I haven't! Regardless of what you might believe, you didn't find favor with God while living with someone you're not married to any more than I did with the sinful things I've done. You're every bit as guilty as I am of breaking our marriage vows. In case you've forgotten, we never divorced. I guess you hadn't ever thought of that, huh?"

What little was left of Simone's dignity dropped to the floor with a sickening thud. She felt weak, as if she had no more fight in her. That Booker had called her out on her own sins had her in a tailspin. *How was she to respond?* That God hadn't been pleased with her sinful living arrangements had crossed her mind more times than she could recall, but she'd always pushed the troubling thoughts away. Analyzing her shortcomings had never come easy for Simone.

But for Booker to call her attention to it had Simone feeling utterly ashamed. Perhaps it was because she was face-to-face with him, witnessing the look of disgust in his expression. Simone was sure that God had frowned upon her in the same way Booker was doing now, but she hadn't been able to see the Father's look of pure disdain. Although she believed wholeheartedly in God, whom she'd only seen face-to-face through His daily miracles, seeing something right before her eyes also spoke to believing.

Simone got up from the sofa. "You can see yourself out, Booker. Good night."

"Coward!"

Turning on her heels, Simone faced Booker, staring him down with fiery contempt awash in her eyes. "Oh, no! I know you didn't have the nerve to go there. Coward! Not me. That's a word that best defines you. . . ."

"This is silly, Simone." Booker arose from the divan, too, coming within a breath of where Simone stood. "You have issues with me and I understand that. But to let them interfere with us coming together for Tyrell's sake isn't what's best for our son. Did you know that he has high hopes of you and me getting back together? He desperately wants the family he never had."

Fainting would be most appropriate in this instance, Simone thought. She certainly felt dizzy with anguish. In her opinion Booker had made that statement like he had no objections to the idea. It was insane. The sooner Tyrell learned that, the better off they'd all be. "No, I didn't know he felt that way. But we don't need to encourage him in his warped thinking. Us together as a family will never happen. It's not something I even want to talk about, let alone consider."

"Why not talk about it, Simone? We're still married to each other. Are you saying you're no longer in love with me?"

Booker could see by her expression that he'd pushed too hard, had virtually shoved Simone's back to the wall, but he had no intention of backing off. Finding out if she still carried a flicker of a torch for him was important to him. If she didn't, he'd move on. But if there was even a spark of hope for them as a couple, he wasn't going to hesitate in adding just enough fuel to start the fire burning between them again. His heart had never forgotten how to love Simone.

Simone had to swallow the huge lump in her throat. His question was one that she hadn't ever expected to be posed, especially by him, and it was making her feel even crazier than she already felt. Did she love him? *No doubt about it.* Could she ever go back with him? *No way on God's green earth would she ever put herself in the position to possibly go through that kind of humiliation again.* Love had already made a big fool of her. Once was enough for Simone.

"This conversation has turned downright absurd, Booker. And I refuse to dignify your outlandish question with a response. It'll do you well to remember that I didn't walk out on you. The question of 'love' is for you to answer." Simone no longer believed in second chances.

Without giving her reaction a second thought, Booker gently placed both his hands on Simone's shoulders. Leaning his head down until it came within a fraction of touching her forehead, he looked into her eyes. "I love you, Simone. I never stopped. It was never about not loving you. Once the color of money stopped blinding me, I began to see things so clearly. No matter how much cash I had, how many true-blue friends I thought I had, or how long party central lasted, along with the number of women trooping in and out of my home, I was never happy and content. In fact, I was downright miserable. It took me a long time to realize what was missing from my life and to learn why I could never find peace at the end of my days. It was the absence of you, Simone. All along it was you, the only one who ever made sense of my life."

Simone felt as if her heart had stopped beating. The tears in Booker's eyes were overwhelming to her gentle spirit. All she wanted to do was bring him to her and kiss the moisture away. Vulnerability made him appear just like he had way back then, way back when all she had to do was look into his eyes to know she was loved and cherished.

God, please help me to forgive him. Booker and I both need your for-giveness.

Wiping the tears from his eyes, Booker heaved a hard sigh. "I've made a multitude of mistakes, colossal ones. I'm human, Simone, just a flesh-and-blood man saddled with all sorts of human frailties. Forgive me for not being perfect. But I'm so glad that you are. Of all the people who I believed had the gift of forgiveness in their heart, you were always at the top of the list."

Booker started out of the room, only to turn back around and again face Simone. "This unfortunate confrontation isn't what I wanted to have happen when I came here to see you this evening. But a man can only take so much of a throttling. I apologize if I thought Tyrell's issues were significant to both of us. Although I know these things weren't very important to me when I was living the life, they're crucial to me now—and I don't apologize for finally coming to my senses. I won't ever come here again and intrude upon your perfect life. Good-bye, Simone."

Scared to breathe, Simone could only stare after Booker. While doing her best to swallow her indigestible pain and regret, she wished none of this had happened. As usual, she'd gone too far in allowing her mouth to come unglued. The horse was long since dead yet she'd continued to beat it to death. She'd been working hard at beating her estranged husband into submission every time she saw him. Making him feel lower than a lowlife seemed to have been her only objective. So busy looking at what Booker had done to her and how he'd screwed up her life, she hadn't taken the time to focus on what was happening to Tyrell, all the while refusing to look into the face of her own problematic situation. Booker wasn't invincible either. He was hurting, too.

Although their son would never have them living under the same roof, Tyrell should have them on the same side, his side. Both parents being on Tyrell's side was desperately needed in this instance, Simone mused. He needed them to come together to help him see his way through. To have her and Booker backbiting and constantly scrapping with each other over every little thing wasn't in Tyrell's best interest. Their son deserved more from them.

It then dawned on Simone that Tyrell had known an immeasurable amount of discord over the past years, more than just what his father had caused in his life. She began to realize that she was just as guilty as Booker of neglecting their son's needs. Just because they'd lived in the same house didn't necessarily mean that she'd given her all to Tyrell. If she'd been meeting his needs, she never would've allowed Jerome to move into her home. Even after Tyrell had told her how he'd felt about Jerome living there, Simone knew she had done nothing to change things.

Simone quickly decided that it was time for her to stop taking Booker's inventory and begin delving into her own issues. She also needed to make some vital changes. With God's guidance perhaps she could put her life back together and help Tyrell get his back on track.

Tara was so pleased at how well the introduction between herself and Carolyn Webber, Timothy's ex-girlfriend, had gone. The warmth and genuinely friendly way in which Carolyn had greeted her had touched Tara deeply, making her breathe a little easier. No one would've guessed that Tara was a perfect stranger to Carolyn. The two women had talked briefly over the phone, when Tara had called Carolyn to tell her who she was and that she wanted to come by and visit her and Timothy's daughter, so they weren't the least bit shy with each other.

Very tall and model beautiful, Carolyn had the prettiest golden brown eyes, a perfect match to her copper brown complexion. Tara could easily see why Timothy had been attracted to this woman. She could even imagine how striking they'd been when together. Timothy's good looks had always magnetically drawn toward him the beautiful females. Tara could only imagine that their daughter had probably inherited a combination of her parents' best features.

Carolyn had the cutest little house Tara had ever seen. Neat and clean, the three-bedroom home boasted modern furnishings mixed in with a few marvelous antiques. While waiting for Carolyn to bring Essence from the bedroom, Tara quietly studied the character of the place.

Tara felt a certain peace seated in the living room, where she rested upon an oyster white sofa. She got the sense from the calm surroundings that Carolyn was a soft, quiet person. Her serene décor definitely belied the turmoil of Timothy's lifestyle. That alone made Tara wonder how Carolyn had gotten together with her brother in the first place. Timothy's life had been a train wreck for what seemed like forever. It gave Tara hope that his life may've been different somehow, that perhaps he had known much better times than what she'd observed.

Tara's breath caught at the sight of Essence, a three-year-old cutie, with a brown sugar complexion and starry amber eyes. With eyelashes longer than Tara had ever seen on any child, and thick reddish brown tendrils spilling out all over her tiny head, Essence was the embodiment of her delicate name. This was one adorably beautiful child in Tara's opinion, niece or not.

Essence stretching out her arms to Tara, someone she'd never seen before, filled up Tara to the brim. Taking the little girl in her arms, she hugged her tightly, rocking her from side to side. "Hi, my sweetie," Tara cooed. "You are so precious! I'm your Auntie Tara."

Essence hugged Tara tightly, surprising the heck out of her. "Oh, baby, you are too sweet." With tears filling her eyes, Tara looked over at Carolyn.

Tara saw that she wasn't the only one in tears. As Carolyn had intently watched the touching scene between aunt and niece, her eyes had become watery, too. It didn't surprise Carolyn that Essence had taken to Tara. Carolyn herself had also been able to feel Tara's warm spirit from the moment they'd met.

Tara came over to the sofa and sat down next to Carolyn, carefully placing Essence snugly on her own lap. "I love her already. You have such a beautiful child, Carolyn."

"Thank you, Tara. She's very special to me. Now let's talk about you. I was so surprised to get a call from you, surprised to learn that you were Tim's sister. This is incredible. Ever since I talked with you I've been wondering why Tim never mentioned you. Do you know why?"

Tara frowned slightly. "I do, but that's not what I'm here to talk about. Tim will explain everything to you, that is, if you don't mind. He asked me to come and see you. He wants you to visit him. He's in Los Angeles Memorial Hospital, Carolyn."

Carolyn looked alarmed. "Hospital! Is it serious?"

Tara pressed her lips against the back of Essence's head, kissing the little girl's curls. "He is ill, Carolyn, but he's going to tell you everything you need to know about it. Will you go see him? He needs to talk with you."

Carolyn looked worried. "I don't know when I can make it up there. I'd have to line up a baby-sitter first. That's not such an easy feat. I don't trust many people with Essence."

"If that's the only thing stopping you, I have that covered. Do you mind if I take Essence home with me while you visit Tim? Or I could stay here with her. Whatever you decide."

Looking totally confused, Carolyn shook her head. "This is all happening so fast. I don't know what to say. Tara, I feel so scared for Tim, for all of us. Should I be?"

Tara shifted Essence around on her lap, making sure she kept the baby comfortable. "All I can say to that is I'm scared, too. As I said before, Tim will explain everything to you. He didn't want to talk to you about his health over the phone. Can you go see him now?"

"Sure, sure. I'll get the baby's things together for you. She'll need her car seat. Do you mind if I put it in your car?"

"Not at all. Let's get moving before it gets too late. I'll write my address down for you so you can pick Essence up when your visit is over. Or I can bring her home if you'd like."

Carolyn shook her head. "That won't be necessary. I'll come to your place. I still just can't believe all this is happening. Tim used to show up here every now and then, but I haven't seen him in over two months. I've asked around about him, but no one I know had seen him either. He loves his daughter, Tara. That's a fact. But he hasn't taken very good care of her recently, and that's probably because he's not taking good care of himself."

"You may be right. I have to ask you this, especially since you really don't know me from Adam. Do you trust me to take care of Essence for you?"

Carolyn smiled gently. "You know something, I do trust you. I know it may seem kind of odd that I'd let a stranger come in my home and take my daughter out of here, especially since I haven't even corroborated who you are. But I have a good feeling about you, Tara. Really good."

"Thank you for that, Carolyn. Your confidence in me is appreciated."

Tara took out her cell phone and dialed the hospital. Since Tim had been moved out of ICU and into a regular room earlier that morning, that meant she could get him on the phone. Carolyn needed to be absolutely sure that Tara was exactly whom she claimed to be. Hearing who she was from Tim would allow no room for doubt.

When no one answered Timothy's phone, Tara got worried. Had something happened to him since she'd left the hospital? Had he gone into a crisis situation? Remembering the horrible things she'd said to him caused Tara to cringe within. While praying that she hadn't bullied him into some sort of setback, she silently asked God for forgiveness and to have mercy on Timothy.

Tara clicked the phone off. "There's no answer. He may be asleep," she said, sounding less than convincing. "I wanted him to assure you that I was his sister."

Carolyn put her hand on Tara's arm. "I believe that already. You two look a lot alike. I need to know something badly, Tara. Are we talking about AIDS here?"

Tara looked mortified. "Oh, God, no. Please. I didn't mean to give you that impression. No, no, not that, Carolyn."

Carolyn sighed with relief. "I'm sorry I took it there, but I had to know."

"I understand that. But why AIDS?"

"Tim has been using for a long time. I don't know if he ever graduated to heroine or other illegal substances that have to be shot up, but I know people share dirty needles and other drug parapher-nalia all the time. My question was more out of concern for Essence's health than anything. If he'd contracted the disease, my child and I may've been exposed. I had to know so I could get the baby and me tested right away if I needed to."

Seeing the tragic look in Carolyn's eyes, Tara couldn't stop her-self from hugging her to offer her solace. "I can understand that. I thank God that you and Essence don't have to go through that kind of painful ordeal. Let's hurry and get out of here so you can talk to Tim and find out all the things you need to know about his health. I just want you to know that I'll be here for you and my niece from now on. We'll all get through this together, Carolyn. We're fam-ily."

Carolyn smiled bravely. "Thanks for including us in your family circle, Tara. I've got a feeling that Essence and I are going to need you in our lives. I'm so happy that you're here with us now. I can see that your little niece is, too. I'll get everything together and be right back."

Still feeling that Carolyn should know exactly whom she was, Tara rifled through her wallet and pulled out an old worn picture of her and Timothy. The photo had been taken in Timothy's early teens. "Just to reassure you, Carolyn, here's a picture of Tim and me."

Carolyn gripped Tara's hand before taking the picture from her. "It's not necessary, but I can understand that you want me to be sure. Thanks, Tara." Carolyn couldn't help smiling at the brother and sister duo. Their entwined hands made them seem very close to each other. "You guys look a lot alike. I'm more than convinced of your relationship to Tim."

Tara sighed with relief. "I'm thrilled. Now we can move forward with our plans."

Chapter Ten

As Hannah opened the front door to her house, the throbbing in her head had her nearly crazy. She'd had to enter the house from the porch because there was a strange car parked too close to the garage door, which she hadn't dared to open for fear of causing damage to the vehicle. Derrick needed to tell his friends to park on the street and not in their driveway. He'd been told that numerous times, but he'd continued to fail at adhering to the simple request.

Noticing that the alarm wasn't on, although she kept it armed even when at home, Hannah proceeded toward the stairwell, taking the steps slowly. Her entire body ached painfully—probably the flu—and she just didn't have enough energy to move any faster. Her workday had proved challenging. It had been hard for her to do her job when she felt like crap, so in the best interest of her patients, coworkers, and herself, she'd decided to take off the rest of the shift.

Upon reaching the top of the stairs, Hannah stood stock still, wondering what were the strange noises coming out of Derrick's room. Thinking it was some of the crazy music he loved to listen to, she moved past his door, only to freeze in her spot when she heard the distinct sounds of physical intimacy. Hannah suddenly felt like her hair was standing on end.

"Oh, yes," came the strangled voice. "You are so sweet."

Before Hannah's brain could reason out her next move, she had the door already open to Derrick's room. Unable to believe her eyes, in total shock over the scene before her, Hannah found herself rooted to the spot. The two people in the bed had no clue they were being watched. Only the bloodcurdling screams from Hannah's mouth caused them to pull apart. Believing she might faint dead away, Hannah gripped the door for support.

Sweat pouring from her face and hair, the rather pretty young woman looked up with a start. Upon seeing Hannah standing there, she quickly jumped out of bed. After grabbing her clothes off the floor, she broke all speed records in getting out of the room.

Derrick quickly followed suit, having pulled the sheet off the bed to cover himself, gathering his clothes along the way. He barely made eye contact with his mother, feeling the worse shame ever. The look on his mother's face told him he'd blown himself out of the water. Finding a place to stay was his second biggest dilemma. Earning back his mother's respect was his first. Derrick was in no doubt that Hannah was going to toss him out of the house for good.

All Hannah could do was break down and cry. She couldn't begin to imagine what had caused her son to show such disrespect to his parents and their home. Any excuse for his behavior was beyond her comprehension. When her husband suddenly came to mind, she didn't even need to consider if she should tell him about this or not. Unless she wanted to visit Derrick in the hospital and then go see her husband in jail, she'd best keep this incident on the down low.

If any comfort was to be found in this situation, the fact that Raquel was not the woman with Derrick helped to bring Hannah some relief. Her spirituality would've been severely at risk had the older woman dared to sleep with Derrick under the Brentwood roof. A holy war would've broken loose and Hannah would've eventually suffered the consequences, but only after taking pleasure in tearing Raquel from limb to limb. Just thinking about what she might've done to Derrick and his woman caused Hannah to shudder uncontrollably.

Studying the messy bed, Hannah had a hard time keeping her anger from escalating. That Derrick had left right behind his female companion was the smartest choice he could've ever made. Him staying behind would no doubt have resulted in a physical confrontation, because Hannah knew that she would've done her very best to beat him down like he'd stolen something from her. But he had. He had robbed her of her peace of mind and had also pilfered her trust. Hannah didn't think she'd ever trust Derrick again.

Deciding that it was best for her to get out of Derrick's room, since it was making her angrier by the minute, Hannah fled and rushed into the master suite. So relieved that Robert hadn't been a witness to what she'd seen, Hannah dropped down to her knees, her heart now hurting much worse than her head. While praying for God's guidance, she wept bitterly. Although Hannah couldn't even think about what she had to do about this situation, she knew she had to do something. This was one of Derrick's sins that she couldn't let go unpunished. Choosing the form of punishment, one that best fit the crime, wouldn't be easy.

Children were a mother's greatest joy, but they could also become her greatest sorrow. On this day Hannah felt deep, deep sorrow.

Once Hannah pulled herself together emotionally, she sat up on the bed and began to think things through rationally. After a few moments of troubled pondering, she decided it was best to just pack Derrick's personal items in boxes and set them at the front door. No, she quickly mused, she couldn't do that. Such an action would cause Robert to ask too many questions, questions she'd be hard pressed to answer. The thought of covering up for Derrick one more time was terribly upsetting to Hannah. But until she could come up with a solution to the problem she might have to do just that. Hannah could easily conjure up the murderous look that would appear on Robert's handsome face if he ever learned about what had happened in his home.

In Hannah's opinion Derrick could never rationally explain how he had thought his bedroom in their home equaled hotel-motel heaven. His behavior was totally out of line, not to mention utterly disrespectful. She hoped that her son would get back to the house before Robert got in. Otherwise the showdown would have to wait until another opportunity presented itself.

As impatient as Hannah was to have it out with Derrick, she wished she didn't have to confront the situation at all. This was something that would be best left up to Robert, since he was also a man, but her husband just couldn't know. But since she had to be the one to confront the situation, she didn't want to wait too long. Hannah knew that she had a way of putting things on the back burner once she cooled off, especially those things relating to her adult son.

If Hannah had thought she was sick before, she now felt even worse. Knowing she had to pull herself totally together, she thought a nap would do her a lot of good. Whatever had brought her home in the first place still needed attention. *Or had her early homecoming been a sign from God?* He did send messages in all sorts of ways. Had she not come home unexpectedly she wouldn't have caught Derrick playing house. The question in her mind was how long had he been doing the unspeakable in their home? She was certain that this wasn't the first time. He'd seemed too comfortable with everything for that. *Was Derrick having regrets?* She was sure he was; regrets of being caught in the act, but not for the act itself. Hannah's thoughts turned to Proverbs (23:13–14)—"Don't fail to correct your children; discipline won't hurt them. They won't die if you use a stick on them. Punishment will keep them out of hell"— one that both her and her son would do well to remember.

Hannah was well aware that she couldn't change all the mistakes she'd made in raising Derrick. With him being an adult, she now had no say over what he did or didn't do. But she did have dominion over herself—and the changes first would have to occur within her.

Continuing to keep Robert in the dark about the things Derrick did wrong while living under their roof was unfair and deceptive. After all, Derrick had two parents. With that in mind, she vowed to go ahead and tell Robert about what had happened. Although her decision to get things out in the open was terribly scary for her, it was something Hannah had to do.

Hannah sighed with relief. "Better late than never."

Finding Jerome sitting in her living room, looking like he owned the place, had Simone going through an internal rage. Instead of giving in to the urge to strike out at him verbally, she calmly walked over to a chair and sat down. "I'm sure you think you have a good explanation for being in my house uninvited, or for being here period, but I can't begin to imagine what it would be. So why don't you just go ahead and enlighten me, Mr. Hadley?"

Simone noticed that Jerome didn't look as though he'd expected his visit to be an easy one. The fact that he appeared downright nervous gave her quite a bit of satisfaction. The thought that she hadn't changed the locks was the first one that had entered her mind the second she laid eyes upon Jerome. She remembered Glenda asking her about the locks. The current locks on the doors would be changed immediately, Simone noted mentally.

Jerome placed his hands on his knees and leaned forward in the chair. "I came here to apologize, Simone. I don't know what got into me that evening?"

"I do. Alcohol and drugs: the two things that are always in you. I'm surprised to see you looking sober right now. But how long will that last?" Seeing him without red eyes and a flushed complexion was a real change. Although she hadn't seen Jerome walk in this time, she had no problem conjuring up the staggering gait always accompanying his drunkenness.

"I don't know if it means anything to you, but I'm on the wagon. I haven't had a drink in over a week. I realized that I couldn't keep doing this to myself. I'd never hit a woman before in my life, and it wasn't a good feeling. I hate myself for hitting you like that."

Simone sucked her teeth. "It's hard for me to believe you even remembered anything about it. You were drunker than drunk, you know. But now that you've apologized, you can leave. I have plans for this evening."

Jerome raised an eyebrow. "It's like that, huh?"

"How else would you expect it to be, Jerome?"

"I don't know, but you haven't even said if you accept my apology or not."

Simone grimaced. "I accept it. Are you happy now?"

Jerome eyed her warily. "You don't sound like you mean it, Simone. I can't believe you're throwing everything away like this, after all we've been through together."

Simone once again tamped down her inner rage. "All that *we've* been through? Don't you mean all that *you've* put me through?" Biting down on her tongue, Simone looked thoughtful. "I take that back. I'm the only one responsible for what I went through with you. I eventually allowed you to behave yourself right out of my life, but I should never have allowed it to happen in the first place. I finally came to see the light; I just didn't see it soon enough. You got away with all that you did simply because I let you. When you dared to raise a hand to me, you woke this sleeping beauty right on up. I need to thank you for at least that much. If it hadn't been for that, your tired behind might still be parked in my private space."

"That's all you have to say? I came here to work things out with you. Are you saying that can't happen? What more do you want?"

Simone had to stop herself from laughing out loud. *Work things out! No, he couldn't have thought that.* After taking a couple of seconds to ask herself mentally why he'd think that, she had the answer. It was what he'd come to expect from her, because she'd always worked out everything with him in the past. She had taught him how to treat her and exactly what to expect from her. No consequences for Jerome had resulted in numerous repeats of the same offenses. *Who other than herself could be blamed for what had occurred?*

"I accepted your apology, and I'll eventually forgive you for nearly knocking me senseless, but that's the extent of my good grace, Jerome. I have nothing else to offer you but my sincere apology. I'm only sorry for allowing you to think you could mess over me like this and then get away with it. If I had stopped you cold the first time you came into my home high on something or other, none of this would've happened. I almost lost my son over this foolishness. So, if I had to go back and do it all again, I wouldn't have brought you into my house in the first place. It was wrong of me to do that to Tyrell. No, Jerome, there's nothing left for me to say or even do. It's over with us, has been since the moment you lifted your hand and struck me in the eye. I wish you only the best that life has to offer, but it won't be happening with me."

Jerome glared at Simone. "Does this sudden change of heart have anything to do with your runaway husband being back in town, Simone? If it does, you also need to remember what he did to you, which was far worse than anything I ever did."

Not daring to respond to his cynical remarks, fearing what she might say in retaliation, Simone got to her feet. "Thanks for the advice, Jerome. I'll take it under advisement. But, for now, I'm going to walk you to the door and bid you a final farewell."

After closing the door behind Jerome, happy that she was finally finished with that chapter of her life, Simone went back into the living room. Once seated on the sofa, she began to go over her entire relationship with Jerome. It had never been a good one, but she'd stayed in it, anyway. He wasn't even her type. That he was weaker than her was what had attracted her to him in the beginning, which was something she'd only figured out recently.

Jerome wasn't strong and confident like Booker was, nor was he the athletic type. He wasn't charming like her husband and he wasn't anywhere near what she considered as handsome. Simone hated to admit it, but she started seeing Jerome because she believed a man like him would never leave her no matter what. Jerome was needy and she had just what he needed in a woman. He'd told her repeatedly that he considered himself so lucky to have a woman like her, that he'd never go astray and risk losing her. Her way of thinking had been sad and even somewhat sick, but that was how she'd viewed the situation.

Jerome's admiration and adoration of Simone had become apparent to her almost instantly. He had told her too many times that he'd never met anyone like her, that she was the first woman in his life whom he could actually be proud of. Her level of education and her profession fascinated him just as much as her looks and personality. Jerome had unwittingly given Simone power over him, the kind of power she hadn't had with Booker in the end.

Never again involve yourself with a fine, strong, confident, and athletic man like Booker Branch had become Simone's motto. Find a relationship that you can control, one in which you get to call all the shots. Only a weak man could fit the description and fill the bill, so she'd let Jerome come into her life thinking she'd have complete control over the relationship.

Jerome had a tendency to make darn good money as a carpenter, when he was sober enough to work, but she made a lot more as a nurse. Her overtime pay alone was often significant. Considering herself as the main breadwinner had made Simone feel even more powerful. Booker provided his family with plenty of money, but Simone only used of it what was absolutely necessary to meet all of Tyrell's needs and the majority of his wants.

While Simone hadn't been fully conscious of all these things in the beginning, she'd begun to suspect her motivation shortly after Jerome moved in with her. It was now plain for her to see in looking back on it. Jerome had been safe, or so she'd thought, before the drinking and drugs had become a major issue. She hadn't had to fear him leaving her because his fear of her walking out on him was even stronger than her own misgivings. Simone now realized that she'd simply gotten caught up in on her own cleverly disguised snare. Everything had backfired.

Looking over at the telephone, Simone wondered if she should just go ahead and accept Tyrell's invitation to dinner at Booker's place. It didn't seem right that she should go to her estranged husband's home to break bread, especially since their last encounter had been a rather nasty one. True to his word, Booker hadn't called her or stepped foot back in her home since that evening. She knew exactly why that bothered her so much, but she wouldn't allow herself to face up to it so she could then come to terms with it.

As infrequent as they'd been, Simone had to admit that she had begun to enjoy Booker's visits to her home. It had been nice to have him around despite the fact that several of their little meetings of the minds had turned into heated debates. She'd also begun to anticipate his phone calls, which had come way more often than his showing up at her door.

Lately Simone had been thinking a lot about all the things Booker had said to her that last evening, especially those remarks she never would've expected to come from him. Booker confessing that he still loved her was one of the things Simone constantly played over in her mind. It scared her as much as it brought her deep satisfaction. She still loved him, too, but admitting it to herself was as far as she was willing to go with it.

How many times had she played out that one particular scenario in her mind? His hands on her shoulders had been firm but gentle. Although their foreheads hadn't actually touched, she'd felt as if they had. A mere touch from him was singeing. Just feeling the heat of Booker's breath so close to her lips had nearly caused her to come completely unglued. It would be so easy for her to fall right back into his arms and into his bed, but her pride would never allow it.

Simone knew that letting Booker know she was still in love with him would be a huge mistake. If he thought for one second that he had a ghost of a chance with her, he'd go to great lengths, and far beyond what she could imagine, to try to win her back. He'd pour on the gooey sweet charm so thick that she'd feel deliciously smothered by it. Booker was a romancer and she had no doubt that he had the ability to romance her right back into his arms. The thought of him succeeding in winning back her heart was what terrified her the most.

How did a woman give her heart up a second time to the same man who'd already broken it into a million and one pieces? Simone wiped the tears from her eyes. *Very easily if she's not extremely careful.*

Following Tara's advice, Sinclair had pulled out all the credit card bills for the last couple of years to study in depth the countless charges. Finding out what Marcus was charging on the cards was imperative. It was when Sinclair learned that the last cash advance she'd made to send to him had sent her over her credit limit, which had instantly increased her interest rate, that she knew she had to do something to try to stop the out-of-control hemorrhaging.

As she scanned the long lists of charges, it amazed Sinclair that she hadn't even bothered to look at the purchases when the bills had first come in. She had simply paid them, never questioning Marcus about any of his monthly expenditures, despite the large debts.

Sinclair then noticed the numerous charges for one particular company, Magical Entertainment Incorporated, located up in San Francisco, where Marcus was enrolled in college. As she closely scrutinized each bill, she saw that the same company was listed multiple times during each twenty-eight-day billing cycle. Deciding that she needed to do a little investigating on the company in question, she dialed information to get the phone number. She could just call Marcus and ask him about it, but she figured he'd probably lie to her, anyway.

Several minutes later, nearly stunned out of her mind, Sinclair could do nothing more than moan and groan. Feeling a deep sense of betrayal, she picked up the phone to call Marcus, only to put it right back down. Since he'd be coming home in a few more days, she decided to confront him face-to-face. Besides, by then, she'd have even more evidence of his bloody deceit.

Computer discs, CDs, ink printer cartridges, paper, pens, and a host of other unexplainable expenditures had Sinclair seeing red in more ways than one. Thousands of dollars had been spent on clothes, socks, and shoes, more than likely designer labels. Marcus loved to dress to the nines in the latest fashions, mostly the hip-hop style. It looked as if he'd even charged his haircuts. She wasn't aware that barbers took credit cards. Everything from combs to hair texturizers and wave caps had been paid for with a credit card.

Marcus must change underwear several times a day, Sinclair mused, seeing all the listings for such apparel. Wearing clean undergarments definitely wasn't a bad thing, since her mother had often pounded the need for practicing such a good habit into her head, but the vast amount of money her son had spent on covering his butt was downright insane.

Overwhelmed by it all, Sinclair lowered her head for a moment of silent prayer. She was going to get through this, she told herself. Marcus might not make it, but she would. She then asked God to forgive her for mentally picking out her beloved son's coffin while she'd been sorting through the mountain of bills.

The horrible mistakes she'd made in raising Marcus were never more apparent to Sinclair than at this very moment. She'd created a five-headed monster. Well, she thought, at least four of those heads had to go. If Marcus wasn't careful, the fifth one might have to go, too. Then she once again prayed for a cleansing of her evil thoughts.

Sinclair needed the strength of an immovable rock. Then she realized she already had one, a solid rock, one with unending strength and extraordinary powers, the Lord.

Sinclair thought about a couple of the Ten Commandments. Although she was guilty of being disobedient to a few of them, a particular two had her standing up and taking notice. As the worst of her sins came clearly into her inner vision, Sinclair's heart trembled with trepidation as she recalled aloud Exodus, chapter twenty, verses three to five: "You may worship no other God before me. You shall not make yourselves any idols: any images resembling animals, birds, or fish. You must never bow to an image or worship it in any way; for I, the Lord your God, am very possessive. I will not share your affection with any other god."

Upon realizing that she had been positively idolizing her son was a bitter revelation for Sinclair. She had bowed to Marcus in worship many times by always letting him have his way. False idols came in many forms: money, automobiles, houses, jewelry—and, yes, even in the flesh and blood of men. Worshiping her son was one of Sinclair's greatest sins.

Sinclair's shame was great, her guilt profound. Knowing that she had constantly placed her child before the will of God was a daunting fact, one that she needed to rectify quickly. Then another revelation came rapidly into Sinclair's mind, written upon a blaze of fire, that she had also placed Marcus before Charles, her beloved husband of twenty-seven years.

Knowing that she'd become the number-one enemy to Charles in his own home, and had unwittingly taught her son to become his number-two adversary, Sinclair began to cry hard. Pride had stood in the way of her even taking Charles's smallest concerns into consideration. Her larger-than-life ego had stepped in and erected an impenetrable wall between them. She had been obnoxiously haughty and downright unreasonable with the man she professed to love, challenging him at every single turn, ignoring him as if he hadn't existed.

Although Sinclair still didn't feel as if Charles had had the right to give the ultimatums he'd handed out to her, outright choosing her son over her husband hadn't been the best way to handle it. Instead of telling Charles that she'd continued to support Marcus financially despite his objections, she should've engaged herself in finding a way for them to reach an amicable solution to their issues. Sinclair's prideful decision had become her downfall, as stated in Proverbs chapter sixteen, verse seventeen.

"Pride goes before destruction and haughtiness before a fall."

Then Sinclair had charged Charles with adultery, the last time she'd seen him, a charge that he had yet to answer—and probably wouldn't. The unreadable expression on his face hadn't revealed to her his guilt or innocence. Without uttering another word, Charles had just walked out on her. Whether another woman was in his life or not, she still didn't know. Sinclair hadn't heard from Charles since that evening, over a week ago.

No matter how hard she tried to stop herself from crying, fountains of tears still fell from Sinclair's eyes. She had to go to Charles, had to tell him how sorry she was. He needed to know that she loved and missed him, that she wanted to work things out with him. She couldn't let their marriage end because of her pride. Sinclair fell to her knees, crying in anguish. "Create in me a new, clean heart, O God; and renew a right spirit within me."

The broad smile on Glenda's face was indicative of the joy she felt inside. Seated at the dinner table with her two men, for the third time in one week, had her quite optimistic about the future. Much to her surprise and pleasure, Anthony and Taylor had been getting along famously.

The first night they'd all had dinner together had been a little tense, but Taylor, being Taylor, had taken the situation completely under control. He'd first praised Anthony on the delicious food he'd prepared. Points in Taylor's favor had begun adding up from that moment on. His stories and jokes about how he'd been raised in a strict home, and the tales of him later rebelling against all authority figures, had had Anthony listening intently. Taylor had told Anthony things about his life that he hadn't ever shared with Glenda. But everything he'd said about his youth had somehow paralleled the troubles Anthony was now having.

Glenda had been amazed at how Anthony had seemed genuinely interested in what Taylor had to say. Since Taylor was such a genuine man, she shouldn't have been so surprised by Anthony's reaction to him, but she was. Never in a million years had she thought her son and any man she was romantically involved with would ever find any kind of camaraderie.

Anthony and Taylor were now into the topic of sports, discussing for the umpteenth time the sporting event they'd attended together. Glenda may as well not have been there for all the attention paid to her once that hot conversation got going. Sports had been the magic spark connecting the two males. However, it bothered Glenda something fierce to know that she hadn't even been aware that Anthony had such a keen interest in sports. He'd never asked to play in organized sports of any kind and she'd never thought to find out if he had an interest in such.

Chalking it up to being just a woman wasn't a legitimate out for her in this instance. As Anthony's mother, she should've known her son's likes and dislikes, all of them. Hearing her son talking about sports with such enthusiasm made Glenda realize she'd been too busy working and worrying to find real solutions to real problems.

It appeared to Glenda that the absence of a real man in Anthony's life was where the real problems lay. While she believed that a woman could successfully raise a son, she had begun to realize that she couldn't teach her son to be a man simply because she wasn't one. Tara had touched upon that revelation some time ago, Glenda recalled with crystal clarity.

Tara, Glenda thought with genuine fondness, was the one who had turned out to be the wisest of the entire group of women. Tara Wheatley, the childless wonder, had made them all do lots of soul-searching where their young sons were concerned. Her advice was invaluable.

It was ironic that Tara would now be faced with child-rearing problems since she wasn't a mother yet. But everyone in their little close-knit circle believed that Tara would eventually come out the victor in both of her current dilemmas, Timothy and Raymond. Whether she stayed with Raymond or not was yet to be seen. At any rate, Glenda knew that Tara would make that decision based on what was best for her. She admired the love and respect the younger woman had for herself. Tara was always in complete control of Tara, a remarkable quality to possess.

"Mom, are you okay?" Anthony asked.

Glenda looked over at her son and smiled. "Yeah, baby, I couldn't be better. I was just lost in a maze of thought. You two were involved in a conversation that I know nothing about, so that's why my mind began to wonder."

Taylor encompassed Glenda in his warm gaze. "I keep trying to teach you all about sports so we can enjoy them together, but you won't let me. Sorry if we shut you out, Glen."

Glenda chuckled. "I don't feel shut out, Taylor. I like seeing you two so animated. It gives me a warm feeling inside." Glenda glanced at Anthony. "Please pass me the potatoes."

"Sure thing." Anthony lifted the bowl of creamy mashed potatoes and handed it to his mother. "After dinner we're going to watch an old NBA championship, the one where the Lakers beat the Celtics, way back when Magic was the man! Why don't you watch it with us, Mom?"

Glenda's first thought was to turn down the invitation. Watching sports was a man's thing. After drawing off her earlier thoughts, she then gave the idea a second consideration. "Maybe I will. But only if you all promise to tell me what's going on. I don't like being in the dark, you know. Although I've been in the darkness about so much over the last few years, I'm now ready to give this little new-found light of mine a chance to shine."

Glenda *had* been in the dark, literally. She had long ago lost sight of what was important to her son's upbringing, had confused doing right by her son with covering up for his wrongs. Overcompensating for the lack of male guidance had been her biggest mistake. Anthony hadn't benefited one iota from her feeling sorry for him because of his father's death. He could've used her courage and strength. What he had needed most was for her to be the best parent possible to overcome the deficit, not to try to make up for it. Glenda could never make up for Antoine's absence in Anthony's life. It wasn't possible. Too bad that she hadn't known that from the start.

Anthony beamed at Glenda. "All right, Mom! By the time Mr. T and I finish with you, you're going to be a walking encyclopedia on sports."

Taylor's heart felt like it was about to burst with his love for Glenda. Although he'd felt confident about fostering an amicable relationship with Anthony from the very beginning, he had come to realize that Glenda had to be comfortable with the idea before she'd take to it. His patience had finally paid off. Getting Glenda and Anthony comfortable with them becoming a family was one of his future goals. When that time came, if ever it should, Taylor planned to take it very slow. Marriage and having a family weren't things anyone should ever rush into, but Taylor was positive that he wanted his relationship with Glenda to end up in holy matrimony.

Anthony's troubles with the law were far from over, but he was now adhering to the strict rules that had been laid down for him. Wearing the electronic leg bracelet had been a rude awakening for him. Having his every move tracked was both disconcerting and embarrassing to him; he wanted it gone as soon as possible. That he wasn't yet eighteen was the only thing that had saved him thus far. That protective covering would soon be stripped away. Where Glenda had failed at making that very point clear to Anthony, Taylor had somehow succeeded.

Taylor had also gotten Anthony involved in quite a few extra-curricular youth activities that he himself was involved in on a vol-unteer basis. At the constant prompting of Taylor, Anthony was even considering continuing his education. He'd have to attend a junior college first since he'd let his studies go begging during most of the last school year. Glenda would be happy to have him in an educational trade program if that's what Anthony chose to do.

Anthony looked from his mother to Taylor. Glenda hadn't missed the slight nod of Taylor's head at Anthony, making her won-der what was up. *What were these two up to now?*

Anthony cleared his throat. "Mom, about the stuff I was charged with, I have a confession to make." He looked at Taylor again for further encouragement, receiving the same response as before. "I did do some of those things, but not all of them. Mr. T helped me to understand how the older guys had used me, 'cause they knew I'd only go to juvenile hall. If they did the same exact things, they'd go straight to prison. I was the fall guy for them. I know you tried to tell me that a hundred times, but I wasn't trying to hear it. I'm sorry."

Glenda fought hard to hold back her tears. This was a time for a show of strength. She'd already shown her son how weak she could be. Taylor had gotten through to Anthony in all the areas she'd failed at. *What would've happened had she allowed Taylor to work his magic on her son from the first time he'd asked? How much time had she wasted by her constant refusals?*

Glenda quickly zapped those thoughts right out of her mind. She had to deal with today and stop harping on the yesterdays, which she had no way of changing. The past was best left in the past. She also had a confession to make, but she wasn't sure if it should be done in front of Taylor since it was a very sensitive issue for Anthony. Glenda didn't want to undo any of what Taylor had miraculously managed to accomplish. Her confession should wait for when she was alone with her son, she decided.

Anthony definitely needed to know that his father hadn't been physically involved with the prostitute. The mystery of why his father had been with her in the first place was still just that, a mystery. Finding out the truth from the autopsy reports was imperative to Glenda's growth, just as it would be essential to Anthony's.

Glenda reached across the table and covered Anthony's hand with hers. "Thank you for that. I won't ask you to go into any details, because it won't do any good for us to rehash the past. All I ask is that you come and talk to Mr. T or me when you're feeling out of sorts with things. I promise to give you the best advice I can, but simply because I'm not a man, there may be things that only a male can help you out with. Mr. T has already told both of us that he's going to be there for you. Can you agree to what I'm asking of you, Tony?"

Anthony nodded, suddenly looking rather forlorn. "Yeah, I can do that. But I have to ask you and Mr. T something. What's going to happen to me if you two don't stay together? Am I going to lose all over again if Mr. T is no longer in your life, Mom?"

Glenda and Taylor exchanged nervous glances. While Glenda was overly concerned with how to answer Anthony's query, Taylor knew exactly how he intended to respond.

"Tony, as I've told you many times before, I'm going to be here for you. You have become an important part of my landscape, so to speak. Your mother has everything to do with the relationship that she and I have built. But the relationship you and I have begun to build is not based on the outcome of what Glen and I do. You're not going to lose me no matter what happens between Glen and me. You have my word on that. Have I broken my word to you yet?"

Looking more optimistic now, Anthony shook his head in the negative.

"And I promise you that I won't, Tony. You've seen most of the youth I work with on a regular basis. Our relationships started out just like yours and mine did. There's no reason in the world why you and I can't continue on just the way we are." Feeling very confident about his next move, though it might prove controversial, Taylor grinned broadly. "Now let me ask you something. Are you saying that you won't have any objections to me becoming a permanent fixture in your life if your mother and I decide to marry?"

Anthony looked downright shocked and Glenda nearly fell out of the chair. Neither Anthony nor Glenda had expected Taylor to come out with such a loaded question. Whether he was aware of it or not, Glenda wasn't sure, but Taylor had come out firing from both barrels.

After a couple of seconds of thought, a huge smile spread across Anthony's face, lighting up his eyes at the same time. "That would be cool, either way!" Anthony then looked over at Glenda, instantly worried about the scowling expression she wore. "But if the wedding doesn't happen, I'm okay with just you and me hanging out, Mr. T."

By the look on Glenda's face, Taylor's confidence was now a little shaken. *What had happened to his decision to take things slowly with Glenda and Anthony?* Now that it looked as if he might crash and burn, Taylor decided to go ahead and finish out the nosedive. Although he knew that he had a lot to lose, Taylor couldn't seem to pull himself up out of the microburst he'd intentionally flown into. "What about you, Glen? Are you okay with things either way?"

Looking more confused than she ever had before, Glenda stared straight ahead at Taylor. That he had dared to open up this can of worms with Anthony present had her a tad shaken. He had certainly put her on the hot seat—and her butt felt like it was on fire. Then the thought to shake things up even more made her laughter bubble within. *Did she dare? Yes, she did dare.* It was time for Taylor to squirm a little, since he had everyone else's behinds wiggling all over the place. "Can I consider your comments as a future proposal of marriage, Taylor?"

Taylor leapt out of his seat, much to Glenda's surprise. Not knowing what was going to happen next, Anthony pushed his chair back from the table, as though he were moving out of the line of fire. His head constantly moved back and forth as he watched his mother and Taylor, wondering what the heck was going on with them. Everything had suddenly gone haywire.

Taylor could barely contain himself. "Woman, I'm not going to waste a minute on trying to figure out what you meant by that one. Since I already know exactly what I want, the heck with anything to do with the future. Here and now is what matters most."

With tears in his eyes, not caring whether he'd once again get shot down by Glenda, Taylor Phillips fell down on bended knee. Taking her hands in his, Taylor looked into her eyes, his love for her shining bright as a silver moon. "Glenda Richards, will you marry me?"

Jamaica Wheatley, his light brown eyes twinkling with stars, reached across the kitchen table and hugged his daughter for the umpteenth time. Each hug was administered as if it were the last chance that he might get to hold her in his arms. He was a big man, six-foot-three, with a big heart, one who took pride in keeping his body and mind well toned. His high blood pressure scare of many years ago had put him on high alert, which had caused him to pay special attention to both diet and exercise.

Tara loved the affection her father always showered upon her. He made her feel so loved and cherished. It was those very generous sprinklings of constant hugs and kisses that had allowed her to grow into a healthy, lovely flower. Despite some of her emotional issues involving her mother and brother, Tara had matured nicely over the years to become the well-rounded woman she was today. Had Jamaica not been around in her youth to water her roots and weed out the bad stuff, she would've withered and died long ago.

Anna Clay, a slightly built woman, who possessed mysterious grayish green eyes, short dark hair painted with broad strokes of gray, and the figure of someone half her age, had an electric smile on her face, one that carried enough wattage to light up an entire country. Anna had made herself right at home in Tara's kitchen, having insisted on preparing the evening meal.

Tara looked at Anna with admiration. She had instantly taken a liking to her father's choice in a mate. Anna had embraced Tara as if she'd known her all her life, as if she were her very own flesh and blood. The warmth in which Anna had greeted Tara had brought tears to Tara's eyes. If only her mother could've given her the same kind of affection, Tara would've been so grateful. Much to her dismay, Tara could barely recall Joanna hugging or kissing her, since those times had been few and far between. On the other hand, Timothy had received more than his fair share of Joanna's love and affection. Tara couldn't help wondering if she'd ever get over it. The desire was strong for such, but her emotions sometimes got in the way.

"Tara, would you show me where you keep the dishes, so I can set the table?" Anna asked, not wanting to rifle through her hostess's cabinets without permission. "Dinner is just about ready."

Tara jumped up from her seat. "I'll set the table, Ms. Anna. That's the least I can do. But I'll go ahead and show you where everything is so that you can locate it when I'm not here."

Jamaica got to his feet. "I'll help, too. This big old man is as hungry as a bear."

While working harmoniously together to get the table set and the food put out for consumption, the trio had the task completed in hardly any time at all. Tara was amazed at how quickly Anna had whipped up the delicious-smelling dinner. As the lightly seasoned salmon steaks had cooked under the broiler, Anna had made light work of tossing a fresh green salad and steaming up a vegetable medley of yellow squash, zucchini, sugar peas, and baby carrots.

Tara could tell that Anna knew her way around the kitchen. It was obvious to her that Anna was also used to cooking for Jamaica by the special attention she paid to his dietary needs. That wasn't all that Tara had taken note of in the short time they'd been together. These two people were in love; of that she was sure. Their golden years hadn't slowed them down one bit. The department of romance was open for business. The affectionate hand-holding and constant romancing with their eyes were a delight for Tara to witness, making her hope that she could have the same kind of relationship when she reached their age. Although she had a twinge of guilt about admitting it, out of loyalty to her mother, Tara had never seen her father happier.

As Jamaica passed the blessing, Tara silently thanked God for this little family reunion. Even though Jamaica and Anna weren't married yet, Tara had already begun to think of Anna as family. It was a great yet somewhat fearful feeling for Tara. Being surrounded by a happy family was all she'd ever wanted in life, but the circle wasn't yet complete. Timothy, the prodigal son, had to be brought back into the fold. Would he be able to accept Anna as easily as Tara had? Would he even allow Jamaica back into his life was another worrisome question in Tara's mind. The battles between father and son had been fierce ones, as well as innumerable.

Timothy's loyalty to their mother was probably still very strong despite the abusiveness he'd pounded Joanna with on a regular basis. There was no doubt in Tara's mind that Timothy loved Joanna with all his might; he just hadn't shown it in the last several years of her life.

Jamaica laid down his fork and looked over at his child. "So, Tara, what's the game plan where Timothy is concerned?" he asked, as if he'd read his daughter's thoughts.

"Funny you should ask. I was just thinking about Tim, Daddy. Since he doesn't know you'll be coming to visit him, I guess we should discuss our strategy. I also want to clue you in on some things I haven't told you. First off, you're a grandfather to the most beautiful child you'll ever lay eyes on. Timothy's daughter's name is Essence."

Jamaica swelled with pride, his eyes filling with tears at the same time. That Tara had shocked him silly was obvious. "Me, a grandfather! Timothy has a child? Will wonders never cease? Essence," he said softly, as though it were a sweet taste of honey upon his tongue. "What a lovely name. Tell me, Tara, does she look like Timothy?"

"She does. She also looks like Mom and me. Actually, I think she has a little of all of us in her features." Tara had added that last statement to make Jamaica feel a part of Essence's life. He *was* every bit a part of Essence's creation. He was her loving paternal grandfather.

Tara went on to tell her guests about Carolyn and how she'd taken care of Essence while Carolyn visited with Timothy at the hospital. Tara's love for Essence was apparent in her every word and gesture. Tara admitted to falling head over heels in love with the little girl on sight.

"Although Carolyn was stunned by Timothy's health situation, she vowed to do all she could do to help," Tara told her father and Anna. "I don't think Carolyn is going to involve herself romantically with Tim again, but she does want to remain a good friend to him. She said there was too much water under the bridge for them to swim through. She does love Tim, Daddy. But as we'll all come to learn eventually, love isn't always enough."

Jamaica looked saddened by Tara's remarks. "Unfortunately, what you've said is true. I can't wait to see my granddaughter, but we'd better take first things first. Getting through this first visit with Tim is an important step in trying to bring the Wheatley family back together."

Anna cleared her throat. "I'd like to offer a suggestion, if that's okay with you, Tara."

"Sure, Ms. Anna. Three great minds are better than two, especially in this case."

Anna smiled delicately. "Thank you, Tara. After giving this much thought, I think Jamaica should go and visit Timothy by himself. It has been a long time since these two have seen each other. And I thought that maybe their first reunion should be a private one. If Timothy has a group of onlookers, he may not give a true reaction to seeing his father. He may feel that he has to act a certain way to keep from embarrassing everyone. Jamaica, if you and Timothy are going to work things out, perhaps you're the only two who should be involved in the initial visit."

Jamaica reached for Anna's hand, then for Tara's. "That's one of the things I love most about you, Anna. Your ability to reason things out so easily is amazing to me. I think you've made some excellent points. What do you think, Tara?"

Like Tara, Anna had had no children with her husband, now deceased, but she was very wise in the ways of effective parenting. She'd been a fairy godmother to many a child in her lifetime. Retired from the department of child welfare services, Anna had been involved with children of all ages and from every walk of life.

Tara nodded. "I agree with you, Ms. Anna. I think you're absolutely right on target. Though I hate to admit it, this plan will definitely take some of the heat off me. Knowing Tim as I do, he may think that I've betrayed him if I walk in there with you, Daddy. I, too, believe that his first reaction to you will be honest and pure if you're alone in the room. He's either going to be angry as a wet hen or happy as all get out to see you. I agree with everything that Ms. Anna has said. You should go up to the hospital alone."

Jamaica shrugged. "Then it's settled. This old man knows that women are the wisest of mankind. If you all had the opportunity to run this plum crazy world, it would be a much better place than it is now. As soon as we have some of that delicious-looking chocolate cake you picked up at the bakery, Tara, I'll be on my way to the hospital. We can't keep fate waiting much longer."

Chapter Eleven

Charles's heart thumped hard with longing. No one would ever know how much he truly missed Sinclair, the woman who'd stolen his heart with a mere smile. Like a bright flash of sunlight, her smile had lit up his world. The raw pain he now saw in her eyes had him wanting to take her into his arms. Their separation had gone on long enough without resolution; that it had taken its toll on both of them was evident. It was time to settle everything once and for all.

Although Sinclair had shown no signs of change in her attitude about their personal issues, he had to admit that he really didn't want her to make any drastic changes. He just needed her to be more responsible, more sensitive to him and his needs, which weren't many. He wanted Sinclair to respect him as a man, as her husband, and as Marcus's father. Charles also desired her to be more up front with things that would affect both their lives and that of their son's.

Sinclair nervously shuffled her feet, looking a bit fearful. "You asked me to come here, Charles, so are you going to let me in?"

Sinclair's tension-filled voice snapped Charles right out of his thoughtful trance. His eyes then swept over her in a warm embrace.

"Sorry, Sinclair. I didn't mean to be rude. Please come on in." Charles stepped aside for Sinclair to enter the town house.

Nervous as an injured bird around a stalking cat, Sinclair slowly moved inside. This was so darn awkward, she mused. *How could two people have lived together for as long as they had and be this uneasy around each other?* At one time Charles had been her equalizer from the stresses of the day, standing ready to give her a good massage to ease the tightness in her tense muscles. His thoughtfulness and cheery moods had always helped to relax her even more after a tough shift. She missed all of that. But most of all she missed Charles, the man she loved dearly.

Charles smiled at Sinclair. "I hope you brought a good appetite. I fixed dinner for us."

Sinclair did her best to hide her surprise. *Dinner!* Sinclair had already eaten, but she wouldn't think of telling Charles that. What harm could come from consuming another meal, especially if it kept him from being disappointed? She'd already let him down enough.

Did she dare to think that things might be changing for the better? After doing so much soul-searching over the past few days, Sinclair had already made up her mind to come to Charles and beg for his forgiveness. Before she'd been able to put a call in to him, he had phoned her with an invite for them to talk. If nothing else, the evening was going to be very interesting.

Sinclair couldn't conceal her pleasure at being in his presence. It was all she could do to keep from jumping up and down with glee. Kissing Charles was out of the question, but that didn't quell her desire. Seeing him had been a long time coming, but she was glad to be there.

Facing Sinclair, Charles placed his hands on her shoulders. "We'll go into the dining room in a minute, but I need to say something to you first." He cleared his throat from the invading lump. "I was dumbfounded when I learned that you believed I was involved with another woman. Disbelief quickly turned to anger. That you would dare to question my integrity had me incensed. That was the reason I walked out on you that evening, not from any guilt. I came to realize that my silence was in part responsible for what you thought, but I no longer knew what to say to you or even how to reach you. I felt as if I'd said everything already."

Sinclair reached up and covered his hands with hers. "Charles, you don't have to . . ."

"Yes, I do, Sinclair." He removed one hand from her shoulder and lifted her chin with two of his fingers. "In all the years we've been married, I've never considered breaking our marriage vows. I admit to looking a plenty at other women, thousands of times, but all it ever did was remind me of how very blessed I was. No one ever compared to you. You constantly test me to the absolute limit, but never to the point of committing adultery. I need you to know that, although I wish you'd known that without me having to tell you."

The unmitigated shame of her false accusations against Charles was hard for Sinclair to bear. She had attacked her husband's dignity in the worst way. She *did* know that he was incapable of cheating on her, especially while living under the same roof, which was why she could so easily believe that it was the reason for him moving out. It was much easier for her to think that he was being unfaithful to her than it was for her to look inside herself to discover that the real problems lay with her. If she had done self-examination from the onset, she probably would've come up with all the very legitimate reasons why he'd chosen to leave.

"If it's any comfort to you, Charles, I knew. Deep down in my heart I knew. But I needed an excuse to remain indignant and continue to be difficult, and also to stay in denial. Reality was unbelievably scary for me. I wish I could express to you how sorry I am for doubting you."

Charles brought Sinclair closer to him, hugging her gently. He then held her slightly away from him to look into her eyes. "You don't ever have to be afraid of anything. Fear is simply the absence of faith, my dear. Trusting God one hundred percent is a tall task, but that's the only pathway to peace." Charles then steered Sinclair into the dining room.

Fighting back her tears, Sinclair was deeply moved by the romantically set table: candlelight and long-stemmed red roses, no less; fine china, crystal, linen napkins, stainless silverware, and sparkling cider chilling in a silver-plated ice bucket. Charles had thought of everything. Not so unusual for him, though. Charles had always been a romantic a heart. Why he had stopped being so romantic with and attentive to her was no longer a mystery to Sinclair.

Sinclair was now aware that she had been unknowingly pushing Charles away for years. That had not been her desire or intent. Earning more and more money to keep poor Marcus enjoying a rich kid's lifestyle had caused her to work too much overtime, leaving Charles behind in the process. Her love for her son had stifled her ability to act reasonably and responsibly. Her desire to please Marcus had cost her dearly. Sinclair prayed that it hadn't cost her Charles too.

Sinclair had to smile inwardly, admitting to herself that things were looking somewhat brighter. At least she hoped so. If Charles were to give her another chance, nothing or no one would ever come between them again. That was an oath she planned to keep.

"The table is beautiful, Charles. As usual, you've done a remarkable job," Sinclair finally managed to say, her normally strong voice unusually shylike.

"Thanks, Sinclair. I haven't forgotten the things that bring you pleasure." Charles pulled out a chair for his wife. "Sit down and make yourself comfortable while I put the meal on the table. I hope you like what I cooked. I decided to try out a new recipe."

Sinclair started to ask if she could help out, but then she thought better of it. Charles obviously wanted to do this for her. It would be insensitive of her not to accept his graciousness with the same spirit in which he'd extended it. Her decision to stay put came with ease.

The second Charles left the room Sinclair started to worry

SACRED SONS

about why he'd really asked her there. Had she read too much into
the romantic setting? Was he trying to soften the blow of them discussing an amicable divorce settlement? Just because he wasn't involved with another woman didn't mean that he wanted to stay
married to her. He certainly had every reason in the book to want a
divorce. Sinclair could only pray that there'd not be a sudden death
experience.

*Was this visit a new beginning for their relationship or perhaps the
very ending?*

Charles came back into the room carrying what he considered his
masterpiece. Black beans and rice accompanied herb-crusted chicken,
a Cuban dish, served with a lemon caper sauce; garlic mashed potatoes;
and a crisp mixture of various zucchinis and squashes. Charles had
prepared everything he'd been served with the chicken at Bosa's
Restaurant in downtown Houston, Texas, while on a business trip.
Much to his surprise, when he'd asked how the mouthwatering dish
had been prepared, he was given all the details on how to cook it.

After placing all the food items on the table, Charles took a seat.
He then passed the blessing, thanking the good Lord for providing
the wonderful meal before them.

While picking up his fork, Charles looked over at Sinclair.
"Once we've had dinner and dessert, we really must get this divorce
thing settled between us, once and for all. It has been drawn out for
far too long, keeping us both from moving forward."

Sinclair's heart dropped to the floor. Her optimism was all but
shot. "Once and for all" had sounded quite ominous to her ears.
The "moving forward" part had her wondering if they were to do it
separately or together. Sinclair had no clue what would come
later—and she really wasn't too eager to find out. *How did Charles
expect her to enjoy the meal after hearing all that?*

Hannah looked up from the plate of snack foods she had in front of
her. Seeing her husband entering the kitchen doorway caused a

slight smile to part her lips. Since she hadn't yet had the opportunity to have a free-for-all with Derrick, smiling hadn't come easy for Hannah over the past few days. Derrick hadn't shown his face since the bedroom fiasco.

Leaning against the island counter, Robert intently eyed Hannah from across the room. "Why didn't you tell me, Hannah?"

Clueless, Hannah frowned. "Tell you what?"

"About finding Derrick in his bed in our house with a woman! How could you even try to keep something as serious as that from me? Have all your senses taken a leave of absence?"

While wishing the floor would open up and swallow her whole, Hannah racked her brain trying to figure out how Robert had found out. She never dreamed that her husband would find out about Derrick's most disrespectful escapade. How he'd found out was a mystery, since she couldn't imagine Derrick telling his father, not unless he'd lost his mind. Although she had planned to tell Robert everything, Hannah had been waiting until after she'd had the chance to confront Derrick. The fact that he hadn't yet come back to the house let her know that their son still hadn't learned to take responsibility for his actions.

The only people she'd told about the incident were her parents. Surely they hadn't given her secret away. When she'd gone to visit Ruth and Edgar at their apartment complex, Ruth had right away tuned into her daughter's troubled state of being. Edgar had also felt the tension in Hannah, but he hadn't commented until after his wife had found out from their daughter what was going on. With much prompting from her mother, Hannah had shared her grief with them.

That her unreasonably strict father had told Hannah she should've kicked Derrick out before her next heartbeat wasn't so surprising to her. She then began to wonder if Edgar may've called Robert and told him what had occurred. She wouldn't put it past Edgar Burrell, since her father had been a no-nonsense parent. Although her brother, Harold, had been deceased for a long time,

Hannah still had a tendency to cringe from the harsh way Edgar had dealt with him.

"You look mighty pale over there, girl," Robert taunted. "Once you recover from your obvious state of shock, I'd like you to answer my question."

Hannah took in several deep breaths. "You already know the answer, Robert. And I already knew exactly what your reaction would be to the situation when I did get around to telling you; Derrick would've been thrown right out on the street, pronto."

"Deservedly so! Don't you get it Hannah? Derrick has gone too far this time. And you can believe it or not, but I don't believe for one second that this was his first offense of that nature. It was just the first time he'd gotten caught. While you and I were out working our butts off, he was laying up in bed with a woman, when he should've been out looking for a job."

"I know, Robert. I know what you're saying."

"Then why does it seem to me that you're minimizing the severity of his actions? If that weren't the case, he'd already be long gone from here. Since all his things are still here, I don't have to guess at your decision. By the way, you still haven't told me why you kept this from me. And while you're at it, can you please tell me how you rationalized this one out?"

"I *was* going to tell you, Robert, though I'm sure you don't believe that. . . ."

"What were you waiting on, Hannah, for Christmas to come around?"

"If you'll just let me finish a sentence, maybe I can tell you."

Robert crossed the room, pulled out a chair from the table, and sat down. "I'm all ears, Hannah. I promise not to interrupt you again."

Although she didn't think her explanation of why she hadn't thrown Derrick out yet would go over very well with Robert, Hannah knew that she had no choice but to make a valiant attempt at trying to get him to see her point of view. After a moment of silent prayer, Hannah began to tell Robert why she'd handled things the way she had. Remembering her promise to tell her husband everything, Hannah held nothing back, though it hurt her heart even more.

Hannah's fast-rolling tears caused Robert to forget about all the unpleasant laws he'd intended to lay down to his wife in no uncertain terms. He could clearly see that she was already weighed down with one burden too many. It wasn't in his nature to add to his wife's grief.

Robert knew for a fact that Derrick had no idea what he'd done to his mother's heart. He had practically destroyed the spirit of the one person who'd always been his best friend, the only one who'd never failed to come to his defense. Yet, with this latest infraction, he'd treated his mother no better than he had the shady kind of women he often got himself involved with.

Hannah sniffled, wiping her nose on the napkin Robert had handed her. "I know I should've told you all this from the very beginning, but I wanted to handle Derrick first. Please believe me when I say I had every intention of telling you. I won't lie. I did think of not telling you, but I finally decided that this wasn't something I could easily get around. I've come to my senses where Derrick is concerned. I hold myself totally responsible for the way he disrespects our home and me, simply because I've taught him that's it okay to do so. Whatever you decide to do about Derrick is okay with me. I won't interfere."

Chuckling, though this was far from a laughing matter, Robert raised an eyebrow. "What I decide to do? Oh, no, not this time, lady! You, Hannah, should be the one to decide the outcome for Derrick's actions. You already know what I'd do, so you don't have to ask me that."

Hannah rolled her eyes. "I know I already said that, so why are you harping on it?"

"Because you've always made me the heavy by demanding that I mete out the punishment phase for his mistakes. You never wanted to be the one to come down on him, so you're always willing to let me play the bad guy so he won't hold you responsible. God forbid that you should find disfavor with your precious son."

"That's not true, Robert. And you don't have to resort to sarcasm."

"Yes it is true, Hannah. Then, after I make a decision on his punishment, you turn right around and tell me I was too hard on him. You can't have it both ways, sweetheart. You saw what happened in that bedroom, not me. So you need to be the one to decide what to do about it. This is one time that you need to stand up and be counted present on the parenting roster. If you let Derrick off, you can't ever expect him to do anything but disrespect you in the future. Respect is something you have to demand, Hannah. People don't just hand out reverence."

Agitated by Robert's unreasonable stance, Hannah knuckled her left eye nervously. "Okay, so I know what I have to do. It's clear to me. Derrick hasn't come back here since the incident, so can you tell me how I'm supposed to go about making things clear to him?"

"You can start by changing the locks. I'm sure he's waiting until we go back to work to show up here, even if he's only coming back for his belongings. If he can't get inside, the message will come through loud and clear. That is, if your intent is to boot him out of here. For good! Is that what you plan to do, Hannah?"

Hannah huffed out a stream of uneven breath. "I don't know what I plan to do, Robert, but you'll be the first to hear. Now that we have that out of the way, how did you find out about this little incident in the first place?"

"Little incident? That tells me a lot about where your head is, Hannah."

Hannah sucked her teeth. "That was just a figure of speech. I definitely know how enormous this problem is—and I don't intend to downplay it one bit."

"Good! As for how I found out, a little birdie dropped down from the sky and whispered into my ear all the details. In other words, I won't betray a confidence." Hannah would find out soon enough how he'd heard about everything, but his wife wouldn't hear it from him. Robert had given his word on that; his word was his bond.

Seated in her living room with Jamaica and Anna, having consumed an evening repast of coffee and cake, Tara had just finished listening to her father's account of his visit with Timothy. So far it sounded as if it hadn't gone over very well. Tara was disappointed in that.

Jamaica frowned slightly. "I don't know what else I can tell you, Tara. I wish I had much better news to share. Our visit was very strained. I don't think I expected it to be any different, but I had hoped for a better outcome. The fact that Tim agreed to let me come back to see him allows me to stay optimistic. This is all going to take time, Tara."

"That's what I'm worried about, Daddy. As ill as Tim is, I don't know how much time we may have left to make all the amends."

"As much time as God grants us, sweetie. You and I have no say over life and death."

Tara sighed hard. "Did you talk to him about wanting to see if you were a donor match?"

"I thought I should wait on that. I have prayed about it, so I'll just have to be patient and wait on the answer. Once I talk to Tim's doctors, I'll know what I need to do. I don't need his permission to be tested. I know at least that much. So I plan to do that as soon as we can get it scheduled. Can you help out with getting the process started, Tara?"

"I'll check on the procedures as soon as I get in to work tomorrow. Then I'll try to schedule us some time with his doctor. Since Tim has given him permission to talk with me about his health concerns, that shouldn't pose a problem."

Anna reached up and ran nimble fingers through Jamaica's wavy gray hair. "You look tired, dear heart, as tired as I feel. Perhaps we should go to bed now. It's already after nine o'clock here. That means it's three hours later on the East Coast. We've been up a long time."

Tara smiled at Anna, deeply moved by her loving attentiveness to her father. "Ms. Anna is right, Daddy. We don't need you getting sick on us. You're going to need all your strength to get through this ordeal with Tim. I'm sure that you haven't forgotten that we're going to have Essence for a couple of hours tomorrow. You'll definitely want to save up lots of energy for your first meeting with your granddaughter. As active as she is, she'll be all over the place."

Jamaica grinned. "Essence! Oh, my, yes. What a grand time that will be for this old man. I know when I'm in a no-win situation, so I'll let you two ladies have your way with me on this one. Anna, since Tara and I have decided that you're going to sleep in the guest room, I need you to help me get this sofa bed ready, if you don't mind. Where do you keep the linens, Tara?"

Tara got to her feet. "I'm sleeping on the sofa bed, Daddy. You're going to take my room. And don't try to change my mind. It's not going to work. Both beds are freshly made up. All you have to do is climb right in. Come on. Let me get you two settled in for the night."

After tending to the needs of her guests, Tara returned to the living room, where she picked up the phone to call Simone, hoping they could get a conference call going with the rest of the crew. Everyone had been so busy with personal issues lately. The entire group hadn't been together all at one time in a couple of weeks. It seemed like their coffee break and lunchtime meetings were suddenly a thing of the past. Tara missed their frequent get-togethers.

Upon hearing Simone's voice come over the line, Tara could tell that her friend had been asleep. "Sorry for waking you up, girl. I didn't think you'd be asleep so early, since you're somewhat of a night owl. I was hoping we could do a conference call, but I'll let you get back to sleep. Hopefully we can talk tomorrow."

"No, no, Tara, we can talk now. It's been a while for us. I talked to Sinclair a couple of mornings ago, but I haven't spoken with Glenda and Hannah for a few days. Hold on while I try to get the others on the line. I'm sure we all have a lot of juicy stuff to discuss. I know I do."

It had only taken Simone a couple of minutes to see that all the connections were made. Everyone voiced cheerful greetings to each other, finding out how the others were doing. Simone was normally the moderator of the conversations since she was the one who always began the hookup for the calls. It was hard to make sense of things when they all started talking at once, so Simone's job was to keep everyone in check. The role of moderator changed from time to time.

"Who wants to go first?" Simone asked.

"Why don't you start us out, Simone?" Tara suggested.

"That's fine by me," Simone responded. "I have so much stuff to get off my chest, but I'll get to the main event first. Booker is still in love with me, that is, according to him." Simone had to move the phone away from her ear to keep from going deaf. The loudly screeching sounds coming out her friends' mouths could easily cause eardrums to burst. "Okay, ladies, you're killing my delicate ears," Simone joked, laughing softly.

"Sorry," Hannah said, "but you can't drop something like that on us and then not expect us to react like certified nut cases. How did you learn that about Booker?"

"How else? He told me," Simone remarked rather smugly.

"We figured that much, Simone," Glenda commented, "but we want to hear all the details. Where, when, and how did this all come about?"

Simone shared the entire scenario that had occurred in her living room, while her friends listened intently. "Tyrell's hoping that we'd get back together was a real shocker for me. Booker had the nerve to ask me if I was no longer in love with him. I thought I was going to faint. Can you all even begin to imagine him asking me that after all this time?"

"Yeah, I can imagine it," Tara chimed in. "Sounds like he's still in love with you, just as he's already confessed. I know for a fact that my father still loves my mother. He had to move on, but that didn't stop the love from flowing inside. He left his wife just like Booker did you."

"True enough, Tara, but the circumstances were certainly different," Hannah responded. "Your father left because he didn't think he had a choice. Booker walked out because he wanted to be free to drive around in the fast lane in a speeding car. It's a wonder he didn't kill himself."

"Okay, girlfriends, your points have been made. But all that isn't nearly as important as what Simone is going to do about it," Glenda remarked. "So, Simone, are you seriously thinking of getting back with Booker?"

Simone sighed hard. "Not even! It's over for us, has been over for the longest. This old girl is not walking that same path of destruction ever again. We're supposed to learn from our mistakes, not keep repeating the same old ones. I've certainly learned my lesson where Booker is concerned. Now that my issues are out on the table who is up next?"

Glenda giggled into the phone, causing everyone's ears to perk up. "Well, girlfriends, you'd better strap yourselves in your seats for this one. Taylor asked me to marry him."

The other women moaned and groaned simultaneously.

"That's recycled news, Glenda. He's only asked you four or five times already! What's so different about this time?" Simone queried.

"This time I'm seriously considering his proposal." Glenda waited for the screaming to die down. "What's so different about this time is he asked me in front of Tony. What do you all think about that?"

"Wow," Hannah said, "this is unbelievable. Since Tony and Taylor are just starting to get to know each other, how's Tony responding to the proposal?"

"He says he's all for it. Tony and Taylor have been seeing a lot of each other lately. I've never seen Tony take to anyone like he's taken to Taylor over the last few weeks. They're doing lots of guy things together, and Tony absolutely loves it. I'm amazed at Tony's positive attitude about everything these days. He's trying very hard to turn his life around. I thank God for that. Taylor has worked very hard in trying to get through to Tony, so I also have him to thank. He's been successful where I've failed. He has also earned Tony's respect. They really get along."

"Okay, so we now know what Tony's response is, but we haven't heard yours," Tara mentioned. "Are you going to marry Taylor, Glenda?"

Glenda giggled again. "I haven't decided yet. Taylor was hurt when I couldn't give him an answer right then, but he understands me better than I understand myself. Tony seemed very disappointed, too. I first had to have a one-on-one talk with my son about some of his unresolved issues, mainly those to do with his father. I told Tony that his father hadn't been intimate that night with the prostitute. He was as relieved by it as I was. Knowing I couldn't move on until I found out the truth about Antoine, I finally sought out the information from the autopsy report. Now that I've put all that behind me, I'm feeling really good about my relationship with Taylor. Unlike before, marriage is now a real possibility for us. We'll have to wait and see. I want to give Tony and Taylor more time. In case you're all wondering, I do love Taylor, very much."

The other women were astonished by Glenda's news about her deceased husband, but everyone was glad that she'd resolved the major issues that had kept her from moving on.

"All I'm going to say to that, Glenda, is don't make Taylor wait too long," Sinclair offered. "He's not going to wait forever. To add even more excitement and drama to this conversation, Charles had me over to the town house for dinner. You all should've seen the romantic setting he'd created, the whole nine yards. It was almost like old times, but throughout the evening I was ever mindful that it wasn't. The food was great and so was the conversation. That is, until we got into the subject of the divorce. Things kind of went downhill from there."

"How so?" Simone inquired, sounding worried.

"Well, when I told Charles that I wanted us to work things out, that I didn't want the divorce, he didn't seem too thrilled about it. He thinks we have a lot of heavy stuff to get through before we can even discuss resuming our marriage. I was terribly hurt, so of course I sort of clammed up after that. All I wanted to do was get home and cry my eyes out. I set myself up by thinking the romantic ambience meant more than it did. However, I did learn that Charles isn't involved with another woman. He made that very clear to me. And I do believe him."

"That's great news," Simone said on a sigh of relief. "At least you don't have to be crazy over that anymore. But I wouldn't give up on Charles if I were you. These things can take lots of time to work out. It doesn't sound to me like he's totally opposed to getting back together. I think he just wants certain things resolved before he considers it."

"You may be right. I'll keep that in mind, Simone. Hannah, we haven't heard from you yet, so what's going on in your neck of the woods?" Sinclair asked, eager to have the attention turned on someone else.

Wishing the line would suddenly go dead, Hannah swallowed hard. "For once, I have nothing to report. All is well with me," she lied with deep regret, hating herself for doing so.

Hannah just couldn't bring herself to tell her friends how Derrick had disrespected her and their home. She was thoroughly embarrassed and ashamed by what had occurred, which made it very difficult for her to share any of the details. Perhaps she could enlighten her friends once the agony of defeat had been lifted from her shoulders. Her pain was still incredibly fresh.

Even talking about it with her parents and then later with Robert hadn't eased the gut-wrenching sorrow. The fact that she still didn't know how Robert had found out was also burdensome. That perhaps someone other than a family member knew about this awful situation was making her crazy. The only other person who knew what had happened was Derrick's partner in crime, the young woman he got caught with. Since she hadn't gotten a really good look at her, Hannah was worried that the woman might be from a family within her own social circle or even from their neighborhood. How embarrassing that would be also plagued Hannah.

Hannah wasn't so sure that the pain would ever go away. Until she had that spirited talk with Derrick, she was in the same boat as Glenda. Committing to anything would be hard for her. Going to work was even a struggle for her despite the fact she loved her job. Her life would remain in a holding pattern until she finally had the opportunity to confront Derrick.

An unexpected knock at her door caused Tara to bow out of the conference call, but with the promise of reconnecting with her friends by phone the next day. They hadn't gotten around to any of her issues, though she was the one who'd had Simone initiate the call.

No one knew about her niece, Essence, or the little girl's mother, Carolyn. Tara had been hoping to tell her friends all about them, also that her father had made it in safely, and that she highly approved of Anna Clay, the only good news she had to report on. Nothing had really changed with Timothy since the last time she'd talked with her friends, except for his visit from their father. Since she hadn't spoken to Raymond in several days, there was nothing new to report on about him and her. That was just as well, as far as she was concerned. He could forever keep his tail high upon his shoulders for all she cared.

Tara was upset that Raymond hadn't even bothered to thank her for watching over Maya until several days later. When Raymond finally did call, Tara had made it quite clear to him that she had no plans of becoming a regular baby-sitter to his teenage daughter, and that he should start working on a permanent backup plan.

Before slamming the phone down in her ear, Raymond had called Tara insensitive and incredibly selfish. Those had been the very last words spoken between them. The biting sting of them was still felt by Tara.

By the time Tara reached the door, the knocks had become almost insistent, making Tara wonder why the visitor hadn't rung the doorbell, which would surely be heard. A quick peek out the security window had her in shock. Tara had no idea why Maya was standing at her door at this hour of the night, especially when she should be at home in bed asleep.

Tara rapidly removed the locks, coming face-to-face with Maya in the next instant. "Hey, what's up?" Tara said softly, taking note of the tears running down Maya's cheeks. This certainly wasn't a time for censure, Tara mused, not if she hoped to find out what was going on with Raymond's daughter. "Come on in, Maya."

Maya threw her arms around Tara's waist, surprising the heck out of her. Tara could feel the force of Maya's sobs, which had the young girl's body convulsing. Feeling sorry for the teenager, Tara led her into the living room, where they had a seat on the sofa. Tara had made sure they were seated very close to each other so Maya could feel her warm spirit.

Tara briefly squeezed Maya's fingers. "What's going on, young lady? That you're in distress is obvious. What has you so upset?"

Tara listened intently to Maya's story, still totally surprised that she'd come to her with whatever troubled her. The deep anguish on the teenager's face concerned Tara, but she decided to wait until Maya finished talking before making any comments. It didn't surprise Tara that her heart would go out to Maya. Despite Maya's nasty attitude toward her, Tara hadn't harbored any grudges against her, even though she had to remind herself constantly that Maya was a child.

The story Maya was telling Tara was not that unusual of an occurrence, especially for this generation of teenagers. In fact, this sort of horrific thing happened all the time to girls around Maya's age. Being a teenager was the most difficult period in a person's life. With all the physical changes to endure, Tara believed the teen years were even more difficult for females.

Maya began to cry even harder as she came upon the end of her story. Tara pulled Maya's head to her chest to let her cry herself out. A few moments of silence would do them both some good. It would also give Tara time to collect her turbulent thoughts. Doling out the proper advice was crucial in this instance. Although Tara wasn't a mother, she was a female. That alone allowed her to relate very well to this situation.

Tara lifted Maya's head from her chest and made direct eye contact with her. "How long have you known this boy, Maya?"

Maya sniffled, her eyes refilling with fresh tears. "I met him when I first moved in with my dad. He also goes to the same school as me."

Tara reached up and gently brushed Maya's tears away with her fingers. "What led up to the events you just told me about?"

Maya's hands began to tremble slightly. "I let him come over to the house when Daddy wasn't home. I know it was wrong, but I trusted Rashad. He seemed like a nice person."

Tara massaged the back of Maya's right hand. "Did he know you weren't supposed to have company when your dad was away?"

"Yeah, I told him. Rashad said no one would ever know," Maya sobbed brokenly.

"Since you mentioned that this was the first time Raymond trusted you to be alone in the house, how do you think he's going to take this?"

It suddenly dawned on Tara that Raymond probably didn't even know where Maya was at this hour of the night. She had to call him and let him know his daughter was safe with her, but she first had to make sure he didn't know. "Does your father know where you are, Maya?"

Maya shook her head in the negative. "I left out and came here after he went to bed. I couldn't stop thinking about what had happened earlier in the day. I was so scared."

Disturbed by the truth, Tara closed her eyes for a brief moment. "You know we have to call him, don't you, Maya? If he wakes up and finds you gone, he's going to call the police before he does anything else. I don't think you want that to happen."

"Miss Tara, please don't tell my dad about this. He will kill me. I don't want him to know. He'll be so mad at me."

"And he should be mad, Maya. He trusted you, and it seems to me that you put your trust in Rashad, who obviously didn't deserve it. I doubt that your dad will kill you. At any rate, it's not my place to tell Raymond about this. But I think *you* should tell him right away. Before we resume this conversation, I need to call your father and at least let him know you're safe. Okay?"

Maya nodded, though she didn't look as if she liked the idea. Fear was written all over her face. She was terrified that her father would hate her once he learned what had occurred. Maya's tears continued to fall as she listened to Tara tell her father where she was. Hearing Tara tell him that his daughter would explain things to him herself and that Maya could spend the night with her brought Maya very little relief. Facing her dad with the truth had her scared stiff.

Tara cradled the phone and then turned back to face Maya. "Listen, Maya, if you want to earn back your father's trust, you have to tell him what happened. He's going to be upset. Make no mistake about that. But his love for you will win out in the end."

"I don't know about that, Miss Tara. My dad didn't want to leave me alone and I convinced him he could trust me. I told him that I knew how to be responsible."

Tara shook her head. "I don't even know that it was about trust. Being a paramedic and all, Raymond knows the accidents and dangers that could befall you, Maya. He wasn't being mean, just a concerned parent. If anything happened to you while he wasn't at home—and something *did* occur—he could be held liable in a court of law. Leaving a minor home unattended is a crime. Parents go to jail all the time for child endangerment. Are you feeling me?"

Maya nodded. "I see what you mean. But I didn't think anything like that would happen."

"Young people never do. Rarely does anyone think of what might happen when getting involved in something they shouldn't. Maya, these sorts of things happen. You're not the first young girl to get caught up in something like this—and you won't be the last. Still, that doesn't relieve you of your responsibility in this situation. You did the right thing by telling your friend that you aren't ready to have sex. And sex is all it would've been."

Maya looked perplexed. "What does that mean, Miss Tara?"

Tara took a deep breath. Getting into the birds and the bees with someone else's child wasn't something she would've ever expected to occur, but that it was so necessary in this case wasn't lost on her. This young girl needed immediate guidance. This wasn't something that should wait until she was back home with her father.

"Sex is a physical act between consenting adults, often an unemotional one. Making love is a wonderful experience shared by a couple who are emotionally involved with one another and care deeply about each other. Sex is instant gratification, nothing more nor less. Lovemaking goes much deeper than just arriving at instantaneous physical pleasures."

"Are you and Daddy emotionally involved?"

Tara chuckled. "Yes, we are, but I don't think that's what you're really asking. However, that's the only answer you're going to get on that matter." Maya's giggling put Tara at ease.

"You read that one pretty good, Miss Tara. How come you're so smart about kids when you don't have any?"

"Because I was one, once upon a blue moon. Even if it was a long time ago, I was also a child. Hard to believe, huh?" Tara laughed along with Maya. "I still remember the days of my youth, vividly. Boys were after me to give in, too, Maya. None of them seemed worthy enough for me to share my intimate treasures with. When a young man or woman decides to give himself or herself to another, the consequences of his or her actions should always be considered first. Although it happens quite often, sexual intercourse before marriage isn't in the best interest of either party. It rarely creates a haven of security, since it often has the opposite effect."

"How's that?" Maya asked, looking quite curious.

Tara had hoped she wouldn't have to go any further into her explanation, but since she'd already opened up the can of worms, it would be hard to put the lid back on. "For whatever reason, a lot of males and females don't value the relationship after sex occurs. Many of them seem to lose respect for their mates shortly after. But that's not always the case. It's risky business either way you look at it. If we respect ourselves, other people won't have any choice but to do the same. Respect is something you must have for yourself and demand from others."

"Why do boys lie? Why did Rashad say he had sex with me when he didn't? His friends think I'm easy now. I'm the butt of every joke at school. It's awful." Maya began to sob again.

Tara brought Maya into her arms, massaging her back in a circular motion. "Maya, if I thought crying was going to help you, other than as a cleansing of the soul, I'd tell you to cry yourself a river. If you have to shed tears, do it for yourself. Never cry over the people who've disrespected you. They're not worth your tears or the tissue you wipe them on, honey. Do not shed a single tear over Rashad. You did the right thing and you should be proud of that. You could've given in to him and then later suffered the consequences for the rest of your life."

"Could you explain that?" Maya asked, on a broken sob.

Tara sighed deeply. "Maya, it's as simple as one, two, three. Babies are not wrapped up in little colored blankets and then delivered to mothers by storks wearing granny glasses and top hats. Two people having sex or making love is the only way a child can be conceived, other than these new methods of artificial insemination and such. No sex, no babies. No sex, no sexually transmitted diseases. Abstinence, abstinence, abstinence is the only surefire method of all the so-called preventative measures."

Oh, God, Raymond may become even angrier with me for saying all that, Tara mused, especially if he thinks he should've been the one to tell Maya everything. Since Maya needed to hear these things right now, Tara instantly dismissed these concerns from her mind. Tara then prayed that Maya wouldn't dare to ask her about how the Virgin Mary had conceived.

Tara stroked Maya's arm. "Have I made things clear for you, honey?"

Maya shook her head up and down. "Yeah, a lot. I guess if my mother had lived we would've one day gotten around to talking about this kind of stuff. I can't go to my Aunt Susan with anything 'cause she'll freak out on me. I'm glad I came here, Miss Tara. I feel much better after hearing what you had to say. As for my dad, do you really think I should tell him about this incident? He's going to hit the ceiling!"

Tara gave Maya a tender hug. "That has to be your decision. Since you're here in the middle of the night, he's going to want to know why. So then you'll be faced with telling him the truth or lying to him and make things even worse for yourself. If I were the one faced with this, I'd talk to my dad. He might get angry and upset with me for disobeying him and making irresponsible choices, but he wouldn't stop loving me because of it. Your dad won't either."

Maya looked skeptical. "I wish I could be sure about that. I've been a witch ever since I came to live with Daddy. He hasn't been too happy with me lately. He really got upset with me the night I stayed with you. I didn't want to come and I really acted ugly about it. I said some awful things about him and about you. I was wrong about everything, Miss Tara. You helped me to see that. But I don't know how to fix it. Can you tell me how I can make it up to my dad?"

Of course Tara wanted to know what Maya had said about her. It was human nature, but she didn't dare ask. A change of climate had already occurred and she didn't want to jolt the thermometer a fraction of an inch in the other direction. Things were not as chilly as they'd once been, but neither were they as warm as she had hoped for in the very beginning. Perhaps trust would come with time. Tara was all for that. Maya had just put herself on the line, had opened up and exposed herself to someone she'd shown nothing less than pure disdain toward. Tara wasn't going to risk tampering with the onset of what could very well be the healing process.

"I wish I could tell you exactly how to go about making things right with him, Maya, but I can't. But I think if your dad sees a drastic change for the better in your behavior, that may be a strong indication of your regret. Raymond Wilkerson loves you with everything in him, Maya. There's nothing you can ever do to change that. Children often have it like that with their parents."

Maya lowered her head. "I might've done it already. The names I called you and the stuff I said about you being a gold digger and all had Daddy ready to knock my head off. He's never raised a hand to me before. Although he just barely stopped short of hitting me, I knew he wanted to slap me onto another planet. The hurt I saw in his eyes made me feel terrible, but it also made me feel powerful."

Tara raised an eyebrow, puzzled by Maya's last comment. "How so?"

Maya shrugged. "I felt in control of his emotions. I saw how I'd cut him down without much effort. But the rush it gave me only lasted a few hot seconds. He barely spoke to me the rest of the week. In a way, that also showed that he'd given up his power to me. It was like I had control over his actions by acting out mine in a bad way. I had gotten his undivided attention."

Tara was absolutely amazed by Maya's very adult-like analogy. Wisdom only came with age. *Didn't it?* How had someone so young figured out all that she had thus far? Tara then realized that she'd also learned about controlling others at an early age. Her brother had worked the art of control down to a fine science. Controlling Joanna had become second nature to Timothy.

Tara thought carefully about how she should respond to Maya. Impact was warranted. Maya shouldn't be thinking like she was. It was dangerous. "Maya, trying to control others isn't a good thing to get hung up on. Controlling oneself is all the power needed. If we can't rule over ourselves, we certainly can't dictate to another. People, places, and things aren't to be controlled by anyone. Lording over someone else's emotions is another no-no. Inflicting pain on other people for self-gratification is plain wrong. Your dad doesn't deserve to be hurt by you. You might want to think about what I've said the next time you feel this euphoric rush of power."

Maya looked thoroughly ashamed of herself. "I know, huh? I got a lot of stuff going on right now, things that I just can't talk about with my dad. Because I don't trust many people, I don't know where to go for help. I feel lost at times."

"I think you did know where you could get help, Maya. That's why you're here. Isn't it?"

Maya scratched her head. "I guess so. It took me a long time to make up my mind to come here since I've been so mean to you. But then I remembered how you didn't react with anger to the things I said and did. That made me feel it was okay to come to you."

Tara smiled with empathy. "I'm glad you did, Maya. Now let's get you ready for bed. You'll have to share the office sofa bed with me or sleep on this couch. Your choice."

Maya giggled. "I think I'd like to sleep with you. Maybe that'll bring me some comfort. Is that okay with you?"

"You bet. And just so you'll know for sure, you can always come to me. I'll be here for you. I'd like us to be friends."

"Thanks, Miss Tara. I'll remember all that. I really like the idea of us being friends."

* * *

As she turned off the office light and settled down into bed, Tara wanted to weep with joy. Realizing that she'd been a little selfish where Maya was concerned caused her to think about what she could've done differently in her dealings with Raymond and Maya.

Tara hadn't given much thought to what she would've done if the shoe had been on the other foot, not until recently, and only after her girlfriends had mentioned it. Thinking about her having a child instead of Raymond had given her a brand-new perspective on things. There was no doubt that she'd want Raymond to accept her child under the same set of circumstances. Perhaps it was time for her to reassess her role in both Raymond's and Maya's lives.

Doing unto others as you'd have them do unto you was the right approach to everything, Tara surmised, happy to be on the right road to resolving yet another serious issue. Although she knew the uphill climb for her and Maya was still going to be hard, Tara was now determined for them to reach the mountaintop together. Whether or not Raymond would join them at the top was another issue that had to be decided.

Chapter Twelve

Sighing heavily, Sinclair rested her back against the living room sofa, praying that her family would get through this awkward session of truth or consequences. She then glanced over at Charles, who was seated in the chair next to the one Marcus had parked himself in.

Marcus looked as if this was the last place he wanted to be, since he already knew this get-together was all about him from past conversations he'd had with his mother. She had called to order this family meeting within an hour of his homecoming. He suspected that it had been set up even before he'd gotten there. His father had shown up shortly after Marcus had arrived.

Sinclair made direct eye contact with Marcus. "You couldn't have come to me and told me that you wanted to become a rapper?"

Marcus scratched his head, looking for the right words to convey his feelings. "No, I couldn't, Mom. I already knew what you would say and I knew how foolish you'd make me feel. You hate rap. You're always telling me to turn that crazy noise off, that it's disgusting."

"I don't hate all rap, Marcus, but there's some of it that's just downright vulgar. Regardless of what you thought I might say, you should've told me the truth. Those innumerable recording studio charges aren't in my imagination, you know. Not to mention all the other music stuff you charged on my accounts. Those humongous bills are very real. And guess who has to pay them? You were using my money and lying to me about it at the same time."

"Our money," Charles remarked, looking Sinclair dead in the eye. Charles then turned his attention on Marcus. "Son, if entertainment was the avenue you wanted to pursue, your mother's right; you should've let us in on it. A lot of money has been totally wasted, needlessly. We wanted you to have a great education, but this is about your life, not ours. We may not have understood your aspirations, but it was still your obligation to enlighten us. When I think of how much money has been spent on your schooling, I have to shudder."

Marcus looked so unhappy, wondering if his parents would ever understand his desire to perform on stage. It was all he'd ever dreamed of doing. "I know I didn't go about it the right way, but I can't change that now. The mistakes have been made and I can't undo them. But, Mom, you never said anything about all the bills until recently. If it was bothering you so much, why didn't you tell me? You could've taken me off your accounts at any time. I'm not trying to be disrespectful here, but I didn't think you cared about what I was spending since you never said anything. The charges made on the cards are all itemized. I admit that I expected you to say something about the large bills, but when you never did, I assumed it was okay."

Sinclair looked as if she'd been shot right through the heart with a bow and arrow—and the arrow didn't belong to Cupid. Although Marcus hadn't written down in black and white his line of defense against the crimes he was accused of, his remarks had come through quite boldly. At that moment Sinclair knew she was guilty of being Marcus's coconspirator. Unlike the financial secrets she'd kept from Charles, secrets that had them on the verge of divorce, Marcus's out-of-control spending sprees had been presented to her every single month.

While Charles had also had the opportunity to check out the monthly statements, it was agreed upon between them that Sinclair would take care of paying all the bills and he'd provide the money for her to do so. Sinclair couldn't argue with the fact that she'd been in complete control of all the finances but had failed to exercise her authority as the family's financial officer.

"Dad, I don't want you to think you and Mom have wasted money on my education. That's just not true. My grades may not be the best, but I've retained everything I've been taught. If I'm going to be in the unpredictable world of entertainment, my business education can take me a long way. I don't want to be just a run-of-the-mill rapper. I need to do more than record in the studio and perform live. I have to learn every aspect of the business so that I can eventually manage and produce other artists. My main goal is one day to have my very own record label."

Marcus reached into a saddleback-style briefcase and pulled out a bunch of papers. He then handed the documents to Charles. "Maybe this will help me get out of hot water with you guys. Please read these over, Dad. Not only do I need your opinion; I value it."

Charles looked closely at the papers. Although he wasn't a contract lawyer, he could read numbers very well, especially a lot of zeros. Charles recognized easily that what he held in his hands was a multimillion-dollar contract, one that had his son's name typed on it. Upon noticing that the contract wasn't signed, Charles looked up at his son. "Is this for real?"

Marcus grinned broadly. "As real as it can get. But it doesn't mean a thing if it's not signed. So, Dad, what do you think?"

Charles chuckled. "It's not what I think. What do you think?"

Marcus looked back and forth between his father and mother. "That I should sign it!"

"Sign what?" Sinclair couldn't help wondering what the devil was going on. She couldn't make hide nor hair out of what Marcus and Charles were talking about, which made her feel as if she'd been purposely left out of the loop.

Charles handed Sinclair the contract. "You have to read it for yourself to get the full benefit of what's happening here."

Looking totally bewildered, Sinclair took the papers from Charles and carefully read them over. Once she realized what the contracts meant and saw the dollar amounts, a heady rush of excitement welled up in her.

Her baby boy was going to be a millionaire. Imagine that!

Then Sinclair saw that the recording contract hadn't been signed. Now she fully understood the strange conversation between father and son. This was so hard to believe, but the evidence was right in front of her in black and white. Still, she wondered if her eyes were deceiving her. Marcus Albright, their only child, had landed a multimillion-dollar recording contract with a major record label. *Was this even possible?*

"Mom," Marcus softly called out to her, "aren't you going to say something?"

Finding it difficult to speak, Sinclair merely nodded. Her marriage was on the rocks over all the financial aid she'd given to her son, and now Marcus would have more money then he'd ever know what to do with. A few strokes of the computer keys had Marcus making on paper more money than what his parents had made in their lifetime.

As she thought about it, Sinclair saw that she couldn't excuse what Marcus had done to her finances, though she realized she'd made it all possible by giving him carte blanche with her credit cards. Regardless of the role she played in the situation, he had to be held accountable for all his deceptions and undercover dealings. A rapper, no less . . .

But how in the world did a parent hold a millionaire son accountable for anything?

"Mom and Dad, if I sign this contract, I can pay you back every dime I took under misrepresentation, and then some. This is my dream come true, guys. Recording and being on stage is what I want to do, what I've lived for. Can you please support me in this?"

Sinclair's first thought was to stonewall this momentous occasion. It was one thing to have money. Being responsible with it was another. She could only pray that Marcus had learned something of value from her irresponsible mistakes in money management. A second thought to ruining the moment had her completely discarding the foolish idea.

Marcus making something worthwhile of himself is what Sinclair had always wanted for him. Achieving great success in life had been her loftiest dream for her son. How could she even think of blowing this incredible moment for him? She couldn't. At this point, Sinclair saw that making things difficult for Marcus would serve no earthly purpose. This was a time for the Albright family to join in a happy celebration.

Sinclair walked over to Marcus and gave him a big hug. "Congratulations, son! You can count on me to support you in all your career endeavors."

Charles embraced both Sinclair and Marcus. "Son, I'm proud of you. Following a dream can be hard work, and sticking to it against all odds can be even harder. You've done both—and it has paid off big time for you. Like your mother, I offer my full support. Congratulations!"

The celebration lasted only a few minutes before Marcus asked his parents to sit back down. He had some things he wanted to discuss with them and he needed their undivided attention. The state of their marriage was the headliner for his part in the little family discussion.

"Mom and Dad, I know I've made things rough for you two. No one had to tell me that a lot of your marital problems have to do with me. I've tried to take this burden on myself, but I can't. This problem belongs to the entire family. We've all made some serious mistakes."

Sinclair sharply raised an eyebrow. "Marcus, are you sure you want to go there?"

"Somebody has to. My biggest mistake was in taking advantage of all your goodness. I'm sorry for that. Although I understand why you did all of what you did for me, Mom, you have to recognize that I got away with it simply because you let me. And, Dad, I see that your biggest mistake was keeping quiet about all the things that have bothered you over the years. I heard a lot of the arguments between you two, especially over the past year. The majority of your disagreements were about me, as well as all the money Mom was handing out. I can now make that right by paying off all my debts to you, but can you two make things right with each other? What's going to happen to your marriage? Are you really going to let it end in divorce?"

Sinclair's and Charles's eyes locked questioningly. Neither of them seemed to have a clue how to answer their son's queries. Since Sinclair had made her position on the divorce issue clear to Charles, she thought he should be the one to answer them. Never for a moment had she conceded to the idea of their marriage ending. Being Charles's wife was what made life worth living.

Charles encompassed both Sinclair and Marcus in his troubled gaze. It bothered him that Marcus was taking responsibility for things that only he and Sinclair were responsible for. Charles could not allow Marcus to believe that this separation had happened because of him.

Charles briefly placed his hand on Marcus's shoulder. "Son, the first thing you need to do is unload the burdens you've placed on your shoulders. They're not yours to bear. Regardless of how many times you heard us arguing about you, our issues go much deeper than any of that. The reasons I left are between your mother and me. And it will be entirely up to us to work them out. You are not to blame for anything to do with us. Do you understand what I'm saying, son?"

Marcus shrugged. "Yeah, I guess."

"Either you do or you don't, son. Which is it?" Charles asked.

"I guess I don't, Dad. Not really. You and Mom have been married forever, so I don't see how you can let it end like this. I hate that you two are living in separate places. This whole divorce thing is tearing me apart inside. I'm having a hard time dealing with it."

Charles felt deep empathy for his son. He hated living apart from Sinclair as well. But there were a lot of things they had to work out. "Marcus, your mother doesn't want the divorce. She's already made that clear to me. If the truth be known, I don't want it either. However, until we can work out all our differences, we should continue to maintain separate residences."

Charles grew thoughtful for a moment, pondering his next remarks. He then looked up and smiled at Sinclair. "I think we should start dating and getting to know each other all over again. What do you say to that, Sinclair? Would you like to date this old man? I'm still very charming, you know. I'm also a great conversationalist and an incurable romantic."

Sinclair felt breathless. Dating? How intriguing, she mused. She'd agree to fly to the moon with Charles if it meant they could work on saving their marriage. Living without her husband had already more than proven his worth to her. No one had to tell her that he was worth his weight in gold. If she were granted a second chance, she'd make sure that he knew every single day how extremely important he was to her. Charles Albright was the only man for her.

Sinclair's bright smile lit up her entire face, while her eyelashes fluttered uncontrollably. "You want to take me out on a date? I am truly flattered, Mr. Albright. I can't think of anything I'd like better. Just give me a few days' notice. This girl needs plenty of time to make herself beautiful."

Charles cracked up. Sinclair had responded the very same way she had when he'd first let her know he was interested in taking her out on a date. She had flashed her big brown eyes at him and her eyelashes had been just a fluttering. On that very same day he'd lost himself in her melting-heart smile; the rest would become history. "If that's the case, Sinclair, then I'm going to give you my notice right now. Today is Tuesday, so it looks like Friday might work out for our first dinner date. Is Friday good for you? Say around seven o'clock?"

"Better than good. I'll be anxiously awaiting your arrival."

Marcus looked puzzled. "Are you two just kidding around or what? And today is not Tuesday. It just happens to be Thursday."

Laughing, Charles slapped his flattened palm onto Marcus's back. "You just heard what actually happened the first day Sinclair and I met at college. Our words were verbatim. I think we both know what day it is, son, but thanks for telling us, anyway. Sinclair, I know it's very short notice, but what about dinner and a movie tomorrow night?"

Sinclair laughed heartily, hopelessly enchanted by what was taking place between her and Charles. "I'm already as beautiful as I'm going to get, so I don't need as much time to get ready these days. So what's wrong with tonight, Mr. Albright?"

Charles smiled broadly. He was positively thrilled to see the old Sinclair busy working her indelible charm and fascinating wit on him. "Tonight it is! Seven o'clock will find me right on your doorstep, Mrs. Albright."

As he looked from his mother to his father, Marcus could hardly contain his joy. "Does this mean you two are going to try to work everything out?"

Charles hugged his son. "We're going to give it our very best shot, son. Is it okay for us to do that, Sinclair."

Tears sprang from Sinclair's eyes. "I can't think of anything I'd like better. Furthermore, I think our millionaire son should pick up the entire tab for our first dinner date."

Marcus grinned. "You got it like that, Mom and Dad. The evening is definitely on me!"

Hannah still found it hard to believe that Derrick was the one who'd actually told his father about the incident in his bedroom, even though she'd just heard it from his very own lips. She studied her son's expression, hating to see him looking so downtrodden. She was happy that he'd finally showed up at the house, wanting to talk things out, although several days had already passed by. Hannah would rather this conversation be just between her and Derrick, but she wouldn't think of asking Robert to leave the living room. She'd already excluded him from too many things that had to do with their son. As a part of her growth, she had made a vow to be up front with Robert on everything. He deserved from her one hundred percent loyalty.

Hannah looked over at Derrick, who was seated on the other end of the sofa from where she sat. Robert had made himself quite comfortable on the floor. "I'm surprised that you shared everything with your dad, but I'm also happy about it, Derrick. Do you realize what you did was plain wrong, not to mention how disrespectful it was to both your dad and me?"

Derrick nodded, sucking in a deep breath. "I do know, and I'm sorry. I don't know what I was thinking that day. It was a crazy one."

"Are you saying that that was the first time?" Hannah asked, hoping he wouldn't lie.

The look of shame on Derrick's face was genuine. "It was the first time that it went that far. I've had other women up in my room while you all were at work, but nothing like that ever happened. Things just got out of hand."

"Just! I'll say they did. I know you came here to resolve this one issue with us, but there are several other things I desperately need to say to you. If you're not willing to listen, we should end this now, Derrick. So what's it going to be?" Hannah asked.

"When I decided to come back here to face the music, I knew you'd have a lot to say, Mom. I want to get everything resolved between us, not just that one incident."

Hannah nodded, happy to have that much out of the way. "That's nice to know. But I have to tell you that you're not going to like any of what I have to say. Dad and I let you come back here out of the kindness of our hearts, repeatedly. The last thing we want to see is you living out on the streets, but you can't keep taking kindness for weakness. You have brought nothing to the table on any of the times you've returned to our home to live. You have kept your room filthy, and I can't even recall how many times I've picked up your dirty clothes off the floor since you've been home this time. You don't even bother to put your stuff in the hamper."

Robert cleared his throat. "Excuse me?"

Hannah turned her attention to her husband. "Yes, I've been cleaning his room on a daily basis, and I already know I've been picking up after a grown man. I'm also aware that I've done things for Derrick that I wouldn't even do for you. So is there anything else you want to know?"

Deciding to let Hannah go ahead and reveal all the things she obviously needed to get off her chest, Robert just shrugged. "I'm cool. You still have the floor, Mrs. Brentwood."

Hannah crossed her arms against her chest. "I guess I don't need to go into all this. Let me just cut to the chase. You have been a guest in our home, Derrick, but that has now changed. The last time I checked your name was not on the deed. You need your own place, your own space, so you can make your own rules, since it's obvious that you can't live by ours. She's out there, and I hope you find your next conquest soon, that is, if you already haven't. You've been staying somewhere. In the meantime, you've got to leave from here. The temporary stay is over."

Derrick scowled. "Mom, did you really have to go there?"

Hannah shot Derrick a hard look. "Yes, Derrick, I did, and I need to go even further. You're too intelligent to be a kept man, but that's what you are. I can no longer stand by and watch you do nothing with your life. We can't do this chummy friend thing anymore. You've taken it too far and I'm guilty of letting you. You are a grown man and you need to start taking on all the responsibility for your actions. I know that I've raised you to be far too dependent on me, but you can consider the apron strings cut, as of right now. I've come to the conclusion that you and I can have a much better relationship if we're not living up under the same roof. With that said, your things are already packed away. You'll find all the boxes neatly stacked in one corner of the garage. I love you and wish you only the best."

Derrick looked at his mother in disbelief. "Just like that?"

Hannah snapped her fingers. "Just like that!"

Robert lifted himself from the floor. He then came and stood next to where Hannah was seated. "Your mother is right, Derrick. You've been given chance after chance to get it right, but I'm afraid you've run out of get-out-of-jail cards. Your game of monopoly is over."

Derrick looked like he was about to break down and cry. "Are you guys saying you don't love me? I've admitted to making mistakes, and I've apologized for them. It sounds like you're willing to just cut me out of your lives. I don't think that's fair."

Robert moved over in front of Derrick and knelt down before him. "This has nothing to do with us loving you, son, because we love you more than anything in this world. This is about us letting go. It's now up to you to stay afloat all on your own. If you really think about it, we can't do anything else for you. There's nothing else we can really teach you at this stage of your life. However, we'll always be here as advisers if you need us. Our door is always open to you as a guest, but no more overnighters or temporary stays."

Derrick shot a pleading look to his mother. "Mom! Are you going to help me out here? I don't have anywhere to stay right now."

It was all Hannah could do to keep from jumping up and bringing Derrick into her motherly embrace. Determined to stand her ground, she steeled herself against the pitiful look on Derrick's face. It would be so easy for her to give in yet again. Giving in to her son all the time hadn't helped him thus far, and it surely wouldn't help him if she were to prolong the agony for all of them. No more excuses could she make for him. Derrick simply had to stand up and become a man or eventually end up getting lost in the ever-shuffling world. One of Hannah's biggest regrets was that she hadn't come to this conclusion much sooner.

Hannah shook her head from side to side. "Derrick, I love you so much, but I just can't continue in this mode. I taught you these behaviors, but you're just going to have to unlearn them. I feel confident that you can do it, simply because you inherently know the difference between right and wrong. I've come to learn that loving someone doesn't mean you always have to give that person his or her way. Discipline is a strong form of love. I've failed in a lot of areas with you, but for me to continue to do so when I know better wouldn't be a very smart idea."

Robert pulled out his wallet and removed several twenty-dollar bills. "This will keep you in a motel for a few days. Call us and let us know where you are. We want to have a relationship with you, Derrick, a healthy one, and this time it has to be on our terms. I love you, son."

Derrick saw no use in further trying to solicit his mother's help. The determined set of her jaw let him know that there wasn't anything he could do or say to change her mind. It would do no good for him to point fingers at her and tell her that he was the way he was because she'd made him that way. It seemed to him that she knew that already. He had come to expect the women in his life to be just as accommodating to him as his mother had always been. When he said jump, he thought they should ask him how high. It had worked well for him up to this point.

Derrick thrust the money back into his father's hand. "I'll make it on my own, Dad. I'm not just saying that to make you feel guilty, either. Like you've told me many times before, I'm very resourceful." Derrick slid down the sofa until his shoulder touched his mother's. "I understand why you feel the way you do, Mom. It's all good. I love you and I know you're not just going to up and cut me off. Everything will be okay," he said, giving her a warm hug.

With tears in his eyes, Derrick looked up at his father. "I love you, too, Dad. I guess it's time that I start showing myself some love." He got up from the sofa and headed toward the door, turning around as he reached it. "I'm going to get it together. Not for you, but for me. You'll see. I promise to be in touch." With that said, Derrick took his leave.

Robert wrapped his arms tightly around Hannah. "It's going to be okay, Hannah. You did the right thing. I'm proud of you and I feel strongly that Derrick's going to be okay. I believe you'll soon join the ranks of all the proud mothers of men. Let us kneel down and pray."

Remembering the day that her brother, Harold, had left home for good caused Hannah to break down and cry. No one had had any idea back then that they'd never see his handsome face again, once he'd walked out the back door. The bad news of his untimely death had come as a shock to everyone who'd loved him. Harold was still missed by his family to this very day.

As Hanna fell on her knees, she prayed to God that history wouldn't repeat itself. While taking everything into consideration, she became more confident that she'd done the right thing in this instance. Derrick would never become a man as long as she kept strangling him with her apron strings. Hannah knew that only she could untie the knot that had Derrick tightly bound.

It was time to let go and let God . . .

Relieved that she'd figured it all out, knowing exactly what she had to do, Tara got up off her knees. After having had a long prayerful session with her Father in heaven, she now felt lighter and more carefree, as if all her burdens had suddenly been rolled away. Completely leaving her troubles with God was an important element in receiving the answers to her prayers. He couldn't work His miracles if she didn't move out of the way and give Him free rein.

Tara had prayed fervently to God that if Jamaica wasn't a match as a kidney donor for Timothy, she would be. Much consideration and continuous prayer had gone into her decision to be tested. It was important to her that she have her testing done before she knew whether or not Jamaica qualified as the donor. Tara didn't want it said that she was being forced to do this for her brother, because that wasn't at all the case. This was a pure act of love on her part.

Tara's love for Timothy was her main reason for reconsidering her earlier negative position on being a possible donor, but little Essence had also played an important role in helping her to decide what she should do. Tara wanted so much for her brother to see his baby daughter grow up and for him to be a big part of her life. Although it happened all the time, no child should grow up without both parents. As was earlier discussed by her friends, she was grown when her mother had passed away, but Joanna's absence in Tara's life was still felt.

If giving up a kidney meant that Timothy could live out his life for a longer period of time, Tara was all for trying to make it happen. Although she was aware that she might not be an acceptable match, her desire to see her brother live as long as possible was what counted most. In the scheme of things, donating a vital organ to Timothy was the very least she could do to help save his life. During her period of deep soul-searching, she had asked herself two extremely important questions: *What would my mother have done? What would Jesus do?* The answers had put everything into proper perspective for Tara.

Tara snatched up the phone, hoping her guests hadn't been awakened by it. Everyone had had a long, hard day, especially Jamaica. He'd practically worn himself completely out trying to keep up with his busybody granddaughter, who had given him a new lease on life. Jamaica's emotions had been running so high. That Timothy had agreed to keep open the communication between them and to try to rebuild their relationship had also overwhelmed him.

"Tara, are you there?"

Tara had gone into a dead silence after she'd looked at the caller ID and seen Raymond's number. She hadn't talked to him in a good while, not even after she'd called him to tell him where Maya was. Tara had assumed that she wouldn't hear from him ever again, since he'd sent his sister to pick up Maya from her house. Not so much as a single thank you for sheltering his daughter had come from his lips.

With so much drama going on in her own life, Tara hadn't had time to decide whether she missed Raymond or not. Hearing his voice on the line let her know that she did miss him, tremendously so.

"Hey, Ray. Sorry for the rude silence. I guess you can say I was shocked to hear from you after all this time. It *has* been a while."

"You aren't the one who should be sorry. I'm the one who has made a mess of our relationship. Do you think we can get together and talk?"

Tara turned her mouth down at the corner. "About what?"

"For starters, us. I'd also like to thank you in person for looking after Maya. She told me all the things you said to her. I don't know if it means anything to you or not, but you've made a big impact on her. She has really changed a lot. She hasn't given me an ounce of trouble since she spent the night with you. She's actually eager to see you again."

Happy that Maya had benefited from their one-on-one, Tara smiled. "It means more to me than I can express. Thanks for sharing the good news with me. About us getting together, I don't know exactly when that can happen. I have houseguests. My father and his fiancée are here. There are a lot of things that you don't know about. For one, I have a brother, and he's very ill. He needs a kidney transplant. Both my father and I will be tested as possible donors. Sorry if you're shocked, but we really haven't communicated that much lately, so there wasn't a good opportunity for me to share all this with you."

Tara realized she'd practically run through that entire scenario in a single breath, but she hadn't known any other way to do it. Getting it all out in the open hadn't been an easy thing to accomplish, especially since she'd kept it all deep down inside for so long.

"I am shocked, Tara. I had no idea you had any siblings. A kidney transplant is serious stuff. I hope it all turns out well for everyone. Beyond that, I don't know what else to say."

"You don't have to say anything, Ray. I just thought I should let you in on the things that have been happening in my life. Both of us are pretty much in the same boat; busy with important family matters. Dad came here from Alabama to see my brother. The reason I've never mentioned Timothy is that we've been estranged for a long time. But all that has changed. For the better, I might add. My father and brother are also doing their best to work out their problems. Hopefully, we'll all be one big happy family again. There's a lot more to this story, but I'll save it for whenever we see each other. Okay?"

"Yeah, yeah, that's fine by me. I'm on duty tomorrow, so I'm sure I'll end up at L.A. Memorial several times before my shift is over. What if I drop by your workstation for a minute or two during one of my runs? There are a lot of things I need to tell you, too."

"I'm taking a week of vacation, but I'll more than likely be in the hospital all day tomorrow visiting with my brother. If you call my cell after you get into the building, I'll meet you downstairs in the cafeteria. Just know that I won't be able to stay too long."

"That's understandable with all that's going on in your life. See you tomorrow." There was a moment of silence. "I love you, Tara. I hope we can work out our differences, too. You're not the only one who's hoping for a happy family, a happy ending. Good night, sweetheart."

Tara wasn't going to touch his remarks, not even with a ten-foot pole. She didn't know what Raymond had meant by it, and right now she wasn't willing to explore the meaning of his curiosity-stirring comments. "Good night, Ray. Looking forward to seeing you to-morrow."

Even though she had refused to voice it aloud, Tara was also praying for a happy ending for her, Raymond, and Maya. Only God knew their final destiny and she was content to let His will be done in this matter.

Tara dropped down on her knees again. "Thank you, God. You have answered so many of my prayers already, for which I'm eternally grateful. I'll be listening for your loving response to this one as well."

Tara began to get up off her knees but then stayed put. "By the way, I also need help in coming to terms with what Tim told me about the night Mom died. Even though I don't believe that he called 911 before I did, but that he panicked instead, thinking she was already dead, I still need to find forgiveness for him in my heart. That he only went through her purse so he could get money to get high on because he couldn't deal with her being dead is also unbelievable. But he's an addict, so he has probably convinced himself that his story is true. Then again, it just may be. Since I'll never know the truth, one way or the other, I need you to help me move past this too."

Seated in the leather reclining chair in Simone's bedroom, Tyrell looked over at his mother with concern. Lying in bed in a fetal position, she looked as if she hadn't slept in months. The puffy bags and dark circles under her eyes made her appear much older than she really was.

Tyrell got up out of the chair, crossed the room, and stationed himself on the side of Simone's bed. Looking down upon his mother, he stroked her hair. "Mama, are you sure you're okay? You still don't look so good to me."

Simone was so weak she could barely manage a smile. "I'm feeling much better than I had been. Just an awful case of the flu, Tyrell. It seems to be going around at work. You probably shouldn't be this close to me. I don't want you getting sick, too."

"You're a nurse, Mama. So you know germs travel through the air. I can catch your cold no matter how far away I stay. If I fix you some soup, would you try to eat it?"

Tyrell's genuine concern for her deeply touched Simone's heart, but just the thought of eating made her stomach lurch. Since she hadn't eaten anything in two days, she knew that it was time for her to force the issue. "That would be nice, Tyrell. I should eat something, but I'm not sure it'll stay down." The deep rasp in her voice was an indication of how sore her throat was.

Tyrell leaned over and kissed his mother on the forehead, more worried about her than he'd let on. His lips on her skin let him know she was running a high temperature, which caused him to lay the back of his hand on her face. Her flesh felt like it was on fire. He'd never seen her this down and out. That she had barely moved a muscle had him really concerned.

Although Tyrell knew Simone would more than likely object, he felt that he should call his father to come over. He remembered how agitated she'd gotten when he'd called Booker to come see about her when Jerome had blackened her eye. But he couldn't waste time worrying about her reaction. If she needed to go to the hospital, his father would make it happen.

"I'm going to make that soup now. I'll bring you some juice, too, if you have any."

"Ginger ale or 7-Up will be better. It might help settle my stomach. Bring up some crackers, too. I'll try to eat those before I tackle the soup."

Tyrell got to his feet. "Be right back."

Simone watched as her son took off running. Having him there to look after her made her feel much better. Being sick and alone wasn't a good situation to be in. She wouldn't think of asking Tyrell to spend the night with her, but she hoped he would make that decision on his own. Another moment in the house alone wasn't an appealing prospect, not when she felt this bad.

When Tyrell had called to say he was coming over to see her, Simone was delighted to have him visit, felt that her prayers had truly been answered. Although she hadn't informed him over the phone that she was the least bit sick, she had told him just to let himself in because she might still be lying down. Tyrell had called her to task on keeping him in the dark about being ill when he'd first arrived, but he hadn't made too much of a fuss over it under the circumstances.

Simone could remember feeling this terrible only one other time. She'd also had the flu back then. Her temperature had soared for several days in a row. Eating had been out of the question, but she'd had to take in plenty of fluids to ward off dehydration. Had she not been running such a high temperature, she would've suspected another pregnancy as the culprit.

Booker then came to her mind. He had been very attentive to all her needs in those days. He'd refused to leave her side during that awful time. When he'd had to leave the house, he'd made sure someone was there with her every minute of his absence. Life had been good then.

Simone couldn't help returning once again to the days when she'd been his black queen. The thought of how he'd dethroned her so easily brought tears to her eyes. The queen had become a commoner overnight and her glorious crown had been unceremoniously stripped away. The fact that he hadn't crowned another queen in all these years, to help him oversee his vast empire, should've brought her comfort, but it didn't. It deeply saddened her to know that she'd never again reign as Booker's queen or hold royal court with him, not in this lifetime.

Tyrell's reentrance into the room quickly brought Simone back into the present. She rapidly dashed away her tears so her son wouldn't see them. It was tough on her weakened body, but Simone managed to sit upright in bed so Tyrell could situate the oak breakfast tray across her lap. She couldn't help smiling when he had her lean forward for him to station a couple of pillows behind her back, plumping them first. Another rash of sweet memories crossed her mind.

Like father, like son, she thought. Booker had tended to her needs in the very same way.

"Bow your head, Mama. I'll pass the blessing."

Simone's heart rate had rapidly increased. Tyrell praying over anything was definitely a new wrinkle. Was Booker's influence on Tyrell that strong? No matter where it came from Simone was pleased as punch. Tyrell had stopped going to church on a regular basis, so she had to wonder if Booker had also gotten him back into the house of the Lord. She hadn't seen either one of them at First Tabernacle, the very same church she'd raised up Tyrell in, but that didn't mean they didn't attend a different service from the seven A.M. one she frequented. Reverend Jesse Covington held three separate church services each Lord's Day, which didn't include the evening session he also conducted.

Tyrell kept a close eye on his mother while she ate her food. He had come there with the specific intent to talk to her about a few important matters, but he no longer thought the timing was right. He hadn't expected to find her in this kind of shape healthwise. The things that were going on in his life were not nearly as important to him as his mother's health.

Always tuned into Tyrell's ever-changing moods, Simone looked over at her son. "How are things going with you, Tyrell? Although we've chatted on the phone recently, we haven't seen each other in a week or more. Is everything going okay?"

Tyrell frowned slightly. "I wanted to talk to you about a few things, but I think the timing is all wrong. My stuff can wait until you're feeling better."

Simone smiled gently. "The fact that you brought it up tells me that it can't wait, and it shouldn't have to. Let's hear what's on your mind, young man."

Tyrell wrinkled his nose. "Are you sure you're up to it?"

Simone chuckled. "There's nothing wrong with my ears other than them ringing a little every now and then. I'm good to go."

Tyrell took a moment to collect his thoughts, though he couldn't take too long. His father was on his way and he wanted everything out in the open before Booker arrived. He had so many things to tell his mother, good and bad. While looking down at his watch, he cleared his throat.

Tyrell then sat down at the foot of the bed. "Mama, I know you're probably disappointed in me 'cause I didn't go into rehab, but I really didn't feel like I needed to. I'm not a habitual drug user. I've smoked a joint on occasion when I was stressed about something, but it isn't something I do that often. Beer is about the only type of alcohol I consume, 'cause I really don't like the taste of hard liquor. . . ."

"Tyrell," Simone interrupted, "have you ever heard the saying 'too much information'? You don't have to go into all that."

Tyrell shot Simone an intolerant glance. "Why is it that you never want to hear me out? Dad listens to everything I say. He always encourages me to talk to him. I guess what's going on in my life isn't that important to you. I see that some things around here don't ever change."

Dad! Simone couldn't believe her ears. She was more in shock by her son calling Booker "dad" than she was by what he'd said to her about not listening to him. It seemed like Booker had scored some mighty high points with Tyrell. That she was jealous of how easily Booker had made such a positive impact on Tyrell's life made Simone feel ashamed of herself, but she couldn't deny the envy she felt. Having Booker around had definitely caused a change for the better in Tyrell. Why hadn't she been able to get through to her son like Booker obviously had?

Simone's sudden distraction bothered Tyrell. "Mama, have you heard anything I've said?"

Simone looked up with a start. "Of course I heard you, Tyrell.

I'm sorry if you don't think I listen to you, but I do. I hear every word you say. Can't you give me credit for something? By the way, when did you start calling Booker 'dad'?"

Tyrell raised an eyebrow. "Is that what had you so distracted?"

"Yes."

"I figured as much. He's earned the title, Mama. I never dreamed I'd ever call him 'dad,' but he's been just that to me. I missed him so much when he was away. I thought he hated me, that I was the reason he left us. But he's been honest without me about everything."

"Everything?"

"Everything, Mama. I know about all the women, too."

Simone rolled her eyes. "How so very gallant of him."

Tyrell sighed with discontent. "Why are you so jealous of our relationship? I thought you'd be happy for us to be back together. You never really said anything bad about Dad, but I knew you were angry with him all the time. I sensed how you felt about him. Why do you think I stopped asking you to try to get him to let me come visit him? I knew it would hurt you if he ever decided to let me visit him. I didn't want to see you hurt any more than you already were."

Simone felt sick to her stomach. This churning sickness had nothing to do with her flu symptoms. Tyrell's right-to-the-point remarks had just landed in her midsection like they'd come from the hard-hitting fist of a prizefighter. She'd had no clue that her son had been so sensitive to her feelings. She had unwittingly done the very opposite of what she'd set out to do, which was never to put Booker down to Tyrell. Yet he'd somehow sensed her ill feelings about his dad, anyway. Simone couldn't feel any more shame than she already felt.

Tyrell sighed with discontent. "You know what, we should talk about this later. This isn't the right time, not with you feeling so sick."

"The timing is perfect, Tyrell. Please go on. I promise to hear you."

Although still a bit reluctant, Tyrell began to open up to his mother once again, telling her about how all his frustrations had built up over the years. He then told her that he'd come to realize that everything he'd ever done wrong was directly linked to the absence of his father. Tyrell revealed to his mother that his anger often got the best of him because he didn't know how to channel it in a positive way. He had turned his rage on her because she was the only target available to him. He then mentioned that Booker had taught him how to better manage his anger and how to turn a negative into a positive. His dad had taught him how to act and not react.

Minutes into Tyrell's discussion on Simone's living arrangements with Jerome, he became emotional and then began to cry. "This stranger had suddenly taken my place with you," he sobbed. "That's how I felt. I didn't know Jerome when he came to live in our house—and you didn't know him either. What if he'd been a child molester? Though he didn't do anything bad like that to me, he still treated me like dirt. His verbal abuse hurt as much as any punch ever thrown and he often shoved me around, but always when you weren't here."

Simone tried her hardest to keep from crying. Seeing her boy so hurt was the last thing she wanted. How she had allowed herself to totally lose touch with reality completely eluded her. Tyrell was saying things to her that she hadn't even thought of. Her son was right. She hadn't known all that much about Jerome when she'd given him an invitation to live in her home. Hearing her son's version of how he was made to feel made her heartsick.

"I resented him being there. You were my mother. Moms didn't do this kind of stuff to their children. I was teased about him living with us. The brothers in the streets can be cruel. They were saying all kinds of bad things about you. I can't count the number of fights I got into trying to defend you. There were times when I had to ask myself why I was defending you. You didn't seem to care what I thought about him being here. Knowing what was going on between him and you made my skin crawl. I never understood how you could be with a drunk like him, how you could even think of letting him touch you. Moms are supposed to be sacred."

Speaking of too much information, Tyrell had Simone wishing she could disappear into thin air. The truth hurt, but she was more than hurting. The sledgehammer pounding around inside her head had her nauseous beyond belief. Hearing these horrible but truthful revelations coming from her son's mouth was almost too much for her to bear. Tyrell's comments had been driven right into home base. The things she'd unwittingly put him through were abominable.

Simone now clearly understood that children didn't just grow up to be rebellious for the heck of it or because they didn't have anything else better to do. When they committed mutiny it was because they genuinely had something to rise up against. Children lived only what they'd learned, especially that which they'd been taught in the home. Parents were their first teachers.

For every parent who had a rebellious child, she now understood that there was a root cause behind it. Hindsight was always twentytwenty, but she had been totally blinded to what her son had needed from her because of her own pain. What she had learned from her son on this day was invaluable. Tyrell had been a victim of circumstances—those unfortunate circumstances that she and Booker Branch had created for him by the bad choices they'd made in life.

Tyrell moved up to the head of the bed and took his mother's hand. "I see I've hurt you, but I wasn't trying to. These are things I had to say so I can finally move on with my life. Everything is much better for me, though I still have a long way to go. Mama, I just needed my dad in my life. He *has* made the difference, but that doesn't mean I don't appreciate all you've done for me. I do. But I want to be able to love both of you without worrying that I'm hurting someone. I know you don't want to get back with Dad, but will you please try to get along with him for my sake? I love you both. We can still be a family without us all living together."

* * *

Booker couldn't stop the tears from rolling down his cheeks, nor did he want to. To hear Tyrell call him "dad" had his emotions in an uproar. To have his son professing his love for him was overwhelming. While Tyrell had already told him that he'd forgiven him, he had clearly heard the evidence of such. Booker knew that he could never make up to Tyrell the time they'd lost, but he had been determined for them not to lose another precious second to being apart. He had needed his son every bit as much as Tyrell had needed him. His deepest regret was that he'd waited so long to act upon what he'd been dying to do for years.

Fear of rejection had kept Booker from his greatest accomplishment in life, his son.

Booker didn't know whether to go ahead and step into the room or turn around and go back downstairs, as if he hadn't ever been there. Tyrell had told his father on the phone that he'd leave the front door open for him so he could just come in. It had seemed like a good idea at the time, but Booker was no longer sure about that. This was an awkward situation at best.

Although Booker had told Simone that he'd never again darken her doorstep, upon hearing that she was ill, he'd let that bit of nonsense fly right out the window. Tyrell wouldn't have called him if he hadn't thought it was serious. But, then again, Tyrell wanted his mother and father back together, so that might've also been a second motivating factor. Booker was in no doubt that Tyrell was worried about his mother's health, that she had been Tyrell's first concern.

Deciding that he should just go on in and get the fireworks over with, Booker stepped into Simone's bedroom, hoping she wouldn't throw a fit. Seeing Simone and Tyrell holding each other in a tight embrace started his tears flowing all over again. No matter what happened between him and Simone, this was his family, and he would move heaven and earth to make sure they always came first in his life. "God," he silently prayed, "thank you for bringing me back into the fold. Please keep me on the straight and narrow path. May your will always be done. Amen."

Seeing Booker coming into her bedroom caused sheer panic to rise up in Simone. How long he had been outside her door and how much he'd heard of their conversation was Simone's first concern. How horrible she looked was her second. Her frumpy nightgown was wrinkled and stained with feverish sweat. Patting down her hair would do no good, she figured, since it was so disheveled and all over her head. Simone quickly picked up the bed tray and moved it aside so she could pull the covers up around her. No woman should ever be seen looking so trifling.

Knowing Tyrell was responsible for Booker being there, Simone looked over at Tyrell, her dismay with him flashing in her eyes. "You could've told me that you called your dad to come over here, Tyrell. A little warning might've helped, but I wish you hadn't done it, period."

Tyrell appeared contrite. "I'm really worried about you. I knew Dad would know what to do. Your fever is kind of high and I thought you might need to go to the hospital."

Appreciative of Tyrell's concern for her, Simone smiled softly. "Thank you for being so thoughtful, son. I now understand. Well, Booker, as you can see for yourself, I'm not as bad off as Tyrell probably made you think. Still, thanks for coming."

Booker grinned. "You're welcome, Simone. I believe Tyrell did the right thing by calling me since he was so worried. You don't look the least bit healthy, woman. How high *is* your temperature, anyway?"

Simone shrugged nonchalantly. "Don't know. I haven't taken it yet."

"Tyrell, go get a thermometer," Booker gently ordered. "The first thing we're going to do is take your temp, Simone. We'll have to see what comes next. Don't even try to pull on us your ranking as a nurse. Nurses are just like mechanics, inasmuch as their needs always come last. Mechanics have the worst-running cars. I won't say more, because I think you get my drift."

Before Simone could respond to his remarks, Tyrell came back into the room and handed Booker a box of disposable thermometer strips. Without further ado, Booker removed one of the plastic strips and then told Simone to open up her mouth.

Simone was fuming inside, but she knew it wouldn't do any good to voice it. Besides, her mouth was otherwise engaged. Having looked at her as if he'd dared her to resist, Booker had all but shoved the thermometer between her cracked lips.

Booker took the strip from Simone's mouth and read it. "One hundred and one is bad, but it could be worse. I guess you already know you need to force more fluids. Tyrell, please go downstairs and make a pitcher of ice water for your mother so we can try to get her temp down. Since I know she's going to fight us on going to the ER, we'll try the home remedies first." Booker chuckled. "Putting your behind in a cold tub of water just might have to come next."

Simone rolled her eyes at Booker. "You *are* pushing your luck, you know."

"Yeah, I do know. But that's what people do when they care about someone. I care a lot about you, Simone." He took her hand in his. "While Tyrell is gone can we make a pact between us? I know you've been wondering how much of your conversation I overheard, so I'm going to tell you. I heard enough to know that we have to put our differences aside and put our son first. He needs both of us, Simone. I can assure you that God will dole out my punishment at the appointed time, but in the meantime can you give this old guy a break? Do you think you and I can start building some sort of amicable relationship while helping Tyrell pull his life together? I desperately want us at least to work on being friends. And not just for Tyrell's sake, but also for ours. Can you please agree to that much?"

The sincerity in Booker's tone made Simone realize that her estranged husband had really changed. He was back to being the man she once knew, the Booker who would've never acted so irresponsibly before stardom. Blinking back her tears, Simone reached out to Booker, giving him a warm hug to seal the long overdue pact. "I think it's imperative for us to become friends, Booker Branch, good friends. Tyrell *does* need both his parents. And I'll do my very best to leave your judgment up to God. Welcome home, Booker Branch."

Silently praising God, Booker reveled in Simone's warm embrace. "I can't ask for more than that, Simone. When you're feeling much better, we'll have a toast to a long, meaningful friendship. And I promise never again to hurt you and Tyrell. Having your forgiveness means more to me than you'll ever know. I love you both."

Stepping into the bedroom, after having heard a good bit of their conversation, a smiling Tyrell pumped his fist in triumph. "Yes, Lord," he cried out joyously. "Thank you for giving me both my mother and father back." Rushing across the room, Tyrell embraced his parents.

With tears running down her face, Simone silently thanked God once again for performing yet another miracle in her life. She then turned to Booker, smiling brightly. "Please lead our family in prayer so that we can properly thank God for all His goodness."

Epilogue

Sinclair was beaming all over as she passed out fancy envelopes to all her friends who were seated at the table in the hospital break room. "I hope you all don't mind that I didn't mail these invitations. I wasn't trying to save on stamps, either. I just wanted to give them to each of you in person. I hope everyone can make the gala celebration in two weeks."

Simone's expression clearly showed her curiosity. "Celebration? What are we celebrating?" Thinking she had figured it out, Simone's face lit up. "You and Charles are going to retake your vows, aren't you?"

Sinclair laughed heartily. "That would be nice, but that's not it. Dating again has been wonderful for us, but we're content in taking things slow. The invitations are actually to celebrate Marcus's recent success. Ladies, my son is a multimillionaire! He just signed a recording deal with a major label. I don't know how I managed to keep this secret, but I wanted the contracts to be signed, sealed, and delivered before I said anything. . . ."

Everyone was all over Sinclair before she could utter another word. The hugs and kisses and heartfelt congratulations from all her girlfriends made Sinclair feel like she was the one who'd landed a multimillion-dollar contract instead of Marcus.

"This is incredible news," Tara enthused. "But how did a recording contract come about? I thought he was studying business administration in college."

Sinclair chuckled. "So did both Charles and I, Tara. After you challenged me on finding out where all the money was going, I did a little investigating and found out he was spending most of it on making music demos. According to Marcus, he's always wanted to be a rapper."

"A rapper! Dear God," Hannah said, "how in the dickens are you going to deal with hearing that kind of vulgarity all the time, especially being a Christian woman?"

Sinclair joined her friends at the table, looking rather thoughtful, wondering how to respond to Hannah's candid remarks. Since Sinclair had only recently come to realize that her own impoverished background was the main reason why she'd become so overindulgent with Marcus, she wanted to choose her words wisely and not respond in the same judgmental way as Hannah. Being the only one in her family who'd ever gone to college and later to enjoy a fair amount of success, Sinclair had scrapped and scraped for every dime to put herself through school. Life had been hard and she only wanted so much more for her son than what she'd had.

Sinclair looked over at Hannah, though she wanted everyone to hear what she had to say. "I've come to understand that Christians aren't anywhere near to being perfect, nor will we ever be. We all have things we need to work on before standing before the King. Learning how to be up front, honest, and nonjudgmental is at the top of my list. To answer your question, Hannah, Marcus has to answer to God for himself. He did tell me that he doesn't plan to do anything but inspirational rap, so I have to believe him. I've heard some of his work and it's very positive and Christian oriented. Charles and I plan to give our full support to his music endeavors. I have also come to realize that this is Marcus's life to live, not Charles's or mine. We've had our shot."

Hannah felt awful about her cutting remarks—and she sincerely apologized to Sinclair for making them. Who was she to judge anything or anybody? She'd certainly made her share of mistakes and then some. Since she was the only one who seemed to have held something back from the rest of the group, she launched into her latest troubles with Derrick and how everything had finally been resolved.

Hannah smiled, feeling much better about everything. "So Derrick has moved out of our house and into an apartment with one of his friends. A male friend, thank God. He's working on himself and I do believe he wants to change. Robert is happy we have the house to ourselves again. He's been making good use of our time alone. He's as amorous as ever. If I didn't know better, I'd think the guy was popping Viagra."

The five women cracked up at that.

Simone entwined her hands and placed them on top of the table. "We all have our crosses to bear with our sons. As I've said before, we just need to continue to support each other. Booker and I have made a good bit of progress. Being friends with him isn't nearly as troubling as I once thought. Although I still suffer the pain from his egregious behavior, I have learned not to dwell on it as much as before. Forgiveness isn't always easy, but it is imperative. He and I have agreed that supporting Tyrell will always come first in our lives, just as it should with all estranged parents. In taking responsibility for my own mistakes, I also called Jerome and had a long talk with him. Though our relationship is over and done with, I've forgiven him, too. He says he forgives me as well. God has been good! I have no other complaints."

"I know you said it could never happen, but do you now think that there's a good chance for you and Booker to resume a life together?" Tara asked.

Simone had to laugh at Tara's question, remembering that she'd dared to ask it once before. "As you've already given us so much good advice, Tara, though we didn't believe you were the least bit qualified, I've taken you up on some of it. 'Never say never' is one of the many wise things you've said to me. While I don't see it happening anywhere in the near future, I'm not going to say that it'll never happen. Time will tell. Only God has all the answers. With that out of the way, what's going on with you and all the drama in your life?"

Tara couldn't help smiling about all the powerful blessings that had been rained down upon her. "My father and I are both matches for Tim. As health-care professionals, you all know how rare that is. Daddy has convinced me to let him be the donor, since I have so much of my life left ahead of me. But we all know that none of us are promised tomorrow. However, he said that Tim might very well need another transplant in the future, so I can donate mine then if that should happen. We pray that it won't. I finally agreed with him. Tim and Daddy are talking a lot and have promised to stay in close touch. Tim is coming to live with me until his health improves. You all didn't know this, but Tim was homeless when he was brought to the hospital. I never did tell my father about that, because I don't believe he could've handled it. There's also a good chance that Tim and Carolyn may work things out between them, but that's still up for grabs. Regardless of what does or doesn't happen for them, they've vowed to see to it that Essence is raised up in a healthy environment."

"And you and Raymond?" Glenda asked.

Tara's face lit up. "All I can say is that we're working on our issues. Maya's happiness is important to both of us, so we've decided to put her first. We've come to realize that we have to work individually on building up our relationships with her before we can even think about making plans for a future together. Once a strong bond is established there, well, we'll then start talking about us," Tara concluded, on a deep sigh of relief. "Glenda, everyone else has already shared their most recent news, so before our break is over, what's happening with you?"

"This should speak for itself." Glenda held up her left hand, wiggling her ring finger, causing flashes of brilliant light to flicker all over the place. "Taylor and I have Tony's blessings on our engagement. He is ecstatic for us. Listen to this. I took both of my men out to one of my favorite restaurants for dinner. After we'd eaten, that's when I asked Taylor to marry me. You should've seen the look on Taylor's face when I got down on my knees. . . ."

Keeping Glenda from finishing her thoughts were the squeals of delight coming from the other women. The joyous noises were loud enough to wake up the dead.

Tara's eyes were wide as saucers. "You actually proposed to him?"

Glenda's smile was as brilliant as the princess-cut diamond on her finger. "I really did, on my knees in public, no less! I wasn't sure he'd ask me again, since I'd already turned him down three or four times, so I took matters into my own hands. Without the slightest hesitation, he said 'yes.' Taylor made sure that Tony was okay with everything. He then promised Tony that he'd take very good care of us. The three of us ended up celebrating."

Hannah pulled a face. "The three of you! Ugh, that doesn't sound so romantic."

Glenda blushed. "Once we got back home, and Tony went off to bed, Taylor and I had a private celebration—kissing only, ladies. Before he left for home, Taylor and I talked about all our issues and how we're going to work hard at becoming a real family. Since Tony is seriously thinking about enlisting in the military, he won't be living with me too much longer. With all that's going on with us being at war and all, I'm terribly scared for my son. But if he makes that decision, I'll have no choice but to support him. At any rate, constantly faced with drugs and gangs, Tony pointed out to me that he's been living in a war zone for years right here at home."

"No one can argue with that analogy," Simone said. "Our sons have had to deal with a lot more danger than we had to contend with in our youth. At least we have them back on the right path. God willing, they'll stay there."

Tara looked up at the clock on the wall. "It looks like we've gone way over on our break time. We'd better get back to work in a hurry. Let's have a moment of silent prayer."

Upon joining hands, Simone, Sinclair, Tara, Hannah, and Glenda bowed their heads, each of them silently thanking God for answering their prayers. Each of the five women knew they had so much to be thankful for.

"Amen," they said simultaneously.

Dear Readers:

I sincerely hope that you enjoyed reading *Sacred Sons* from cover to cover. I'm very interested in hearing your comments and thoughts on these five sister-friends, Simone, Sinclair, Hannah, Glenda, and Tara, all of whom supported each other in good times and bad. These women fought courageously alongside their troubled sons, hoping to bring about a positive change. Even when the situation seemed hopeless, they knew they'd find renewed strength only through prayer.

I love hearing from my readers and I do appreciate the time you take out of your busy schedule to respond. Please enclose a self-addressed, stamped envelope with all your correspondence and mail to Linda Hudson-Smith, 16516 El Camino Real, Box #174, Houston, TX 77062. Or you can e-mail your comments to LHS4romance@yahoo.com. Please also visit my Web site and sign my guest book at www.lindahudsonsmith. com.

New York City: Same Day

Alison drove straight through to Courtney's Manhattan apartment. Heavy traffic slowed her progress once she reached the outskirts of the city. She hadn't left her house in Delmar until nearly three, and it was after seven by the time she found a place to park near the girls' apartment building.

While sitting in traffic, she'd called Len to find out if he'd made any progress in tracking down their daughter. "Did you get my text?"

"Yes," Alison replied. "I'm glad you see it my way."

"I do. Since I'm busy trying to prevent a major event, it's good that you can focus on finding Courtney. I asked Meir to research the NYU group. I'll let you know if he comes up with anything relevant."

"Len, since you've other things to worry about, why don't you send me Meir's report as soon as you get it? I'll go through it and let you know if there's anything relevant."

"Point taken. I'll do that. By the way, the Regency is booked. Ed put us into a hotel over on Lexington. I'll send you the reservation info. I'll meet you there late tonight unless you want to come here."

"Okay, but I won't be able to sleep until I find her."

Standing at the entrance to Courtney's apartment building, Alison kicked herself metaphorically for not having gotten a key when they signed the lease. *We're paying the damn rent. I ought to have a key.* She kicked herself a second time, realizing how Courtney would have reacted to her demanding a key. Alison knew better than to do so at the time, but now she was stuck with the consequences.

The rental agency had checked the apartment earlier that day and had informed her that no one was there and nothing looked awry. She doubted they would be as cooperative if she had to call them again to let her in, but what were her options, other than sitting on the stoop and waiting for Courtney or Doreen to show up?

When someone came out of the building, Alison grabbed the door before it closed. She took the elevator up to Courtney's floor and knocked on the door to her unit. No answer. She knocked again a little louder. Still no answer.

I guess it's time to call the rental people, she told herself. She started to dial the number, but saw only one bar on the top of her phone. Something in the building must be blocking the signal.

Just as she got outside and started to make the call, she spotted Doreen Rupert coming up the street. *Thank goodness.*

Doreen didn't see Alison until she started up the front steps. She stopped, backed down, and started to run back in the direction she'd come.

"Doreen. Stop," Alison called. "Where are you going?"

Doreen turned back, hesitated, and then started running again. Alison took after her. Fortunately she was wearing more sensible footwear than the younger woman, who had on high heels. Alison also had the advantage of being in excellent physical condition. She caught up with Doreen in middle of the next block.

"All right. I give up," Doreen said, as Alison cornered her between two stairwells.